THE CHILD LEFT IN THE DARK

J M BRISCOE

Reader reactions to
The Girl with the Green Eyes,
the first book in the Take Her Back trilogy:

5.0 out of 5 stars Very interesting, heart-breaking and gripping.

5.0 out of 5 stars **Cleverly constructed story draws you in to the start of a series**. Beautiful example of show not tell.

5.0 out of 5 stars **Delicious Book** This book is like a perfect chocolate torte – rich, dark and bittersweet. As soon as you've devoured it, you'll be clamouring for seconds!

5.0 out of 5 stars **Gripping from the first pages** I am not a sci-fi fan but this book may well have changed that for me. Bella and her story caught my attention from the first pages. It was hard to put down because I wanted to know more about her journey both as a young child and older adult. A great read with dark and twisty turns.

The Child Left in the Dark

by

J M Briscoe

Copyright © J M Briscoe 2022

I, J M Briscoe, hereby assert and
give notice of my rights under section 77 of the
Copyright, Design and Patents Act, 1988
to be identified as the author of this work.

All Rights Reserved. No part of this publication
may be reproduced, stored in a retrieval system
or transmitted at any time by any means
electronic, mechanical, photocopying, recording or
otherwise, without prior permission of the publisher.

All characters in this publication are fictitious and
any resemblance to real persons, living or dead,
is purely coincidental.

Cover photo by Dmytro Tolokonov-unsplash

Cover design by Jason Anscomb

Interior design by BAD PRESS iNK

ISBN: 978-1-8384577-5-4

published by www.badpress.ink

To Mum and Dad, for always leaving a light on

Thank you

I'm going to kick these acknowledgements off with a massive apology for forgetting to add any to my first book. Author noob here, learning as I go, etc.

A huge thank you to Iain and Pat at BAD PRESS iNK for believing in me and my words. I'd received so many 'It's good but not quite right for me' emails by spring 2021 I'd almost given up hope of finding a publisher for my quirky, unconventional sci-fi. Turns out a quirky, unconventional publishing house was the one (who'd have thought!). Thanks too for your endless patience with me and my occasional tendencies of indecision/nit-pickery/made-up phraseology.

Thank you to The Bridport Prize for choosing *The Girl with the Green Eyes* as one of the (few) long-listers for the 2020 novel award. It was this achievement which gave me the confidence to renew efforts to find a publisher as well as write books two and three.

Thank you to Alison, my mum, for being my first reader, my loudest cheerleader and for explaining the difference between a deltoid and a bicep (Ethan thanks you too).

Thank you to my small team of beta readers: my husband Gary for your support, patience and teaching me the correct way to pronounce segue. My awesome stepmother-in-law Mandy and your eagle eyes for finding things I'd overlooked even after 368 read-throughs. And my excellent friend Celine whose notes were simply: 'Bloody love it.'

Thank you to my eldest daughter Lara for being an excellent girl with (fake) green eyes for my first book trailer (and several BookTok posts). Hopefully it will be an asset and not an embarrassment if you ever do launch that YouTube career in a few years. Thank you as well to my brilliant niece Alyssia for being my Ariana in the trailer for *The Child Left in the Dark*. You took my vague direction to 'look angry with the world' and did such an amazing job I had to go back and edit Ariana's hairstyle to match yours.

To my wonderful family: Gary, Lara, Annabelle and Ben. You inspire me every day.

Lastly, I want to thank all the readers of *The Girl with the Green Eyes*, especially those who took the time to leave me a rating or a review. I am so grateful to each and every one of you. I hope to do you proud with this follow-up.

1

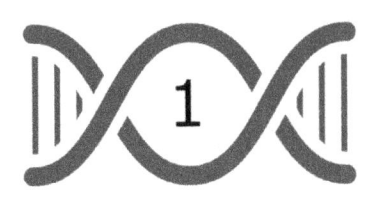

April, 2019

She wakes herself screaming, the sound bitten off by the firm hand clamped over her mouth. Her panic recedes immediately; it is her own hand and it's the same way she has woken almost every day for the last six months. As she waits for her heart to slow down, Ariana tells herself that the images, still blazing agonisingly against her eyelids, are not real. The sounds are harder to forget, the shrieks caught somewhere between a helplessly tiny animal and something old, wretched and full of anguish. Not dying though. Tortured, ruined, haggard; it's the sound of something that wishes it could die. Or it would, if it had enough of a mind left with which to wish. But it doesn't have a rational mind because it isn't real. It isn't, it can't be… she won't let it be until it is safe to take her hand away from her mouth. Until the adrenaline of the memories stops writhing jaggedly along her veins. Until she absolutely, definitely, is not going to scream. Because as long as she is hiding in the back of a moving van, having stowed away on her dad's latest, not-so-secret rescue mission, screaming is not the wisest thing to do.

Ariana shakes herself a little and listens, her body a tightly-wired hunch. She hadn't meant to fall asleep here in the back of Ethan's old Ford Transit, but she'd been awake long into the previous night finalising her plan.

The Child Left in the Dark

There's no sound above the engine's low rumble except the buzz of the radio and Ariana relaxes a little, knowing that if anyone up front suspected her presence they'd act instantly. She takes her hand away from her mouth and squeezes her fists into her armpits, wondering whether the trembles of her body are caused by the shuddering vehicle or the shadowy remnants of the nightmare. She squints in the darkness to read the hands of her wristwatch. Twenty past ten. They must be over halfway there now. She tries to focus on something else but there's nothing here in the dark burrows of the van except blankets and old painting supplies left over from when Ethan worked as a tradesman. She knows Felix keeps them in here as a reminder of him, but Ariana never knew Ethan. To her, they are just useless old cans, brushes, and sticks that she keeps a wary eye on whenever the van lurches round a corner. They provide no distraction from the wailing memories. *It isn't real.* The words create a moment of comfort, a fleeting glimpse of a candle's flame in the heady darkness. Before she remembers Tess's shriek ('Don't!') and her father reaching anyway, wrenching the door open and scouring the horror into her eyes and ears.

At first she'd thought the huddled creature in the cage was some kind of dog, although the thought had instantly clouded over itself with confusion because it had feathers. The cage – more of a crate, she realised, once she looked closer – stood in a dark room just inches from the open doorway. Giant bird had been Ariana's next guess, and this one bore up a few moments longer than the first. Pale, golden feathers bloomed downwards over its back and the ground was patterned with what looked like the tips of enormous wings, folded but still impossibly huge. Then Ariana's eyes travelled back upwards and she wondered why the feathers grew more sparsely the higher they went, how they were interspersed with thick, downy hair which caught the light in gingery glimmers, and why the skin beneath was so visible, so pale, and were those human ears?

Then... then the next second had arrived and the creature responded to the sudden gush of light from the room they'd been standing in, and the head had lifted, the very human tumble of hair nestled with feathers turned and Ariana found her brain stumbling to catch up with her eyes. It wasn't a bird, but it also wasn't a person. Somehow it was something like both. The face was almost human. The small nose was hooked like a beak but was skin-covered and smooth. Eyes shone brightly, darkly, and swept between the three astounded figures with birdlike speed and human intelligence. The body was covered in feathers whose golden tone darkened as they swept downwards, and the hands, drawn protectively around the torso, were clawed. For a moment Ariana stared wordlessly into the creature's eyes and the being blinked slowly, raised its head a little more and, without warning, gave a shriek in a voice caught somewhere between a gull's and a child's. It was the sound of pure unfiltered pain and longing, and something more... something, Ariana realised as she stared uncomprehendingly at the bird-girl, furious.

'Come on,' Ralph had muttered, his large hands around Ariana's shoulders. Ariana wrenched her eyes from the creature in the cage, which had begun to unfurl itself from the cocoon of its tawny-gold wings and seemed to be mustering itself for an attack. More noise ripped through the air as Ariana was tugged backwards and she caught the glint of more cages set in rows beyond that of the bird-girl. Her ears and eyes struggled to make sense of it – the

The Child Left in the Dark

strangled grunts of a pig-boy, the anguished eyes of a dog-man – at the same time her nose was only just beginning to register the onslaught of terrible, unremitting foulness. Ralph pulled her through the door just as the bird-girl gave another shriek, louder than all the others, her talons gripping the metal mesh separating her from Ariana. Ariana caught her gaze one last time before the door was thrown closed between them.

Afterwards, when she lay in the unfamiliar bed in what was once an office belonging to a grandmother she'd never known, listening to the wind screeching around the strange, muddled-up-castle-slash-house everyone called The Manor, she tried to tell herself that it wasn't real. That none of it had been… surely. It had been a large bird, that was all. A bird, a dog, and a pig. And several other injured animals. They were fixing them. Trying to, anyway. Ariana had met some of the scientists working at the Futura Lab after all – studious, nervy Tess, bumbling sweaty Alec, and all those other white-coated rubber-clogged people – they'd shown her their experiments, let her feed the test rabbits and try out the lasers and stuff… She must have imagined the rest. Maybe she'd banged her head and not realised or perhaps her brain had had some sort of delayed reaction to whatever Tess had put in her drink to make her sleep. Or maybe it was all just a stress response – it *had* happened during the same weekend she'd been kidnapped, drugged and met her real dad, after all. That had to be it. The people who worked there… they were all a bit weird and geeky maybe, but none of them had seemed like they spent their days experimenting on wretched half people/animal things before locking them in cages and leaving them in the dark. Then she'd remembered Dr Daniel Skaid and Dr Josiah Lychen. The creepy, empty eyes. The pull of danger. And she wasn't so sure of anything anymore.

Her dad won't talk about it. Neither will Tess, who has moved into the room next to Dominic's on The Manor's second floor. Whenever Ariana broaches the subject of Futura (or Graysons as most of the people who'd worked there had called it) with either one of them, they both get that odd, closed-off look in their eyes that adults get when you ask too much about a thing they don't fully understand themselves. It's similar to the look Ralph got the time she asked him to buy her tampons (she hadn't actually needed any, she'd just become bored of him trying to bond with her about Minecraft). Or the look Dr Blake, her new grandfather, sometimes wears when she says or does something that she knows is making him think of *her*.

She's learning, though. The ways around them – her new family. She knows how to exert her presence just enough so that they remember that she is there and needs money and food and lifts to town, but not so much that they start getting crazy ideas like putting restrictions on screen time or making her go to bed before ten. She knows how to fade into a room unseen, where to sit against the wall just inside her bedroom door – which she chose for its position on the first-floor landing, not because she feels any connection to some old woman who had the same name as her – so she can hear what's being discussed in the rooms ('offices') downstairs. She knows how to open her clear green eyes to their widest and put them fully behind a question so that she can be sure of the answer. So even though Ralph won't talk about what happened in that lab, and Tess avoids her, Ariana has learned over the past few months that they, as well as the other adults now in charge of her – Felix, Dr Blake, Dominic, think the same thing as her. That the Futura Lab is, in part, in the business of housing human/animal hybrids. That Dr Daniel Skaid is the one in charge of it. And that he should probably be stopped, though this isn't their priority today. It *is* Ariana's, though. Which is why she is hiding in the back of the van and they are up front, without a clue.

April, 2019

I know trouble. Even when I was a child, I could usually tell within a few minutes of meeting someone whether they meant me harm, and, within a few minutes more, whether they were capable of doing it. I suppose it was all part of what made me the way I was. Am. My resilience, as Dr Blake would put it. It's why the prickling hatred from Ramona, the Blakes' old housekeeper, never troubled me much; and why the spiked glances and sharp fingers of Ana did. In much the same way, I know the older woman in the second row with the wire-rimmed glasses and the try-hard mum-bob is not who her name tag (Dr Ellen Kneck) says she is. She laughs when I joke, her large, bulbous eyes trained upon me the same way the nineteen other pairs of eyes are, as I talk and talk... She follows my gestures and she nods when I say things that should be nodded along to. There is absolutely nothing that would make anyone else pick her out as a foe. But I can tell. It's just there... it's the care with which she listens, the misplaced pinches of concentration. She's trouble. But she doesn't trouble me.

'...the earliest Guard models were all named for the Greek alphabet – Alpha, Beta, et cetera. The researchers then deemed these monikers too personal and the next batch, including T here, were each simply given a letter of the English alphabet. When this ran its inevitable course and the research had proven itself successful enough for everyone concerned to know that no matter what you called them, the Guard would never retain or recall any facsimile of their bodies' former characteristics, the names became anything two syllables or less. This, of course, has been for the convenience of BFI staff thus far. Once the Guard are made available to the public and each has been assigned a primary client, that person will be free to call them whatever they want.

'As explained, the average bonding process encompasses the length of a good night's sleep. By then the client's particular model will be linked psychically to them for the trial period of two weeks. By which point the client should be well-positioned to make their decision on whether or not to purchase. Hardly a difficult one, as far as we at Beaumont Futura Industries are concerned.'

I smile, dipping my head forward as a few of them chuckle. There is no mirror, of course, but I can tell the soft lighting of the functional meeting room is gleaming upon the dark waves of hair spiralling from the neat clips behind my ears, that my eyes are ablaze in all their jade glory. I need no mirror but my audience, who watch me with a mixture of intrigue, amusement, lust, wonder... all the usual things. Even 'Dr Kneck' glances between me and the three stoic Guard Assistants behind me, her mouth twitching in acknowledgement of my hint of a joke. I wait for the three seconds it takes one of them to ask the question, just for the fun of seeing who might be bold enough to try and catch me off guard. It's Professor Pillsboom in the front row – old, cynical, misogynistic. Good. This will be fun.

'How exactly do you expect us to believe all of this? I mean, you *do* realise this has all been peddled to us before, don't you? Must have been what, five, six years ago, your colleague came to see me in Oxford. Creepy guy, pale. Came with a great big entourage of those weird robot people and tried to do a sales pitch. We were all so freaked out by the things that none of us were sure, at the end of it all, whether he'd been trying to sell them to us or asking us to buy more for him... He was almost as weird as they were. Softly-spoken. Charming but in a horrible hypnotic kind of way. Odd name...'

'Dr Josiah Lychen is the Managing Director of Beaumont Futura Industries—'

'That was it, Lychen.'

'Like all of his successful predecessors in the field, Dr Lychen has learned a great deal from past endeavours, including the earlier applications of this particular research.'

'Seemed to be more of a pitch problem than an error in application.'

I silence him with a glance.

'But in answer to your more pertinent query, of course I don't just expect you to believe this. After all, it has come from a former partner of the ARC Institute, and I know you'll all have seen the press regarding the recent court cases and settlements from their past experimentations. However, this research has been in development for more than a decade and operates with full transparency. It is rock solid and, moreover, our sourcing of subjects is fully government-approved. The Prime Minister himself has shown personal interest in the project after his private tour of the Beaumont facility at the start of the year. But, of course, you are scientists. You need to witness...' I lower myself abruptly backwards and sense rather than see the Guard Assistant nearest me sweep the desk chair across with one swift movement. I sit back as my audience raises its collective eyebrows. I smile until they all can't help but echo it.

'Parlour tricks,' mutters Pillsboom, the first to find his frown.

'Perhaps.' I stand up again and the same Assistant tugs the chair back into place and joins the others in their at-ease positions against the wall. 'So why not try it for yourself, then?'

'What?'

'I have the necessary instruments here. I have a spare Assistant. It will take mere moments to bond them to you—'

'But you said it would take eight hours!' he exclaims, visibly alarmed. I let him see how happy this makes me.

'It takes eight hours to bond an individual to an Assistant for the two-week trial period. A few seconds would be sufficient for, say, an hour. The process is painless, I assure you.'

'I... I don't know— I'm not sure if I...'

'I'll do it,' the imposter stands up, as I suspected she might. I smile from her back to Pillsboom, urging his inner chauvinist not to let another upstart bitch get the better of him... Come on, old man. His brow unfurrows and he holds up his hands.

'OK, I'll bite,' he laughs, gruffly. 'Can't have you all thinking I'm scared. Where do you want me?'

I force myself not to glance at fake-Kneck as she sits back down, every inch of her bristling with disappointment. I guide Pillsboom into the chair in front of the briefcase on the desk next to me. From the case I gather a small device which I place behind his ear and he makes some asinine comment about mind control which goes unacknowledged as I position a slightly larger probe behind the ear of the second Guard Assistant. The female, T, just because. Professor Pillsboom looks at me and raises his eyebrows as I remove both devices after ten seconds.

'Is that it? I don't feel anything...'

'You wouldn't. Nothing has been added to you, just extracted. As I explained earlier, the bond works with the copying of your basic desires and needs. Obviously, after ten seconds these will just be surface-deep. There will not be able to tell us anything *too* incriminating,' there's a smattering of laughter as the old man turns puce. 'But have a go at thinking about something basic and—'

There's a gasp as the female Guard moves suddenly, swooping down over one of Professor Pillsboom's shoes and scrubbing at its surface with the corner of her own sleeve. His mouth forms a perfect O as she then crosses the room to where he had been sitting, plunges a hand into his briefcase and emerges with a water bottle. She brings it to him without so much as a glimmer of expression.

'That's— how did she know—?'

'The mind is a complicated thing. I could go into the ins and outs of impulse desire and control, the layers of the minute things that make up what we want and need, not to mention what we *think* we want and need on just a minute-by-minute basis. But perhaps you have seen and heard enough now, to get the idea...'

Pillsboom is staring at T, who is now balancing on one foot, holding the other in her hand as she continues to stare blandly ahead. She hops three times facing forward, three times facing the window...

'Extraordinary...' the professor mutters. 'How much did you say you needed, for the initial roll out?'

I smile, unable to stop my eye meeting the frowning

gaze of trouble in the second row. She is the only one still watching me and not the hopping robot-woman next to me.

3

April, 2019

A little after midday the van slows to a grumbling stop on gravel. Ariana burrows deeper into the blankets, but no one opens the door to the boot. Ariana hasn't been to the former-boys'-school-turned-laboratory since the autumn, but she'd been allowed to sit in the last time Felix and Ralph returned from one of their 'fact-finding' missions. She'd been quite excited to see them return, having spent most of the day imagining them on their quest – both dressed in black, her father long and lean, Felix short, blocky and tough, waiting for the cover of darkness. After the last of the white-coated workers had left, the two of them would break a window, Felix using some sort of high-tech, handheld device to disable the alarm system before they would slither and weave along the long school-like corridors. Perhaps dodging laser beams and booby traps along the way – Lychen and Daniel were bound to have put *some* new security measures in place since last October when Ralph and the others had broken in – broken in with *her* help, not that anyone seemed to remember that anymore.

In reality Felix and Ralph had shuffled into the front room (once Dr Blake's office, now more of a living room with a new flatscreen TV shoved into one of the corners) a little after seven pm. Neither looked particularly ruffled;

Felix appeared as pale and annoyed as she always did, Ralph seemed almost cheerful despite a large, blood-like stain on his jacket. Ariana had been expecting to be sent to her room at the very least, as Dominic and Tess had joined her and Dr Blake in the room, but no one had blinked an eye in her direction, so she'd remained where she sat, cross-legged in front of MTV.

As it transpired, absolutely nothing exciting or dramatic had happened at all. Felix and Ralph had spent most of the day in the Futura car park waiting for a 'sympathetic' contact of Tess's to emerge for her lunch break. Once identified, this person had informed them, rather bemusedly, that there were an increased number of Guard people – Guard Assistants, they were supposed to be called now – working at the facility but she had no idea if one of them might once have been called Ethan Bryden. Yes, she would take a look at the photo but no, she didn't recognise him. They all looked the same to her and, to be honest, they creeped her out so much she preferred not to look at them at all if she could help it. The whole interrogation was over before lunch, so they'd stopped at KFC on their way home, which explained the stain on Ralph's jacket. Annoyed, not least when Ralph had looked up, seen her and grinned instead of barking at her to go straight to her room, Ariana had decided around that point that nothing exciting was probably ever going to happen to her again. She had begun to suspect as much by the end of her first week living in Cumbria, at which point her grandfather had called her by her mother's name about fifty times already, and had looked perplexed when she'd asked for the Wi-Fi code. At least she had persuaded her dad, who luckily did know the Wi-Fi code, that she should be allowed to go to the local high school in the neighbouring town rather than be home-schooled like he had been.

The kids in Cumbria aren't quite the same as at home, but Ariana has never had trouble making friends... Still, the days seem longer somehow than they had back in Flintworth, less fringed in spiky danger when she glances over her shoulder; logs into her new Instagram account; lies in bed trying hard not to think about what her mother might be doing in her new, glamourous life hundreds of miles away in London. And then she wakes, half-suffocating on her own hand, heart thundering, adrenaline coursing... alive, awake, ready to *go*. The nightmares aren't fun, but at least they remind Ariana that there is something else out there beyond the endless grey and green mountains lumping through her bedroom window, that those half-human creatures *are* real... and they need her help.

She waits for ten minutes after hearing the door slam behind Felix and Ralph. They've made an actual appointment this time. Ariana can't help but roll her eyes, even in the solitary darkness of the back of the van, as she recalls the parts of the plan she has overheard during the past week. With Dr Blake's help, they've cooked up a cock-and-bull story about some old research papers to do with the B-Project and given Dr Skaid just enough information to persuade him to grant them a meeting with one of his colleagues. Ariana knows it won't be long before the Futura person realises they're full of it, so she must move quickly. She stretches her legs, flexes the cramps out and, her limbs still spasming with pins and needles, scurries to the van's back door, which opens easily from the inside. She barely spares the large squat building a glance as she blinks in the weak sunlight of the cloudy day, pulls her hood over her curls and tucks the loose strands in. Then she dips her head low and walks purposefully toward the far eastern end of the building where she knows, thanks to an overheard conversation between Tess and Dominic, that there is an old fire door with a dodgy catch.

'I'll give you ten minutes,' the snide, greasy-faced youth says to Felix's chest. She feels her arms flexing in response and battles the urge to plunge one of her fists into his wet-looking forehead.

'We've come a long way with data from Dr Blake himself,' Ralph snaps from her left side. She doesn't need to look at him to know how his jaw clenches around the words. The sallow man smirks at him and this time Felix has to look away to force herself to stay still. The carpeted entrance hall of the former boys' school is much as she remembers it. She, Ethan, and the others hadn't entered this way back in October, of course, that would have been foolish even without the Guard placed either side of the plain double doors behind them. But there to the right is the corridor from which she had followed Ethan after he'd thrown his first home-made hand grenade into an unmanned laboratory. Opposite is an identical-looking passageway where she'd been separated from the group after receiving an unexpected blow to the back of the head. Felix can still feel the bruise to her skull sometimes, late at night when she grinds her teeth into her pillow. And there, just beyond this pimple-nosed cretin's gesturing arm as he explains just how busy he is and just how little the name of Dr Frederick Blake means to *anyone* these days, is the polished door through which Ethan had burst and never returned. Felix can still feel the way he'd looked straight through her when she'd gone in to see him on the surgical bed hours later. This time she can't keep the anger from her voice as she cuts into the man-child's monologue.

'Listen, *mate*. We've been given this meeting for a reason. *You* know what you're doing here. *I* know what you're doing here. Your boss Daniel... well, we all know he's up to his slimy little neck in it. And yes, we all know Dr Blake's been all over the journals and the papers with the Project A court cases. I know you all think he's a massive failure or a senile old sell-out or whatever for settling. But he's also the reason you're here. He's the reason why all of this is here. So I suggest you stop pedalling your little power trip and take us somewhere a bit quieter so I can show you this tiny wodge of papers which might go a little way towards explaining why your Project B freaks aren't communicating meaningfully.'

The boy raises his eyebrows and she knows that she's surprised him. *This must be what it's like to be Bella,* she thinks briefly, as the power of his discomfort swarms through her veins like hot wire.

'How did you know they don't speak?' The voice is reedy and thin and comes from the corridor off to the right. Felix hears Ralph's gasp before she can turn and the sudden surge of power drops from her like a swallowed shadow.

Daniel Skaid is standing, all wispy hair and grubby lab coat, in the entrance to the corridor on the far right. Held firmly by his side and wearing an expression caught between fury and sheepishness, is—

'Ariana,' Ralph groans. 'What are you doing here?'

'Answer mine first,' Daniel snaps, tightening his grip around the girl's arm. The fabric of her black hoodie pinches visibly where his fingernails must be digging into flesh, but Ariana only spares him the merest twitch.

The Child Left in the Dark

'I read up about our old work on B,' Ralph says, quickly. 'The consciousness barrier was always insurmountable, even with the earliest of experiments. There was nothing that could be done to make it happen. That's why our lot gave up on it.'

'Is that so?' Daniel rolls the words around slowly, like a boiled sweet.

'Yes,' Ralph says, shortly, 'I know it now, Dr Blake knew it then, and I'm willing to bet your pal Lychen knows it too, but goodness knows he has to give you *something* to play with.'

Daniel's greyish face clouds over briefly and Felix knows that the suspicion is not a new one to him. Then he wets his lips and moves his head a little closer to Ariana's. The girl, who is only half a head or so shorter than him, throws him a look of pure loathing and tries to inch away.

'Maybe I'll find something else to play with then, Blakey boy.'

'She's a twelve-year-old little kid you sick fu—'

'Do you think that bothers me?' Daniel shakes the girl, his eyes bulging wildly from his skull. 'Do you think I give a damn how old she is or who her parents are? Do you know who *I* am? I've done things you couldn't even begin to imagine, Blake. I don't answer to *anyone*!'

He throws Ariana to the ground and spits next to her. She rolls away from the glob of moisture gleaming on the old floor tiles and springs to her feet before anyone can reach down to help her.

'*I* know what you've done!' she exclaims, her voice choking with fury. 'I've seen it! I saw it again today; I could have let them all go if that stupid lab assistant hadn't forgotten her glasses!'

Daniel looks at her and yawns slowly. Felix darts

forward to catch the girl round the shoulders before she can lunge at him. Ariana shrieks wordlessly and Felix is surprised by the force she has to use to keep her back. The greasy-faced man-boy from earlier has retreated to a safe distance, eyes stretched to their limits as he watches.

'This is all very tiresome, Blake,' Daniel says, blandly, 'I know you're not really here to pass on some long-disproven theory about whatever my project used to be, so I'll save you the trouble of bothering us again. Ethan Bryden is not here.'

'Where is he, then?' The question hisses from Felix before she can stop it. Ariana falls still in her arms and looks at Daniel as well. Daniel just smiles, slowly. It doesn't reach his eyes. It barely reaches his mouth.

'I could expose you, you know,' Felix blurts, desperately. 'I could go to the police, the press, the government – I know your boss has his puppets but can he really survive it going viral that his precious empire is making innocent people into Guard without consent?'

'Ah, but you see, I *did* have consent, dear Fee. You yourself signed a form allowing us to do whatever it took to save Ethan. He was brain-dead. This was the only way.'

'Bullshit was he brain-dead!' But she remembers, even as she says it, the ashen slackness of Ethan's face as two men had heaved him onto a stretcher, muttering about blood loss. A piece of paper and a pen thrust into her hand. *Consent for surgery*. Had they really said that? Had they said more?

Daniel watches her as if he can see the memory stammering into place as the fight seeps out of her. 'Is it *my* fault you didn't read the small print? I'll let you go this time. Not because I want to. I hate waste. If it were up to me, you'd all be given new lives here. Maybe I'd meld you with a weasel, Blake. Seems to match your character. A rat for Blake junior here, who likes to squeeze into places she's not supposed to be. And Fee-Fee, you'd be joining Ethan. I've never had a married Guard set before. Could be lucrative, in certain circles... There are people out there who'll pay for some *very* strange things. Trust me.'

He leers horribly at them all before slouching away. Ralph snorts contemptuously and reaches for Ariana. She shakes him off with a filthy look and stalks towards the front doors.

'Really? You sneak into the back of the van and put us all in danger and *you're* the one who's mad at me? Come on, Ri!' He jogs after her. Felix follows slowly, her mind still fumbling through those desperate, blood-soaked moments following the gun-shot which had ripped her world apart. Had Ethan really been brain-dead? Would she ever know?

'Don't call me that!' Ariana spits over her shoulder at Ralph, 'Only Mum calls me Ri! You'd know that if you knew anything about me at *all*!'

Ralph stops and glances at Felix as they follow the girl out of the double doors.

'What the hell did I do now?'

Felix sighs, shaking the image of Ethan out of her head. 'My first guess would be calling her a little kid in front of Daniel and master mouth-breather back there...'

'But she *is* a—'

'My second would be that you called her a *twelve*-year-old little kid. Her birthday was on the fourteenth, last week...'

Ralph stops. They've reached the car park now, Ariana striding stiffly several paces ahead, her entire frame edged in fury. A sudden break in the clouds throws a blanching light across Ralph's tired features.

'Oh. Oh, *crap*!'

'Yep,' Felix nods grimly. In a different lifetime, she ponders, she would laugh. If there were a soul-intact Ethan nearby to catch her eye, to roll his own back at her.

'She didn't say anything...'

'Can you blame her?'

'No. God, I'm *terrible* at all this. Even *my* dad always remembered my bloody birthdays...' He starts walking, one stride for every two of hers so she has to jog a little to catch up. Ariana is waiting by the van now, determinedly not looking at either of them.

'How did *you* know?' Ralph squints down, sees she's jogging and slows his pace. Felix shrugs.

'I let her help me out with the computers. She's pretty good, actually. We chat. We miss our people... not exactly together but, you know, at the same time.' She thinks about telling him about the nightmares. About the mad, desperate panic of the child's eyes in the darkness when Felix rushes into her bedroom. The teeth marks scoured into the flesh of her hand. The wrack of shudders so hard, so violent that sometimes she can't tell who they're coming from as they huddle together on the bed.

'I'm sorry, Fee,' Ralph sighs.

'What for?'

'Everything. All of it. You and Ethan... always wanting to be parents and not getting the chance. Me getting it thrown into my lap and crapping it all up...'

No. Ariana never speaks of the nightmares so neither will she.

'If you're looking for someone to stroke your ego, you're barking up the wrong tree here...'

He grins and she smiles quickly, tightly, back at him. It

feels weird, like the sun's kiss of warmth on bare limbs after months of winter.

'It's not all about long lengthy bonding sessions, Ralph. Talk to her, find some common ground, but don't make it all intense. Kids are good at saying more when their hands are busy and they don't have to look at you.'

'Right. Thanks... And, well. I suppose today wasn't a total bust. We did find out that Ethan's alive and not here anymore...'

'True. Shame we've no idea where he actually is... or if we'll be able to bring him back to himself once we *do* find him. If what he said is true about Ethan being brain-dead...'

'Look, you remember what Daniel was like as a kid. All he cared about was getting what he wanted, he lied as easily as he breathed. And he hated everyone, especially us lot. Of course he'd have taken the chance to turn Ethan if he ended up on his operating table. Brain-dead my arse.'

'Still doesn't mean we can turn him back,' Felix mumbles, though Ralph's words have lightened her mood considerably.

'Well. Dad and I are on the case there at least with Serum X. I really do think we're onto something with the incorporation of the dementia medication...'

They've reached the van too now. Ariana gives no sign that she's been joined by anybody whatsoever.

'Hey, R—... Ariana... Ari. Maybe I can call you that instead? I mean, I like Ana too but it was my mum's name so that's a bit weird, isn't it...' Ralph looks up, remembers what Felix said and looks down again, flapping his hands a little. Felix unlocks the van doors and Ariana climbs delicately into the back seat, folding her legs neatly into the footwell. It's a graceful movement so reminiscent of Bella that Felix has to blink and shake her head a little, catching

Ralph doing the same just before he props the front passenger seat back into place and climbs into it.

'Anyway, I'm sorry about saying you were twelve back there. Of course, you're thirteen now. Maybe we can stop off on the way home, now we know you're with us. Do you like KFC? I could murder a Zinger Tower burger...'

Ariana sniffs and Felix, now in the driver's seat, glances into the rear-view mirror to see a confusion of expressions cross the girl's face. Stubbornness, anger, sadness, wanting... She doubts living with Bella facilitated many trips to the local fast-food establishments.

'I like *normal* burgers...'

'I'm sure we can manage that. And... there's a shopping centre not far from here... Maybe we could stop off there.'

'You want to take me *shopping*?' Ariana snorts as Felix taps the shopping centre into her Sat Nav and starts the engine.

'Not for clothes and such... But you complained the other week about your laptop being all slow...'

'Only because the broadband at The Manor is from, like, the nineties...'

Ralph chuckles and is rewarded by the twitch of a grin's shadow from the backseat.

'So you *wouldn't* like a nice new one for your birthday, then?'

'Yeah,' the answer comes quickly. Felix pulls backwards out of the parking space and glances in the mirror again. More conflict battles across Ariana's face. *This is how she's different to Bella,* Felix thinks. *Bella never questioned a thing about herself. Not in a way that was visible to others, in any case.*

'Yes, please. That would be good. Thanks.'

'You're welcome, Ari.'

Ariana accepts the nickname without comment and Ralph smiles at Felix. She rolls her eyes back at him, but she lets him have this small, expensive victory. Catching Ariana's eye very briefly in the mirror as she prepares to pull away from the squat, grey building behind them, Felix winks and receives the smallest glimmer of a smile in return.

April, 2019

By the time it's dark outside I can tell they're all in. Every single one of them. The Guard Assistants have completely captivated their attention. They watch the solid bulky forms with their bland unassuming expressions and they think about how much easier their lives would be with one of these doing the laundry, picking up their kids from school, walking the dog on wet, freezing days. Responding to their every whim and desire before they even know it's there... Well, almost all of them. Fake-Kneck still watches me from a corner of the room, her expression inscrutable.

'So, as I said, the investment packages are all outlined in the material we have emailed. We do ask that any initial offers are made by the end of the month. Are there any further questions at this point?'

My feet are beginning to protest in the high heels I have been wearing for seven hours and I'm looking forward to the cool, soft leather of the back seat of the limousine, the dark windows, the absence of sentient beings, their eyes, their questions, before we arrive back at the Beaumont and I have to don the next mask. I glance around the room, sensing hunger, tiredness, bladders under pressure, a general need to be out of here and away to warm, safe houses. Except the imposter, who waits until I am watching before she raises her hand, a smirk flicking across her flat features.

'Ms D'accourt? Or is it Mrs?' She pokes without knowing what it is she does.

'Dr Kneck. Was that your question?'

'No. I was wondering if you would address the rumours that the Beaumont have begun using teenagers under the age of eighteen as source material for these Guard Assistants?'

'I am not here to address rumours, Dr Kneck,' I say, cordial but icy-firm. She frowns and looks down and up again.

'But you do *know* what's going on in the place where you work, don't you? It wouldn't exactly be the first time the BFI has been linked to the exploitation of children...'

'I am not here to address rumours. Now if there are no further questions about the Guard Assistance Programme, I think we are finished here. Thank you all for your time, and we will be in touch.'

Fake-Kneck opens her mouth to keep arguing, but then she looks past me, towards the Guard man who moved the chair earlier. I don't need to turn to know his head has moved, that his eyes have focused on her. Something shadowy moves across her face and she looks down again. The rest of the audience have already descended into excited chatter and there are three, no four, eager men waiting to talk to me, invite me for drinks, see what else they can find out about BFI and me, its mysteriously alluring new spokesperson. I respond charmingly, smiling where it is needed, flirting here and there but carefully matching their intelligence every step of the way, watching out of the corner of my eye as the imposter makes her way slowly out the back door, a lumpy leather handbag clasped to her side. I give her five minutes' head start before I make my excuses and leave, my Guard Assistants following behind with my case.

Darkness has fully descended once we are out of the tall municipal building and into the gravel-lined car park. I'm glad to see fake-Kneck standing off to one side of my limousine as I approach with my entourage. Saves a tedious chase at least. We both pretend I haven't seen her while the rest of the businessmen disperse to their cars or down the road towards the town's pubs and train station. My Primary Guard man places the briefcase in the boot of the car while T opens the front passenger door. The third goes to the driver's side and climbs in to begin warming the vehicle. It's late April but the sky is clear and the ice-tinged night air clouds lumpenly in front of our faces.

'Does Felix Bryden know what your colleagues have done to her husband?'

I take my time turning from the boot of the car to face her, not letting my surprise show on my face.

'As a matter of fact, she does.'

She twitches irritably and I can tell my reaction has not lived up to the expectation she created when she rehearsed this moment. She tries again:

'You're Bella, aren't you?'

'I didn't realise my first name was omitted from the invitation to tonight's meeting. It shouldn't have been.' I check my nails impatiently. I'm cold despite the fur lining my coat, and my feet are really starting to ache now. I'm sure I used to be able to wear high heels for far longer back in my late teens. All those years as Elodie Guerre in her blocky flats have ruined me.

'No, I mean... You're Bella D'accourt. From the ARC... The last surviving Project A designer baby.'

'Ah.' Finally she has my full attention. She flinches to

receive it. 'Now I do know that the newspapers and journals withheld my name from the court case reports. Who are you, then? A relative of one of the other A-Subjects? Someone connected to the Blakes? Is that how you know Felix? Or are you one of our own... A disillusioned worker from Futura, perhaps? I know you're not Ellen Kneck.'

I stare at her so she can't look away. She has to answer, though the words stumble reluctantly.

'I'm not linked to Project A,' she says, trying to keep her voice icy. 'And I don't know Felix or the Blakes anymore.'

'Good. So you must be linked to the Futura. I know they're a little more... open-minded... about their hiring policies than Beaumont.'

'I'm not... I used to work... Argh, what are you doing to me?' She smacks herself on the forehead, but she can't look away. I have her and she knows it. A spasm of fear crosses her face.

'Who are you? How did you come to acquire Kneck's invitation for tonight? It'll be quicker if you just tell me the truth. After all, isn't that what you wanted to talk to me about?'

'I intercepted Kneck's invitation. I work with her at Shaker University... I know her by sight, we're a similar age and I knew that no one here would notice... Not with you about, anyway.'

'OK. And who are you? How did you come to know about Project A?'

'I... I know someone who works at Futura... I'm not sure what in, exactly, she's all NDA'd but she's getting fed up of it all. Apparently something big happened there last year and she's got ongoing issues as a result, didn't get properly compensated... She told me that all the funding to her project has been redirected in the last six months to the Guard developments going on at the Beaumont and she's facing redundancy as a result. I asked her what the new developments were but she didn't know much, she doesn't like the Guard projects, they freak her out. But she did tell me the rumours that are going around about a new Guard programme using teenagers, some as young as sixteen...'

'Fifteen, actually.'

'They're children.'

'Actually, they're not. We don't use pre-pubescents. They're not... stable enough. Fundamentally changing the thought process of children before they have reached the self-actualisation of adolescence can result in some extremely... unbalanced... individuals.'

'Like Project C? Like *you*?' She hisses, her eyes now torn from me to the Guard man approaching her from my left side. I smile brightly as if she has just complimented me on my shoes.

'Yes, precisely. Now, please.'

She doesn't have time to scream. She barely gives a yawp of horror as the Guard man walks up to her, locks an arm around her mouth and uses the other to restrain her arms, which have grasped outwards in defence. I wait and then approach, nodding at him to loosen his hold a little.

'If you co-operate you will live. Understand?' She nods. 'Good. Now I will ask you this one more time – who are you? What's it to you what we do with our Guard projects?'

'You don't remember me, do you?'

I frown, caught momentarily off guard. I scour my memory for her pallid, paunchy face. Dull, muddy eyes behind thick glasses. A fashionable hair cut which couldn't quite compete with that of her prettier, slimmer colleague... So she'd made up for it by being the best, sucking up to those in charge... Dr Blake... then Lychen... She sneers and suddenly I recognise her.

'Melinda. From the ARC. Melinda... Brown?'

'Burton. I didn't expect you to recognise me straight away. I know we weren't exactly close once you wormed your way to the top... But I'd have thought the infamous Bella D'accourt would have been able to identify an adversary far more quickly.'

'You're giving yourself too much credit. I barely remember you, even now.'

She flinches and I know my insult has hit her deeply.

'Well I remember you. I remember the day Dr Blake first brought you to the ARC when you were a dinky, pretty little scrap of a girl. All twinkly and sweet, even with poor Robbie. Especially poor Robbie. He became a bit obsessed when you disappeared. Drove him a bit mad in the end. Lychen fired him, said that it was getting creepy and inappropriate. Guess he thought he owned the copyright on that...'

'So what became of you, Melinda Burton? Dominic told me you went with Lychen, after Rudy died.'

'After Rudy was killed, you mean. Yes, I joined him,' she sniffs, peering disdainfully down at the Guard's arm around her front as if it were an unfashionable scarf. 'Is it any wonder? I still see those dark, cold rooms in the basement of the ARC where they took those poor Project C children when they turned inward with the madness... But then I learned a bit more about what Lychen was actually doing, developing those *things* that used to be people,' she gestures behind her at the impassive face staring into the middle distance. 'On top of the ghastly Project B rumours and what became of the poor Subjects he brought with him – Daniel, little Nova... That was around the time I made my excuses, said I wanted to get into something a bit tamer. Lychen didn't care. I was already getting on in years, wanting to settle down, have a family. Once I signed all the exit NDAs he let me go without a fuss.'

'But you broke one of the rules, didn't you? You kept in touch with someone from the Futura Lab, didn't you? Who?'

The Guard tightens his grip at my silent urge. Melinda's eyes bulge even further, and her voice, when she next speaks, comes out as a tight wheedle.

'What'll you do to her?'

'If you were so concerned for her, you wouldn't have drawn attention to yourself. What is her name?'

'They all heard me. All the... the *salivating* delegates in there, argh! They know now about the children you're using, even if it's just the rumour... What?'

'The rumours don't matter,' I smile, though I know my eyes are still spitting fire. I can feel it melting pinpricks of her hammy skin. 'In fact, they generate intrigue. We were going to feed out mention of the Youth Programme in the next few weeks anyway.'

'So... why all this?' She frowns, even as she starts to choke. I have the Guard release his grip across her chest slightly more without letting my gaze leave hers. 'Is it just because I questioned you in front of them? Christ! Make him stop, I'm bloody asthmatic!'

'What is her name?'

'It's Miriam Jones! Please, Bella! I've got kids!'

The Guard puts his hand back over her mouth as he reaches into his pocket.

'I'll do it,' I say. Not because I need to out loud, but because I want her to hear it. I want her to see me. He hands me the syringe without a word and I plunge it into her neck.

'And it's *Dr* D'accourt, FYI,' I mutter, as her eyes float upwards and finally, finally, she stops watching me.

'Take her car to Skaid and tell him who she is,' I say, as the Guard man takes her weight easily. 'Find Miriam Jones while you're there and report her to Skaid as well. Make sure he knows who caught them. A gift, for his ongoing patience, tell him.'

The Guard man nods and reaches into Melinda's pocket for her car keys. He presses the button and an old Peugeot flashes itself unlocked across the gravel.

'Thank you, Ethan.'

5

Autumn, 2005

> Bella, what's going on? You sounded so strange on the phone.

>> How would you know what I normally sound like?

> OK, OK, good point. I more meant what you were saying... all this cloak and dagger secrecy. What on earth is going on?

> Bella? Can we meet? I would love to see you.

> Bella, are you getting my messages?

>> This afternoon, 4pm, Covent Garden tube station.

> Yes, of course.

>> Tell no one and come alone.

> Bella, are you in some kind of trouble?

>> Yes.

I chucked the cheap Nokia into my small plain rucksack and approached the narrow mirror. It was pocked and stained with blemishes but showed my reflection well enough.

Standing sideways, my hand hovered over my stomach. There was just the slightest hint of a curve when I flattened my loose T-shirt, the skin already taut underneath. My jeans were beginning to feel tight in the mornings and by the evenings I often had to undo the top button. I would have to go up a size by the end of the month at this rate.

Turning away from the mirror, I shrugged a long hooded cardigan on and checked the pockets for cash. Nothing. I turned back to my rucksack and dug out a leather wallet. I'd acquired a very good price for the car I'd left The Manor in; the car Dr Blake had bought me when I'd passed my test two years earlier, but even so there weren't many notes left now. I'd been staying in the hostel for just over two weeks after realising that hotels were not as cheap or anonymous as I had been hoping, especially on the outskirts of London. Luckily my loss of a private bathroom had coincided with the ease of the horrendous – and often untimely – bouts of early pregnancy nausea. At least my bedroom was my own, though I never left anything of value behind when I went out each day.

Placing the wallet back into my bag, I reached for the sunglasses on my nightstand, slotting them on top of my head ready to be pulled down over my distinctive eyes. Hair pulled into a ponytail, make-up minimal; jeans, trainers, faded colours, high-street brands. None of it was me, but that was the point. I wasn't me anymore. I cleared my throat, smoothed my top once again and swallowed hard against the lingering threat of sickness until it faded. Then I looped my backpack over my shoulder, crossed the room and left, locking the door behind me and passing through the shabby door-lined corridor without looking up. I emerged onto the street and brought my sunglasses down. Just another student making her way across London

The Child Left in the Dark

to meet her dad for money.

The years had not been kind to Marc D'accourt. I remembered him as impossibly tall, with a generous mane of the dark curls I'd inherited and the large brown eyes he shared with my brother and sister. His full-lipped mouth had curved a constant smile and his hands had been large, strong and comically hairy. I tried to banish all sentimental thoughts and memories as I stood under the overhang of the shop opposite the tube station, watching the jumble of commuters and tourists flood unremittingly from the exit. I tried to block out the expanse of his hands around my ribs, tumbling my small body high up into the air and then back down into the soft melt of his cuddle. The whiskery burrow of his chin against my soft skin and the way his voice lifted into a songful caress when he said my name. It was impossible not to, though. I didn't know if it was the pregnancy, the swoosh of irrational impulses which assaulted my brain daily and far more irritatingly than the nausea had or just the fact that I hadn't spoken to a person who knew my real name for over two months now. Still, it was a shock when I turned from the tall handsome man in his fifties who'd clearly just spotted his wife somewhere off to my left to spot a sweaty, balding man in a shirt which strained over a burgeoning stomach making his way towards me, grinning nervously.

'Bella!' He opened his arms wide but stopped short when I lifted my sunglasses a fraction and shook my head. His smile faltered. As he drew close I could see he was indeed still tall, and when he rolled his sleeves up, his arms were whittled in muscle and the dark wiry hair I remembered.

'I took the stairs,' he said, apologetically. 'Too crowded to wait for those flaming lifts... Forgot how many there were though, hence looking like I've just attempted a marathon in a work shirt. Would you like to go and grab a drink somewhere? I know a good coffee place slightly off the beaten track...'

His voice took me straight back to childhood – lace dresses, a pink bedroom, barbed glares – and I battled to keep my voice level as I replied with a simple: 'Fine.'

He stole glances at me as we walked, the crowds jostling us back and forth, as if unsure if I were real or not. Conversation was stilted and mostly one-sided. It was only when we had reached the coffee shop – reassuringly filled with older, business-meeting clientele – and were sitting opposite one another that I removed my sunglasses and settled back into my chair, letting a small fraction of the tension I carried like armour lift a tiny bit. I looked up to see him staring at me almost hungrily.

'What?'

'Nothing... Just... It's been *ten years*. I can't believe I'm actually seeing you, sitting here with you.' He laughed incredulously and passed a hand over his forehead. Now he'd stopped sweating so much he looked more like the man I remembered, just with a few less hairs on his head and a few more kilos on his front. 'I mean, just hearing from you in the first place was enough of a shock. And now you're here. God, you're just so beautiful. *So* beautiful... I'd imagined, over the years, you know. But... wow.'

He chuckled nervously. I stared, unflinching. A waiter approached, took our order – cappuccino for him, peppermint tea for me – and bustled away again. Marc cleared his throat.

'So... how are you? Did you say you were staying in Catford now?'

'Yes. A hostel. It's not brilliant but I've got my own

room and it's cheap enough for now.'

'I wish you would let me help—'

'I am. That's why I'm here. The cash I've been using is running out...'

'How much do you need?'

'I don't know, exactly. There are things I want to do...'

'Such as...?'

'I've been going to one of the London universities, sitting in on lectures. Their security is pretty lax. You can practically get a degree without ever registering, as long as you get hold of a student card and that's easy enough to do once you work out where they go drinking...'

'Right...'

'But what's the point of doing the work if I'm not going to actually get a degree out of it? I *want* a degree. It's kids' stuff, some of what they're doing. Concepts and theories Blake taught me when I was barely into my teens. But it means something, getting those letters. I want to do a BSc, and maybe even a PhD...'

'OK, well I'm sure we can manage that... It's not like you'll have any trouble getting in by the sounds of things. We might even be able to arrange something for a January start, a lot of places do that nowadays...'

'No. I can't do it this year. There're people... from the ARC. They'll be looking for me. I already have a deferred place at UCL, that's the first place they'll try.'

'Blake? He doesn't know where you are?'

'No. I mean he doesn't, but it's not him I'm worried about. He knows why I left... sort of. He'll respect my decision, in any case.'

'So who?'

'Look. You must know a bit about what it's like, what they do there. You used them to make me and Silas and

Maya, after all. I'm not trying to understand why you did that. But I'm important to them. And I've got... something... that's important to them as well. Or would be, once they realise what it is.'

'I don't understand. You mean you took something? Like stole it?'

'No... it's mine. They don't know about it but if they do, they'll want it. He will. I'm not... I don't want to tell you his name, but he's bad. He's the worst person in the world. He can't find me. Not again, I *won't*...'

I stopped and put a hand over my mouth. Wretched, *fucking* hormones. I breathed slowly until the rise of it all fell away, until the feel of hands on my throat, cold skin, wrenching pain... all of it... went back down. Down to the dark pit in my centre. My abdomen gave one of the strange, bubbling twitches I'd been noticing over the past few days, as if the thing growing within could sense the shame pushed upon it and was trying to writhe away. Marc was staring at me in horror and I knew that he knew. That he had connected the dots that Dr Blake had failed to back in August.

'Bells... What did they do to you?' He glanced, briefly, from my eyes to my stomach and I nodded.

'Shit.'

'Yeah.'

'Was it...?'

'It's not your concern. It's not a science experiment or a genetic aberration like I was. You don't get to know more than that.'

'But you're in danger? Both of you?'

'Yes.'

'This person... this bad man. He's the father?'

'Yes.'

'And if he found you...?'

'He wants to control me, possess me... He's already tried. If he finds me, he will never let me go. Or the baby.'

His face clouded over. 'And the Blakes? They just let this happen to you, did they?'

'They have no power against him. He owns more of the research than they do now. The stuff with momentum, anyway. Ana tried to warn me. Years ago, before she died.'

'She's dead?'

'Metastatic cancer. When I was fourteen.'

'I'm sorry. She was... a formidable woman.'

I frowned. 'You knew her?'

'A little...'

Our drinks arrived and I watched him blow thoughtfully into the foam of his cappuccino. His gaze dropped to my abdomen again and he smiled a little, though his eyes were sad.

'How far along are you?'

'Almost four months. She's due in April.'

'She? You know it's a little girl?'

'I know. It's too early to see on a scan or anything but... I know.'

'Right.' He sipped. 'So... what do you want to do? Come home?'

'Of course not. I want to change my name. I want to become someone else... Hopefully Blake's bought me some time, but it won't be long before *he* starts looking for me, if he isn't already. Bella D'accourt, 19-year-old London student... she can't exist. A single, foreign mother-to-be in her early twenties, living in a one-bedroom flat south of the river won't even cross his radar.'

'OK... So you need—'

'I've found a place. It's less than eight hundred a

month, I met the landlord and talked him down a bit... Here are the details... I'll need a deposit, a guarantor and I want to rent it in a new name. This one.'

'Going back to our French roots, I see...'

'It's an easy accent. And the Blakes are predictable. When they start looking for me – it'll take them longer, but eventually they will too – they'll search for an Italian name. They wouldn't consider that I'd seek to connect myself with my birth heritage. With you.'

He frowned as the swipe hit him easily.

'But I thought you said Dr Blake knew about the pregnancy—'

'He doesn't know about the baby. But he knows enough about *him.* And he knows I'm in some sort of trouble and that I need to hide.'

'So why would he come for you?'

'Because that's what parents do.'

I stared at him, watching the second blow land and not feeling one bit sorry as he crumpled into a sigh. He drank more coffee. I glanced at my tea, but I knew it was still too hot to sip.

'Well. They also help sort out sticky situations. I just... well, I'd feel better if I knew you were safe...'

'You will,' I frowned, tapping the brochure for the flat in Peckham Rye.

'I mean...'

'You mean at home. *Your* home at Weston-on-the-Hill with the pink bedroom where I lived for nine years and two months. Until the day my mother finally persuaded you to let her abandon me on a stranger's doorstep. Forgive me if the idea doesn't exactly fill me with security.'

He sighed again and looked at the table, at my forehead, my stomach, back to the table.

'You'll have to cover your tracks with the payments.'

'Bella, when you were little—'

'Cash only where possible. Maybe a new bank account.'

'Bells, seriously, your mother—'

'Make it look like you're investing in somewhere to stay when you're in London on business. Christ knows you're rich enough that no one will question it.'

'I never wanted to abandon—'

'I *don't care*,' I hissed, making him flinch back in his seat. 'I don't want to know about it. Not today. Maybe not ever. I just want you to help me now. If you won't, I'll manage without you, but it will be harder—'

'I'll help! Of course I will! And I won't tell your mother, not if you don't want me to…'

'Absolutely not.'

'Well. I can respect that. Maybe one day… But anyway, never mind that now, let's have a look at this place then…'

He reached for the brochure with one hand whilst retrieving a pair of slim reading spectacles from his breast pocket with the other. As he began to read, I settled back in my leather chair, my pulse slowing again after my outburst. As I reached for my tea, which had finally cooled enough, I realised with some surprise that actually, for the first time in months, I did feel just a tiny bit safe.

April, 2019

The limousine reaches London a few minutes past midnight and by the time it draws up on the private driveway of the Beaumont, I can see only a handful of windows alight in the facility's southernmost building. Having dozed on and off during the four-hour journey, my body feels springy and ready for action as I slip my shoes smoothly back onto my feet. I wait for the female Guard Assistant to open my door and peer at her closely as I slide out of the car. She shows no signs of anything – no conflict or confusion, no inclination to be elsewhere, which means the connection with Pillsboom has most likely run its course. Still, to be sure...

'Primary Human Connection status report,' I check her lanyard to remind me of her name, 'T.'

'Connection established at eighteen forty-eight, expired at twenty seventeen. No existing PHC at present.'

'Good.' I glance around at the imposing shard of the outermost point of the triangular-shaped building in front of us. A narrow passageway, almost impossible to see from the gated driveway we've just come through, runs between this building and its tall identical triangular neighbour. I sigh and turn back to T. 'I suppose you'd better take Ethan's place as my Primary while he's gone. We'll do the connection once we're inside.'

'Affirmative.'

The male Guard takes my case from the boot of the car and the two of them flank me as we make our way towards the corridor between the looming triangles. There are eight of these buildings in total, all of them triangular with their own small gardens in the middle, all of them angled round one large green space replete with paths, trees and a pond. This space – known as The Yard – gives the impression of natural wilderness, but every inch has been landscaped down to the last lily pad. Viewed from above, the whole facility would look like a perfect octagram with the spherical pond at the very centre, a pool of dark green surrounded by clinically-striped lawns, dotted trees at calculated intervals and perpendicular pathways.

Passing between the two triangle buildings, we approach one such pathway now. The Yard is deserted, even outside the residential buildings off to the left, though several lights still shine from windows there. I pause as a Guard Assistant emerges from one of the laboratory buildings to my right, his face set as he strides purposefully, a tray of test tubes in his arms. I look around but can't see anyone in perceptible control of him. I turn to the male Guard on my right side.

'That Assistant is taking laboratory equipment out of bounds. Find out who is in charge of him and report back.'

'Shall I apprehend him?'

'No, follow him until he has taken the samples wherever he has been told, then proceed.'

'Yes.' He turns and strides away, handing my case to T. I turn back and notice a few faces watching me with interest from the brightly lit buildings on my left. I blink slowly and set a brisk pace on the pathway leading around the outermost edge of the gardens, T half a step behind.

Most of the workers at the Beaumont like to spend their breaktimes out here in The Yard, chatting over coffee under the cherry blossoms, skimming stones across the pond, feeding the small collection of birds which have found their way through the spires of the surrounding buildings, and down into the tiny patch of tightly-controlled nature. The employees aren't supposed to eat out here – too messy – but there are picnic benches in the smaller gardens at the centres of the triangular buildings.

I don't tend to spend much time out here. Not because of the people or the way my presence seems to silence the huddles and send their gazes skittering anywhere else and then back to me like magnets as I pass. I feel the blaze of their attention, I feel it now as I pass under their windowpane-filtered stares, I feel it but I don't really register it. It's not like how my life was before – then I was always alert as to who it was watching me, who was interested in me for more than my appearance, who might be working for... well, this place; these people. Lychen. Now I live in this place, I lay my head to sleep on Lychen's silk pillows and they can all look at me as much as they like. Their small lives, clustered around these manicured gardens and pointy buildings where they sleep and eat and shit and work and do so under complete and utter control, are not so much a flicker in the pulse of my day.

No. It's not the people in this green space which drives me from it, it's the space itself. The tiny sprigs of nature are all so pruned, so contained, so walled and so very, very far from the Lake District that when I'm here, *there* is all I can think about. Even now, I have to face away from the dark spray of pine to my right so the fresh scent doesn't take me back to the pathway between The Manor and the ARC, the sweet bloom of spring in the air, the lightness of being young and *stupidly beautiful*. It's almost tortuous, coming out here, attractive as it is with its neat landscaping, carefully spaced pagodas and strings of festoon lights glowing softly in the corners of my eyes. You almost can't see the high walls of the octagram which surrounds it, the glare of the windows, the small, almost-hidden exit in the furthest-most corner from the direction I'm currently heading. It's the perfect prison.

They certainly don't see it that way, though. The people who work here. Who live here. This place is the ARC of its time, only bigger, richer, and less ostentatiously secretive. All the young scientists want to be part of this place, but only the best are accepted. The vetting process for potential employees is long and arduous but the benefits are unique, and not just in terms of cutting-edge equipment and discovery. The eight triangles of the octagram are each named for different compass points according to their location – four are given over to laboratories and offices, four to living quarters. The buildings we are passing now, where the lights still blaze and the stares still buzz like gnats against the left side of my face, are called West and North West and contain the apartments belonging to the scientists, technicians and analysts. Being located in central London, the prospect of living at work certainly has its perks for many, and the apartments are basic but practical. Rent and living expenses are taken from wages, but there are, of course, other costs. All live-in employees must sign contracts forbidding any outsiders entering the premises and all are subject to a nightly curfew, and urine tests once a month. I thought at first this was primarily to rule out any drug or alcohol misuse but, once I reread the standard employee contract, I realised that pregnancy was also an eviction-worthy offence. I suspect they have me to thank for that.

Not everyone lives in, of course, but there are certain benefits to being a jog across The Yard away from ongoing experiments in the middle of the night, and each block of eight apartments has its own pair of personal Guard Assistants to help with anything from fetching a midnight sandwich to message delivery, dictation taking, and probably a whole host of other things too tedious for such brilliant minds to concern themselves with. As a result, many who didn't sign up for Beaumont living at the beginning of their contract here often do so within the year. Those that don't – those with children at home, for example – often find themselves slowly relegated to the less desirable projects. Nothing official, of course, nothing that would stand up in any sort of workplace tribunal, but still. There's a reason why most of the workers are unmarried, untethered… There's a reason why those who aren't end up relocating to the outskirts of York to work at Grayson Boys.

The path takes a turn to the right as it skirts the North West building and I glance briefly across The Yard to the North East building, home to the Guard people's prison-like dormitories. Despite there being at least as many Guard people as normal at the Beaumont, their living quarters are so basic, so tiny and soulless, that they don't even fill the building they have. They live like inmates, sleeping in bunk-beds, eating a basic ration of specifically nutritional gruel and energy bars with zero taste, and their particular outdoor triangle is a circuit of fitness equipment designed only to keep their bodies in optimum condition. A person might feel guilty about their pitiful situation until you remember that they feel nothing at all.

The lights are softer around the entrance to the North building, and though the pillars outside the sandstone walls are spaced exactly the same as those outside all the other triangles, these are carved in the more intricate Corinthian style to mark the more luxurious setting. As we turn towards the dark lacquered doors leading inside, two Guard people spring into action from the shadowy alcoves on either side of the door where they have been positioned like Beefeaters. The first opens the door while the other scans T's eyes briefly with his own, checking for anything untoward. Once satisfied, he resumes his former position and we pass into the chandelier-lit hallway. Unlike the other buildings, which mostly have practical, spill-friendly tiled floors, the vast majority of North building is carpeted in plush rich pile. Our feet don't make a sound as we step onto the scarlet carpet of the hallway. Straight ahead is a wide staircase leading to the upper floors of offices and laboratories and the top-level living quarters. To our right, the eastern arm of the triangle leads towards a private kitchen and dining room; to our left, stairs descend to a gymnasium, subterranean swimming pool, jacuzzi, and sauna. Beyond the staircase are windows and double doors leading to the triangle of garden used, perhaps, the least of all the Beaumont's green spaces, yet kept to the highest standards. Perfect, symmetrical flowers bloom along the beds at any given time of year – camellias, tulips, hyacinths soon to be overtaken by roses, dahlias and hydrangeas. Vibrant, dayglo colours sneer from their glossy, perfect shells of petals even through the gloom of night pressing against the window pane.

T pauses as I hesitate at the bottom of the stairs. There is no sound in this building. There rarely is. I head up to the first floor and she follows. Unbonded Guard tend to match their physicality to the human currently commanding them, and though her feet are twice the size of mine and clad in thick-soled mules, T barely makes a touch of noise as she tails me. One level up and the carpets are cream, leading to purpose-built laboratories and offices. For all his careful extrication of association with the ARC over the last few years, Lychen cannot claim that his facility's design isn't influenced by it. For one thing, when it comes to laboratories and offices there is no hierarchy here. All of them contain exactly what they need and no more. Some, over in the South East building for example, are the size of Olympic swimming pools, and bedecked with robotic surgical equipment. Others are no bigger than broom cupboards. There are animal enclosures, libraries, rooms kept entirely dark or light, even a self-contained terrarium somewhere over in South West. The research arms of the Beaumont are many, varied, and, for the most part, nothing more than a front for the more controversial enterprises. The Prime Minister was most impressed with the variety of cacti, the piano-playing chimp, and the sensory labs when he visited. His tour did not include my lab, which lies just down the cream corridor on the North building's second floor, and currently contains twenty-one individual desks, a smart board, bean bags, games consoles and a bookshelf stocked with everything from Nietzsche to A A Milne.

'Take my case to my office, please, T,' I say, quietly. She turns to the left and approaches a mahogany door half-way down the corridor. The marble name plaque bearing my moniker winks gently in the glow from the chandelier as she opens the door. I carry on up the next two flights of stairs, past conference rooms of various capabilities and guest suites kept scrupulously clean despite no one having ever used them in the six months I have been here. Aside from the carpets and swimming pool, the living quarters are what really set North building apart from its siblings. Enclosed behind double doors set a few paces from the top of the stairs, the entire top floor is off-limits to all but me, Lychen and a few sanctioned Guard people. The double doors open to a large outdoor terrace taking up most of the building's northern-most corner. A bi-folding roof enclosure shelters elegant iron furniture, potted plants, even a water feature in the far left corner – all positioned just so to complement the almost 360-degree view of London. Every direction throws up a tangle of tall and short buildings, monuments, blurred glimpses of the Thames, balconied flats, glowing landmarks, offices, traffic, the odd breath of tree and, of course, thousands upon thousands of people scurrying among it all like ants. Up here, you can't see The Yard; the illicit dalliances under the weeping cherries, the secret cigarettes in the shadows of the Doric pillars outside South East's walkway, the tedious misuse of Guard Assistants. Up here there is nothing but city as far as I care to look. Few birds, little nature; just metal, glass and the beckoning breeze. This is the furthest from the ARC I can be.

Tonight, the city blinks and blears in the cool night, a distant siren threading through the thrum of base beats caught on the wind. I gather my fur collar closer around me and glance to my left. There is no soft glow of light around the edges of the sliding doors leading into Lychen's living quarters, so he must be either occupied in one of the other buildings or in his office downstairs. Letting the wind gust a little of my breath from my body, I turn to the right and approach the other entrance. There is a pad on the outer wall which responds to my fingerprint, unlocking the glass doors with a subtle but reassuring click. I slide them back and enter my rooms, stepping delicately out of my heels and allowing the soft pile to swallow my toes. The carpets in here are a dark mauve and the furniture is all shining mahogany. The four-poster bed is queen-sized and draped with diaphanous white, the wardrobe is walk-in and there are several ornate mirrors with heavy, gilded frames. A door on the far side leads to a bathroom which is larger than all the living rooms of every flat I've ever lived in put together, complete with whirlpool bath, wet room-style shower and one of the ever-present crystal chandeliers.

It is the other door which I head towards tonight, however. This one is straight across the bedroom from the sliding door and leads to one of the few above-ground uncarpeted rooms in the entire building. The ten square metres of floor is sprung. Mirrors line one side and on the other, the view of London is impaled by a ballet barre. This is *my* room, my studio; carefully refurbished under my orders during my first week of living here. I switch the light to a dimmed setting, head into the small dressing room built into the far wall and change my clothes. Without looking at the figure in the mirror so I can't catch my own eyes and see the new layers of darkness there, I sweep my hair up and fasten it neatly into a bun, plug my phone into the speaker system and select a flowing instrumental piece. Tightening my core, feeling my body taut and responsive, I rise onto relevé and, for the first time since Melinda Burton locked eyes with me this afternoon, gradually feel myself relax.

7

April, 2019

Ariana isn't supposed to go to the ARC anymore. Not because of any exciting secrets to uncover or dangerous equipment to explore. Not even because of the broken glass and boarded windows. None of them are supposed to go there. It doesn't belong to the Blakes anymore. When Ariana first moved to Cumbria there were still around twenty people who worked there, not to mention the handful of weird Guard people keeping watch over everything. Then, within a week, she'd woken to hear a rumble of heavy vehicles over the usual birdsong and had peered out of her bedroom window – which looked out over the back garden and the path to the ARC but also held a glimpse of the road leading towards it – to see two large artillery lorries pulling up at the base of the shining dark tower.

Ariana had spent the rest of the morning watching from the limbs of a sprawling oak on the path between The Manor and the ARC as the Guard had loaded random objects into the back of the trucks. She'd spotted microscopes, some as big as her, telescopes, oddly-shaped machines that looked like they should belong in a hospital, several computers, microwaves, refrigerators, children's toys, and even what looked like a dentist's chair. They'd still been at work when Felix had tracked her down and told

The Child Left in the Dark

her to come back for lunch.

A day later, the Guard had abandoned the ARC along with all but a handful of people. Felix, Dominic, Tess, a blonde woman called Jemma who had been part of the group sent to 'rescue' Ariana back in October, Jemma's partner Stephen, the two Blakes and a strange old man called Bert who never went anywhere without a cat following him. The ARC had been left almost completely empty save for a few tables, desks and books. Ariana wasn't stupid, even back then; she knew that most of the important stuff had been squirreled away into The Manor long before the trucks had arrived. There were several stacks of bulky hard drives which looked as old as she was atop a locked filing cabinet in one corner of the room she now slept in. Felix had taken over one of the downstairs rooms as her office and had filled it with computer bases and monitors. Another room on the ground floor – a former dance studio judging by the ballet barre along one side – had been filled with what looked like X-ray machines and body scanners (Ariana was largely basing her guesses on TV medical dramas because everyone always seemed deliberately vague when she asked what the purpose of it all was). She couldn't imagine that Lychen wouldn't know about all these pieces of equipment, but as time went on, she'd had to conclude that he didn't deem anything his Guard had failed to retrieve important enough to bother about. Or perhaps he had come to view the ARC and The Manor a bit as she was beginning to; as a place where interesting things only used to happen. In any case, the Guard had not been back.

With so little left to work with, it hadn't been long before Jemma and Stephen had decided to move on. Bert had gone next, wringing Blake's hand and apologising long after Ariana could tell her grandfather had ceased to care, saying that he and all his cats were going to retire and live with his sister in Penrith. He'd been the one Ariana had been sorriest to see go, he was one of the few people at The Manor who'd never had trouble looking her in the eye and had told her strange, often rambling, stories which hid snippets of intrigue. Like the time he'd lost one of his cats up a tree in the grounds of the ARC and one of the Project C kids had scaled the trunk like a spider monkey to retrieve it. Or the Christmas her own mother had persuaded him to dress up as Santa for the children, despite him being Jewish, and one of them had been so surprised to see him she had accidentally set fire to a wardrobe. It had been Bert's stories which had led Ariana to explore the now-deserted ARC building, trailing her fingers along gleaming walls, snagging on cobwebs, imagining she could still hear the laughter of scientists, the shouts of intrigue, the play of extraordinary children... Dark conceptions of impossible ideas... Stolen, green-eyed glances and whispers of secrets, forbidden discovery, everything.

Burning curiosity was not the only thing Bert had left Ariana with when he'd departed The Manor. The morning he'd gone she had opened her door to find a small box on the landing outside her bedroom. Thinking it probably contained some mortifying relic of her mother's – Bert used the same wistful tone to his voice and eyes as most men did when he talked about Bella – Ariana had been as relieved as she had been delighted when she'd cautiously opened a corner and a small furry black and white head poked out. Marble has been her loyal companion ever since. He still prefers to sleep in Bert's former attic bedroom – now occupied by Dominic and, when they don't think anyone is paying attention, Tess – to the bed Ariana made for him under her desk in her room, but he has a knack for appearing on the path to and from the ARC whenever Ariana makes the journey, no matter the time of day.

Marble trots next to her now as Ariana crosses the back garden and eases open the gate to the overgrown field beyond. The morning has brought a drizzling chill and Ariana wishes she had thought to put on one of the unattractive raincoats ever present on the coat hooks just inside the back door of The Manor. She pulls the hood of her sweater closer around her hair, the memory of doing the same yesterday sending a hollow spasm of embarrassment around her insides. It had gone so horribly, despite what Ralph said about the overall success of finding out the snippet of information about Ethan. Ariana sighs, pausing under the patchy shelter of a pine tree and squatting to scratch Marble behind the ears. His back bounces upwards and he leans his furry face into her hand.

Ariana tries to care about Ethan. She likes Felix well enough, in a cool brilliant-computer-nerd-with-really-weird-style aunt way. Felix is the one who took her into town to get her hair cut when Ariana became so fed up of Blake calling her Bella that she'd kicked a hole in her bedroom door the second week she'd been here. She was the one Ariana went to when she actually did need tampons. She's the only one who knows about the nightmares. Ariana can see the pain in her dark pinched eyes when Felix talks about Ethan – what he liked to eat and the ways he always made her laugh and how it had taken her a while to think of him as more than a friend – Ariana can almost *feel* those feelings right there alongside her. Particularly when they sit together in the dark, Felix's voice a calm, monotonous soothe settling over the quaking remnants of Ariana's nightmares. She understands Felix's grief, and not just because of the part of her that aches with conflicted longing for her mum. She just knows. But she can't bring herself to care quite as much as all the others do, because she doesn't know Ethan, and to her he is just a story that Felix tells. A large man-shaped blank hole who should be here, sharing the biggest room on the first floor and driving them all mad with his legendary snoring, but isn't, mostly because of her. She *should* feel guilty, she supposes, bemusedly, as she straightens up and brushes loose strands of Marble's fur from her hands. But, well. She shrugs.

The drizzle has insisted its way into fat droplets of rain now, so Ariana takes the path from the relative shelter of the trees at a jog. The gate leading into the ARC's boundary is bolted, but she climbs it easily. Technically the building is up for sale, but Ariana has never seen anyone looking around and she knows, with the same underlying sense of privilege with which she had jimmied open the fire door at the back of the former boys' school yesterday, that she won't get into very much trouble, really, if anyone catches her. There are advantages to being the prodigal daughter/granddaughter. Felix is the only one who gets half-strict with her about coming here, and that was only because she caught her skulking around the creepy dungeon rooms a few weeks before they'd fitted a padlock to the front doors. To be honest, Ariana hadn't needed the lecture. She'd decided way before she'd seen the awful scours on the wall, matched her fingernails to the desperate claw marks, that she wouldn't be trailing *those* particular corridors again any time soon.

As she reaches the bolted front doors of the ARC and skirts around the back to the window she'd put a brick through last month, Ariana wonders why they are all so fussed about keeping her out of here. Sure, it isn't really their property anymore, but it isn't like she's doing any damage – one measly window aside – and it isn't like there's anything dangerous in here anyway, unless you count the odd stapler. The building is old and unoccupied, a few window panes on the upper floors are missing and there's a bit of broken glass under some of the chandeliers where the Guard weren't too careful with their removals, but it's a long way off being perilously dilapidated.

Ariana slides easily through the window, over the old towel she'd filched from the airing cupboard at The Manor to cover the sharp bits sticking up at the bottom of the frame. On the other side of the window is an old bathroom; toilets and sinks long dried up. The floor is slick with rainwater and she wonders, a little guiltily, whether she should maybe try and put up some sort of screen. Technically it's spring, but who knows how long the rain will last up here. Months, probably.

'Back again, Ariana?'

Ariana jumps backwards so violently she has to catch herself on one of the old sinks to stop herself slipping in the puddle. Dr Blake is watching her sternly from the doorway, though his eyes sparkle with mirth at her surprise, and his mouth twitches.

'What are *you* doing here?' Ariana winces at the accusation in her own voice but, if anything, it only amuses the old man more. He gets that look on his face, and she knows she's doing something that reminds him, probably painfully, of *her*. Mum.

'I might ask you the same thing. Perhaps we should pose our questions to one another somewhere a little less... wet?'

Ariana pouts but follows him as he turns, surprisingly graceful for one so ancient, and lollops down the dark corridor up ahead. They don't speak as they make their way — somewhat precariously in places, as the walls are dark as midnight and there is no electricity to power the lights — up a staircase. Ariana hasn't explored much of the upper levels, finding the long corridors and endless locked doors or empty dull laboratories not worth the treacherous climb. But Blake shows no sign of stopping and is as sure-footed as if he has made this journey every day of his life. *He might have,* Ariana thinks. She is far more puffed out than he is when he finally turns to a door, swipes a card through a slot on the wall and swings it open. She follows him down another corridor, past a defunct lift and several closed doors until they come to one which looks as unremarkable as the rest, a bare patch where the name card used to be. He stops, swipes his card again and ushers her inside.

'How come you've got a swiper thing that works?' Ariana asks as she steps into the room. Empty shelves stretch along one length of it, interspersed with large glass cabinets of nothing. A writing desk — presumably too heavy to bother taking — still stands in front of the shelves, looking defunct and lonely without a chair. There are marks on the floor where another desk presumably stood in the middle of the room, and more over between the window and the bookshelves. Apart from a few work benches fastened to the left-hand side of the room, with sinks and taps set into them, the room is empty. There isn't even a stool to sit on. Blake passes the desk and heads for the far side of the room, which is made up of floor to ceiling windows. Ariana joins him wordlessly, seeing the glaring empty spaces of the room and wondering what used to fill them. The view from the window seems to span endlessly, and the closer she gets to it, the more there seems to be. She feels like she needs ten extra pairs of eyes just to see it all; the wonky, asymmetrical mountain peaks, the snow scattered across distant valleys, the icy jags of frozen waterfalls.

'The ARC pass keys are fairly basic mechanisms. Felix was able to clone and update mine after the Guard changed the locks. It wasn't hard to do, we have all the original security codes and programs, after all. And the system runs on a different power source to the mains electricity. Still, the BFI could have prevented it if they really wanted...'

'Which means they probably didn't care if you got in or not,' Ariana says, thinking about the ease with which she had broken into the back window, the computers and equipment now dispersed around The Manor.

'What's to care about? What threat could I possibly be, without all my gadgets and toys?'

Ariana squints up at him, knowing he's being sarcastic but not quite understanding how.

'You guys don't seem to be doing too badly for gadgets,' she mutters, thinking about the elaborate den of monitors in the downstairs room Felix uses as an office. The room the Blakes still sometimes refer to as 'the schoolroom'.

'Yes, well. I only wish we'd managed to save a few more of the books. The Guard were particularly meticulous about emptying *this* room. But you should have seen this place back in its heyday... Not just this office, though goodness knows it was full of enough curiosities to keep one busy for a lifetime...' He turns and looks behind him, his sharp blue eyes lingering on the empty shelves and the far right corner, where an odd circular mark shows where something has been ripped away.

'This was your office then, I'm guessing?'

'Yes,' Blake focuses back onto her and smiles.

'So... *what* are you doing here again? When all your stuff is back up there?'

He shrugs. 'Nostalgia. Peace and quiet. Tortuous contemplation of my own futile existence. Sometimes I just like to come up here and look at the view and think about how I should have spent more time out *there* among the wildness and beauty, instead of viewing it all as a big shield from the rest of the world while I hid behind my microscopes and calculations.' He smiles at her sadly. 'And, if nothing else, there's always the additional perk of keeping an eye on trespassing descendants...'

'I'm not really trespassing...'

'This building does not belong to us anymore, you know that.'

'No, but...'

'Ah. You think that your mother—'

'It's got nothing to do with *her*,' Ariana spits, staring back out at the mountains mutinously. Blake smiles to himself and waits a few minutes in silence.

'You could try answering the phone to her once in a while,' he says, quietly. 'There are easier ways of getting her attention than risking your life...'

'Breaking a window is hardly risking my... Oh. You mean...'

'Stowing away in the back of a van, breaking into a working facility run by a mad man and deliberately attempting to thwart his research single-handedly at the age of only-just-turned-thirteen with no back-up or, indeed, much of a plan at all beyond simply opening a few cages and letting havoc reign...?'

'It wasn't about getting mum's attention. And anyway, it's not like I got the chance to set any of them free, is it?'

'No. What happened there, exactly? Ralph said you mentioned something about a lab assistant coming back unexpectedly...?'

Ariana reddens and looks down, blurring the grey-green countryside into shapeless colour beyond the toes of her shoes, just nudging the glass.

'I thought that if I went back there... if I helped them... you don't understand what they're like. Those things. No one will talk to me about them, not properly. Tess looks scared to death if I even mention Graysons, let alone the things we saw. I... still hear them, at night. I wake up because of it. I thought that if I could just help them, set them free, whatever... That it would stop. I could actually get a proper night's sleep again. I mean, do you know what it's like to see and hear something so awful that your mind is, like, *burned* with it?'

'Yes,' he says, quietly. His face is rivetted in sadness and Ariana believes him without question.

'Yeah. Well. Anyway, when I got to the place...'

'*How* did you get there? I can't imagine such an area isn't heavily guarded, particularly after what happened in October...'

Ariana grins briefly. 'I know how to get people to do what I want. I set off a few distractions and when I saw people I confused them, acted like I was meant to be there by mentioning details or people I remembered from the last time. I also played the whole, *Don't you recognise me?* thing a few times... It worked, mostly. And if they looked confused, I just threw Lychen's name into it. They're all terrified of him.

'Anyway, I managed to get back into that room and opened it up... And it... The things... There were more of them than I'd remembered. Rats and birds and cats and... a pig. All with humanish bits, like they'd been stitched together wrong... The noise was crazy and it *stank.* Worse than I remember before... it took me like thirty seconds just to concentrate on not throwing up. And then I found her. The bird-girl from last time. Her *eyes...* She recognised me, I'm sure, but it wasn't like I thought – she wasn't... she wasn't *glad* I was there. She looked at me and she had her claws – her talons – up like this and it was like... Like if there wasn't a metal cage between us, she'd have ripped my throat out.'

Ariana shudders and keeps staring out at the mountains, blinking away the tears which have sprung, annoyingly, into her eyes.

'And then they found you?'

'It didn't take long. I'd... backed away from the bird-girl, thought I'd start with something smaller. But I was still faffing about with the first cage when they came. I should've taken bolt cutters. It was stupid...'

'It was brave.'

'Yeah, really brave. Standing there trying not to pass out from the smell, fiddling about with a stupid lock while this pig-boy looked at me like he was saying, *Just kill me, will you?* And that bird-girl... When I left, when they found me and pulled me out of there... it was like she looked right *into* me, like she could see everything about me, all the worst things I've ever thought and felt and she kind of snarled... Her voice... it wasn't human but it wasn't really bird-like either. It was like a bird was trying to growl. Not words but *almost* like words... I couldn't make it out, though. It was so loud in there by then... but I think if she was saying anything it would be, *I hate you…* I don't know why… I was only trying to help.'

Her voice tightens into her throat and this time she can't stop the tears spurting onto her cheeks. She swipes them angrily. Blake puts a hand on her shoulder and squeezes, just once, before letting her go. They stand solemnly for a few minutes more.

'Did he hurt you? Daniel?'

'No. Not really. He kind of shoved me on the floor, but he didn't really hurt me. He scares me, though. More than the creatures. Even bird-girl. The way he looks at me… it's like I'm one of them… He said… he said he'd turn me into a rat if I went back there… And I believe him…'

'Yes… he always was a bit of a shit.'

Ariana looks up at him, her surprise chasing away the remnants of sadness. Blake smiles, but this time it's humourless.

'I think he was the one we struggled with the most from the C-Project. Not his abilities. He was right up there with the best of them, could disappear right before your eyes, and he was one of the few who didn't lose his talents at adolescence like most of them… but… his personality. It's like it just… never got filled in properly. He'd hurt other children and be surprised when they cried. He'd see what he wanted and take it without even thinking about whether or not it was his right. The only way to control him was through threats or bribery and as he got older the stakes only got higher. It seems some things don't change…'

'No.' Ariana sighs. 'And the worst thing was… Ralph said there wasn't even any point to it. The animal-human Project B stuff. That Lychen was just letting Daniel do it, cause all that awfulness, just to keep him busy.'

'Did he now?'

'Well, isn't it true?'

'Possibly... Partially, I suspect, at least,' Blake sighs, and squints out of the window as if trying to read words etched into the snow of the mountains. 'But, you know, none of the projects were started without a purpose in mind. With B, it was to explore the transference of consciousness... Whether it could be achieved. We shut it down when the scientists working on it realised the pain caused wasn't worth the meagre results... but there are rumours... There are suggestions that what Daniel is doing has made a little more meaningful progress than what we were able to achieve here...'

'But how he's done it! Those creatures are suffering – it's awful!'

'Abhorrent, abominable, yes...'

Ariana doesn't like the way he says the words, like they're nothing but a check list. She narrows her eyes at him and he glances at her almost sheepishly.

'In any case, yesterday was not without its merits.'

'Yeah, we found out that Ethan wasn't there.' *Big deal,* she almost adds.

'Not just that. We found out more about these creatures. That there are a few of them, more than ten...?'

'Definitely more than ten. Twenty, maybe even thirty, some of them were small...'

'And that the key to their salvation isn't going to be breaking, entering, and simply freeing them...'

'No, because Ralph thinks we should put them all down for one... I heard him say that when he thought I wasn't listening.'

'That might well be the kindest course of action.'

Ariana opens her mouth to argue, but then she

remembers the desperate, pleading eyes of the pig-boy. She shuts her mouth and nods.

'But that's not to say we condemn them all. What we need is a way to determine whether any of them are salvageable...'

'How can we do that with Daniel in charge?'

'We need to use the tools at our disposal...'

'What tools?' Ariana frowns, though she can feel her spirits lift a little with his enthusiasm. She half expects him to reach into his moth-eaten tweed jacket and produce some bolt-cutters.

'Your phone, for one,' he smiles. She stares for a moment and then, realising what he means, screws her face into a scowl.

'*God*. Really.'

'Really.'

'I'd rather take my chances with the bolt-cutters,' Ariana mutters. Blake just smiles in that irritatingly amused way of his, as if this entire conversation, all the theoretical pondering and discussion of the poor B-creatures and their consciousness has all been part of some bigger plan to get her to decide to call her mother. Which, knowing him as Ariana is beginning to, it could very well have been.

8

April, 2019

The sky over London tumbles with heavy clouds and the wind brings a scent of rain as I lean on the glass balcony edge, cup of coffee in one hand. My hair is gathered into a neat chignon, but I can feel tendrils of it tickling free in the breeze. I sip my coffee. It isn't quite as good as Ethan's but it isn't far off. T will learn, until he is back.

'Bella.'

I take another sip before I turn, my smile ready. Lychen moves so silently, one of our agreements is that he announces his presence around me.

'Good morning.' I gesture to the cafetière and cups laid out on the terrace table. 'Help yourself. I didn't hear you come back last night; you must be tired.'

'Thank you,' Lychen says, smoothly, not confirming or denying my assumption. His waxy face is as passive as ever, but there do seem to be slightly darker shadows beneath his black eyes. As if the general pallor has been shaded with a crayon just one degree darker. His forehead is only slightly lined and, of course, there are no hints of laughter creases at all.

'Where is Ethan?' he asks. I've been able to feel the question burning at me from the first moment the blind was drawn silently across his window and his eyes found me, being served coffee by T out here. Behind him, his

Primary Guard, Delta, stares impassively ahead.

'I had to dispatch him on a personal mission. There was a complication with one of the delegates last night. A former ARC employee – Melinda Burton – posing as Dr Ellen Kneck from Shaker University. She questioned me, brought up the Youth Project... I did a little digging on the journey back here, I'm fairly sure she wasn't reporting to anyone else. She said she hadn't been in touch with the Blakes for years. She lives alone and hasn't any close relatives, despite what she said about having children. I double checked. I've had a memo sent to Shaker to tell them she was offered a new position effective immediately.'

'Why would she confront you?'

'She was in touch with a Futura employee and had caught wind of the Youth Programme, seemed quite concerned about their age. But I'm starting to think it was more personal than anything else... she didn't *really* become cross until I failed to recognise her straight away. Yes, I'm willing to bet she saw my name on Kneck's invitation and took a chance...'

'Tedious,' Lychen, level with me now, is watching my face rather than the city, 'Did you ascertain her information source?'

'Miriam Jones. I suspect she is the one who has been feeding the ARC collective their information as well. She worked in the same department as Tess Cochran. I disabled Burton with a mild sedative and told Ethan to drive her to Daniel.'

'Good. He has requested a video conference at 9am. Perhaps this is what it is concerning.'

'Wants to make sure I'm not overstepping my bounds, no doubt.' I roll my eyes. Lychen gives a twitch of a smile and reaches for the hair at the nape of my neck. I don't flinch, though I can feel the soft skin tic with a tiny nerve as his icy fingertips make contact. I don't flinch, though. I have learned not to, these past few months. Another one of our agreements.

'It's a mess. I need to redo it. The wind... it's too cold still to have coffee out here really, but I've always been so partial to a spring morning. There's something about the air... it's so...'

I wait for him to finish my sentence. For a hint that there might be anything whimsical, anything resembling an imaginative thought process. But he just stands there, his fingers winding into my hair, snatching it from the wind's tease territorially. He watches me, waiting for me to finish, his gaze steely as always, the growling wolf lurking beneath.

'So fresh,' I say, finally. I move my head away, feigning drinking the last of my coffee and turn to return the cup. T steps swiftly forward to take it from me.

'Thank you, T. I'd better go and freshen myself if we are conferencing at nine.'

'Leave your hair,' Lychen commands, as if I were a Guard person myself. I turn back, eyebrows raised. He is closer than I'd thought, the wolf straining, his hand twitching.

'What, all wind-swept and *chaotic*?'

He smiles again, tightly, though his eyes tell me he knows exactly what I'm doing with this gentlest of needle touches.

'With you, Bella, a little chaos is allowed. Only with you.' He gives his empty cup to Delta and takes my hand.

'We have some time before nine. You can *freshen* in my apartment.' He turns to the two Guard people and I keep my shudder inside, blocking the sudden dread and nausea away and dampening it all down like flames. *Time to disappear.*

'See we are not disturbed,' Lychen says, and the two of them nod, T taking the tray of coffee things and Delta holding the double doors leading down the stairs. I let Lychen lead me, swallowing everything inside me so that by the time he holds the sliding doors to his quarters open, I am as smooth and cold inside as any other robot.

⁂

The main conference room is on the second floor of North building. Like all the rooms in the building, it is trimmed in luxury with its large lacquered table, plush office chairs with inbuilt lumbar support and large flat-screen TV. The windows all boast automatic shutters which lower at the press of a button. Lychen and I are the first to arrive, naturally, but we are joined by three department heads from different corners of the Beaumont by the time Daniel's wispy little head fills the large screen on the wall.

'Hello all, I shouldn't be too long today. Firstly, I've got a few project developments...'

'Did creature 5PY have any continuation of the problematic behaviour you noted in last week's report?' Lychen cuts in, his voice a silken knife blade.

'No,' Daniel colours, but doesn't stumble. 'It reverted back to its normal habits. Creatures 8CY, 9CX and 14AY were all terminated in the last seven days, and a further creature – 2FX – died of natural causes.'

'14AY, that's avian, right?' Dr Gibbs from my right side pipes up, shuffling through some papers in front of him. 'That's not the one you were making a modicum of progress with...?'

'No,' Daniel replies, impatiently. 'That's 16AX. As in X chromosome. Female. She remains stable.'

'Any language?' Lychen looks up from his phone. He's answered three text messages and checked four different email accounts since Daniel first began to speak.

'Not as such… More attempts at attacks, though, especially if I'm anywhere near her,' Daniel says quite cheerfully, though his eyes slide shiftily. 'She really doesn't like me and when I look into her eyes, I *know* that visceral hatred is human.'

Lychen looks up at him and smiles with thin lips. 'Well. Aren't we poetic today? Continue with the progress report.'

I tune out as Daniel goes through various pieces of data about the labelled creatures in his laboratory. Surreptitiously, I check my phone under the table. No calls. No messages. I tap on the message icon just in case I've missed a notification. Nothing. Just a long, sad string of sent dating from last week all the way back to the autumn.

> Happy Birthday. I love you.
>
> I have topped up your account with a little extra for your birthday next week. Hope you are doing something fun. Love you.
>
> Your orthodontist called last week, you were due to get braces next month. I've told Ralph but he may need reminding. I love you.
>
> One day you will understand why I did what I did. I love you. I will never stop.

I sigh and put the phone away before I can start to feel the pathetic well of it all. Daniel has come to the end of his report now and is exchanging a few snippets of data with the other department heads. Lychen has his head down, scrolling on his phone through test results from some experiments being carried out on Guard pain response over in the South East building. Eventually, Daniel clears his throat importantly enough for us both to switch our focus back to him.

'My last point of business regards some more... ah... personal issues. Dr D'accourt, firstly I would like to thank you for your late-night contribution to my research.' He inclines his head towards me, his eyes glittering and cold. 'I was also grateful to receive the intelligence of Ms Jones' indiscretions. I was, of course, fully aware that she had been feeding information to Tess Cochran and was in the process of dealing with it, but yah, thanks all the same.'

'It didn't sound particularly *dealt with* from what I gathered,' I say, icily, 'Seeing as she was able to talk freely with one of my audience members last night – a former ARC employee, no less – and share classified information about the Youth Guard...'

'Oh come on, we all know that programme is well on its way to launch. Any publicity at this stage can only do it good—'

'That is not for *you* to—'

'Enough,' Lychen snaps, and we both instantly drop into silence. 'Is that all, Daniel?'

'No,' Daniel keeps his eyes on me, his voice battling between sulky and snide. 'We had another *interference* from the Blakes – this one far more serious than the last. Ralph and Felix engineered a meeting with one of my project handlers while their little rat girl snuck in round the back and attempted to relieve me of some of my best assets.'

'You mean Ariana?' I'm sitting up now, my entire attention on the odious little man on the screen. He smiles and takes his time to continue.

'Your daughter, yes, Bella. Pretty little rodent, isn't she? A bit rough round the edges. She actually tried to *bite* me at one point...'

I very carefully don't smile.

'Are you looking for an apology? You know full well I relinquished custody months ago...'

'I know, I know. No, it's not the damage she did which concerns me... She didn't do much, really. Smashed a few bits here and there, but that was mostly in the struggle once she was discovered. By all accounts she couldn't actually get *into* the cages once she got to them – not the sharpest mind, perhaps...' This time he grins, and I know I've let the wash of irritation prickle across my face.

'Get to the point, Daniel,' Lychen murmurs in a bored voice.

'Right, yes. No, the thing that concerned me was *how* she got to the cages. I've got several locked doors between her point of entry to the facility and the area where I keep the hybrids. Locked doors *and* posted guards, both human and, well, Guard. And yet this little slip of a thing manages to get round all of them.'

'Well.' I'm smug. I can't help it. 'Maybe you should ask your—'

'I did. They say she confused them, made them think she was supposed to be there. Some of them recognised her from the autumn, thought she'd been brought in for something again, didn't want to get involved... I'm not buying it. I think she had help.'

'You think *I* told her how to do it?'

'Charming her way around people, using her *wiles* to get what she wants... Certainly sounds like you, D'accourt. Not to mention the convenient timing of your little *gift for my patience*, or however you put it.'

Everyone is looking at me now. I can feel their gazes prickling like the spit of burning oil. I keep my expression placid, though. My voice calm.

'I merely referred to your patience in dealing with the Blakes and their little stake-outs. I do, after all, employ the reason for their interference as my Primary Guard. What on earth would *I* have to gain by releasing your poor pathetic little science projects? And even if I did want to, why would I send my own daughter to do the job?'

Daniel pouts. He looks utterly ridiculous.

'The Blakes have been trying to meddle with my research for years—'

I sigh and turn to Lychen, eyebrows raised. It does the trick and I know it infuriates Daniel more than anything I could say.

'That's enough, Daniel. I trust Bella. I will make contact with Blake and extend a further warning about trespass, if you would like.'

'I told him that this would be the last time I let them get away with it,' Daniel says, his voice twisting in spite.

'Yes. Fine.' Lychen says, boredom creeping in once more, though he is watching me again. 'When can Bella expect Ethan returned to her?'

'Are we still calling him that?'

'Yes,' I say, quickly. Daniel shrugs, though he regards me with slightly more curiosity.

'Interesting decision. Maybe you're more twisted than I am.'

'I doubt it.'

'I'll be sending him on his way this morning. Can't have him hanging around here when I assured your long-lost *ex-family* that he wasn't here anymore, can I? Although it wouldn't be the worst timing in the world if they *did* decide not to heed my warning and make a return visit. I am down a few creatures this week after all, and progress is so slow. I could use some entertainment. I promised your Ariana I'd meld her with a rat if she ever came back, but knowing what I do now... If she does take after mummy dearest so closely, maybe there are other uses for her. You certainly seem to have yours, after all...'

'If you lay a *finger* on her, you tedious little scrotum...'

'That's enough.' Lychen puts a cool hand on my arm and I realise I'm standing. I sit down abruptly, though my heart is trembling with the effort to keep still, to stop myself rushing at the screen. Daniel pauses mid-flinch, his hands halfway around his own throat. He blinks and removes them, staring from them to me bemusedly. I look at Lychen instead and the fire inside instantly wrenches into fear because I recognise that dangerous blaze in his eyes. It's not the lustful wolf but, in a way, it's worse. It's his calculating look. The one when something's occurred to him, an avenue of possibility he hadn't even noticed before.

'If you should encounter Miss D'accourt... Or Miss Blake, or whatever Bella's child is calling herself these days, you will call *me* directly, Skaid. And then you will put her in a room, guarded and *untouched,* understand?'

'I was only joking,' Daniel says, sulky once more.

'You were not,' Lychen replies, calmly.

There is a silence. No one moves. The other three department heads look as if they don't dare to breathe lest someone remember they are here and sends them away.

'Fine,' Daniel pouts again. 'The rest of my report is classified.'

'Alright. I will call you in ten minutes,' Lychen says, as coolly as if they're discussing a game of golf. Four minutes later, Daniel's face has disappeared from the screen and Lychen and I sit alone at the dark shining table. I turn to find his eyes burning into mine.

'What?' I bring a hand to my face when he doesn't look away.

'I forgot how glorious you are when you're passionate about something. You *radiate*.'

The wolf stirs. But, just as I'm wondering if I'm going to have to muster myself into a second disappearance in one morning, he gets to his feet, businesslike once again.

'It's interesting what he said about Ariana. I didn't realise she possessed so many similar… talents… to you. Has it always been the case?'

I shrug, keeping my manner insouciant while, beneath the surface, I pedal furiously.

'She's always been pretty… persuasive, when she wants to be. And clever, despite what that *turd* said about her. I always taught her to act as if she knew more than she did if she was trying to find something out. I suspect yesterday was mainly a result of these things, as well as a good dose of luck… Not to mention the relentless self-righteousness of being thirteen. I certainly don't think there's anything particularly *enhanced* about her, if that's what you're wondering. After all, Project A was designed specifically for each genetic enhancement to be contained to the individual subject, it doesn't pass on to offspring. That was one of the control rules.'

'Mmm. You're right, of course. Still, she sounds like a particularly enigmatic young person. I'm sorry I didn't make her acquaintance more back in October.'

I give him a half-smile and he returns it, to my relief.

'I might try and call her again,' I say, as he makes to leave the room. 'Just to check in, berate her a bit for taking risks… She probably won't take my call, but it's worth a try.'

'By all means,' Lychen smiles, though there's slightly more confusion in it now. There always is, when it's a matter regarding emotional attachments. 'This separation, it was always your choice, you know. I would never keep her from you.'

'Yes. I know.'

He'd keep you from her, though.
It's not how he sees it.
Are you making excuses for him, now? Has he tamed you so, Bella? Or simply lobotomised you?
No. I'm beginning to understand him a little better, that's all.
Oh yes? Is that between the times when he does the things that make you disappear?

I shake the argumentative voice off as I draw my phone out of my pocket. Lychen has gone. I'm alone in the room, with the table, empty chairs and the screen now blazing a blank royal blue. I swipe my phone into life and almost drop it with surprise. Three missed calls. One voicemail. All from Ariana.

Winter, 2006

> How are things? Did you have a nice Christmas? Did you get the card and cheque?
>
> Bells? Everything OK?
>
> Bella, I know I've agreed to respect your privacy but when you don't answer your phone I worry. There's another letter for you here. This one's got different handwriting. I will bring it round tomorrow afternoon at 3pm unless I hear from you.

>> I'm fine. Don't come round, I won't be at the flat.

> I'm glad you're OK. Where will you be? I'm free all afternoon, I could meet you?

>> I have a midwife appointment at St Mary's at 2.30. You can meet me after if you like.

> Yorke Coffee, 3pm?

>> Fine.

LOVE YOUR BUMP, the slogan shrieked from the poster advertising stretch mark lotion in the antenatal waiting room. I did not love my bump. I sat cocooned in a large trench coat I'd found in a vintage shop, my stomach swelling over the top of my jeans, which were fastened only with the use of a hairband looped through the hole and round the button. In another week or two they would be too uncomfortable to do up at all. I glanced around the waiting room at the other bumps, all in various stages of protuberance from the barely there to the distortion of polyester flowers stretched so widely they were blanched white in places. Hands draped lovingly, stroked, rested, used as a prop-up for phones, paperbacks, magazines. I glanced away again, sitting up a little straighter as the midwife emerged into the waiting room.

'Elodie Gu... Garr?'

'Guerre,' I said, smiling graciously as I got to my feet and handed the woman my blue folder of pregnancy notes. She took them without comment and led me silently down the corridor away from the other bumps. I hid my small breath of relief as I followed her into her office. I'd seen a variety of midwives and had already learned that smiley tended to go hand in hand with irritatingly inquisitive.

'So,' she held the door of a small, medical office open for me, 'This is your thirty-one-week appointment, yes?'

'Yes,' I said, battling to keep my demeanour meek and unassuming. It was always harder when faced with a forceful personality. Particularly an older woman. The midwife looked over my notes as I sat in the chair next to her desk. She opened a file on her computer and clicked a few times as my information – Elodie's information –

appeared. Finally, she looked at me. She had short grey-streaked hair and full stern eyebrows which bristled over the top of neat rectangular spectacles.

'You opted out of having the genetic screening tests?'

'Yes. It was an unplanned pregnancy. By the time I found out, it was too late to have the tests. It should all be in my notes.'

Calm down. Not so abrupt.

'Hmm,' she frowned.

'Sorry. I just… I get the same questions every time,' I smiled, trusting in my face to soften hers. 'I had the scan. It was fine.'

'And you've also declined all blood tests—'

'I don't do needles.'

'I really would recommend—'

'No. Thank you.' I narrowed my gaze at her, skewering a little Bella through Elodie's bashful docility, pinioning back the woman's questions, her prying. *So much for less smiles equalling less interference.* Eventually the midwife shrugged and tightened her jaw, not quite masking her disapproval but not fully trying to, either.

'I'll just check your urine sample, then.'

I could sense her wondering if that was something I'd fight her for as well. I handed over the yellow vial with as serene a smile as I could manage, feeling Ana chuckle in my head.

It's harder than you think, isn't it, Miss Bella? Letting them underestimate you.

'Have you begun working on your birth plan yet?'

'Oh… er, no. Not yet. I've still got plenty of time for that, haven't I?'

'Well, yes, hopefully. Though you never know, especially with your first. Sometimes these things are hereditary, though. Do you know if you were late or early?'

'I was born on my due date.'

'Really?' She perused me briefly before glancing back at the dipstick in her hand.

'Urine's fine,' she said, pouring the rest of the contents down the sink and peeling off her gloves. 'Well, we'll be discussing your wishes for labour and birth at your next appointment, so it might be time to start thinking about it. Just to warn you, some of the pain relief options will include needles. Discuss it with your partner, if you have one?'

'I don't…' I smiled apologetically, though it took some effort. 'The baby's father and I are not together.'

'I see. Will he be present at the birth?'

'No. I don't want him there.'

'Are you sure?' Her eyebrows softened for the first time. 'It's a lot to go through, particularly when it's your first…'

'I have other people I can call on…'

'Your parents?'

'Yes… My dad. He's in Surrey. My mother lives in France. Lyon. She'll come over once the baby is born. My parents divorced when I was little, I get on better with my father…'

'Well, as long as there's a good support system in place. And not just for the birth but afterwards as well. I can refer you to—'

'It's fine, really. I've got a sister as well. Ma- Marie. She's said she will be there for me too, if I need her.'

I'd said the right thing, at last. The midwife's face relaxed. 'Oh, that's good to hear. We don't mean to pry, of course. Younger mums can find it hard sometimes, so a good system in place is always key. Why don't you hop onto the bed and we'll measure your bump and have a listen to baby's heartbeat?'

I nodded, mumbling something about how I was older than I looked. I lay back on the fold-up table, feeling the paper crinkle and tear beneath my unfamiliar body. My bump seemed to explode from my abdomen and the baby shifted as I undid my shirt and exposed my taut skin to the harsh, fluorescent light. As well as dark brown eyes and glasses, Elodie also had short, choppy curls and the press of a pillowed surface against my bare neck still felt odd as I rested my head back. I nudged the feeling aside as the midwife approached with the tape measure. She dug her fingers into my abdomen, ignoring the baby's kick of protest, and drew the measure all the way down to just beneath the edge of my haphazardly fastened jeans.

'You're measuring quite small for your weeks,' she said, her mouth pinched as she surveyed me again.

'I don't feel small,' I muttered.

'Well, it could just be because baby's moved position,' she dug her hands into my mid-section. I winced and shut my eyes briefly, counting slowly in my head. I still wasn't used to how much touching was involved in pregnancy. It was far worse than the questions. The speaking part could be controlled, even with my eyes veiled and my manner demure. The touching was an entirely different endurance.

'Yes,' the midwife murmured, finally drawing away, 'Baby's head down. Nonetheless, you're a few centimetres behind the line you were following so I'd like to refer you for a growth scan... That is, if you *consent*, of course.'

She's testing you. Just agree.

I hate this.
I know.

'Yes. Fine.'

'OK then,' she turned and picked up a small, handheld wand. 'Let's have a listen.'

She gelled my stomach and placed the wand on top. The silence dolloped awkwardly as she moved it around and then, like an impending steam train, the heartbeats thundered between us. For the first time since she'd called my name, the midwife caught my eye and smiled.

༺༻

'Wow, I like the haircut!' Marc boomed predictably, though his eyes were on my stomach as I approached his table in the busy café twenty minutes after leaving my appointment.

'What would you like? I'm buying,' he said, when I didn't reply.

'It's fine, I've already ordered. They're bringing it over,' I murmured, 'Perk of being a walking blob.'

'You look wonderful, Bells. Blooming. Your eyes, though, and the glasses… I almost didn't recognise—'

'Shh,' I glanced around us furiously, though the café was full of bustling bubbles of people, mostly couples, and no one spared us a glance. A few pink hearts were draped from the windows and red balloons paunched sadly from an empty corner table. Valentine's Day had just been, I realised with a small sprig of surprise.

'Sorry, sorry,' Marc stage-whispered, holding his hands up in placation. I scowled at him as a waiter placed a steaming Chai latte in front of me. Marc's brow was creased into an expression caught between amusement and worry.

'All this... cloak and dagger business... It's a bit much, isn't it? I mean, your hair looks great. A *bald cap* would look good on you, but changing your eye colour? Wearing glasses... Bel— I mean... Elodie,' his mouth hinged around the name carefully. 'If you're really that worried, we should go to the police.'

'I'm not going to the police,' I said quietly, taking a sip from my drink. The milky spice flowed down my throat and settled warmly over the remnants of irritation left by the midwife. A couple on the table next to us were exchanging heart-emblazoned cards. I blinked and in an instant I was svelte, high-heeled Bella D'accourt walking into my own plush, chandeliered office which was greater than the entire square footage of this grotty little café and that midwife's office put together, to discover a bloom of two dozen long-stemmed red roses in a crystal vase on my desk, a card poking out with delicate, spidery cursive across the top. I suppressed a shudder.

'Where's this letter then?' I turned back to Marc, who was still watching me somewhat anxiously.

'Oh, yes. It came the other day. Though I think it might actually be a card,' He reached into his pocket and pulled out a burgundy envelope. 'I'd forgotten about Valentine's Day.'

I stared at the envelope on the table between us. The writing was scrawled carelessly, as if it were an inconvenience. I let a little of my breath escape.

'Like I said, this one's writing is different to the others.'

'Have there been any more of those?'

'No. Not since Christmas. I burned them, like you said.'

'You didn't read them?' I stared at him carefully. He didn't look away.

'No, of course not. I said I wouldn't. You can trust me,

you know. I've proven that over the last few months, haven't I?' He frowned.

'It'll take more than a few months,' I muttered, frowning back. Silence fell between us. He took a gulp from his coffee. I reached for the envelope and swept it into my bag.

'What about that car you mentioned the other week with those men?'

'Ah, well like I said then, I'm sure it's nothing. They were just parked up the road for a bit. Annie from next door happened to mention she thought she'd seen the same car a few weeks before. Old bat needs to get a hobby if you ask me.'

'What kind of car was it?'

'Black Merc I think she said.'

'Not a Fiesta?'

'No. Why?'

'Just… let me know if you see it again. Or a red Fiesta.'

'Sure. How did the appointment go, anyway? All OK?'

'Yes. Measuring a little small…'

'Well, *you're* small.'

'Yes, she said it was probably fine. Berated me about the blood tests again.'

'Well, you know they're only testing for the common genetic abnormalities.'

'I can't take the chance of anything being flagged up. Anything. For all I know the ARC has an alert for Project A blood samples on the entire medical system. *I* don't know what was in those contracts you signed.'

Marc opened his mouth as if to argue, but, catching my glare, he closed it again, shrugged and glanced from me to the balloons on the corner table.

'Aren't you going to open it?'

'Not here. Later.'

'OK...'

'It's not from...'

'No. Not the dangerous one.'

'I didn't think so. But you do know who it is from?'

'Yes.'

'Right.'

'There's something I need to ask you...' I hated the words as they left my mouth. I hated having to ask him, hated the eager look on his face, his keenness to help... It made the taste I had in my mouth whenever I saw him all the more bitter.

'Anything. What is it?'

'The midwives... they're obsessed with me having a stupid *support system.*'

'Ah, well, you know. You *are* young...'

'I'm in my mid-twenties, according to my records. I'm separated from the father of my child but he's supportive and keen to co-parent. I've got a nice flat which I can afford thanks to a small trust fund and I've plans to go to university in September.'

'Ye-es, but all they really want to know is that you're not going to go off the deep end when the baby's a week old and screaming all night long and you've no one else there in that tiny little apartment to help take care of *you* while you take care of her...'

'I'll be fine.'

'I've no doubt, Bella. But put me down as your support system to satisfy the powers that be, all the same.'

'It doesn't mean anything—'

'I know.'

'...I'm not going to be calling you in floods of tears in the middle of the night...'

'I wouldn't mind if you did.'

'...and I don't want you *anywhere* near me when I'm giving birth...'

'I wouldn't dream of such a thing.'

He held my gaze firmly, though something flickered in his eyes. I couldn't decide if it was amusement or sadness. I drank the last of my latte. He mirrored me.

'As long as we're clear on that,' I said.

'Perfectly.'

'Good.'

'But, Bella?'

'What?'

'Just so you know... if the impossible *does* happen, with any of it... Labour, birth, needing anything at all, even if it's extra baby wipes at 4am... I'm here, OK? You've got my secret mobile number, no one else does. If it rings, I'm there. OK?'

I sighed and looked down so he wouldn't see the irritating lurch of feelings. Sodding bloody pregnancy. I waited until they were gone and then, when I was sure my voice wouldn't betray me, muttered: 'Fine. And it's *Elodie*, remember?'

Two weeks passed before I remembered the burgundy envelope. It had slipped between the pages of one of my text books and fluttered to the floor when I took the book out one evening, having finally given up trying to pass as a normal university student. I held it between my fingers, wondering why I didn't feel more. Why I hadn't remembered it at all until now when just the thought of every spidery-written missive from Lychen, Marc had told me about had seared itself into my jugular for days.

Breathing out, I slit the seal open. The card was plain white, a small, red heart in the middle. No cheesy slogans, no awkward proclamations. I opened it.

Beast,

I am sorry for all the things I said to you. I shouldn't have. Of course I don't really blame you for Rudy, I was just being... well, me. I'm an arse. Always have been. I can't blame you for turning me down. But I wish you would come home. It's not the same without you. I used to think that you'd come along and changed everything for the worse... Dad and Mamma and the ARC and me. I'd obsess and brood about all the ways I could get them to take you back. I don't think anyone noticed, actually... Least of all you! And it wasn't long before I realised that things weren't worse at all. They were better. And it wasn't too long after that that I realised... well, that things had changed again.

I keep going over it. The awful things I said to you that night you left. I said you loved yourself so much no one stood a chance. You thought I meant that nobody else stood a chance of being loved by you. But what I actually meant was: no one else stands a chance of loving you as much as you love yourself. I was wrong. No one, not even you, can or will love you as much as I do.

I'm sorry. I miss you. Please come back.
Ralph

I sighed and, slowly, read it again. I read it until the words blurred and lost their meaning. I read until my sadness swirled and whispered that maybe it meant something else, something more. The baby kicked and turned, undulating my skin into strange and terrifying shapes. I slid the card back into its envelope and stood up slowly, crossing over to the small kitchenette and placing the burgundy rectangle into one of the drawers. I would leave it there until the feelings – the something more – came.

10

April, 2019

'Ariana? Are you OK?'

'Finally, I've been calling all morning!'

'I know, I'm sorry, I was in a meeting… I didn't see my phone.'

'Oh right, I should have known you'd be *busy* being all *Executive Vice President* or whatever…' Ariana can't keep the sneer out of her voice, though she had tried very hard to keep herself neutral when answering the call. Just the sound of her mother's calm, musical voice seems to trigger all the dark, burning parts of herself.

'It's Executive Head of Development actually, but I'm glad to hear you're taking an interest,' her mother trills. Ariana can *hear* the amusement in her voice now, can picture her smiling in that irritatingly perfect way. Then, before Ariana can make a sardonic remark about missing the point, her mother adds: 'What was it you wanted to speak to me about, darling?'

Urgh. Ariana doesn't know how she does it. Six months she's kept her stoic silence, refusing to answer calls, deleting voicemails before her mother's voice could curve her finger into returning the call, rolling her eyes and ignoring the messages about money and orthodontists. Six months she has been the one with the upper hand and now here's her mother, all snipped vowels and businesslike on the phone, probably flicking her perfect hair about and signing contracts at a big, head-teacher-style desk in some executive board room or something at the same time, making it sound like Ariana has been the one chasing *her* all this time.

'I went to Graysons yesterday…'

'The Futura Lab? Yes, so I hear… Why on earth did Ralph take you there?'

'He didn't… Well, I mean he did, but he, er, didn't exactly know about it…'

'Ah. I see.'

'Do you know about what they're doing there? The creatures they're making? They're… it's awful, Mum. Seriously, have you seen them?'

'I know, but Ariana if you're asking me to stop Daniel, I'm afraid I just don't have that kind of—'

'Have you *seen* them?'

'No. Not in person. No.'

'So you totally ignored what Dad told you back in October? Figures.'

'Ariana, I have been a little busy—'

'Being extremely important, yes I know. Well, *I'm* telling you now. You need to see them. You have to get yourself to Graysons or get Daniel to bring them to you… Then you can decide whether or not you can be bothered to get yourself the sway or power or whatever it is you're so obsessed with—'

'I am not obsessed with power.'

There is a definite edge to the voice now. Ariana has annoyed her. Good.

'Oh, really. So you just got tired of parenting after twelve-and-a-half years, then?'

'Ariana. You know that's not why I left you…'

'Do I?'

'Yes. You do. I did it to protect you...'

Ariana turns away from the glare of the ARC looming through her bedroom window and sinks irritably onto the bedspread.

'Protect me from what, exactly? I'm *still* having nightmares from seeing those things. No one here understands me, there are no other kids about at all except for at school, there's nowhere to hang out unless you count the derelict building just over the hill. Most of the time I'm either learning how to hack computers with Fee and Dom or being talked at by an old man who thinks I'm you... I started my weekend by stowing into an old Transit van so I could try and actually *do* something before I go mad... I know all about the *bad men* now, Mum. I'm not a little kid you can scare with your stories and lies anymore, I've got nightmares of my own. What exactly are you trying to save me from?'

'*You,* Ariana! Your own bloody-minded self! So perhaps all the *real* bad men will stop having meetings about you!'

There's a pause. Ariana frowns, turning back to the window, gazing absently out at the grey mountains in the distance, the blurry smudges of wild animals. She can hear her mother breathing loudly as if trying to suck back the hiss of her own words. She pictures her differently now, not in the glossy boardroom but hiding somewhere, maybe a small cupboard or an alcove in a corridor. Looking behind her shoulder, touching her hair nervously, eyes glittering as they sweep for danger...

'They held a meeting about *me*? Who, Daniel or Lychen?'

'Both of them... It wasn't really just about you, but you

were mentioned, somewhat…'

Ariana can tell her mother is holding back. She shuts her eyes and concentrates on nothing but her, letting her voice, the voice she had heard every day of her life until six short months ago, trickle deeper into her. *What aren't you saying?* she thinks. *Let me hear it… Let me in…*

'Mentioned? Because of the break-in?'

'Yes. Ri… How did you get through to the creatures?'

The question comes quietly but with a desperate urgency that tells Ariana far more than she's sure Bella intended.

'They think I'm special, don't they?'

'What?' There's real alarm now, the same wild fear Ariana saw in her mother's face back in October when she'd come down the stairs in that remote little cottage in Cornwall and admitted she had been talking to a random man on Twitter.

'Dr Blake asked me the same thing. Seemed quite interested in it, so I know it must be important. And especially if you guys are having *meetings* about it…'

'This isn't a joke, Ariana. You need to be careful…'

'Why, in case Lychen decides I might be worth keeping around after all, despite what you want?'

'Yes.'

'So?'

'You have no idea what he's capable of…'

'He doesn't seem so bad. Daniel's the real psycho… What's Lychen done?'

'He gave Daniel the means to do what he's doing, for one… He knows exactly what's happening at Futura and signs an invoice every month to allow it to continue, to progress… He came up with the whole concept of the Guard…'

'I heard a rumour that was you.' She hasn't, not really, but she says it just to needle her, try and nudge her into more interesting revelations. There's still something Bella is edging around, some deeper reason why she is so worried about Ariana coming to Lychen's attention.

'There was once a rumour running round the ARC that I was Ana Blake's biological child and that Ralph and I were *actual* brother and sister. You know what that would make *you*...'

'Ew.'

'Precisely. Don't pay too much attention to rumours, particularly those about me.'

'But you still haven't answered my question—'

'If you're asking whether my genetic enhancements administered as part of Project A passed down to you as well, the answer is no. Project A was always a one-generational thing, the genes which were altered were designed only to do so in one individual. Ask Dr Blake if you don't believe me.'

'That's not what I meant, though. I'm not talking about the beauty and the grace and that stuff. I know I'm not beautiful and I can't do pirouettes or walk like I'm balancing ten books on my head... I'm talking about the stuff that makes you, you know, *you.* Bella D'accourt. The person who just *looks* at someone and they instantly do exactly what she wants...'

'Sounds an awful lot like a rumour...'

'It's not, though, is it Mum? I've *seen* you. You don't think I remember it all, but I do. When I was small and I started having a tantrum in the middle of a supermarket and you told me to, *Be quiet.* I remember it. My mouth was still open but it was like my voice had just shrivelled up. I couldn't make a noise at all. I just stood there like a stupid fish. And then there was the time when we lived somewhere else, before Flintworth, when I was really little, like three or four. I was meant to be asleep but you were having an argument with a man – I guess you were in a garden or a different room, I think there was a window or something I could hear you through. You told him to leave… He didn't want to. I saw him, he went past me on his way out and he was crying. I remember that because it made me cry as well, I could *feel* how much he didn't want to go… But he *had* to, because you said so.'

'I didn't realise you remembered that.'

Her voice has softened. Ariana still has her eyes shut in concentration, but she can't reach where her mother has gone now. There's something so sad and strange at the other end of the phone, so much harder to grasp between finger and thumb than the bitter edge of her earlier anger.

'Well, I do. I remember all of it. And I know that's why you came up here in the first place. That's why your mum abandoned you when you were a little kid. They never did fix you, did they? The Blakes?'

'I wasn't broken.'

'Really. Tell that to the little girl whose hand you burned on a stove top.'

There's a pause. Ariana can't hear anything now. She wonders for a moment whether Bella has simply put the phone down somewhere and walked away from it.

'Who told you about that?'

'What does it matter? I know about it all, so there's no point in lying to me about it anymore. Where did it come from? That power over people? How do you know that I haven't got it too?'

'Because you haven't. Because you're normal. I know that's not what you want to hear. I know you're up there surrounded by these stories and rumours and that old relic of an institution where children used to disappear into thin air, and walk through walls, and fly... But you're *normal.* Nobody fiddled around with your genes, I didn't take any super-secret potions when I was pregnant. You're just... good at persuading people to do what you want. Probably because you've seen me do it so much. I'm sorry... Like I said, I know that's probably not what you want to hear...'

'Oh no, I've been dying my whole life to hear my mother say that I'm not special, that's every kid's dream isn't it?'

'I didn't say you weren't special...'

'Just that the only things that make me special are things about *you*...'

'Ariana, that's not what I meant.'

'I'm going to save those creatures, *Bella*. Whether you like it or not. It would be easier with your help, though.' She's quite proud of the cold authority in her voice until she realises it's a direct copy of her mother's.

'How exactly do you expect me to help you?'

'I don't know! Use your powers of persuasion on Daniel? Go and *demand* it of him? You're the one who's so *gifted* aren't you, after all?' She sounds petty and childish once again but she's tired now she's stopped trying to work out what her mother is doing and feeling. She doesn't care.

'It's not that simple—'

'I don't care. I want you to do it. Or I'll try again. And you know he won't go so easy on me next time...'

'Ariana, you can't!'

'Don't tell me what I can't do.'

She presses end on the call and throws the phone onto the bed. She stands in the middle of the bedroom without remembering when she got to her feet. Catching sight of herself in the floor-length mirror, Ariana scowls at her reflection. Her fists are balled and her hair is wild – it always seems to become more frizzy when she's angry, like her emotions carry some sort of electrical charge – and her eyes glimmer as green as her mother's. *She's wrong. I can feel it. There's something... Something more.* But isn't that what every kid wants to think? Why, if she's so sure her mother is wrong, is Ariana so angry? So scared that actually Bella might just be right all along, as she so often is?

11

April, 2019

My argument with Ariana stings in my ears for days. Her warning about returning to Futura, placing herself deliberately within Daniel's grasp, panics my heartbeat every time I think about it. Something is unlocked though, between us. Despite the bitterness, the awful hiss of her voice when she'd called me *Bella*, it's as if part of the wound festering between us since October has finally begun to scab over at the edges.

> Tell me more about them. These creatures.

>> They're the worst thing I've ever seen. They aren't human, but you can tell they used to be. It's not like the Guard. You can look in their eyes and see them hurting, feeling. There's a bird-girl who tried to attack me. I think that if the cage hadn't been there she would have killed me. And there's this pig-boy. He didn't look much older than me. He was crying. It sounded like nothing I've ever heard… Like a baby and a piglet all in one but with the knowingness of grown-up feelings

behind it. It was desperate. Awful.

> It sounds it. I'm sorry you had to see that.

So what are you going to do about it?

> I'm wor

'Bella.'

My fingers stiffen over the screen and I quickly swipe the conversation away. I look up from where I am leaning on the balcony and blink as Lychen approaches the twisted iron table on the terrace. The sun blazes from behind his smooth features, illuminating tiny hairs which have resisted the smooth, doll-like sweep on his tawny head. He glances at my phone and smiles tightly.

'So the prodigal daughter has finally deigned to return your messages, has she?'

'Something like that,' I stretch my mouth into a rueful smile as he pauses by the table and gestures for Delta to pour him coffee. Delta does so with his usual precise, even movements before returning to his position at the double doors behind us. Ethan waits there too, having returned to my service the night before.

'We had a conversation about her... indiscretions... the other day, after our morning meeting with Daniel. She is rather upset about these creatures of his. Is insistent that I should see them. I think she wants me to save them.'

Lychen takes a measured sip of coffee as he walks over to join me. His steps do not falter and the hand holding his cup does not waver, though he moves without once taking his eyes from mine. He raises a narrow neat eyebrow.

'Well, as it happens, Daniel and I have decided that it is time he bring some of his research here to the

Beaumont. He has had some, ah, *interesting developments* in recent days. Certainly some which warrant a closer examination using certain tools at our disposal in this facility.'

'Oh? Was that what the classified part of his report concerned the other morning?'

'Mostly. Yes. So there you are, you can tell young Ariana that you'll be able to observe the creatures – those he deems fit to travel – soon enough. Though I can't promise you'll be able to, er, *save* any of them. Indeed, if the whole matter is proving too overwhelming for the girl, perhaps it would be best for her to come here as well and observe them more closely for herself, see that their lives are not all cages and misery...'

'Really?' Confusion battles with the usual dread at the suggestion of Ariana being anywhere near him. Or Daniel for that matter. 'That's... generous of you.'

'It's the least I can do for you, Bella, after all you do for me. For us. Which brings me to my next matter – I thought I would observe the Youth prototypes this morning. You've done so well in the ambassador role for the Guard Assistance Programme – all twenty attendees from the Manchester proposal signed up to the beneficiary package, including the absent Dr Kneck, once the invitation error was explained to her. Marketing is well underway with the roll-out of the first round of press releases and media coverage. I want you at the forefront of the entire campaign. Not just the initial Care Programme we're launching next month, the whole thing. Your face – this face – this is what I want people to see when they think of BFI. The next few weeks are going to be extremely busy. I thought it would be prudent to see where we are with the Youth Project, perhaps some of their supervision can be delegated while you're in the public eye…'

'Is this because of Burton?'

'Who?'

'Melinda Burton, the woman who threatened to expose the Youth Project?'

'Ah, Daniel's latest recruit. I think he turned her into a Guard in the end, though I know he was looking into bovine experimentation. No. It's not about her, but it *would* be best to ensure the impact of the GCAP coverage is not diluted with any further leaks.'

'So we'll vet the journalists, pre-arranged questions only, that sort of thing. I don't want to give up the Youth Project, Josiah. It's mine. *They're* mine.'

He watches me and, slowly, reaches for the hand which I've clenched unconsciously around the railing between me and the empty air over the city.

'So ambitious,' he murmurs.

'Yes, well…' *What else do I have?* I think, looking from him down to the streets below. A gaggle of women push prams towards a playground lurking out of sight behind a large grey office building. I sense him follow my gaze and I draw back, blowing my cheeks out and inserting the shine back into my eyes as I turn to him once again.

'So, all twenty signed up? Even Pillsboom, hmm?'

'Pillsboom signed the executive deal,' Lychen smiles, snake-like, though there is a question lingering in his eyes. 'Evidently your presentation skills are far superior to my own.'

'He did mention something about you having made a similar proposal several years ago.'

'Back in the earlier days of the Guard application, back when I still called it Project D, I used to undertake demonstrations myself with Delta here, and a few of the other early models.'

'Really?'

'Oh yes. Not particularly successfully, for the most part. I have my ways of commanding others, but clearly when it comes to sales I lack certain people skills.' He smiles again, but this time there is a shadow behind it. A brief, contemplative shadow, something inward and secretive that I have never seen from him before. I smile back at him, desperate to nudge but not wanting to shatter the tentative glimmers of humanity.

'*People skills* is one of those vague terms for a skill set that is completely multi-faceted,' I say, measuredly. He watches me keenly. 'Yours are more attuned up here,' I raise my hand to my eye-level, 'Where the stakes are highest and the persuasion counts the most.'

'You flatter me.'

'No, I tell you the truth.'

'Do you, Bella? Sometimes I don't know if I can truly tell with you...' He reaches his coffee cup backwards and Delta, who began moving at the same time Lychen did, takes it smoothly from him. Without taking his eyes from mine, Lychen takes my cup as well and hands it to Delta too. He takes my hand, which is still at my eye level, lifts it as far above my head as it will go and then grasps my other and stretches it downwards. Like we're about to do some sort of strange, open-armed dance. It almost hurts, but not quite.

'This cannot even come close to the span of *your* power over people,' he murmurs. 'Over me.'

Then he stretches forward and kisses me quickly on the mouth, and lets me go. I blink in surprise.

'Well... that's my job...' I say, slowly, as he turns back, takes his cup from Delta again and drinks more coffee.

When he turns around again, his eyes are steely once more and the glimpse of something else, something so fleetingly soft and distant, has disappeared.

'Yes,' he says, briefly. 'Along with the Youth Project. Shall we go?'

12

Spring, 2006

The flat was pristine. I had had so little else to do since I stopped my visits to the university – once I hit the seven-month mark it became too difficult to slide into lectures unnoticed – that I had sorted and organised and scrubbed until every surface gleamed far brighter than it had when I'd first moved in. The midwives had visited and deemed the space acceptable accommodation for a mother and baby, I made sure Marc was also present at the time so they could tick their 'support system' box. The flat was on the ground floor of a generic block. The upper levels had balconies and, in recompense, I had private use of a tiny square of concrete set behind the little cubicle of my bathroom and overlooked by windows belonging to at least every other resident.

'It's not all that different to normal student accommodation,' Marc had remarked on his first visit, as he'd peered around the small living space, a kitchenette lining one wall and fake fireplace on the other. 'At least you've got a separate bedroom with a decent wardrobe and space for a cot,' he'd added.

The cot stood ready now, sheets clean, blanket fresh, a pretty white Moses basket I'd found in a charity shop within it so I'd be able to move the baby from one room to another without waking her. Next to the cot, the chest of drawers which had come with the flat waited, bedecked with piles of nappies, wipes, muslins and changing mat all squared neatly. The drawers contained more of her clothes than mine. I reached into the top drawer for a pair of tiny yellow socks and placed them inside the open bag at my feet. I breathed slowly as the pain began to build again, holding onto the drawers with one hand and desperately paddling the other over my rounded back, trying to find the spot I'd read about, the one which was meant to help relieve some of the burning course of agony. I squeezed my eyes closed as the pain mounted, letting a moan escape.

You need to call again.
No. They said there has to be three in five minutes. It's not that bad yet.
Then call Marc. You can't walk for the tube or catch a bus like this. How will you get there when the time comes?
I'll call a taxi. I have a plan, just... butt out...

'Arrrrgh.' The pain had become part of me. It was a snake which wound around my tenderest parts, squeezing them until they screamed, until they became sound and that sound had nowhere to go but out. I put my hand over my mouth and bit.

I can't do this.
You can, Bella. You can.
I wish you could do it.
I know. I wish I could too.
This is worse than anything. This is worse than what he did. This is—

I moaned again as my entire body seized. My hand throbbed as my teeth sank into the skin, the distraction only a tiny pinprick of relief in the sea of unyielding brutality. I opened my eyes. The yellow socks hazed in and out of focus, impossibly intact as my whole being tore itself apart just heartbeats away. I breathed in slowly and reached for the phone.

'Elodie? Elodie? Love, you have to focus, you have to listen to us... Elodie?'

I blinked and tried to concentrate. *That's her*, I thought. *Elodie*. But in the next second I wasn't sure who or what Elodie was. I lay on my side, pain coursing through my body as someone tried to lift my leg away. Lychen's hands wrenched my skin. The icy fingers of night air on my softest, palest parts...

'No!' I shouted and kicked. '*No!*'

I hadn't said it then. That's why it happened. I hadn't said it and I let him. I let him. It was my fault. I didn't do what Mamma said, I wasn't careful. I should have listened to her and told him he couldn't have me, not like that. I'd wanted some of it, though. I'd bathed in the burn of eyes on me, the scorch of his gaze – him, the most important, who wanted me. I'd wanted that. I didn't tell him no.

'...not responding, any emergency contact?'

'...already tried, no answer.'

'...how long fully dilated?'

'...need this baby to come out now...'

Voices swam in and out of reality. I blinked a few times and, at some point, someone with a kind face was right in front of me, talking to me in strange, dolloping words which seemed to bounce away. Someone mentioned something about psychosis, reactions, babies... Baby. Where was it? Was that Elodie? I looked up and my stomach clenched massively under my hands. I turned my face and screamed into my pillow.

'Bella? Bella, I'm here. Bella, you've got to listen to me.'

I looked up. I knew this one. This wasn't one of the Elodie aliens.

'Daddy?'

'Yes, sweetheart. Listen, you've got to move onto your back so the doctor can help you, do you understand?'

I moved, his large hands guiding me.

'I didn't tell him not to do it, Dad. It was my fault. I didn't tell him no. I shouldn't—'

'Shh, never mind that now...'

'But I let him, you don't understand... This is my fault, this child is going to be half a monster and it's my fault—'

'Sir—'

'Marc. It's Marc.'

'Marc, you need to tell her to push when she feels the contraction, she needs to push otherwise we'll have to—'

'Bells, listen to the midwife, you need to push when the pain comes.'

'No! You can't make me, none of them can! I'll stop it, I can make it stop—'

'No, you can't,' he leant close. Too close. I squirmed away but he let go of my hand and took my head instead so I couldn't twist the other way.

'I don't want it,' I murmured, squeezing my eyes shut. 'I don't want her.'

'I know, I know,' he kissed my forehead, and I tried to writhe away again but he held me. 'But she's coming all the same. You have to help her, just push... and it will all be over. I promise.'

I opened my eyes and narrowed them at him as another impossible surge ravaged. I could feel it more now, the drug they'd given me was wearing off, my brain was struggling out of the foggy confusion. I was naked from the waist down and my father was *right there.* I stared at him and he removed his hands from my head immediately.

He's right. I can't do it for you and neither can he.
I don't want it.
Yes, you do. You said you would protect her, as long as it took, as long as you're still breathing. You're still breathing, aren't you?
I've changed my mind. This isn't love. This didn't come from love.
Then don't do it for love. Do it for hate. Have his child and use it to destroy him.
I'm scared.
No, you're not. You're Bella.

I gave a long, anguished cry. It came from the place he'd hurt me. It came from the dark, swollen spot I'd buried and burned and hidden from all those long months as my abdomen had grown. It came from the very core of me and I couldn't have stopped it, no matter how hard I commanded. I stared around at them all, the medical people at the foot of my bed, exchanging worried words I couldn't hear, Marc near my head, glancing from them to me and back again. I opened my legs, propped myself up, climbed to the top of the surge with bloody torn fingernails, and pushed for hate.

13

April, 2019

'So, Bette,' I press pause on the TV screen at the front of the laboratory and face the room full of perfect, passive teenagers. 'What can you tell me about this interaction?'

'It was primarily between two individuals, a man and a woman, who are currently involved in a romantic, most likely sexual, relationship. The conversation was about hosting a celebratory event for a mutual friend's birthday. There was a third party, another woman, who observed the conversation from behind a door, undetected by the couple.'

'Yes, that's basically correct,' I say, smoothly. The girl blinks and the blankness of her expression flickers as she looks at me. From the corner of my eye, I see Lychen staring at her avidly. 'Now think about the subtext of this scene. Tell me about this person,' I point to the woman frozen on the screen, standing behind the door between her and the couple, her face a fixed prison of anguish. Bette stares at the woman. Her grey eyes remain focused, blinking at perfectly regular intervals, but her forehead twitches.

'She is unhappy with what she hears.'

'Yes. Why?'

'Jealousy?' Bette looks at me, face marked only by question. I look from her to the other members of the class.

Most of them are looking hard at the woman on the screen, though one or two are staring instead at Lychen, a few watch me, and a handful remain blank.

'Tom?' I address one of the males who is staring at Lychen. He immediately refocuses on the screen.

'Jealousy,' he repeats.

'OK. Why is she jealous?'

'They are discussing a birthday party. Perhaps they forgot her birthday party?'

I smile and a few of the Youth smile as well, though I can tell most of them are just mirroring, as I have taught them to do when unsure of the situation.

'Perhaps. But I think it goes deeper than that. Think. Did she look unhappy at the start of the conversation?'

'Yes,' Tom replies.

'Yes. In fact, her unhappiness is apparent throughout the conversation and doesn't change with the other characters' reactions. Which tells us that it is likely unrelated to the primary subject matter of the birthday party... Eve, do you think the character's discomfort is residual or superficial?'

'Residual,' Eve says without hesitation. I have saved calling on her until this part of the lesson because she is one of my more reliable observers.

'Good. What else can you tell me?'

'She looked unhappy from the start, but only began to frown when the male character began speaking about how much he cares about his friend Michael.' Eve's voice rises and falls with the words and, to an outsider, she sounds almost normal. 'That is when her left hand makes a fist and she brings it up to her chest. This shows unconscious agitation. She is having a physical reaction. I think her jealousy is rooted in a deep attachment. To this character,' she points at the man on the screen. Then she shrugs and smiles, 'Or Michael.'

'Not the woman?'

'No. Her reactions to her voice are relatively minor. Besides, same sex relationships are rarely portrayed in daytime soap operas from this particular era.'

I smile at her and she smiles back, though of course her brown eyes remain glazed behind their rhythmic blinking.

'Thank you, Eve. You may all take a ten-minute break.'

The class blinks in time and, as one, lower their chins to their chests, hands spread evenly on the surfaces in front of them, eyes fixed.

'Remarkable,' Lychen says, from the corner. 'And this is the time they use…?'

'To consolidate what they have learned. I have found that regular rest periods like this help significantly with retaining knowledge.'

'Almost like real children…'

'Well, they were, not so long ago. It makes sense that their fledgling brains require similar periods of rest, stimulation, leisure…' I gesture at the books, computers, and games consoles in the rear end of the laboratory.

'This one,' Lychen approaches Eve, hands behind his back as he peers at her. 'She appears more advanced than some of the others.'

'Yes, her file shows an elevated IQ. I took a personal interest in her particular recruitment because of it. She is an exceptionally fast learner. Of course, all those predisposed to intelligence are at an advantage.'

'Yes,' Lychen turns from the motionless girl in front of him to the screen, which is still frozen on the image of the woman, the couple blurred in the background. 'And all this... emotional response learning...' he wrinkles his nose slightly.

'The focus group testing largely showed that the public are far more agreeable to Guard Assistants who show a thorough understanding of human emotion. Imagine, for example, a person who has a fear of the dentist but who is in need of a check-up. An ordinary Guard might perceive the fear as an insurmountable barrier. One these would understand that it is not so...'

'I see.' He looks unconvinced. 'Have they been tested on different masters?'

'Yes. All results have been consistent, for every single one.'

'But they answer to you, too?'

'For my safety, I have been bonded to all of them on a basic level. But it can be overridden as easily as the bond with T last week. And it certainly doesn't go anywhere near as deep as my bond with Ethan.'

'No, I should hope not.'

'So, what do you think?'

Lychen stares around the room. His gaze falls on Bette, on her blonde hair braided closely to her head, her clear grey gaze unflinching upon the far edge of her desk.

'They're good. Better than I thought they would be. Their youth...'

'... it can appear a little unnerving at first, I know.'

'No, it's not that. I know it's necessary for this level of intervention. It's just... they remind me of... the C-Subjects.'

'Yes. Me too. But they're not the same, I promise you that.'

'Still, seeing them *think*... The original Guard were created to eliminate the messy intervention of emotion.'

'As a result of the failures of Project C, I remember.

But there is a difference. These teenagers do not *feel* – they question when they do not understand, and they simulate. In all other respects they are just like the Guard Assistants being prepped for roll-out over in South East as we speak. They've undergone the same alterations, the same transitions. And because of their age, their sourcing has been particularly scrupulous.'

'No loose ends?'

'I made sure of it. You would not believe the lives some of them were living, how many of them were salvaged from drink or drug-related brain death. And even with those whose recruitment required some creative intervention,' my eyes linger on Eve briefly. 'I can personally vouch that each and every one of them is better off now than they were six months ago.'

'Admirable as your dedication to them is, your priority must remain the GAP ambassador role. Are you sure you can keep up both?'

'I would like to try. They know me… my teaching style… They've come to know what to expect, as much as they can, anyway. I think anyone else could risk setting them back.' I keep eye contact. Lychen blinks and shrugs.

'Fine. But my standards remain high. I will come and observe again next month, by which time I'd hope they will all be closer to the level of this one,' he indicates Eve. I nod, smoothly.

'They will.'

'Thank you, Bella.' He smiles tightly and checks his watch. 'I had better go, I've got an eleven o'clock with Dr Gibbs over in South. Will you join me for dinner later?'

'Yes.' I return his smile until he turns on his heel and walks out, each step a measured, precise clip. I wait until the door closes and the sounds of his neat little footfalls padding across the hallway carpet disappear down the staircase. Then I turn and touch Eve briefly on the shoulder. Her dark brown eyes blink twice before she looks up at me.

'What can you tell me about that interaction?'

Eve looks towards the door once, as if Lychen were still there, but I know it's just a move to gather her thoughts. A tic she's observed from me, while internally she organises, sorts and smooths.

'The power balance is precarious. He wants to control you, but he does not know if he can. He doesn't care about this programme as much as he thinks you think he does, however he is more impressed than he shows by the progress you have made. He has little intention of marketing the Youth Guard anytime soon, however. It is a means of engaging you, he has recognised your enthusiasm and drive for the project and sees that this is where your passion lies. He knows that your other roles here do not fulfil the same need, so he thinks it is important to continue your role with us because he is afraid that you will attempt to leave him otherwise.

'He is terrified of your influence over him, he is worried that his obsession with you is masking his judgment, making him weak. But he cannot contemplate living without it.' Her heart-shaped face furrows far more humanly than it did earlier, making her appear for all the world like any other teen struggling to interpret adult emotion.

'This visit was about making sure that you are still under some semblance of control. You have done well elsewhere in his estimations, secured something important. He is happy about this but threatened by his growing dependence on you. He is so entirely preoccupied by you that he completely fails to see what is truly happening here.'

I smile. 'Which is?'

'That he may control the surface, but your power is deepening, like roots burrowing under the foundations of everything he is building. That your plan, when the time comes, is to yank the roots clear and watch everything crumble into the spaces they leave.'

'Thank you, Eve. Wake.'

As one, all nineteen of the other heads rise and focus their eyes upon me. Every gaze is clear, focused and waiting. My army of tree roots.

14

May, 2019

'Ralph! Dom! It's on!'

Felix presses pause on the TV and sits up straighter as Ralph turns from the bookshelf where he's been browsing in a determinedly casual manner for the last twenty minutes. The double doors leading to Felix's adopted office – once Ralph's schoolroom – are ajar, Dominic and Tess leaning over one of the six separate monitors Felix has had on continuously ever since she moved them there from the ARC. The two of them look up and make their way through the doorway to the front room.

Felix waits as Ralph sinks onto the cracked leather sofa next to her, Dom perching on the far arm and Tess hovering in her nervous, awkward way behind him. Dr Blake looks up from the book he is poring over at his desk but does not move closer to the screen. On it, Bella sits across from seasoned interviewer Christine Fairley, legs crossed neatly at the ankle, her microphone positioned just so at the hem of her pristine silk blouse, smiling as if giving TV interviews is as natural to her as breathing. Her dark hair sparkles in the studio spotlights, one loose curl tumbling delicately to the front, the rest flowing neatly behind her. Her eyes blaze like twin jades and seem to pierce right through the screen. Felix glances around in the second before she presses play. Everyone else in the room is transfixed and the bloody woman hasn't even begun speaking yet.

'So... Dr D'accourt, tell me a bit more about the Guard Care Assistance Programme... Where did the idea come from?' Christine Fairley leans forward with an easy grin. Her neat blonde hair bobs around her pointed chin, her clothes are just as tailored and smart as Bella's but she looks tired and dull in comparison. Like a tarnished penny next to a nugget of radiant gold.

'The research has been ongoing for well over a decade now,' Bella twinkles at Christine, dipping her head slightly. 'So it's hard to say where the idea originated. It was more a natural evolution of several avenues of research aimed to address the issue of whether it was possible to create a bespoke workforce devoid of certain hindrances of humanity...'

'Hindrances? So you're saying the presence of humanity in, say, a carer for a disabled or elderly patient, is a bad thing?'

Bella smiles, though her eyes narrow dangerously. Felix can feel the chill of them even here, and she watches Christine blink rapidly, though she doesn't squirm. *Good for you*, she thinks.

'No. I'm not. What I mean is, humanity encompasses a margin for error – clumsiness, tiredness, boredom – which is eliminated by our programme. And it can be applied beyond the care industry, that's just one small aspect of it... With the correct training, we can place Guard people in almost any industry.'

'Won't that mean massive job losses for ordinary people?'

'Our programme is designed to alleviate those jobs with the lowest levels of employee satisfaction. Our research shows that these often fall in sectors which tend to involve menial, repetitive tasks with the lowest levels of pay… But we're here to talk about the Care Assistants, let's stay on subject, shall we?'

Bella smiles icily; Christine returns it grimly.

'Quite. There is an emerging body of protest against the ethics of this programme – putting loss of human jobs aside, let's address the issue of the Guard individuals themselves. Who are they, exactly, and how are they turned into these unfeeling, robotic beings?'

'For the most part, they're criminals under life sentences who have consented to donate their bodies to science. A small proportion is made up of patients in persistent vegetative states – ie, no chance of brain activity recovery. Those whose souls have already departed, if you will.'

'And the soulless?'

'Well, that's one way of looking at it. All of the people who undergo the procedure have given consent, one way or another, though sometimes it is through family.'

'Liar!' Felix snarls at the TV screen. Ralph puts a hand on hers and she realises she's trembling.

'…why would anyone consent to their dying loved one being used for such a purpose?' Christine is asking, her expression torn between fascination and horror.

'Not many do,' Bella says, levelly, 'But those that do tend to take the viewpoint that their loved one has already gone, that their body is something entirely separate. But that, maybe, it would be nice for the skin to feel sunlight again, for the hands to reach out and help another person, for the voice to be something someone, somewhere, is happy and grateful to hear…'

'Mmm. Even if it's just to ask if they would like a cup of tea?'

'Whatever they need.'

'So how do they *know* what a person might need? If the patient is unable to communicate?'

'There's a bonding process. It's completely painless, it just involves a small device worn by the person for a few days, the longer it's on, the stronger the bond, so it is variable depending on the person's needs and situation. The device records part of a person's inner thought process, both conscious and subconscious – their habits, needs, decisions, desires… The longer the device is worn, the deeper it perceives. Then it is uploaded to the Guard Assistant and they are able to process and predict what that person needs or wants without them having to say it out loud.'

'Incredible.'

'We've already introduced several trials across a variety of voluntary participants from those in need of fulltime care to those who just require a little assistance in their day-to-day lives. All the uppermost-level employees at the Beaumont have their own Primary Assistant and there have been several assigned to our live-in workers as well, their help with research tasks has been invaluable. And, among our voluntary recipients, we have had a consistently high level of satisfaction.'

'Well, that leads me nicely to my next guest – one such volunteer, Mary Freightworth, who joins us from her home in Aberdeen. A home she's recently been able to return to after a spell in a care facility after breaking her hip. Hello, Mary, what can you tell us about your Guard Assistant and how they've changed your life?'

Christine turns to the screen behind her showing a grinning woman with white hair and thick glasses sitting in a floral armchair. A stoic Guard person stands beside her.

'What do you think?' Felix turns to Ralph as the old lady's voice bubbles into the background. He blinks a few times, seemingly coming out of some sort of reverie.

'It's... God. It's bigger than I thought. They're going to roll this out everywhere, aren't they? It starts with hospitals and care homes but what's next? Law enforcement? A Guard in every household?'

'Can you imagine one of *those* in your home, watching you all the time, always *on*, always there...' Tess gestures at the screen and shudders. 'Bad enough when they were at work, but at least then they kept to themselves... Back when I worked for BFI, they were only about two dozen doing the cleaning, working in the canteen and doing general maintenance stuff in the living quarters. You never saw them in the labs or offices and there was none of this *Assistance* business...'

'Well, *she* seems happy enough,' Dominic nods at the old woman, who is now patting the arm of the blank-faced man beside her. He is dressed in hospital scrubs and is smaller, more wiry than the Guard people Felix has come across in the past.

'Of course she does,' Ralph says, quietly. 'She's got a personal man-slave to do all her bidding and listen to her ramble on about cats and grandchildren without so much as cracking a yawn. Do you know how many lonely old people there are out there?'

'But it's like having... having a little bit of Lychen everywhere... it's *creepy*,' Tess shudders. Felix glances at her witheringly, but it is Dr Blake who responds first.

'But these people do not know Lychen. They have no experience of the earlier generations of Guard, who were entirely his slaves. These Guard Assistants have been designed to bond to them and them alone. When they look at them, they'll see only a reflection of their own wants and needs, in a body able to give it to them.'

'Unless it's not that at all… Unless it's all just fake and the Guard really are still Lychen's and he's trying to use them to spy on everyone…' interjects a voice from the corner of the room. Felix shuts her eyes briefly and then turns around. Ariana is standing inches from the doorway, her eyes wide and staring at the screen, which has now panned back to Christine and her mother.

'We're going to hear now from one of those opposed to the whole idea of Guard Assistants,' Christine segues, smoothly. 'Dr Hedgeson from Brywick University, hello there…'

'Good evening,' the screen formerly occupied by Mary is now filled with a large man, suited and tired-looking but bright-eyed as he stares keenly from what looks like a small, teacher-style office.

'What is your opposition to the programme, sir?'

'Well, putting aside the question of what are essentially reanimated corpses brought back for the purpose of servile degradation… I'm concerned about the dubious origins of this research, the foundations of which we mustn't forget lie with the disgraced Aspira Research Centre. A facility which has recently been exposed as having used children in its experimentations into genetic mutilation…'

There is a pause. Christine turns to Bella, who raises an eyebrow delicately.

'Did you have a question?' Bella asks, sweetly. Ralph snorts with laughter and immediately looks ashamed of himself.

'Is it true that the research for this programme originated from the ARC?'

'The ARC was an institution of scientific research for many, many years. It did a great deal for the research of genetic engineering, eugenics and science as a whole. It wouldn't be far-fetched to claim that most advancements in human enhancement and improvement over the last few decades have originated, at least in part, from there.'

'So you're defending the use of experimentation on children?'

'I am merely placing credit where credit is due. I wouldn't like to comment on the rumours surrounding the now defunct programmes once researched at the ARC. It is no longer relevant.'

'But you yourself once worked there, correct? You are the very same Bella D'accourt who grew up at the institute as a ward of Dr Frederick Blake, right? There are even rumours that you yourself are an example of genetic experimentation...'

Christine's mouth drops open. Felix watches Bella closely. Her careful face does not so much as tic but one of her fingers flutters very slightly in her lap. A small flicker of movement from somewhere at the very edge of the camera's focus catches Felix's eye briefly, but then the picture zooms closer to Bella to catch her response.

'There are a number of injunctions in place as a result of several recent court cases concerning the ARC and its former projects, should you care to look it up, Dr Hedgeson. I am here to talk about the Guard Care Assistance Programme. Did you have a question about it?'

Dr Hedgeson blinks a few times and looks down at a piece of paper in front of him. He clears his throat. 'Does Beaumont Futura Industries hold any current ties with the Aspira Research Centre?'

'Apart from the ownership of an empty building in

Cumbria, no.'

'And what, exactly, is in place to stop BFI going down the same route as the Blakes and delving further into human experimentation, teasing the boundaries of what is possible as opposed to what is right...'

'We have strict policies with full government backing. The current Prime Minister, Roger Metcalfe, himself has seen and signed off on our work. Everything we do is done with transparency. And, as I mentioned, the individuals selected for the Guard programme are done so with full consent wherever possible.'

'And is the process reversible... Should the family members change their minds?'

Bella's eyebrows flicker upwards as Felix catches her breath. Her heart waits, as if it is scared of beating too hard and drowning out what she hears next.

'At the present time... it is not. But we do have a team working on it.'

'Dr Hedgeson, thank you for your time. We are now going to move on to seeing one of these Guard Assistants in person. Dr D'accourt, would you like to introduce us to... er, Sigma, is it?'

'Yes,' Bella beams. 'No need for any introduction, really. Sigma, would you come here, please?'

Felix watches as the camera pans to the backstage area and follows a short, stocky Guard woman who looks vaguely familiar. She lets Bella's voice warble over her, barely taking in her brief explanation about how each Guard's name indicates which generation they're from but can easily be changed once bonded. She doesn't listen as Ralph snorts along with Dominic, muttering under his breath. She doesn't even notice Ariana sidling up to crouch next to her on the rug. Her eyes feel like they're burning.

In that split second of panning, the camera picked up another figure standing backstage. It was only the briefest glimmer, a fragmented whisper of a silhouette, but a fragment was all she needed to identify him.

'Ethan,' she breathes.

'What?' Ariana turns to her. 'Where?'

'He's *there*! I saw him in the backstage bit just now and earlier, I thought I saw him before, when... she... *Oh*! He's got to be hers. When that man said that thing about the genetic experimentation rumour and pissed her off, she twitched and I saw him move at the edge of the screen. Because he sensed her distress... What did she say before? Each upper employee gets their own Primary Guard Assistant... And he's hers. Ethan is Bella's Guard...'

There's a pause.

'Are you sure?' Ralph turns a furrowed brow to her. 'I didn't see anything. And it seems a bit... risky. I mean, sooner or later our paths are bound to cross. Why would she do that?'

'Why wouldn't she?' Felix snorts, on her feet, staring at the screen with an odd mixture of repulsion and eagerness as the camera continues to pan. 'Look, there he is again!'

'Well... maybe she's doing it to protect him? You know, keeping him close so he's not mistreated...'

'Right,' Felix scoffs, 'because we all know how warm and cuddly Bella is deep down inside. No offence,' she glances at Ariana, who shrugs.

'It's alright,' Ariana says, with a half-smile. 'I actually think you're probably right. It is the sort of thing she'd do.'

'Whatever the motives,' Dr Blake cuts in, just as Felix opens her mouth to unleash some of the fury bubbling in her gullet, 'We've been given an awful lot of information over the last half an hour. We have an idea of BFI's short and long-term plans regarding the Guard programmes. We know that Bella is continuing on in her role as spokesperson among other things. We know where Ethan is and what his role presumably entails. *She* has given us all of this. Do you think it was by accident?'

He fixes the others with one of his stern looks and they all fall silent. On the screen, Christine thanks Bella for joining her and Bella glows beatifically, her eyes sweeping graciously over the interviewer and the camera and it's as if, just for a moment, she too is scrutinising each and every person staring back at her on the screen in Dr Blake's office.

15

Spring, 2006

> How are things? I'd love to come round if poss?
>
>> I'm fine.
>
> How is the baby?
>
>> Fine too. Back to birth weight. The midwife discharged us yesterday.
>
> That's good news, when can I come?
>
>> This afternoon?
>
> Do you need anything?

I looked around my small living room and remembered how it had looked before. My basic Ikea furniture interspersed with the faded, corduroy sofa which had been here when I moved in. The pristine kitchen counters and stove top, uncluttered as a show home. Now you couldn't even see the electric hob underneath the pile of dirty muslins and bottles. The washing machine next to the oven was half-full of tiny soiled garments. I hadn't yet found the energy to bring the many, many more dirty things in from the bedroom to complete the load. The coffee table in front of me held three dirty cups, a cereal bowl from whenever it was I'd last remembered to eat and more baby bottles, despite the baby having taken quite happily to the breast. Before, I hadn't given much thought to breastfeeding, having decided fairly early on in the pregnancy that bottles seemed a more practical option. It wasn't like I was going to be around much to breastfeed, once I'd started my course, after all… But then the midwives had asked if I wanted to try and, at the time, I had been up for anything that might make the moment I could close my eyes come sooner. Ariana had latched on straight away, and now… Now it was the only way to get her to shut up.

> Bella? I need to leave in a few minutes
> if I'm going to beat the traffic…

Traffic. What time was it, anyway? I glanced at the clock on the wall opposite the tide of mess spilling from the kitchenette and realised it had gone three. I supposed it must be a weekday. I looked down at the baby. She had fallen asleep on my breast, her mouth puckered around a growing patch of bruised, shiny skin which, according to the midwives, I was to keep an eye on in case it should turn into something called mastitis. I put my finger into her mouth and gently tried to break the suction. She made a small, guttural squeak and instantly began sucking again with the vigour of a parched marathon runner. I sighed and swallowed heavily against the wash of utter, bone-deep exhaustion. I couldn't stop the tears; I'd stopped noticing them by that point. I reached for my phone.

> Can you bring some food, please? Just
> the basics. Milk, bread, etc.

> Of course. I'll be there as soon as I can.

Just over two hours later I stepped out of the shower,

wrapping a large towel around my body without looking down at it. I felt clean, at least, though no less wrecked. My heart hammered furiously around my skull as I bent forward, carefully drying around the parts of me that still felt raw and wounded. It wasn't as bad, I thought, as the awful, searing feelings of dirtiness and shame I'd felt in the weeks after Lychen's attack. (I couldn't call it rape yet. Not then. Especially not then.) My body would heal; my rational mind told me that even as my irrational side, the side that had been raging louder and louder over the last tumultuous months of pregnancy and was now almost a constant siren, screeched at what I'd done to my perfect, flat stomach, my creamy unblemished skin, the glowing face of a person who took eight unbroken hours of sleep a night for granted.

I dressed quickly in clothes I wouldn't have looked twice at a year earlier – leggings, a vest that was already baggy from being pulled down so many times, a loose woollen jumper which had once belonged to Ana. I rubbed the worst of the wetness out of my hair and walked back to the living room with an odd mixture of dread and anxiety. It was quiet. Stepping into the room, the first thing I noticed was that the washing machine was running and that all the dirty bottles, plates, cups and cutlery had been gathered into the sink. The kettle shuddered loudly, two cups and tea bags at the ready. There was bread in the toaster. My surfaces were clear, if not entirely clean. I turned around and there was Marc, standing in the centre of the room with his granddaughter in his arms, making those odd squeaky noises adults made around infants. Her face slumped over his shoulder, eyes glimmering under heavy lids.

I crossed the room and began to fill the sink with

soapy water.

'I can do that, love, if you want to take this little one...'

'That's OK, she seems happy enough with you.' I plunged my hands into the warm water and began to scrub, omitting to add that after ten solid days of breastfeeding around the clock, my body was screaming out for time on its own again.

'She does seem content, don't you, little chick?' Marc chuckled, making the noises again. 'Oh, I forgot to ask, did you finally decide on a name?'

'Ariana.'

'Oh... after, um...'

'The woman who raised me, yes.' I paused and turned to look at him. I could tell that, though tired, my gaze hadn't lost any of its piercing intensity because he quickly looked away.

'Of course, of course. I just thought, well...'

'What, did you expect me to call her Julia?'

'No, no, I just didn't think the Blakes... Well, anyway... It's a lovely name, isn't it, little Ariana? Ari? Ana? Ri-ri? We'll see what suits, shall we?'

I rolled my eyes and let him prattle on until Ariana began to make the snuffling squawking noises and my chest began to throb with the masochistic urge to be tortured once again. I draped the last plate on the draining board, dried my hands and headed back to the sofa.

Once he'd seen me fed and watered, watched as I changed Ariana's nappy, and checked that the boiler, plumbing and all the lightbulbs were working correctly, Marc hovered as I detached Ariana from my breast and put her on my shoulder.

'I could come back next week, if you like?'

I shrugged. 'If you want to.'

'Bells... help is there if you need it, you know. You just have to ask. And in September, when your course starts...'

'There's a nursery just down the road from uni, they take babies from three months. I've had her on the waiting list since December.'

'Oh, right... Well... I was thinking of cutting down to three days a week in the autumn... I could help out one of the other days, if you like?'

I paused, my rational head struggling against the emotional screech. Ariana gave a tiny, wet-sounding belch over my shoulder and I resisted the urge to shudder as I felt the inevitable creep of dampness.

'I'll think about it,' I said, eventually, bringing the tiny girl lower so I could dab my shoulder with a muslin. Ariana nuzzled into my neck and I sank back into the corner of the sofa. I shut my eyes and the lids instantly turned to stone. I felt sleep pressing into me at all angles like the hand of a granite giant holding me down. I didn't even have the energy to feel disturbed by the sensation.

'Isn't that perfect? Can I just take one little—' my eyes beat open and I jolted forward at the image of him standing, camera in hand.

'No! I told you, I don't want any photos!'

'But you look wonderful, darling. Honestly, no one would know you'd only just given birth, you look fresh off the catwalk, as always—'

I sighed as Ariana made one of her squeaky, sleeping rodent noises into my neck. His reassurance hadn't been what I'd been looking for, but it was comforting, all the same, to know that I hadn't quite lost everything about myself. That the Bella of before wasn't perhaps as far away as I'd thought.

'It's not that, it's her.'

'Your mother? I told you, she never looks at my cam...'

'No, not *her.* This her,' the exhaustion swatted me with his maddening confusion. My brain struggled past the simple equation of what day it was and which breast I'd last used, to try and piece together what I'd told him and what I'd only told myself.

'The baby? What about her?'

'I just... I don't want photos of her. Not taken by anyone else. Please. Just... just take a mental picture or whatever.'

'Fine,' he held out his hands, smiling sadly. 'Well, I'll leave you to it. Try and get her into that Moses basket and see if you can get a little shut-eye while she's down...'

I let the rest of his words ramble around my ears, my eyes already half closed by the time the door clicked shut behind him. Shaking my head gently, I eased a hand under Ariana's head, cupping it neatly in my palm as I swung my legs over the sofa. So tiny. So fragile. So easy to break, with just a flex of my arm and a jolt of a twist... I kept my body close to hers as I eased forward, dipping lower and lower... And then she was there, in the Moses basket on its stand next to the sofa, her eyes still closed, her lips puckering but only absently, without the ferocious need that would come again all too soon... I watched her for a few moments and then covered her with the blanket, careful to tuck it under the edges of the mattress like they'd shown me in the hospital. I didn't want to hurt her. I didn't want to hold her. I didn't want anyone in the whole rest of the world to ever come anywhere near her. I sat heavily back onto the sofa, swung my legs up and was asleep in seconds.

16

May, 2019

I wake slowly, the noises of the early morning city chirping through my open window like birdsong in Cumbria. Somewhere far below a bin lorry trundles along an alley, its wheezy engine noise taking me, with a shocking wash of memory, back to the flat in Peckham Rye. Lying in my rented bed, holding my breath as I listened to the bin men's laughter, the smell of rubbish mingling with the fresh summer morning air, willing the tiny baby in the basket next to me not to wake up.

I roll over and blink myself away from the tangling confusion of the past. It's early. Not yet 6am, though the light filters beckoningly through the shutters. I sit up, stretch and cross over to the large wardrobe. My casual clothes hang on the far right side of the rail, disused and untouched by the stylists who visit almost weekly now. I think about the ballet studio, but my heart pulls to be outside, away from the silk and the muted air of this building. I pull on a dark grey, off-the-shoulder jumper and jeans which feel loose around my hips. Stress, probably, I think abstractly. Glancing in the mirror, I'm glad to see it's not showing in my face, at least. The old fear trembles in the back of my mind, the sickness and disease that might be lurking even now, waiting to blemish my skin and my body… The old curse of Project A. I'd mentioned to Lychen months ago that the dust-covered report from October would need to be updated, but he'd dismissed my questions with a firm assurance that the matter was in hand. I'd assumed that would mean more tests, perhaps even a summons of Dr Blake himself or a trip to visit him and whatever machinery remained in his possession, but nothing had transpired. If such human frailty were possible, I'd assume Lychen had forgotten.

I comb my hair and gather it into a messy bun. Ethan is waiting, of course, by the sliding door to the terrace as I ease it open. I glance over at Lychen's apartment, but it remains dark and Delta isn't positioned outside, which means Lychen is still asleep. I haven't seen very much of him since the launch of GCAP over the last few weeks. He's been busy overseeing production and send out, I've been touring the TV and radio studios giving my interviews. Even my weekends have been scheduled over the last few months, taken up by appointments or travel, preparations and research. Still, my last interview wrapped yesterday and now I've got what I haven't had for so long I can't even remember the last time – a day off. It sits like a stone in my throat. I have to get out.

'Your blood sugar is low; would you like me to get you any breakfast?' Ethan murmurs as he holds the doors to the staircase open. Delta doesn't blink as we go past him, but I know he will have recorded the movement.

'A large coffee, please,' I reply as we step lightly down the stairs. 'Oh, and an almond croissant if there are any, please.'

'It is Saturday. There will be plenty,' Ethan replies. I look at him sideways. 'Have you eaten yet today, Ethan?'

'No. I shall replenish when my nutrition levels dip below optimum. I have my daily allocation of energy bars with me.'

We reach the lower level of North, where the kitchens are. He stops, sensing my strange mood, perhaps. The restlessness of a morning devoid of a schedule.

'Is there anything else you require assistance with, Bella?'

'I just... wondered. Do you miss real food? Bacon and eggs? Toast? Fried bread? Sausages? Do you remember the Cumberland sausages they served at the ARC? Some of them were as big as my forearm. I once saw you eat five of them in a row, one after the other. You grinned at me afterwards, like they'd been no larger than my little finger... then you started on the mountain of mashed potato...'

I watch him carefully, as I have watched him so carefully these past seven months. He blinks a few times, his formulaic mind flicking over the questions and sorting out the trivia, pushing it to one side.

'I do not recall my former life. The energy gruel and bars provide all the nutrition I need now. If that is all, I will meet you in the North East courtyard in ten minutes with your breakfast.'

'Thank you, Ethan.' I sigh. He turns away and walks smoothly towards the kitchens.

Well, what did you expect? A sudden flicker, a click of the fingers at the mention of really big sausages? You know they've tightened their confusion traits now. Not like that half-witted robot you encountered at the ARC back in October.

Oh good. You're back.

You never did cope well with enforced leisure time.

I wonder why. My thoughts are so calming and peaceful.

Even when you were a child. If you weren't practising

your ballet you'd be reading. I don't think I ever saw you sit and actually watch the big TV you had to have in your bedroom. The only times I saw you play were when Ralph made you. Weird, really.

Is it? Ariana was the same. Never happy just playing alone, always pestering me for something to do.

Well. Neither of you are entirely normal, are you, despite what you want them all to see.

I sigh, halfway across The Yard now. The festoon lights glisten with morning dew and the trees beam with armfuls of freshly green leaves. For a moment, if I block out the distant sounds of traffic and blur my eyes against the grey of the buildings surrounding me, I could be on the path to the ARC on an early summer's morning.

No, you couldn't. The air is completely different here. It's clogged in fumes, even down between the trees. You've just been away too long. You're forgetting.

Wow, OK. What is your problem today? I'm sure you never disagreed with me this much when you were alive.

Do you really want me to answer that?

No. Not really.

Because you know I did. She did. All the time. Are you forgetting that, too?

No.

I've reached the silent North East building now. I put a hand against the cold stone of one of the pillars of the covered walkway between the entrance and The Yard, wondering abstractly why I'd chosen to walk through the gardens instead of alongside the building. I sigh. Tiredness, low blood sugar. Trying. Pretending. Lying. Every day. Every single day.

You can't keep doing this, Bella. You can't keep living like this.

What do you mean? I've lived like this ever since Ariana was conceived.

Not like this. You were only hiding, keeping a low profile. You got so good at it that it wasn't even an effort after a while. Even being shy, silly little Elodie. You miss her, don't you?

Yes. I miss that life. It was dull but it wasn't this. This constant... work.

Take your hand away now. You look strange.

No one is watching.

Someone is always watching! You can't afford to stop, even for a minute. You have to be the mask. You have to keep it on.

I'm so tired. It's so hard. I miss her so much.

I know.

And it rises, with her acknowledgement and my own, a sudden, tremulous wave of unfiltered pain. I take my hand from the pillar and watch as my fingers shudder under the tide, breathing slowly against the battling, hitching sobs that have come so close to the surface.

'Bella.' Ethan is there, holding a steaming cup in one hand and a paper bag in the other. He stares at me and I wonder if there's a flickering in his large, dark eyes. If it crept into his voice, curving around my name with something other than the usual metal.

'You are hurting,' he says, and the words sound as brusque as they usually do, but still I stare into his gaze, wondering if I imagined that flicker, that chance.

'I'm fine,' I say, and to my relief, my voice is as level as his. 'I just... miss my daughter.'

'Yes,' he agrees. And in blinking, I realise I wasn't wrong, because his eyes are normal now. They weren't, a second ago. There was something beyond me in them. A shadow of a memory. Missing someone? A child? I take the coffee and the bag from him and he opens the door for me.

So maybe that's his thing. He lost a child, perhaps. You knew he and Felix were trying for years.
Yes. Maybe that's the way in.
And what then? When you break him? Will you send him away, back to her? You know Lychen will know it was you.
What more can he do to me?

Even as I ask it, my mind echoes with images of degradation, chains, my prison walls narrowed further. Ariana, taken and placed somewhere out of reach, under his control. *No.* Shaking my head, I pass through another door and take a seat on a wooden bench facing the running track in the centre triangle of the building. Six of my Youth Guard are already here, clad in grey tracksuits, mechanically running. Four more lift weights at the far side. Eve is among them. I focus on her, remembering the pale, pudgy girl she had been when she'd first arrived here. Now her thick muscles strain under honey-brown skin as she folds a dumbbell to her shoulder, her strong legs planted. I tear a shred of croissant and place it in my mouth. It's buttery and soft, but I barely taste it.

Watch them. Use them. They're your way back to her.
And what if she doesn't want me to come back to her? I can't blame her, after what I've done. She doesn't even know the truth.
What would you want, if it was you?
But it's not me! It's Ariana. She's different. She's more... everything than I ever was. God, I hate days off.

I glance at Ethan. He is standing, hands behind his back, next to the bench. Across the courtyard, Eve places the weight down evenly and begins to stretch her arms. Bette and Tom arrive. I sip my coffee and put it down on the ground, sit back and rest my head against stone. I shut my eyes and try to sift past Ana's voice to find my own.

'Delta was approaching the kitchen as I came out,' Ethan says, suddenly. I open my eyes.

'How long have I got?'

'Dr Lychen has an international conference call at seven-thirty. Once he establishes you are not in your quarters, it is my prediction that he will not pursue you here.'

'Good.'

'But he will be displeased that you have not chosen to linger at North this morning.'

'I know.'

'I would advise heading back to North building by eight am.'

'Yes, thank you.'

'You know you don't actually have to say please and thank you, D'accourt. It's not like it has feelings.'

I twist swiftly. Daniel is standing just inside the courtyard, leaning against one of the Doric pillars. He's wearing faded jeans and a patched jumper, his insubstantial hair lifting a little in the breeze as he stares openly at the teenagers stretching and lifting weights.

'Daniel. Some of us were raised with manners.'

'Some of us were barely raised at all.'

'Careful. I was there, remember.'

'How could I forget?' He leers at me. I look away contemptuously, picking up my coffee and taking another sip.

'So what brings you here, Dan? Really?'

'I'm looking to move my entire project here,' he says,

reverting back to his usual bored drawl as he stares back at the exercising youths. 'I've been wanting to do it for years. And with recent developments... Well, let's just say your little brat's visit triggered something of a breakthrough for my programme.'

'Ariana?' I glance back at him, unable to stop the sharpness. 'What did she do?'

'Oh, nothing much,' he chuckles. 'It didn't really have anything to do with her, really. More... you.'

'Me?' I frown. He enjoys my confusion, looking me up and down deliberately slowly.

'Josiah hasn't mentioned anything, I take it?'

He knows he hasn't. He's nettling you, trying to get an emotional rise. Don't let him.

'If Dr Lychen hasn't told me something, I can only assume it's because it isn't essential for me to know at present,' I say mechanically, staring straight ahead.

He smirks again but I can sense the frisson of his frustration as I carry on not asking. Eve and the others jog past us, their faces stoic. He glances from them over to Bette who is spotting Tom as he lifts a bar weight.

'*Dr Lychen,*' Daniel mimics softly, eyes still fixed on Bette. 'Do you call him that when you're in bed together?'

'Don't you?'

'Careful, Bella... Mustn't lose your delightful poise. Anyone would think you're actually human underneath all that... exterior.'

I can feel his gaze on me again like a rash. I sigh, crumpling up the brown paper bag still containing most of the almond croissant, and get to my feet.

'Off so soon? You only just got here. Though I suppose you'll want to be ready for him, if he needs you... Everyone has their uses here, after all.' He's looking at Bette again. I can practically see her golden head with its neat Dutch braid beaming from his eyes. Beside me I feel Ethan clench his fists. Daniel notices it too and gives a high-pitched, almost pre-pubescent sounding laugh.

'You'll need to watch that, too! Can't have your man there expressing all your messy frustrations like that just because you're so good at suppressing them.'

'*You'll* need to watch that I don't let him.'

Ethan takes half a step towards Daniel and the shorter man's eyes flicker up to his, doubt flaring briefly across their dishwater surfaces. I'm reminded suddenly of him as a boy, squaring up to the bigger, more popular Rudy over some silly argument during rehearsals for the presentation.

Don't push him, Bella. Don't forget what happened to Rudy. Daniel's a vengeful creature at heart.

Don't forget what happened to Katie. So am I.

'I'll be seeing you later, I should think,' I say, keeping my voice light as I call Ethan back to my side silently. 'You've seen *my* work, after all.' I gesture at the Youth as they continue to exercise, seemingly impervious to our entire exchange.

'We're over in South,' Daniel remarks as I turn my back on him. 'Labs fifty through sixty-four. I strongly suggest you bring your man here. For protection.'

I spare him a brief glance, a quick roll of my eyes to let him know I don't give a flying fuck what he suggests. Ethan carries straight on. I don't let either one of us show a whisper of how much Daniel's sickly knowing smirk disturbs me.

17

May, 2019

Felix stares at the computer monitors dotted about in front of her. She sips absentmindedly from a cup of tea, her gaze flickering from one screen to another. To someone who doesn't know her, she appears absorbed in her work, in the streams of unintelligible code streaming across the screens, some rapidly, some painstakingly slowly. But Ariana knows that if there was something truly there, Felix would be transfixed, both eyes locked, fingers sweeping expertly over the keyboard, tea left to go cold and make a ring on the old mahogany table. She also knows that Felix is not really concentrating, that her eyes aren't really looking at what's in front of her, that perhaps all they are really seeing is that brief outline of Ethan that she insists she saw on TV the other week. Otherwise, surely, she would have seen the pattern.

'Fee? You OK?' Ariana says it softly, but Felix still jolts with surprise. She turns around and squints up at Ariana. Her eyes look bruised with tiredness and the ashy roots of her bleached hair are clumped and oily.

'Shouldn't you be at school?' Felix croaks, before clearing her throat. She glances at the clock behind Ariana as if to confirm that it is indeed half past ten in the morning and not the evening.

'It's half-term,' Ariana says, not adding the

'remember', but she sees it clunk into Felix's head anyway.

'Ah… damn. I was going to run a workshop for you, wasn't I?' She glances over at Ariana's new laptop, which she'd plugged into one of her own to download a string of new programming tutorials on the morning of Bella's TV interview. It still sits there, more than a fortnight later.

'It's OK,' Ariana says, though she can't help the disappointment stinging in her throat. Ever since the phone conversation with her mother when she'd threatened to return to Graysons again, she has been feeling restless. Felix had noticed the very next day, sitting her down and getting the whole story from her before persuading her that there might be an easier way to free the creatures without having to step foot into the York facility. Ariana had been daydreaming about hacking the building's security system ever since, imagining herself dressed all in black like a ninja, sitting behind a laptop and murmuring into a walkie talkie before pressing a few buttons and – *voilà* – one hundred miles away one hundred locks on one hundred cages all sprang open…

If she could just do that much… If she could just *free* them… Then they could do what they wanted. Spring for Daniel and the others who had experimented upon them and turned them monstrous. Run away and live however they wanted in the world. Or stay, silently, in their cages until someone came along to snap the doors shut again. For her part, she hoped it would be the first one.

'…just been distracted after that bloody interview. I mean, I'm sure you probably have been too, it can't have been easy seeing your mum again after so many months. We didn't really mean for you to see it, at least not before we'd seen it first. Sorry. We should have done a better job of keeping you out of the way.'

'S'OK,' Ariana shrugs, 'It didn't really bother me. I mean, seeing her. Doing that sort of thing. Putting on a show. It's not really like actually seeing her.'

'No. I suppose not,' Felix frowns.

She's wondering whether seeing Ethan as he is now is the same as seeing him. She has to see him again. Felix has never been hard for Ariana to read. But even so, today her desires swarm from her with a particular rawness. Probably because she is so tired. *Or I'm getting stronger.*

'What are these programs doing then, still trying to hack the main system at Graysons?'

'These are,' Felix gestures to the three monitors to the right. 'These, on the left, are trying to get into different parts of Beaumont. I haven't got much to go on, unfortunately. Tess isn't the most helpful source anymore – she has a good foundation but all her information is completely out of date. Looks like they've totally overhauled server security since she worked there...'

'What about this one,' Ariana gestures to the screen second from the left, the one with the pattern.

'That one is tracking the... HR... hang on...' Felix puts her tea down with a heavy clunk and a slosh. She doesn't spare it a glance as she slides her chair over to the screen, her stubby fingers skimming like a ballerina's toes on the keys beneath. Ariana grabs one of the other office chairs which have replaced the old, heavily carved furniture now shunted to the edges of the room.

'It's a pattern, isn't it?' Ariana says, when she can't keep quiet anymore. Felix frowns, typing a few more things, then blinks, seemingly registering what Ariana has said. She turns to her.

'How did you...'

'I saw it. Like, as soon as I came in.'

'You can read this code?'

'Not... exactly. No. I just sort of... looked at it. And tried not to think too much. Like when you're staring at those optical illusion books...' *Or trying to hear someone's thoughts.*

'And...?'

'Here and here, there's something the same, like a repeated sequence. And here. It's the password, isn't it? The way in, I mean?'

'I think so,' Felix turns back to the screen. 'I just need to work on it a bit more, get past a few more layers. But it's amazing you can see it... no one... I mean, maybe Dom, when he's in the right frame of mind... but I don't know anyone who can actually *read* a bit of code like that without any training...'

Felix gazes back at her oddly, not quite in the same weird way Daniel contemplated her after catching her breaking into the lab, but there's a certain similarity in the measurement of it. Like she's trying to weigh her in exact ounces just by looking.

'I'm sure it's just a fluke—'

'Stop that. It's not just the code, is it? You do it with people too, don't you?'

'I dunno...' Ariana squeaks her chair away, twisting towards the door. 'I don't think I'm anything *special*. My mum certainly doesn't.'

'What do you mean by that?'

Ariana shrugs again, starting to wish she hadn't mentioned the code in the first place. Why had she wanted to show off?

'Only, you know, the way she's been my whole life. Like I'm more of an inconvenience than anything she actually *wanted*. Figures, really, as I'm the whole reason she had to give up her cushy life here and go it alone as a single mum when she was still a teenager…'

'Her life here wasn't always so cushy,' Felix mutters, her look dark the way it always is when she talks about Bella now. 'If you ask me, you were the excuse she was looking for to get out…'

'You're not saying she *planned* to have me?'

'No… Maybe not. But maybe. Who knows, with her. But going back to this stuff,' she gestures at the screen with its unmistakable pattern beckoning Ariana in, whispering of secrets and passageways, rabbit holes and wonder…

'If you can see this sort of thing, well that *is* something special… And I've *seen* you do it with people, too. I see the way you get round Ralph when you want something from him and again, when you know to leave him alone…'

'That's just being a person, surely?'

'What is it, mind-reading? Perception of mood?'

'Look, slow down, OK? I'm not some Project C freak of nature… My mum didn't make me in a test tube or take funny potions when she was pregnant. That's what she says, anyway…'

'Yeah, that's what she *says*…'

Ariana sighs and looks from the pattern on the screen down to her hands. The nails are torn and one of the cuticles is bleeding slightly where she's been chewing on it. She begins to pick absently at a shred of skin on her thumb.

'I dunno… I know she lies… but I mean, she was, like, nineteen and at the top of her game… Why would she plan to have a baby? Her and Dad were just having some fling or something, weren't they? I mean, it's gross because they were practically brother and sister, but I always just thought I was a bit of an accident.

'But I can't be like those C-kids. For one thing they all

got weaker when they got older, didn't they? With me… Whatever's going on is getting stronger, it's getting worse. Or better. I dunno… I've always been good at getting people to talk to me, tell me what they need or want… But lately, it's been more like I don't *need* to get them to talk to know it… Like I can sort of just feel it. Like with that pattern. It's all patterns, really. The way people want things, the waves and flows going with what they need in their body and their minds… sometimes they sort of wrap around each other and sometimes they spike about like weird little zigzags. But whatever they are, I can feel them… I think.

'It's like Mum said in the interview last week – with the implant thingies and how it lets the Guard know what you want. Ever since then, I've been thinking it's like everyone around me has been wearing one of those devices and they're all connected to me. Like I'm one of those Guard Assistants, only I'm, like, *me.* But maybe not, you know. Mum said it's just being able to read people and it's come from watching the way she can control people. She said everyone *wants* to be special…'

'And you don't think she was just telling you that… so that you would doubt it?'

'Why would she do that?' Ariana stares at Felix.

'To protect you? I mean, far be it from me to defend your mother, but I do know the sort of people she's wrapped up with…'

'What, Lychen? He doesn't seem all that bad,' Ariana snorts, though part of her remembers those cold, dead eyes and their irresistible pull. She feels a sharp little pain and looks down to see she's shredded her thumb bloody. Felix reaches into her pocket for a packet of tissues and hands them to her.

'He is. You don't know him. I remember back when he worked at the ARC. The way he was around the kids who showed the most promise, the keenest abilities... and your mother. She was only a slip of a thing, your age or so. Once he noticed her... that was it. He was obsessed.'

'Yeah. She seems to have that effect on people. Specially men. You should've been at some of my parents' evenings. Last year, Dr Goldstein actually *salivated* over the desk when she asked him about the year eight geography curriculum. It was obscene.'

'I can imagine,' Felix says, drily. 'My point being, she knows what Lychen's attention feels like. She's known it since she was fourteen years old...' her eyebrows deepen the grooves in her forehead. She falls silent. Ariana watches her, but there's no desire or want bumbling around the surface of her, nothing that she can read.

'So...?' She prompts, when Felix doesn't speak. Felix blinks.

'So, what I'm saying is that if *you* don't realise you have this weird power, then there's far less chance of Lychen ever coming across it... Why else would you be here, when she's there?'

'Oh, I don't know, someone gave her the chance she'd been waiting for for twelve years to ditch me and get on with her shiny, sparkly new life as some top executive in London?'

'Oh, Ariana... Is that really what you think?'

'I don't know what to think. She always told me we were hiding from *bad men* because of something she had that they wanted. A work thing. Then I met Lychen and he said he's only concerned for her wellbeing. Now you're saying he was all weird and obsessed with her. So why would she agree to stay with him? I know you've said it was to save everyone back at Graysons but after all that calmed down couldn't she just, you know, look at him in that special way she has and tell him to sod off?'

'I think it must be more complicated than that. I do know that, whatever else there is going on, Bella does what she does to protect you.'

'How could you possibly know that?'

'Because everything she's done as your mother is, essentially, exactly what I would have done. Would do.'

Ariana sniffs as Felix looks away, awkwardly. Ariana blows her cheeks out and stares at the screen, not seeing the pattern this time as she lets her eyes unfocus. She pictures her mother as a young girl her own age, standing, perhaps in this very room. Tiny, delicate, beautiful, innocent. And Lychen, the shadowy-eyed predator, his body angled around her like a giant, malignant spectre hovering, honing in. Then she blinks and the image is gone. And beside her Felix is frowning and this time her intentions tumble from her as clear as a loudspeaker. She wants to see Bella. She wants to talk to her, and not just about Ethan... Ariana sighs, gets to her feet and wanders out of the room, wondering how on earth a proposed workshop on programming had, like so many things, tumbled into the orbit of her mother.

18

Autumn, 2006

I heard Ariana before I saw her. Motherhood hadn't come naturally, but I was relieved to find that, just as the baby books had promised, I was able to pick out the sound of her voice from a dozen other squalling infants. She was on the swings, barely able to move in the stiff, fleece-lined snowsuit I'd bought for her just the previous week, her body slipping ever more diagonal as my father pushed her backwards and forwards. He caught my eye and smiled as Ariana gave another chirrup of pleasure, pumping her legs up and down. She saw me and her mouth beamed wider, she lifted her arms and seemed to vibrate with excitement.

'Hello, you,' I said, reaching down and pulling her into my arms. She wriggled her solid little body into mine, searched my eyes briefly with her own clear gaze, now devoid of the murky new-born blue, and as green as my own, before laying her head on my shoulder.

'She's had a bottle, but she didn't want any of her banana,' Dad says. I look at him and smile briefly.

'Yeah, she's starting to get a bit fussier about them.'

'I gave her the jar instead, she liked that.'

I nodded. The playground was darkening by the minute. Ariana wriggled and leant down towards the swing, grunting urgently.

'OK, one more turn,' I smiled.

'She knows what she wants, alright,' Dad ginned. 'Just like you when you were little.'

'Is she?'

'Yeah... Well, she's not quite so neat and tidy with her eating,' he showed me the sleeve of his coat where small, starfish handprints patterned a variety of texture. 'This is where most of the banana ended up,' he chuckled.

I smiled briefly before glancing back at the baby in the swing. 'What about other stuff, though? I don't have anything to compare her to. I've not been around babies... There were little ones at the ARC but none under four or so. I don't really know what's normal in terms of behaviour...?'

'And you think I do? With three kids fresh out of that designer baby factory?'

The laugh in his voice turned bitter. I peered at him, wrapping my scarf slightly tighter around my throat as a chill trickled through the air.

'Sorry,' he said, and smiled again as Ariana squawked happily. His hair had thinned further since the previous year, I noticed, and his eyes seemed smaller, more heavily framed with lines. He had learned not to talk about home life too much around me, though I didn't mind hearing the odd piece of news about Maya – on placement in the USA studying neuroscience – and Silas, dithering between sports brand sponsorship deals. Still, I couldn't help but wonder why Marc was looking so rough, particularly since, as promised, he had cut down to three days a week at the firm he managed.

'Is there something worrying you about Ri-ri's behaviour?' he asked, quietly. 'Has nursery said anything?'

'Not exactly... I mean, they said she's a lovely baby and very socialised for her age. They were surprised she didn't have siblings or close cousins... Apparently she has a real knack for playing with other infants, usually the older ones as the babies her age aren't really interested... They said it's the sort of thing they usually see from toddlers at least a year older...'

'Doesn't sound like anything to worry about to me...' Marc beamed down at his granddaughter. 'You were always very popular with the other kiddies too... I remember when you started nursery—'

'The other kids all flocked around and followed my every move, yeah. I know.' My mother's scathing description still stung around my head like a trapped wasp. 'But I *was* a toddler then. Ariana is only seven months old. She can barely sit up on her own, she shouldn't be trying to communicate with other babies...'

'I'm sure it's nothing *sinister*, Bells...'

'Not like me then,' I sniffed, reaching into my pocket for a small, pink hat which I tugged onto Ariana's head. She frowned briefly, reached up and pulled it swiftly off.

'Is that what you're worried about? That she's like you?'

'Well...'

'The Project A programme was never multi-generational. That was in the contract. I remember signing it and thinking that they'd done it to cover themselves, so if something had gone wrong and Si had turned out to be nine-foot tall or something, at least he wouldn't be having giant, nine-foot babies... But seriously, she isn't like you in that way. I mean, she's *gorgeous*, of course... but she's not like you.'

'It wasn't *that* I was worried about.' I frowned, worry making me cross. 'Come on, Ri. Time to go home.' The lights had come on along the footpath leading out of the park. I reached down and Ariana immediately started to cry as I extracted her from the swings. I thrust her into the pram before she could work herself into a rigid-bodied tantrum.

'She seems pretty normal to me,' Dad smiled again, pulling a pair of leather gloves from his pocket. 'Can I give you a lift home? You don't want to be grappling with the pram on the bus at this hour.'

'You have your car today?'

'What can I say... I'm a creature of luxury. Besides, I found some on-street parking *just* outside the congestion charge zone... Come on, it's not far.'

I attempted the hat again but was met with a withering death-stare.

'Fine,' I said to them both, tucking a blanket around Ariana's snowsuit. She peered at me imperiously, tears still glistening on her cheeks. I used the blanket to wipe them away and reached into the bag for a rice cake for her to chew on. Dad held the playground gate open for me and I pushed the pram through it and matched his pace on the tree-lined path. Leaves crunched underfoot and the streetlights beamed through half-naked tree limbs. I let my eyes slide in and out of focus until the lights blobbed into indistinct, glowing orbs. The words I needed to say tumbled against my lips, my old self – my proud, before self – battling with the newer, strengthening instinct to protect the small, dribbling human in the pram before me. I sighed and let them go.

'When I was younger... I don't remember a lot of things. But I do remember being able to get what I needed. Whether it was putting on a pretty smile and a cute lisp, or turning cold and vindictive. There's always been this instinct, this voice... that told me what to do... What I needed from people and how to get it... And... I don't know... I know I'm a *young mum* as the health visitors like to tell me, and that I'm inexperienced... but I'm still me. I'm still the same person who smiled and twirled and flirted and... well, did whatever else I needed to do to get wherever I needed to be... I still do. And sometimes I think I recognise... bits... of it. In her. Even though she's just a baby...'

The silence was broken only by the gentle sucking noises coming from the pram. I glanced down and saw remnants of rice cake strewn down the front of the blanket and over Ariana's chubby little fingers, but it wasn't worth taking it from her now. I glanced sideways. Dad was staring at the path in front of us, but there was a tic chewing at the side of his temple. I wondered if he was about to bring up the things we'd been dancing around since the night Ariana had been born. The things I'd said. He passed a hand over his eyes and cleared his throat.

'When you did these things as a child, when you used your powers of persuasion to get things, do you remember *why*?'

I frowned. 'Well... I suppose it was to get what I wanted, like most kids.'

'That's not what you said just now. You used the word *needed.* Which seems to be a very different thing. If Ariana has inherited this particular trait from you, the ability to get what she needs, is that such a bad thing?'

'Ask Katie Jennings.'

'No, thank you. You know she runs her parents' toy shop in town now? They bought her a flat as well. She's never known a day's hard graft in her life, that one...'

'People could say the same about me. And whatever she's like, she didn't deserve what I did to her. I still remember the things I said to her, you know. To make her put her hand in that open flame… What did I *need* then?' I shuddered as the smell of burning flesh, always there, always waiting for those moments when I questioned myself, singed delicately around my throat.

'I don't know, Bella, but you were only a little girl yourself… Maybe she *didn't* deserve it, maybe you were just acting on a wild impulse. Kids do all sorts of stupid things. *You* certainly didn't deserve what happened afterwards… I mean, we didn't even really *know* the Blakes. They could have been anyone.'

'Well. This isn't about me. It's not about then. You're helping me now, aren't you?'

'Of course I am, I'm your father! And after what I did, it's the least I can do.'

'Is it? Or is it just because I asked? How can you be sure?'

We reached his dark blue Lexus and he unlocked it with a chirrup that startled Ariana from the beginnings of sleep.

'I haven't got a car seat,' I said, suddenly. 'I have one at home, for taxis, but I didn't think…'

'It's OK, I've got one in the boot. I bought it just in case. Hid it under my gym kit. That's where Ju— well, let's just say that's my cover story.'

He busied himself digging the pristine car seat out of the boot and securing it in the back seat of the car. It was the closest we had ever come to discussing what had happened when my mother had left me at The Manor when I was nine. The subject bumbled between us like a clumsy child as I unbuckled Ariana from the pushchair and Dad loaded the nappy bag and my textbooks into the boot of the car.

'She knew they weren't just anyone,' I said, quietly, as I let him take Ariana from me and strap her into the car seat.

'Hmm?'

'The Blakes. Julia knew they weren't just anyone. She'd been talking to him for a while about me. And her. Ana told me, on my first morning there. She said she'd known for some time that I would be coming back to them. That it was always my home, because I'd been born there and she'd been the one who made me and all sorts of other weird stuff...' I breathed slowly, deeply, so that the memory of Ana's sinewy arm, crushing around my skinny, nine-year-old chest didn't overcome me. Dad straightened up, frowning.

'Eh?'

'I'm just saying... you shouldn't feel so guilty. There were things at play that went beyond your control... The thing with Katie's hand, it might have been the final straw, but Julia had been wanting to get rid of me long before then. My bag had been packed for weeks. Maybe months. And it's not like she made any effort to check back and see whether or not I was *fixed* or whatever... I realised a long time ago that that whole line must've just been an excuse. That there must have been something else going on, some deal or something... Why else would Blake not have actually tested my blood when he had the chance?'

'Bella, we... *I* tried—'

'I don't care. Not really. And I'm not saying that to be hurtful. I know what Ana was like. She was fierce, and not just in the way she loved us... I remember when I first met the other scientists at the ARC and Blake told them her cancer was getting better. They all acted relieved but I could tell they weren't really... they were unnerved. I didn't understand it then but I did afterwards, when time went on. She was... she pushed boundaries. Whether that was with her work at the ARC or the way she loved her family... That's just what she was like.'

I looked up and, instead of the confusion I'd been expecting, caught instead a knowing nod, a failure to entirely meet my eye.

'What?'

'Nothing... I just... I used to phone up sometimes. I suspect you didn't know that, did you? No. Well, it was almost always Ana who spoke to me. I'd go into the conversation ready to tell her that enough was enough and I was coming for you right then... and somehow once she'd begun speaking... I don't know how she did it but she had this persuasive way about her. Telling me all the extraordinary things you were learning, the progress you were making, how happy you were... She made me feel as if there could be no other place for you but there. That I was the selfish one for wanting to take you back... I'd come off the phone convinced that we'd done the right thing... until the next time I came across an old photo or saw something that reminded me of you. I never agreed to let them formally adopt you, despite the repeated requests... Still, I should have tried harder to get you back.'

'It doesn't matter now.'

'No, I suppose not. But I really don't think you should worry so about Ariana. I think kids... well, it might sound strange, given the whole Project A thing, but actually, I do think kids are who you make them, not how they're made... does that make sense?'

'I'm not sure.'

'I'm saying, the way you are is because of how you were brought up as much as what was put into you when you were a tiny bundle of cells. That's on me, your mother and them, your other parents... And the way Ariana will turn out is as much to do with how you raise her as it is whatever passed down from you and her father, whoever he might be, *whatever* he might be. I, for one, am not worried in the slightest.'

I watched him collapse the buggy in one swift movement and lift it into the car boot. I could hear Ariana beginning to fuss as he slammed the door.

'OK,' I said, as I opened the passenger door and climbed in.

He doesn't get it. He doesn't get you. He never will, you'll always be his little princess. You'll always outgrow him before he outgrows you.

Perhaps. Or he's lying about something.

About Ariana?

About me.

19

May, 2019

If Lychen is displeased that I did not wait for him this morning, he does not show it when I find him in his office a little after Ethan has informed me of the end of his conference call.

'Good morning, my love,' he says, looking up from his computer. He is dressed in a pressed shirt and neat suit trousers, his designer shoes unblemished. I still wear my casual clothes, keeping my hair in its messy bun with the tendrils spilling over my bare shoulders, because I know he likes it best when it looks like it's trying to escape.

'Good morning, Josiah.' I cross the room and he reaches for me, drawing me onto the desk in front of him. His hand finds my hair and he winds his fingers in. Not so tight that it hurts, but snagging enough to tell me that it will if I try to move away.

'I'd hoped you would come to see me before my call with Paris this morning,' he murmurs, inches from my face. I swallow. My body barely registers what he's doing to me now. It's like I've manifested a cloak which cannot be felt, and allows me not to feel.

'I'm sorry. You've been working so hard, I didn't want to wake you,' I say, peering at him through my lashes. 'I thought I'd take a little walk, oversee my Youth Guard. And then I bumped into Daniel.'

'Ah, yes,' Lychen unwinds his fingers from my hair and takes my chin between his thumb and forefinger. 'I wondered when your paths might cross. He has been here a few days now. Are you angry?'

'No,' I say, truthfully. He is so close he catches my brief glimmer of surprise.

'What?'

'Nothing… just, you don't usually… question… that sort of thing… My emotional responses, I mean.' It was like before, the other morning, when I'd seen that glimmer of softness. Again, things stir behind his eyes that go beyond the usual blankness of control, wolfish lust, empty callousness.

'Perhaps you are changing me,' he murmurs, and this time the amber glow is unmistakable. He leans forward, his hand finding my throat once again. I ready my cloak, but the panic has crept under its hem. I swallow and fight the sudden rush of nausea.

'Josiah… Please. Can we… Can we go upstairs? I… It's the desk…'

He pulls back and stares at me. Again, there's more in his eyes, but this time I see exactly what it is. It's a challenge. Why. I did nothing wrong. I was just taking what you had offered me, in so many words, in so many actions. And you let me. And you will let me again, whenever and wherever I want. Wasn't that your price? Whatever I want.

'Can we go somewhere else?' I put everything into it. It shouldn't matter, where it happens. It happens all the time, after all. My cloak simmers over the fluttering now, shushing it back down, willing my body into cold, empty acceptance. But something makes me ask all the same. He blinks once, twice. Then he shrugs, slides backwards and pulls me by the hand over to the door. The cloak is firmly in place now, but still I feel the wonder of the tiny inconsequential victory.

It is late afternoon by the time we make our way across The Yard to the South building. Delta and Ethan follow behind us. Workers look up, see us and scurry. The braver souls attempt to accost one or both of us as we go, but we don't stop for them. My head swirls with too much darkness, too little sleep. I remember the thought I'd had that morning about the Project A curse and ponder when would be best to pose the question to Lychen without sounding like I'm just looking for an excuse to reconnect with the Blakes.

And when did it become so important, to make sure he thinks you want to be here? To seek him out and call him Josiah and let him hold you by the throat?

I don't know. But life is better for me when he gets what he wants. I have more opportunities. I would never have hung onto the Youth Guard project for so long otherwise.

What does that say about you?

That I have always known how to guard myself. How to make myself a robot. How to disappear within myself until what others do doesn't hurt me. You taught me that; you and my other mother. In any case, I'm more concerned with what it says about him. Maybe he's right, maybe I am influencing him. Maybe he is becoming more human, because of me.

The love of a good woman, eh? Or the tolerance of a bad one.

As we reach the South building, the scientists fall away, as if they know what we're about to go and see. There is an unusual silence about the place and, when I look at Lychen curiously, he glances behind us, at the two Guard men, before he takes my hand in his. I wonder for a moment if he is about to warn me that what we will see is going to be unpleasant. Whether he will give me the chance to change my mind, turn back, not sully my pretty little head with these smelly, monstrous beings. Instead he gives a strange tight spasm of a grimace and nods at Delta to come forward and open the door.

The building, usually bustling with white-coat-clad men and women as well as several Guard Assistants, is quiet. We take the stainless-steel lift up from the deserted lobby to the fifth floor in a silence which throbs heavily against my ears. Even Ethan seems a little twitchy around the edges and I know it's my tension coursing through him. The doors slide open and my heart starts hammering, my head swims cold and I feel caught somewhere between fainting and being hyper-awake. It's a little like the sensation of stepping into the spotlight on stage, except the exhilaration has been replaced by dread. Ethan's hand meets my shoulder as I step out of the lift and, when I meet his gaze wordlessly, I feel a little steadier. Lychen, a few steps ahead of us, notices nothing. The corridor is icily quiet.

'Ah,' Daniel bursts out of a door halfway down. 'The King and Queen of hearts, at last! Bella, I expected you hours ago after our little *tête-à-tête* this morning, but I suppose you've probably been *busy*.' He grins wildly. He's full of energy, practically bobbing up and down on the balls of his feet. Though I feel calmer, the sight of his exuberance only makes the pit of foreboding in my stomach worse.

'Boundaries, Daniel,' Lychen murmurs. Daniel pulls himself up short.

'Of course, sorry Dr Lychen,' he gestures to the door through which he came and winks disgustingly at me behind Lychen's back. I give him my most withering glare. He sidesteps quickly into the room.

'Now, of course what we have here is only a small selection of the creatures we are currently hosting at Futura,' he says, letting the door swing behind him so that Ethan has to catch it for me. The smell hits me first and I cover my nose with my sleeve as, a few paces in front of me, Lychen does the same. The laboratory is roughly the same size as my own classroom-style workplace, but the similarities end there. The floors are laminate and the walls are utterly bare. The lights are dim, though bright enough to glint off the large chicken wire cage in front of us. Inside I can just make out a pale pink shape half buried under sawdust and a rough-looking blanket. Next to the cage is a ten-by-ten feet square of mud, straw and, I can only assume judging by the smell, faeces.

'Meet PY06. Porcine, though you probably can't tell from here... He's usually a bit more sociable than this, I do apologise,' Daniel sounds anything but apologetic as he crosses around the cage to the corner nearest the huddled shape. 'I would give him a prod but I've been told that undue physical pain causes a stress response which is *detrimental to our research*,' Daniel scowls over at a small collection of white-coated people huddled around a desk near the open window. One of them, a young woman, looks up and returns the filthy look before catching my eye and looking away again, disdain replaced by fear.

'What progress have you made here?' Lychen asks, through his sleeve.

'Ah yes, sorry about the smell. I've rather gotten used to it, but I know it can be unpleasant. He *is* part pig, after all. But anyway, yes, this one has shown some progression in behaviour over recent weeks. Mainly concerning feeding

The Child Left in the Dark

habits – he has begun to use his hands.'

Daniel stares at Lychen like a small boy looking for a pat on the head. Lychen raises an eyebrow.

'Is that all?'

'Well... his grunting is still fairly sporadic... but he was entirely trough-fed until a month ago...' Daniel has lost a little of his eagerness now. I remove my hand enough for him to see my smirk and he glowers at me in return. I move closer to the open window. It must have been the smell that caused the strange reaction in the lift, I think, as I breathe heavy gulps of sweet, early summer breeze. I'm feeling better by the minute.

'...more progress with the rodents, if you want to come through to the next lab,' Daniel is saying, ushering Lychen through a door on the far left of the room. I glance at the workers just in time to see a few exchanging surreptitious smiles.

'Bella?' Lychen is waiting for me at the open door, 'The air is not so pungent in here, I promise.'

I step away from the window and glance briefly at the pig thing in its huddle. A pair of eyes flash at me from the depths of the darkness. They do look miserable, though there is no sudden projection of pain or anguish. No sweeping sensation of pity. I must lack Ariana's empathy, I think to myself, as I walk quickly away from the heinous smell. Or perhaps she encountered a more fragrant pig-boy. I enter the next door hurriedly. This lab is smaller than the last and holds more cages, all of them roughly the size of a large dog crate. This time we get a much better view of the specimen, a rodent roughly the size of a chihuahua with a human nose, human hands and feet, though its glittering quick eyes remain wild and its body has most of the grey downy hair of a rat. I watch it glance at us disinterestedly before turning and using its human hands to dig through a food tray of nuts, seeds, and what look like chocolate buttons.

I let Daniel's monotonous voice wash meaninglessly over me as he explains about success with mazes and something about a Rubik's cube. I wander past another cage with a similar looking rodent – this one bearing a long tail and human ears – and come to a halt outside another door. This one is, again, set into the wall opposite the one through which we've come. Without warning, the cold wash swipes over my head again and I feel suddenly breathless. Ethan is beside me in an instant.

'Are you alright?' he says. I look up. His words are as mechanical as ever, but, though it's dark, there seems to be something similar to what I saw this morning there in his eyes.

'I'm fine. I've probably just had too much coffee, not enough food.'

'Your blood sugar levels are not abnormal.'

'Well, then. I don't know. Maybe I'm coming down with something.'

'It is not a physical ailment. It is a reaction. An intuition...' he looks from me to the door in front of us. 'You should not enter.'

'Why? What's in there?'

'You should not enter.'

'Oh, now... But this is the *best* one,' Daniel bounces in front of me, his face more alive than I've ever seen it.

'Bella?' Lychen is next to me. His question isn't for concern, he is merely waiting for me to walk forward. I shrug and Daniel opens the door.

It's an aviary. The cage walls reach all the way to the high ceilings and I realise that this room is the entire reason

The Child Left in the Dark

Daniel has been given this particular floor. Something is making a huge racket on the far side of the room; I barely have time to blink and feel the clutter of dread once again before there's a swoop and a rush of wings and she's there. I stand and stare in horror as Lychen remarks, almost excitedly, about the flying and Daniel says, *Yes, this is the real success story here,* and something about finding her wings just a few short days ago... I don't really hear it though. Their words just bounce off me and it's all I can do to stand upright. She is perched at my eye level, talons clawed around the mesh wire of her cage wall, which sways under the impact of her. Her body is covered in thick, coarse feathers which lighten as they climb to her head. Her nose is longer, hooked, but her eyes are the same bright, beading pearls of deep blue staring at me from a mop of strawberry-blonde hair, now grown matted and tangled with feathers. I haven't seen her for almost fourteen years. I open my mouth, her name already on my lips, already gasping from my heart, but she gets there first. She gives a scream of utter, ear-wrenching hatred. Lychen steps back but Daniel approaches the cage.

'Now, now, is this any way to greet our guests?'

The bird-girl leaps away from the cage wall, shrieking at him with a mixture of wild fear and spitting vitriol. She turns back to me.

'Ah, but of course... you've already met, haven't you?'

He turns to me and, for a moment, I think she has leapt straight through the cage. I think she must be shrieking again, tearing through the metal to rip and wrench that awful look from his face, for where else could that wild rage possibly come from? Then I feel Ethan's hands around my arms, turning me, lifting me, and I realise that it's me. I'm shrieking; I'm raging; I'm tearing my way through the air between us to try and rip him apart with talons I don't possess...

'Bellaaa!'

She says my name. We all stop. We all turn. She stares for a moment longer, at me. And it's full of everything – all the trust, the love, the loyalty she had for me, when I was everything she had and all she wanted to be – all of it, torn away when I'd disappeared. When I'd given her up for my own child, the child she could never have been. Then something wild shutters over her face and she beats her great wings and flies, heavily, far more clumsily than the light-boned girl I knew, back to the far corner of the cage, where a perch has been wired in.

'Speech!' Lychen turns to Daniel in triumph. Daniel grins back at him.

'I *knew* it. It was the Blake girl's resemblance to Bella that triggered the human responses we've been tracking for the last few weeks. Then, as soon as we got here, flight. Now speech! It's the familiarity—'

I don't listen to any more. I turn and make for the door across the room, the one leading out into the corridor. I think it is Ethan beside me and I don't slow my stride as he falls into step as we make for the lifts, then a hand catches my arm and it's icy.

'Bella, I'm sorry.'

'No, you're not,' I mutter. Because he isn't. He's just guessing at it. My distress is waving a flag in his face and this is the only thing he can think of to try and stop it, because it's messy and displeasing to him.

'I didn't realise you still felt so strongly about the Subject—'

'She has a name! It's Nova Messenger. She was four years old when I met her. I saw her every day – I gave her the best crayons to colour with, I plaited her hair… I taught her how to do a bloody pirouette! How can you think I wouldn't be upset to see her like this?'

I jab my finger onto the lift call button. Ethan is here now, standing just behind Lychen. He frowns slightly and shakes his head. I know he's warning me. My head is shrieking with the same high-pitched wail I emitted minutes earlier, warning me not to push too far, not to lose control, but my hands are shaking and my chest pounds with the echo of my furious heart.

'Bella, I—'

'You should have told me the minute her name cropped up. The moment you knew what he'd done to her. You should have told me.'

He blinks and I see the truth in the sudden shift of his gaze. My arms are wrapped around myself, I can feel my whole body vibrating with rage and sorrow and shock beneath them.

'What? What now? Tell me!'

'Daniel came to me. Years ago, when he was establishing his project. He said he wanted to experiment on one of the former C-Subjects. She'd shown signs of the madness which overcame so many of them, he said there was nothing to lose and everything to gain. I authorised it.'

The lift doors open. Ethan steps into them and stands so they won't close. He holds a hand out to me. I stare at Lychen, some of the feeling trickling slowly back into my brain. My body is still trembling and I feel a swarming wash of utter exhaustion. It's so heavy I sway a little under it.

'You are a monster. You are worse than him. He was born and raised to be monstrous… You… You're just… *unfathomable*.' My voice is a hiss. I've never spoken to him like this before. No one does. I see it register in his shark eyes, my words settling heavily before being parcelled up and placed to one side. He reaches for me but I spring away, towards Ethan. I can sense him tensing next to me, and I know he would spring to my defence in a heartbeat, even if it cost him the rest of his own.

'You are upset,' Lychen says, his voice carefully blank. 'I will give you some time.'

Lychen steps back at the same time Ethan steps into the lift and presses the button for the ground floor. Lychen's empty eyes never leave my face as the doors close between us. There is a warning there, shining clearly. It says: *I will not tolerate this again.* But there is a warning in my eyes, also. I can feel it beam back at me as the steel doors slide closed, ricocheting off and hitting me like a punch square between the eyes. I breathe slowly, thinking only about staying upright. Then I look up. Ethan's face has settled back into its usual blankness.

'Ethan. I'm going to need a large glass of wine. Make it red. And make it a bottle.'

'Yes,' he agrees and, again, there's something there. A spark of amusement or warmth. Of the old Ethan. Only for a second, then the blandness resumes once again as the lift doors spring open on the ground floor.

'Welcome back, friend,' I murmur, as we step out into the fading sunlight.

20

Spring, 2010

I kept a steady eye on the large clock above the fire exit. Time seemed to be dolloping by at a strange rate – the hours between getting the keys to the community hall and setting up the party had swept by in a flicker, but once the kids and parents had started to arrive, it had slowed completely. Each five-minute segment of greeting, fetching teas and coffees, directing children towards the bouncy castle and entertainer at the other end of the hall seemed to take an age. Finally, though, it was four pm and children were being ushered into small puffy coats, baby siblings were dragged from under the party table and Ariana had been cajoled into giving out party bags at the door.

'Want me to start taking down some of the balloons, El?' Josie, mum of three including Ariana's current best friend Sylvie, asked in a solicitous sort of way. I beamed at her, 'Would you mind? That would be a massive help, thank you so much.'

'Of course!' Josie practically skipped off to begin untying the same balloon strings she herself had provided and hung just a few hours earlier, calling to her two older sons to help. They ignored her. Darren, dad of twins Rupert and either Eddie or Freddie, I could never remember which, caught my eye and mimed clearing the party table. I gave him the same grateful, so-good-of-you-thank-you-so-much response and he set to. Five minutes later all the children save those belonging to the helpers – now five of them – had gone, Ariana and Sylvie were playing hide and seek around some of the dismantled trestle tables and Dad sloped up, pink frosted cupcake in hand, to where I was sorting through the remains of the food in the small kitchen.

'Quite the band of assistants you've got here, *El*,' he remarked, winking. I smiled tightly and turned to place the sticky, stacked party cups in the bin.

'What can I say, I'm a single mum... I'm not going to pass up offers to help.'

'Well, quite,' he mumbles through a mouthful of cake.

'Elodie, do you want to keep any of these balloons?' Josie appeared at the hatch, bunches of pink and white balloons clutched in her fists.

'Let the kids have one each and then get rid of the rest,' I said, smilingly, 'they won't fit in my flat.'

Josie smiled and wandered off, dispensing balloons as she went.

'It's nice you've made so many good friends with the nursery parents...'

'I wouldn't say they're exactly *friends*...'

'I don't know... we hosted a fair few parties for you and the others when you were little. We never got so much as an offer of a balloon tie. And there you've got one sweeping, one loading chairs away...'

'Yes, well. I'm me, aren't I.'

'Certainly looks like you,' he smiled, though I couldn't help a small flurry of anxiety at his words.

'Yes,' I touched my hair, pinned in its neat chignon. 'I really should cut my hair again, shouldn't I?'

'Or you can face the fact that no one has come looking

for you in over four years now… No more letters, no knock on the door, not so much as a threatening phone call… Haven't seen hide nor hair of those goons in the black Merc since long before Ariana came along. Maybe, just maybe, you could lose those contact lenses as well?'

'Dad. Have you heard of Facebook?' I hissed, as I gathered a collection of dirty coffee cups and emptied the dregs into the sink, glancing around to make sure no one else was listening.

'Course I have…'

'No one might be looking for me around here, but all it takes is one photo to end up there, one glimpse of my eyes… Have you ever seen anyone with eyes like mine?'

'No… Apart from Ri-ri of course.'

'Yes,' I sighed, sadly, 'I wish she didn't.'

He made a small snorting sound as the two of us looked up and gazed through the small hatch to watch Ariana, lying on the floor in her white party dress, attempting to blow her pink balloon across the floor. One of the twins kicked it up into the air, narrowly missing her face with his shoe, but instead of squealing she laughed delightedly and made a grab for him. I glanced at Dad and watched his gaze slip to Darren as he strode quickly towards the tangle of kids on the floor.

'So, any of these dads… you know… single?'

'I've no idea.'

'So you haven't… there isn't anyone… special?'

I sigh and roll my eyes, turning from the sink to wrap a paper plate of sandwiches in clingfilm.

'I know, I know… None of my business.'

'Exactly.'

'I just, you know… You're only twenty-three. I'd be more than happy to babysit if you ever wanted to go out with your friends. I could stay the night or even for a few days, if you'd like – if you ever wanted to visit your friend's cottage in Cornwall, you know, that you mentioned the other day? Everyone deserves a break, a social life...'

'Dad. Thanks, but let's just... not go there, OK?'

'As long as you're happy...'

'I am,' I smiled at him. A real smile this time, because it was true. I *was* happy. Ariana was a sweet, talkative, and popular child bursting with confidence. Sure, she sometimes said or did things that gave me pause. Like the other week when the nursery teacher had told me, in a dazed, bemused way, that Ariana had made her a special card because she'd thought she looked sad. ('I'd just lost my grandma that weekend, but I didn't tell any of the children. What a remarkably perceptive little girl she is!'). Or the time I'd woken up with the buzz of a headache and Ariana had turned the TV down and dimmed the lights in the living room without my saying a word. These were just oddities, though; flecks of pepper in what was otherwise a smooth, sweet existence. Ariana loved nursery, I loved my work as a first year PhD student. There had been flirtations along the way, the odd, brief fling with other students, a professor or two (never in my own field though, never anything that could be used to discredit how hard I worked), but no one I would bring home. If ever I did take up the invitation I had carefully solicited from one of the university professors to use her remote cottage in Cornwall, it would be alone. As a test run, should we ever need the escape option.

There were moments of emptiness in my new life, too. I didn't really crave other company when at home with Ariana – the flat was cramped enough as it was – but sometimes, when she was sleeping and I hadn't any work to spread out over the coffee table as the TV buzzed in the background, I missed small things. The smell of Ramona's cooking reminding me that I didn't have to worry about that aspect of my life, that however taxing the other things in my brain, I didn't have to think about what to make for dinner. The gentle crackling of a fire as Ralph and I debated some silly detail about Project C over a bottle of wine as Dr Blake read obliviously in his large armchair in the corner. Those brief, heady nights when we would sneak to his car afterwards, dipping, tasting, tracing a new exploration of one another's bodies. And sometimes, very occasionally, I'd take a book from a shelf or pounce on the one free computer in the library and remember my large, plush office at the ARC, the soft carpet, the wink of crystal-filtered light, the polished wood of my desk... but then the desk would cool and charge against my face and I'd stop before the memory changed. I didn't miss the uncertainty. The boil of stress in the pit of my stomach, the constant burn of gazes at my back, the tremble of other people's desire a relentless threat at my throat... I didn't miss that, even in the quietest, most boring moments of parenthood. Even in the darkest, loneliest hours of the night. That's what I told myself, anyway.

'I'm heading off then, El, if there's nothing else you need me to do?'

'Thank you so much, Darren, I really appreciate it.'

'No problem at all...'

'See you on Monday, Elodie!'

One by one, they all left in a flurry of grateful helpfulness. I waved, smiled, hugged the huggers and prettily blushed at the flirters. Dad watched it all, a wry smile playing about his mouth.

'Mummy, are we going home now?' Ariana asked, her

small, sticky hand finding mine as she stared up at me. Her fringe mopped heavily into her large, darkly lashed eyes. Her mouth still bore traces of pink icing. I smiled and glanced over the top of her head at the small playground just outside the hall window.

'Well… It doesn't look too busy out there. Maybe we could have a quick go on the swings before we go home, if Grandpa's got time?'

'I've got plenty. But I also have one condition… lose the contacts and the glasses. Come on, just this once. Just for me.'

'Dad—'

'Your friends have gone home, you said yourself the playground isn't busy… Please, Bells? I just want to see my girl. My girl with the green eyes.'

I sigh and roll the eyes in question.

'Fine. But you're taking out the rubbish while I'm in the bathroom.'

'Deal,' Dad beamed, gathering bin bags to take out to the large skip bin round the back of the hall. Grabbing my handbag, I left Ariana prattling excitedly at him and made my way to the small cubicles at the back of the hall. Three minutes later I emerged, hair loose and eyes unleashed. Dad grinned and opened his mouth, but stopped when I held up a finger.

'One more word of sentimental girl with the green eyes nonsense and I'm putting the brown back in.'

He held his hands up and chuckled as we made our way outside, Ariana catching a hand from each of us in cheerful oblivion.

'Where does she think you are today?' I asked Dad, as I helped Ariana onto one of the swings in the small playground. He looked at me in surprise, but didn't remark at the rarity of my mentioning my mother.

'Golf. I couldn't keep up the gym pretence any longer, not with this growing ever wider,' he slapped his stomach, which did seem to be overhanging his trousers slightly more than it had. 'Plus she mentioned to Silas that I'd become a gym nut and he offered to come with me. Can you imagine?'

I chuckled.

'Who's Silas?' Ariana piped up, unexpectedly.

'No one, little darling,' I answered quickly, 'Just one of Grandpa's friends.'

'Oh. Mama, you wana swing wi' me?'

'Oh I don't know... I don't know if we'll both fit now you're a great big four-year-old...'

'Yes we do! C'mon, *please?*'

I lifted her off, slid gracefully backwards onto the swing and tucked her onto my lap. Her legs intertwined with mine and her curly hair tickled my nose as I held her with one arm and wrapped the other around the chain. It must have been then. That tiny speck of a moment when I pulled her back into me, laughing into the side of her face as she giggled, her feet flying upwards. I wasn't looking forward so I didn't see him produce the camera, there was no flash because it was a bright, sunny day, there was no audible click... When I next looked up, Dad's hands were in his pockets and his gaze had been caught by the ice cream van which had appeared, music blaring, across the green.

'Hey, Ri-ri, how about an ice cream?'

'Yeah!'

'She's just had a whole party tea and cake!'

'Oh go on, it's her birthday...'

'Please, Mummy? *Pleeeeease?* It *is* my birthday and I *am* four...'

'Oh, alright then...' I rolled my eyes. Ariana gave another high-pitched emittance of joy as she leapt from my lap and took Dad's outstretched hand. I watched the two of them make their way to the small café at the edge of the park as I slowly raised myself up from the swing, lightened by the lift of my daughter's weight, the early hints of summer in the air, the beam of everything going just right, just now.

Summer, 2010

It was early on a Saturday morning and I was making use of Ariana's newfound ability to sleep past seven-thirty to sort through the last few things in the kitchen cupboards. An old breast pump and several dusty bottles went straight into the bin. A hand-painted mug given to me by Nova over ten years ago went into the open box by my feet alongside my good wine glasses and a faded, burgundy envelope. The post thumped onto the doormat. I hopped down from the chair I'd been balancing on, padded out of the living room and down the hall to retrieve it. There were several letters addressed to the flat's new tenant, due to arrive next Monday. I placed them carefully on top of the radiator lining the hallway and bent to retrieve a jiffy bag addressed to Elodie.

I slit it open, a strange sense of dread shivering along the surface of my skin. Out slid a photo of Ariana and me. I was laughing into her cheek as she beamed up at the camera, our eyes twin shades of delighted, sparkling jade. It took me a minute before I could place it, the bow on her head, my pale blue spring jacket, no contacts or glasses masking my eyes... Then I realised, with the strange, heady blow of both sadness and vindication. *This is why*, I thought, as I tucked the frame back into the jiffy bag and strode back down the hallway and into the living room. I held the bin open, the package hovering over the discarded baby bottles.

Go on, get rid of it. It's not safe.

It's just one print. He doesn't know where we're going. What harm in keeping it now?

I pulled my hand back and placed the brown, padded bag in the open box instead. I thought about the stark soulless new flat waiting for us in the stark, soulless town of Flintworth. The photo could go on my bedside table there. I would look at it every night and be reminded that no one, not even a parent, could ever really be trusted.

21

May, 2019

Felix sits in the large bedroom she used to share with Ethan. It's been their room for more than ten years now, but apart from the large crocheted quilt they inherited from his mother covering the king-size bed, it doesn't look all that different to how it did when they arrived. A large, neatly carved chest of drawers punctures one side of the room alongside a built-in wardrobe. Opposite the bed the windows are wide and interspersed with stained glass patterns. They overlook the large oak-lined driveway. Felix stares unseeingly at the bright green leaves as they sway slightly in the breeze. In one hand is her phone. The other hand clenches unconsciously around the soft yarn of the blanket. She looks down when she realises her little finger has gone through one of the holes in the pattern. It seems to resolve something in her mind as she drops the quilt, brings her phone onto her lap and searches for a number. She is about to press the green call button when the knock comes on her door.

'Fee?'

'Ralph.'

'Can I come in?' he asks, as he's already halfway into the room. She shrugs and nods. He looks pale, his dark brown eyes shining brighter than normal, as if he's had too much coffee. His hair is smooth, though, which means he hasn't been running his hands through it for once. He looks at her, chews his lip awkwardly, then puts his hands in his pockets and crosses over to the window.

'I always preferred the outlook on this side of the house,' he remarks. 'It's just wild enough, you know? The drive, the big trees, a hint of mountain in the distance... No moorland or wildlife. No ARC.'

'Did you come here to discuss the view, Ralph?'

'No,' he turns back and smiles tightly. 'Ari said you'd managed to decipher some of the coding... find out some of the movements at Beaumont...?'

'Did she now.'

'Fee, are you OK? You look... weird.'

'I don't know, Ralph.' She sighs and looks at her phone, at the name which seems to groan at her from the screen. 'Sometimes I wonder... if it would be easier just to take a job somewhere on the other side of the country, some little data analyst thing which pays well and includes a bunch of pension benefits. Live in a house by the sea in Scarsby or Whittleworth, get a dog. Leave all this... mess... behind.'

'You don't really mean that.' He smiles, though there's a little uncertainty in it.

'Actually I do... That's the thing.'

'What about Ethan?'

'What about him? He's gone, isn't he? You heard what she said on TV the other week, there isn't a reversal...'

'She said they were working on it, and we are too, remember? Don't forget Serum X.'

'Ah yes, the great un-Guarding chemical fairy tale.'

'Give us some credit, Fee. The research is solid and we've got reason to believe it should work to enhance memory and emotional response—'

'But with no test subjects, how can you possibly know—'

'Yeah. I know, I know...'

Felix sighs and looks down again.

'She took it all from us, didn't she...'

He crosses the room in long strides and sinks onto the bed opposite her, taking her hands. Her phone tumbles onto the quilt between them. He looks down at the screen and sees the name.

'You were going to call her? Did you think she would answer?'

'I don't know... I just... I needed to hear her tell me that it's true, that she has him.'

'Fee...'

'I know, it's stupid. I know where she's supposed to be next week. We managed to hack some of Beaumont's HR calendar files. She's supposed to give a presentation about something called GHAP to a bunch of investors in North London...'

'That's brilliant! So, come on, let's tell the others – we can plan a course of action. Maybe we can ambush them on the way out... I'm sure we can handle Bella and Ethan, especially if we ask Jem and Steve for back up—'

'It won't work, Ralph. Don't you think I've been going over and over it in my head, trying to think of how we can get to him? All she needs to do is look one of us in the eye and tell us to jump in front of a bus...'

'She wouldn't do that.'

'Wouldn't she?'

'No. Anyway, if we catch her by surprise we can disable her. Use chloroform or something.'

'And what, leave her by the side of the road? Down an alley? And how do you think you're going to manage

The Child Left in the Dark

Ethan? Even if one of us managed to knock him out, do you think any of us could carry him?'

'Together, we might...'

'Ralph. It won't work. There are a million things that could go wrong. Plus, the minute he wakes up, he'll just go straight back to her and then it will all be for nothing...'

'Not necessarily. If the Serum X—'

'It's untested, Ralph! You don't know what it might do to him!'

She pulls her hands away and scratches irritably at her temple. Her hair flops limply, the tips still a startling blonde against the darkness of the roots.

'So what was your plan then, call Bella and attempt to reason with her?'

'Maybe...'

'Let me,' he says, quickly.

'What?' she frowns.

'Let me call her. You're too... you'll get angry, then she'll clam up and cut you off and you'll never get through to her again.'

'And you won't?'

'I grew up with her,' he grins. 'I know when to push but also when to stop.'

Before she can say anything else, he grabs the phone and presses the green button. Felix stares at him as the ringing tone blares into the room. It feels strangely juvenile, sitting with a boy on the bed, calling a girl who has made his cheeks flush... Then Bella's cool, smooth voice finds her and the illusion comes crashing down.

'Felix? Is that really you?'

'No, it's Ralph.'

'Ralph? Is Ariana—'

'She's fine. I... er... We saw you on TV the other week,'

he looks away from Felix, back out of the window. She can tell he's regretting his impulsive offer to ring already.

'Yes?'

'You... Ethan's your Guard person, isn't he?'

There's a pause, a small sigh of sound as if Bella's just sat down. Felix imagines her reclined on a chaise longue in a plush conservatory, Felix's husband hovering close by with grapes on a crystal dish.

'Yes,' she replies, simply. Then: 'How on earth did you work that out?'

'Fee spotted him in the wings.'

'Ah. Of course. Well, you can tell Felix that it's not the heinous act she might think. Believe it or not, I'm trying to help.'

There's something strange about Bella's voice. Felix frowns as Ralph catches her eye. He hears it too, she can tell, it's almost as if...

'Beast, are you drunk?'

There is a long sigh and another soft noise.

'You would drink too if you'd seen what I saw today... But then, I suppose you did, didn't you?'

It isn't so much that her words are slurred, Felix thinks, more that they are being pronounced with extra care. The musicality to Bella's voice has flattened too, though that might just be due to the heaviness of her tone.

'What d'you mean? Look, do you want me to ring back when you—'

'The creatures, Ralphie. The hybrid animals. In the cages. Ask Ri, she certainly remembers...'

'You mean Daniel's Project? What about it? Are you at Futura?'

'No. He's here in London. He came with the hybrids. Some of them, anyway. There was a breakthrough, after

Ri's little interference last month. She saw her. It triggered a whole lot of shit and now she's here and she can fly and she said my name.'

'What, who?' Ralph's face is a picture of utter confusion.

'Nova. Nova Messenger from the ARC. He... he used her,' her voice wavers into something very small and very young. Felix stares at Ralph in horror. The image of a small girl with gingery blonde hair flutters through her memory and, a second later, she sees her swoop through Ralph's as comprehension clunks across his face.

'Little Nova from Project C? Shit, that bird thing... I saw her... I didn't even think—'

'How could you? It's unthinkable. She recognised Ariana because she looks like me... started making more meaningful attempts at communication. So they brought her here to see if putting her with the real me would trigger anything else. *Et voilà*. Mission accomplished,' the bitterness winds out of the phone and snags at Felix. She snatches the phone from Ralph before she thinks about what she is doing.

'It really sucks when arseholes experiment on the people you love, doesn't it?'

'Fee. How are you?'

'Oh, you know. Missing my cyborg spouse.'

'I know. But listen, it's not what you think, Ethan's not like the others. Our bond, it's changing—'

'I don't want to hear about your *bond*—'

'That's not what I mean, I'm trying to help him, Fee. I want to bring him back...'

'Really. And what exactly would be in that for you, hmm?'

'You don't believe me.'

'You're a fucking liar, Bella. Going on TV talking about how every Guard person has given consent, one way or another. You know as well as I do that neither Ethan nor I would have signed that form under normal circumstances.'

'It wasn't my choice to turn Ethan—'

'What about Melinda Burton?'

'That... That was different. She came after me—'

'Bullshit. You expect me to believe you felt threatened?'

'You don't understand. There are ways I must act now, certain behaviours which are expected of me, despite how I might feel about actually doing them...'

'Is that how you justify it? You're right, I don't understand. I think you lie to yourself as much as anyone. Why else would you still be there when your child is here?'

'It's... complicated.'

'Is it? Because I've been going over it and over it in my head... And there's only one answer that really makes sense to me. About why someone would choose to leave their child with practical strangers and go to live with a vile monster who will never leave her alone...'

'You were there, it was the price I had to pay for you all to be safe...'

'...especially when that someone has the power to get what she wants whenever she wants.'

'It's not that simple. I have to live this way to protect her. To protect you all.'

'That only proves my theory. You *can't* just command him to fuck off, can you? Because then he might just see the truth. The real truth. Why you stayed hidden for so long. Why you gave her up rather than risk him finding out who she really is.'

'Felix. Please. Ralph's there, isn't he? Don't. Not like

this.'

'What the hell are you talking about? I thought this was supposed to be about getting Ethan back,' Ralph says, his face a picture of utter bemusement.

'It's true, then?'

There's a pause, another shuffle. Then:

'Meet me. I'll be in North London next week. I have a presentation at the Celeste Exhibition Centre, Tuesday at 2pm. I'll meet you afterwards... I should be able to get away by five...' she sounds breathless, as if she's just finished a lengthy ballet routine on stage.

'Will Ethan be there?'

'Yes.'

'And...?'

'Just a Guard driver and a couple of demonstration models, but I can leave them in the car. Bring Ralph. No one else. I'll know if you do. I'll get it from him. You know I will...'

'Yes. Where?'

'There's a back entrance, off Marley Road.'

'Five?'

'Five. And Felix? If you breathe a word of any of this to Ariana, I will take a knife and I will bury it in his neck. Understand?'

'Perfectly.'

Felix presses a button and drops the phone on the bed triumphantly. She enjoys the feeling, the new lightness in her chest and the tingling of victory in her fingers for a few seconds before she meets Ralph's gaze. His eyes have darkened almost to blackness and his forehead is so furrowed it has brought his hairline forward.

'What the bloody hell was all that about? What truth... what risk?' She can tell he's halfway there already, though.

He won't be able to wait until next week. He'll implode before then. She puts her hand on his, bites her lip.

'That code we broke to access the HR calendar... I wasn't the one who solved it. Ariana saw the pattern before I did... She's different, Ralph.'

'She's got Bella's talents of persuasion, yeah...'

'Not just Bella's. She understands what people need; she uses it to her own ends... she sees things that she shouldn't... It's more than Bella...'

'OK...'

'I'm saying it's not just Bella... I see it in her, when she gets angry. She has this look, this darkness in her eyes... A hardness... It's him, Ralph. Lychen. I think he's Ariana's real dad.'

'Don't be stupid!' Ralph gives a short, humourless laugh which doesn't catch up to his eyes.

'Call Bella back if you don't believe me. She basically admitted it to me just now.'

'But we... She... She was seeing him, too?'

'No. I don't think so. I think he raped her, Ralph. I think that's the real reason why she left and why she never got in touch for all those years...'

'What? What?' He throws himself off the bed, his hands trembling into fists.

'Ralph, sit—'

'I'll kill him. I will gut him.'

'Yes, this is probably why she didn't tell you...'

'And she's working with him, living with him now! How can she do that!'

'Because of Ariana, Ralph! Look, I'm sorry. This isn't how you should be finding out... And far be it from me to defend Bella but I really do think this whole damn charade is to protect her from him... We can't go mouthing off about this... It can't get back to him. Can you imagine what he'll do?'

'He'll... He'll come for Ariana... He'll want to control her, too... Bella said to me, once, that she raised her away from here because of him. Because she didn't want him lurking over Ariana the way he lurked around her... I thought she meant... God, but she lied! She bloody lied about everything!'

'Yes. Like I said, I think she lies so naturally that it becomes part of her life. I think she wanted Ariana to be yours, Ralph. More than anything.'

'I just... I need to think...' He sweeps away out of the room. Felix sits in the exact same position she's held for the last thirty minutes, staring at her phone. Ralph's distress settles heavily in her lungs but she still feels the novel trickle of hope underneath it. Ethan. She's seeing him in five days. Nothing else matters.

22

May, 2019

My head feels as if it has turned into a lump of grit. I burrow into my pillow and groan as yesterday sifts back into focus. Nova, her eyes full of recognition, pain, fury. Lychen reaching for me, Ethan's eyes twitching in warning. The grin of Ralph's voice in my ear: *Beast, are you drunk?* Felix's cold hard words which had hooked past the layer of winey befuddlement and pierced somewhere deep and unknowable. *Fuck.* She knows.

'Oh, God.' I open my eyes. The room is dim, the blinds fully drawn across the sliding doors. My jeans and jumper hang neatly on the clothes stand and the only evidence of last night is an empty wine bottle on my dressing table, a dirty glass by my bedside and this horrendous pounding in my head. At least, I think, I'd had the sense to send Ethan to stand guard outside my door and he hadn't heard any of my conversation with Ralph and Felix. The inkling of humanity I'd seen yesterday had disappeared by the time we'd reached the North building, the last thing he needed was me prodding at it without all my wits about me.

I reach for the bottle of water on my bedside table and gulp at it hungrily. Then I glance at my phone. It's not quite seven yet. My head filters a little clearer and I begin to feel slightly better for the water and the long night's sleep. My phone beeps with a notification from my calendar. A conference meeting at nine am regarding the Guard Home Assistance Programme roll out, scheduled to begin next month. Followed by another meeting at noon. The afternoon to be spent with the Youth Guard, teaching the next level of emotional response. Lychen's next assessment of them is imminent, I realise with an echoing shiver of last night's blaze of emotion.

You are a monster. You are unfathomable. That look in his eye, that glint of utter contempt as if I'd thrust a mirror at him and forced him to see.

I can't face him. But I have to. Felix knows the truth. That means Ralph probably knows by now, too. I picture them standing in his old laboratory at the ARC, her putting the phone down in triumph, him confused, asking what on earth we'd been talking about.

It wouldn't have been in the ARC. The ARC is empty.
It hardly matters. He won't let it go. He'll force her to explain.
And he'll think you betrayed him. He'll think you were playing them both.
Well. I was, in a way. Wasn't I?
Oh, Bella. It hurts too much in here to talk about this now.

I sigh and ease myself out of bed, rolling my shoulders and trying not to shake my head too much. A gentle knock comes at the sliding door and I know it is Ethan. I silently tell him to come in. He slides the door open quietly, a small box in one hand and a fresh bottle of water in the other.

'Painkillers,' he says, shutting the door behind him.

'Thank you,' I murmur, taking them from him and shaking two into my palm. He holds his hand out for the rest of the box and I hand it back over with a wry smile. Everything controlled. Nothing left to chance.

The Child Left in the Dark

'Did you know I would have a headache today? From the wine, I mean?'

'I deduced the likelihood was high, given your body mass index, the strength of the wine and the lack of food eaten with it. And, once in closer proximity, I felt it.'

I swallow the pills one by one and take another long drink of water. He watches me instead of staring straight ahead, and I can tell a small amount of him has returned further.

'You felt it?'

'Yes. I felt it in my own head. I feel all your pain, your needs... I have been designed that way...'

'But the bond is meant to be based on a copy of a person... It shouldn't go that deep.'

'Ours does.'

'But wh— oh. *Oh.* Lychen made you that way, didn't he? So you could report to him. So you can detect any faults, any sign of degeneration...'

'Yes.'

'Due to my being Subject A. That's why he hasn't suggested I have more testing. How often do you report?'

'Once a week. You are disappointed...'

'No... I just... thought more tests might mean going back to Cumbria. The chance to see Ariana.'

'Yes. I feel that. I feel all of it. All the time.'

I look up in some alarm.

'You hear it all? Even my—'

'Your conversations with your dead mother. The turmoil within yourself. Your determination to destroy Lychen's empire battling your love for it. I feel it all.'

'But... you don't... you wouldn't...'

'I would not tell Dr Lychen. His orders concern your physical self.'

'But if he had the slightest inkling of what I really felt, half the time...'

'Dr Lychen does not place weight on emotional responses. But if he knew your true motives, he would seek to punish you. That is where my programming to protect you overrides. I will never tell him. I will die first.'

I stare at him, struck by the oddity of such a proclamation delivered in such unemotional, stoic tones.

'You must protect yourself too, Ethan. I saw you yesterday. Even now, the things you are understanding are beyond what you should know as a Guard person...'

'Yes.' His face spikes with a tiny trickle of awareness before smoothing back into passivity.

'We got lucky yesterday. Lucky Lychen was so distracted by me having a small breakdown,' I grimace as my own heated words glare around my head again.

'But if he sees even a glimpse of this,' I gesture at his face vaguely. 'He will have you destroyed.'

'Do not concern yourself for me. I know what is expected.'

'Good. Because we're in this together now. Any way you look at it... God, my head. Is there any coffee?' I ask, feeling a tiny sprig of guilt to still be giving him orders. Appearances, though. Also, hangover.

'Coffee is on the terrace... with Dr Lychen.'

'Of course it is.'

'He has given you thirty minutes.'

23

May, 2019

Ariana is bored. She blows her cheeks outwards and watches her own reflection lazily in the old full-length mirror. She checks her phone for the eleventh time that minute. No new messages. No calls. She went to the cinema with her school friends yesterday and one of them, Molly, is having a sleepover this Friday. But today... today stretches in a miasma of dull nothingness. Homework has been done, mostly. She's read all the books they've been assigned this term for English. Ariana sighs and droops her head back further over the end of the bed. She had always thought that, once she didn't have to be so careful anymore, she would be busy all the time, that these spoonfuls of long empty hours would be eliminated.

Marble steps neatly into her line of vision, staring at her strange upside-down form with an aloof sort of nonchalance. She makes a kissy sound at him and he blinks slowly before turning away as if embarrassed for the both of them. Ariana watches him as he climbs delicately onto her work desk and settles himself onto the A3 paper containing the beginnings of a project on abstract art. She wonders if she can use her strange, pattern-seeing powers of perception to unlock Marble's secret desires, see what it is about the crackling, cold paper on the hard plane of wood which called out to him as the optimal resting place in this room of soft furnishings. Ariana feels the blood trickling to her head and places her hands on the wooden floor, her elbows by her ears. From there she walks her feet up the bed, arches her body and flips the right way up. The movement is neat and graceful but still it sends Marble skittering off the desk and out of the open doorway. Ariana sighs and turns back to her phone, which is lying on the duvet where she left it. She closes the WhatsApp group she shares with her friends, checks Twitter, Snapchat and Instagram and then opens the text messages to the brief and frankly odd conversation she'd had with her mother last night.

> You were right. I've seen them. They're here. They're awful.

>> What? Mum, I know you love to be all cryptic and dramatic, but you need to make a bit more sense than that.

> Sorry. I mean the hybrids. Daniel's experiments. He's moved a few of them here to London and I saw them today. A pig thing. Rodent creatures. And her, the bird-girl. She's someone I used to know, actually. A former C-Project child. She recognised me. It's why she tried to attack you.

>> Oh. That makes sense I guess. It wasn't something I'd done, it was because she thought I was you?

> Something like that.

>> So... are you going to help them?

I'll try. They will want me to work with
her, I suspect. She spoke to me, said
my name. She flies, too. They think I
am key to her progression.

> You have to help all of them, not just
> her. They need to be set free, out of
> those cages. They just need a chance.

Yes. Well. We all need that.

> Huh?

Nothing, never mind.

> Are you OK, Mum?

I'm fine. Just tired. Maybe I'll go to
bed.

> But it's only 6.

> Mum?

The main thing, Ariana supposes, is that the matter of the poor hybrid creatures is now out of her hands. Like Blake had said, if anyone has the influence to do something to help them, it's her mother. Still, Ariana can't help feeling a little redundant now the problem which has been haunting her for so many nights has suddenly lifted away. She hasn't even had one of the screaming nightmares for at least a week… Mum *knows* bird-girl. That has to be a good thing. That ensures that whatever happens with her at least, it won't be too awful. Ariana frowns, wondering if that's the right way of looking at things. Whether perhaps it's a bit *off*… Whether she should care, just a little bit more, about that weird comment her mother had made in response to the creatures being released. *We all need that.* Then she shrugs. She said it didn't matter. And her mother can take care of herself, she's proven that more than once over the last year.

Ariana stretches and wanders lazily to the door of her room. From here she can see down to the flagstone tiles, partway into the two front rooms/offices and some way into the dining, kitchen and utility rooms at the back of the house as well as Felix's makeshift computer suite. It had been from here that she had learned all she'd needed to know about the last trip to Graysons and how she'd be able to get into the building. It had also been here she'd sat the other week when the sound of her mother's voice on TV had filtered up from Blake's office. There is nothing exciting to overhear today, though.

Ariana steps lightly out onto the landing. The carpeted floor stretches in a generous curve around the wide winding staircase. Ariana finds Marble sitting on the landing, tail swishing as he watches something lazily in the air beyond the wooden banisters lining the hallway. Ariana sits next to him, stroking him absently as she glances along the floor. The door to the bathroom directly opposite her bedroom is open and so is the one leading to the large room with the colourful crocheted quilt on the bed where Felix sleeps and Ethan used to. The room between the two is closed and, as far as Ariana is aware, has remained so since her first week here when her grandfather had told her that anything in it was hers if she wanted it. Ariana had perused the large purple velvet-covered sleigh bed, desk, stripey rag-rug eerily similar to the one she remembered from the old flat in Flintworth and the rows upon rows of neatly hung clothes in the wardrobe. Many of them were wrapped in protective plastic as if they'd been freshly dry-cleaned, and Ariana felt strange just touching them, as if she were disturbing a grave. The shoes lining the shelves along the bottom of the closet were all designer, and impractically-heeled apart from a pair of fur-lined, leather ankle boots with a fine layer of dirt on the soles. These Ariana had taken possession of and, providing she wore thick socks, could wear comfortably enough. Her legs looked overly long and a little noodly when she'd checked her reflection in the wardrobe's full-length mirror, but at least she hadn't been reminded of Bella.

Remembering the boots now, Ariana heads back into her own room and pulls them onto her feet, thinking she might go to the ARC. She hasn't fully explored the upper floors yet and she has a feeling she's seen the flash of the key card pass in her grandfather's coat pocket. She's just opening her bedroom door when she hears the voices coming up the stairs. It's too late to retreat, though she freezes for long enough to catch the end of their conversation.

'...take Dom and Tess, just in case?' Ralph's voice is tense and slightly gruff as if he's coming down with a cold.

'No, she said to come alone,' Felix, in contrast to Ralph, sounds stronger than she has in weeks and her footfalls fall solidly on the stairs as the two of them round the corner. 'I'm not doing anything to jeopardise— oh.' She spots Ariana at the same time as Ralph. They both give her a strange look, as if they'd completely forgotten she even existed.

'Ariana, I thought you were at Molly's today?' Felix says, recovering first.

'That's tomorrow. It's a sleepover.' *I could go for a week*, she thinks, *and they probably wouldn't notice*.

'Will you be wanting a lift?' Felix smiles at her, though Ariana sees the strange set of tension in the hinges of her jaw and follows the tiny nudge Felix gives her father. Ralph is still looking odd; his eyes shift from Ariana to Marble to Ariana's boots and back again. It's like he's watching a flea hopping from thing to thing and Ariana actually looks down to check there isn't one.

'I was thinking I could take the bus…? There's a bus stop only a mile or so from here. It goes all the way to town and Molly said she'll meet me there…'

'Hang on, you mean the stop near Pickerton? That's a good twenty-minute walk away, mostly on the main road…' Felix frowns.

'There's a footpath for a lot of it,' Ariana says, directing her words to Ralph. 'It'll be in full daylight and we've gone that way in the car tons of times… I know the way… Dad?'

He looks up almost absently. 'Hmm? Yeah, sure. Fine.'

'Great, thank you!'

'Ralph, I really don't—'

'I said it's fine, Fee. She knows how to take care of herself, don't you, Ariana?'

'Yeah, course. I'll have my phone on me too, I can text you when I'm on the bus and stuff… if there's any issue I'm only a bit up the road, someone can come get me…'

'There you go then.'

'Ral, I'd be happy to drive her—'

Something weird is happening, Ariana can see. She watches the two of them shrewdly, trying to get her brain past her small triumph and into the right head-space to probe. Felix is easy, her concern bubbling all over her as obvious as steam from a kettle. Ralph is less so… He's barely thinking about the conversation at all, his mind dipping in and out of weird swirls and confusion all skimming the surface of a huge well of deep unknowable sadness. It hits Ariana all at once and her breath catches in her throat as tears swarm into her eyes.

'What's wrong?' she asks, before she can stop herself. 'Dad?'

He just looks at her and shakes his head. 'Nothing, Ari. I'm fine. I'm just tired. I didn't sleep well... You know. I might go and have a lie down now, actually.' He turns from them without another word and drifts distractedly up the next flight of stairs to the room directly above Ariana's. She frowns. She's become so used to falling asleep to the sound of his pacing she can't remember if she heard it last night or not. She shakes her head, the tears subsiding, though the aching chasm of his pain lingers like a bruise.

'What's wrong with him?' she asks Felix, though she can already tell that whatever it is, Felix has decided not to tell her.

'Don't worry about it. We haven't caught up today, have we? Were you alright last night? I didn't hear you—'

'Yeah, I think those dreams are starting to go away. I haven't had one for a while.'

'Oh? That's great! How was the film? Did Dom pick you up at the right time? He wasn't embarrassing, was he? I told him to stay in the car...' She crosses the landing, smiling at Ariana. Her head is full of trivial things, and Ariana suspects she's doing it deliberately. She sighs.

'It was fine. He was a bit late, but it was OK, he waited in the car. What were you guys talking about before? When Dad said something about taking Dom and Tess with you somewhere?'

'Oh. You heard that, huh? We're... We've got a lead on somewhere Ethan might be next week. We're going to go and see if we can intercept him...'

'Oh,' Ariana's thoughts begin to tumble. 'Will Mum be

there?'

'Yes. We were right about Ethan being her personal Guard guy... And *you* were right about that code, missy. Good job there. In fact, if you're not too busy now I'd like you to come and take a look at a few more programs I'm running, see if you can spot some more patterns for me?'

Ariana knows the thought has only just occurred to Felix, that she's trying to distract her so she won't ask to go with them.

Why should I go? If they can't see how I can help them, if they're too witless to see how powerful I'm becoming, why should I help them?

The words surprise even her. They're so callous, so cold... And they're not, to her surprise, in her mother's voice. They belong to something else, the empty un-focus she reaches for when she tries to read people... it's like they belong to the intention itself.

'OK,' she says, shrugging. She follows Felix back along the landing and down the stairs, her mother's boots clumping loudly on her feet.

24

May, 2019

Twenty-nine minutes after my conversation with Ethan I stand on the threshold of my room dressed in a tailored, sleeveless blazer dress in white. It skims neatly over my body and highlights the vibrancy of my eyes whilst also disguising whatever lingering pallor I've not covered with make-up. My hair spirals from crystal-encrusted barrettes in the style that makes my stylists clasp their hands together and sigh. I need to look better than good today, hangover be damned. Today I am taking the floor and talking to all the most important heads of departments about the roll out of the GHAP programme. Today I need to show them that I am the only person who can tow the public by its nose. They will never suspect how little I care about it all right now. I open my shoe closet and quickly select a pair of never-worn ivory Louboutins to match the dress, and I'm ready. Ethan gives me a quick nod as he opens the door and I brace myself, painting my face clear and cold and letting my body do the rest.

'Bella. I'm glad to see you.' Lychen stands as I step over the threshold. His face is guarded and he regards me with a mixture of approval and something that on anyone else might be apprehension.

'Dr Lychen. Good morning,' I say, shortly, perching on my chair and nodding for Ethan to pour my coffee. I know

Lychen will not notice my detour from the polite way I usually order my Primary Guard. He does not notice things like that. He sits down, his gaze still a scour upon my face as I drink deeply.

'You are still upset about Daniel's hybrid?'

'Yes.'

'And you are still angry with me?'

I sigh and put my coffee cup back down on the table. I look him directly in the eye.

'Do you want me to be truthful?'

'Always.'

'I am angry because I want you to be something that I don't know if you can be. I want you to understand *why* I became so upset yesterday and why I am still sad about what happened to Nova. I want you to not need to question whether I am upset because you know me well enough to know that I would be, or that I am. But mostly... I want to know *why* you're like this. Almost like them,' I gesture behind me at Delta and Ethan. 'It's like you don't *want* to be human so you block off the impulses that make you that way... Except the ones which it suits you to turn back on.'

'You called me monstrous last night.'

'Well, in a way... Your lack of empathy means you can make decisions which can be potentially monstrous... You authorised taking that defenceless child and turning her into a beast...'

'A glorious, unique beast...'

'A half-thing who will never know a normal life, may never be let out of that cage in that building behind us...'

'Not necessarily, with your help.'

I sigh and take my coffee cup up again. I can sense his frustration mounting as I continue not to bend like I usually do. Like everyone always does. My instincts screech but I ignore them, recklessness shooting bolts of lightning into my words.

'And you don't understand, do you, why that might be a lot to ask of me? Someone who watched this child grow up, who loved her like a little sister...'

'I don't see—'

'No, you *don't see*. That's my point. That was my point yesterday, too. Daniel... He was brought up at the ARC, trained to disappear at will... His upbringing required him to *want* to disappear. I watched the scientists in Project C... They did all sorts of things – ignored him, shunted him aside, left him alone in a dark room for days and days... All to bring out that talent. And he's not the only example of the ARC's horrifying legacy. I know that for my part I can be cold when I want to be, that I use *being a robot* as a shield – goodness knows what neurodivergent label I'd be given if I were a child in mainstream education nowadays. But that's me, that's Daniel. We were not raised to be ordinary. But you? *You* didn't grow up at the ARC. You must have been a normal child once... and yet I don't know anything about you. Where did you come from, Josiah? Why are you the way you are? Are you a Subject like me? Are you just fucked up? What happened to—'

'Enough!' He throws himself to his feet and takes two furious steps away from the table. Just as I begin to breathe, he turns back, swift as a loosed arrow, rips the coffee cup from my hand and throws it into shards on the terrace beside us. I sense Ethan beginning to move to my defence and silently command him to be still as Lychen places a hand on either arm of my chair and brings his face close to mine. His eyes glitter dangerously and his mouth is clenched. I've never seen him so furious.

'I thought better of you, Bella. I prided your *coldness*, as you call it. I thought you were more like me... not so... messy. That you turning your back on the Project C children showed – just as your relinquishment of Ariana – a ruthlessness, a narrowly-focused ambition I prized. I did not think all this... muck... of emotion and *feeling* was so important to you.'

'It is in a partner,' I breathed. 'It is if you want me to truly settle here, with you.'

'You seem to think that you have a choice in the matter. That you have any other place other than by my side, or wherever else I choose to put you.'

I wait, keeping my face calm even though everything in me is crying to fight, to force him away from me, to run and never stop, even if the only direction lies in front of me, over that balcony.

'I will tell you, but first I want something from you.'

'What is it?'

'You will swear never to use your power of command on me ever again.'

I lie to him every day anyway. What difference will one more make?

Because it will only take one time for the balance to tip, for him to see the cracks in the mask. It's all you have, Bella.

It's not all I have. What about my Youth Guard? What about Ethan?

The Guard are all ultimately his, you know that. Ethan is just one and he will be destroyed before he so much as moves a finger against Lychen. The Youth are still new and untested, you haven't had the time to dedicate to them. There is no one you can rely on, Bella. Just yourself.

But I have to know.

Why?

Because I can't see any other way of destroying him.

'OK,' I mutter. He looks down, almost as if disappointed. Then he removes his hands, stands up and walks away, towards the balcony edge. I glance quickly at Ethan to let him know that he needs to stay away, stay stoic. Then I get to my feet and follow Lychen. We stand side by side at the edge of the city, his hands resting lightly on the balustrade. When he speaks, his voice is determinedly flat.

'I was not a Subject like you or Daniel, though there are similarities in our stories. I grew up with my parents in a small, nondescript village in Somerset. My parents lost twin sons two years before I was born. My father was a cruel, obsessive man who pushed all of his ambitions for three sons onto me. When I could not deliver, his punishments were unyielding. Beatings, mostly. Sometimes he withheld food. Other days I'd be locked in my bedroom or in the understairs cupboard for days at a time. My mother had her share of it as well and became a hollow shell of a soul, unable to help herself, let alone me. She committed suicide when I was five.

'My father was furious that she had escaped his control... He drank more, descended into a brutish, messy filth of a person. His obsession with making me into his skewed image of the perfect son only got worse as I grew older. He'd set me ridiculous, irrational tasks to demonstrate strength, stoicism, athleticism... I was not strong, stoic or athletic, and so I would fail over and over again, often becoming injured through trying or through punishment... He stopped taking me to the hospital when questions were raised and a file was opened. I don't recall a lot of the period after that, only a pervading sense of weakness. Of being often alone, left behind, left, like

Daniel, in the dark to disappear. I believe I might have perished before the age of twelve if my father hadn't heard rumours of the human eugenic experimentation being done at the ARC.

'We travelled there a few months before I turned thirteen. I remember meeting Dr Blake and his wife, Ana. I saw Ralph, though he was a very young child then. My father and I had become increasingly isolated by that point, it'd been a long time since I'd been around other families... I remember being confused by the way they acted around one another, though now of course I realise *we* were the oddities. My father asked them to change me into something better. I asked if they would keep me. I begged them to take me. I didn't care what they did, I just didn't want to leave with the man who had made me.

'They turned us both away, of course. Their work still concerned Project A at the time, the moulding of children who hadn't even been born yet. They did not have an application for a twelve-year-old pre-adolescent and they saw through my father's intentions. I'm not certain what they said to him, but whatever it was changed the way he behaved towards me. He gave up. He no longer barked at or beat me, but nor did he speak to me. I was given a basic monthly allowance directly into my bank account and left to make my own choices. I chose to survive the only way I could, by putting emotional ties and hindrances behind me. What good, after all, had any of it ever done me? The last time I had asked for help the door had been closed in my face. I realised that the only person who could save me, who could be relied upon, was myself. And what did I want? To get as far away from the life I had been born into as possible.

'So I worked. I saved what I could and used the

advantage of a free house to live in until I had gained enough qualifications for university, which I paid for using wages from menial jobs as well as all the loans I could acquire. I left home for university when I was eighteen, changed my name, never went back. I don't know if my father is alive. I don't care. It no longer occurs to me to care.'

He stops and carries on staring straight ahead, like a Guard person finished with a report. There's more. I can tell. He is mustering.

'Josiah... that's horrendous.'

'Is it?' He turns to me, fury creeping back into his eyes. Not for the parents who failed him, not for the Blakes who had refused him. For me. For bringing it all here, to his unblemished empire a thousand miles away. 'Do you like the bed you sleep in? The luxurious clothes you wear? The personal shoppers and stylists who visit at your beck and call? Those pretty shoes with the red soles upon your feet?'

'Of course...'

'Do you enjoy your position of power? Your dominion over everyone here? Running your own ground-breaking project, overseeing a dozen others? Appearing on television, radio, the internet... Your position, everything you have ever meaningfully worked for... Ten years too late but here all the same?'

'Yes.'

'Then never again question who gave it all to you. All this exists because of the way I am. I have had to do some monstrous things to build it all, and maybe I am a monster. Maybe that is the only thing I will ever be, but if that is what is required to create all of this, to give the world a taste of all the possibilities, all the avenues that can be reached when one removes the hindrances of messy, wasteful emotion… That is a reality I embrace. That is the reality I have chosen…'

'So you've become what your father wanted all along?'

'My father was an ignorant brute who drank too much. I no longer waste energy on deciphering whatever it was he wanted me to be.'

'And the Blakes?'

'They kept in touch, out of guilty obligation. Made sure my father was sticking to whatever agreement he had made with them. Frederick helped pay some of my university fees. And when I graduated, he offered me a position at the ARC. Once there, I tried to put my application thesis into practice and discover whether genetic enhancement could be applied to adults, as it had been applied to the C children… I even experimented upon myself, when resources were scarce. None of it was successful enough to warrant further research, though I believe one of the side effects has been an enhanced ability to command – which, of course, was essential in the development of the Guard project. They already had a similar application there, at the ARC, you see. It had already been used successfully, but only once. But you know that, don't you…'

'Yes.'

'I was put on the C-Project, but those children… They were already too ruled by their emotions, too unpredictable. It wasn't long before I began to develop Project D. That's where our stories collide.'

He turns back to me. His face is impassive once more, though I can still see the fury tumbling behind his gaze.

'I own who I am, Bella. I learned to when I was twelve years old. I do not feel a kinship for you out of our shared experiences of parental inadequacy. Nor do I resent you for being the child the Blakes *did* decide to take on as their own after rejecting me. I love you because you are incandescently beautiful and you wield power over others. I love you because of everything that makes you Subject A. I love you for all the monstrous things *you,* too, have done to get to where you are… Perhaps it takes a monster to truly love another monster. But I have limits to my tolerance, too, Bella. I can and *will* destroy you if you push me too far. Do you understand that?'

He stares at me and I stare back. I see the truth in his conviction. I see his own longing, his hunger, his need for me to bow obediently under the rearing hand of his control. He really, truly believes he can kill me if he chooses to. I smile at him quickly, sweetly, until the fury dies away.

'Thank you, Josiah. I understand perfectly now.'

Do you?

Yes. I know what I have to do now. He just told me. I have to push him too far.

Summer, 2010

Marc stood with his feet planted firmly on the worn carpet, facing the street-level window. He watched a small cluster of shoes walk slowly past. I knew what he was going to say.

'You know, you really should think of moving, Bells. Putting a deposit down somewhere with a garden, maybe Surrey or Berkshire... You can commute in for your course, Ri-ri can go to a school with a little bit of land to play in...'

'The application for primaries went in months ago,' I said, quietly. Ariana slumped on the sofa next to me, her eyes half closed as she watched Iggle Piggle chase Upsy Daisy on the small screen in the corner of the room. A small trail of milk crested her upper lip and she barely flinched as I wiped it gently with my thumb.

'I'm sure you'd be able to transfer it... Bells, this place is too small for one person let alone two... Look at your desk!' He gestured to the small writing desk I'd slotted into the cramped space under the window between the TV and kitchen sink. A laptop and printer took up most of the space, there were also notebooks stacked haphazardly on the floor, interspersed with Ariana's drawings. Text books balanced on the windowsill, a Tupperware box perched on top, overflowing with lidless pens, crayons and biros.

'I do most of my work in the library,' I muttered as the strange, bean-shaped hero of the piece finally settled down to sleep in his boat amid the gentle plinky plonky theme music. 'Bedtime, Ri.'

'Can I have two stories?' Ariana bounced up, all signs of sleep momentarily vanished.

'Only if you ask Grandpa nicely,' I said, glancing at him. His eyes crinkled at the pair of us.

'How could I refuse?' he grinned.

Ten minutes later, with Ariana pyjama'd, face washed, teeth cleaned and talking gently to her teddies from the cot bed she was almost too big for in the corner of my bedroom, I offered Dad a glass of wine. I could tell he was surprised, but pleased. Usually, Ariana's bedtime was his signal to make his way home.

'Shall we go outside? It's so warm out.'

'Sure.' He followed me out into the tiny concrete square. I'd squeezed two wrought iron patio chairs and a neat little table – all far too over-priced for the little time I ever used them but irresistibly stylish – out into the space and, in the soft glow of the overlooking windows, providing you ignored the slight smell of drains, it was almost nice.

'So...' Dad sat heavily in one of the iron chairs before immediately shifting his weight around it, trying to get comfortable. I perched on the other, the coolness of the metal seeping gently through my jeans. Mild as it was, the sun had begun to dip behind the buildings surrounding us and I was glad of the wool cardigan I'd brought out with me. The window to the bedroom was slightly ajar behind us and over the sounds of TVs, laughter, talking and gentle-if-somewhat-incongruous violin playing which drifted down around us, I could still hear Ariana's little voice chirruping away.

'Yes, I know, I know. It's not really big enough. And Ariana's only going to get bigger, need her own room... I know. And I've been saving a bit here and there—'

'Bells, you know you don't need to do that.'

'But, you know... I like it here. It's been hard; I miss the ARC, Cumbria, The Manor... everything, really. It was home. Even when everything happened... it was still hard to leave. Harder than I thought. And when I came to London I never thought I'd feel safe. But I do.' I sighed and drank a little more wine. It slid easily down my throat, warming everything it touched on the way down. Two moths danced dazedly towards the light in the window of the flat above.

'Well... You know I'm happy to help with a deposit if you want to buy somewhere, get a rung on the property ladder. Possibly not this central, but certainly Greater London if you'd like to stay in the area. We paid towards Maya and Silas' university fees after all...'

'And you'll still be paying mine for another three years,' I murmured, softly. I glanced over at him. His face seemed more rounded in the moonlight; softer. Sadder.

'Yes, well, you're doing a PhD...'

'There are grants, stipends. I've looked into it. I'm sure I'd be eligible, as a single mum. I was thinking of applying for my second year to be funded, as a matter of fact. It's slightly more exposure, but as you like to remind me, no one has come looking. No one has even come close... Maybe it's time I stopped leaching quite so much...'

'Bells...'

'I know you still feel like you owe me. I know you look at Ri and think about when I was little and what happened... But you know, I couldn't have done what I've been able to do over the last few years without your help. Hell, I wouldn't have got my coursework last term finished at all if you hadn't looked after Ariana so I could go down to Cornwall for the weekend…'

'Bella, it was a pleasure, I told you. It's always been a pleasure to help—'

'Has it? I haven't exactly made it easy on you—'

'And why should you? I put you in harm's way, in *his* way. That bastard Lychen never would have done what he did if we'd kept you where you should have been all along…'

'I knew I shouldn't have told you his name. Look, let's not go over all that again. It is what it is and possibly would have all happened anyway. I told you what Ana said – maybe I was always going to go back there… Let's just… move past it. We're good.'

I took another drink, glancing over at him when he didn't reply. He was sitting hunched forward a little, his wine almost untouched on the table next to him. He was looking down at the tips of his shoes and for a moment, as the light glanced off his bald patch and the strands of silver spidering from it, he looked older than Dr Blake.

'What?' Something trembled inside as I asked it, like the beginnings of an earthquake. As he opened his mouth, I had to resist the sudden urge to jump up and slam my way back into the flat.

'It… It's not just that. I didn't just let your mother send you away when you were little. I… I'm the reason why she did it.'

'What?'

'Having a third child was my idea. Your brother and sister were always so self-sufficient, even as really small children. Especially Maya. She had already potty-trained herself by the time she was fifteen months old, for goodness' sake. I was selfish… I wanted a child who didn't beat me at chess at three or out-bowl me at cricket by four. Your mother agreed, but she didn't want a normal baby. She didn't know how she could treat it the same as the other two, knowing it wasn't gifted or special like them... She wanted another exceptional child, a beautiful, graceful girl she could dress up and parade around for the world to admire.

'I should never have agreed to it. We had the children we'd planned. We had a nice house, my work was booming and Julia had just had a promotion... But once the idea took hold, we couldn't forget about it. So we contacted the Blakes again. And they were only too happy to oblige.'

'I know all of this already, Dad—'

'Not this next bit, you don't. I had reservations, you see. I wasn't a fool. I feared for you, even then... I imagined this perfect child, painted to be pleasing, always having to perform, engaging the world to an obsessive degree... We met with the Blakes. We sat in their garden up in Cumbria. Maya played with their little boy, Ralph. Silas ran laps around them. At some point Dr Blake took your mother off to see some flowers or something, and it was just me and her. Ana. I can't remember if I voiced my fears first or if she brought it up, but before I knew it we were both talking about this child that my wife and I had proposed, and she said that she feared the same as I. That she worried such a child would be forever used by others, forever judged on her beauty, forever held as an object to admire... Ana said it best – she said it sounded as if what we wanted was a living doll. A child doll is one thing – it can be prettied and dressed and paraded but also protected. What of an adult doll?'

I shuddered. The trembling feeling had returned. I imagined Ana sitting in her sunny garden, my brother and sister running around with Ralph among the flower beds.

Ana still had all her hair, her eyebrows, her beauty. My father was the full-headed, powerful man I remembered. They should have left it there, I thought. Shook hands and parted as satiated parents of the children they already had. But, of course, Marc was already talking again, already voicing the dreaded truth which I had long come to suspect.

'She was the one who suggested that we add a further alteration. Something that would work alongside the beauty and grace, something that wouldn't detract but would complement, strengthen.'

'Resilience.'

'Yes. It hadn't been done before. She didn't know whether it would even work, but she assured me that it would be safe for the child. That there wouldn't be any heightened risk of miscarriage, birth defects, that sort of thing... Dr Blake... I don't think he knew. Your mother certainly didn't. She just wanted the beautiful child, any suggestion of something else and she would have disagreed to the whole thing, I knew it. So did Ana. She wanted to do it. To *try* it. I could tell. Her eyes shone with the possibility, she practically vibrated with it... I knew she could do it. I just knew...'

'But you didn't know what you were doing, either of you! You didn't know if the application would work! I use enhanced genetic hypotheses all the time at the lab, it takes years to get from the stage of discussing something like that to the application... and that's just on bloody mice!'

'I know. I know. I got caught up... I imagined this beautiful, superhero of a woman... I imagined *you*, Bella... Once that idea took hold, I couldn't give it up. I couldn't give you up.'

'Until your brilliant idea landed another child's hand in an open flame! Until your wife decided that I wasn't beautiful enough to ignore the fact that I used my brilliant *resilience* to manipulate everyone around me…'

'I know, I know… I panicked…'

'And instead of owning up to it, you let her ship me back to the Blakes! To the very people who'd done it to me!'

'I thought you'd be better off! I thought they'd be able to help you control it, use it to better the world. And they did! They taught you incredible things, they brought you up to be a scientist, a pioneer!'

'They put me in the path of the man who took everything,' I hissed. I realised I was on my feet, my wine glass broken in my hand, blood dripping onto the concrete below. Marc stood up, holding his hands out for mine, but I turned away. Ariana's voice still burbled gently through the window.

'And it's not just me, is it? That resilience edit… It went to her as well, didn't it?'

'I… I don't know… Bella, you're bleeding.'

'Don't touch me! Don't you come anywhere near me! This is the real reason why you never came back for me, isn't it? Because you knew all along that it was your fault, that you'd let her go too far… And now… This is why you've been paying up for everything, isn't it? This is why you never complain, this is all guilt. All of it.'

'Bella, please, just calm—'

'It's why you brushed me aside when I told you I was worried about the things Ri does and says… It's why you don't push me about seeing my mother… It's why you continue to come back, to offer help and money and everything else you possibly can… Because it's your sodding fault I am what I am!'

'I'm sorry, Bells... I should have said no the minute Ana suggested it...'

'You should have said no the minute my mother said she wanted another Project A freak.'

'I... You don't understand, Bella... The influence you have. You always have had, even when you were just an idea...'

'Do you know who you sound like?' My voice had become guttural as I pulled my sleeve down, wrapping it around the cut on my hand that I could still barely feel through the pound of my fury.

'Going on about how resilient I am, how irresistible, perfect, cold... You sound like the man who raped me. Who saw me for exactly the thing you and Ana were so worried about. That superhero resilience didn't exactly help me then, did it?'

'Bella,' his face had drained of all colour, leaving him sagging and ghoulish in the dying light.

'You're going to leave now. You're going to get the *fuck* out of my flat and away from me and my daughter and never contact us ever again. Now.'

He didn't resist. He pulled his coat up from the seat, shuffled back into the flat, down the hallway and out of the front door, pulling it gently to a close behind him. I waited until I heard his slow footsteps slump up the steps and the sound of his car pulling away, then I crossed calmly into the kitchenette and held my bleeding hand under the tap. My heart punched loudly in my chest but my thoughts were smooth and ordered, almost as if I'd known ever since the moment we'd sat down what he was going to tell me, and what it would mean.

I would give notice on the flat in the morning. Ariana

and I would move somewhere cheaper and bigger, out of the city. I would apply for the loans I had already begun researching. And I'd get a job... maybe in a chemist's or as a laboratory assistant. Something I could've done with my eyes closed by the age of fourteen at the ARC, but with people that wouldn't ask questions, would allow me to establish myself and climb the ladder. We'd be fine, I told myself, as my blood swirled and thinned into patterns alongside the cool water. I took it out from under the tap. My cardigan was ruined. The cut was in the pad of my thumb joint, not deep, but it continued to bleed long after I'd fetched a new glass, gone back out into the small, concrete terrace and drank slowly into the darkening night.

26

May, 2019

By five pm the sun has tipped into most of The Yard and it is full of workers. They stand about, voices jarring and jumbling, pale skin exposed, hands clutching eco-friendly cups. Someone has a flask of something that wafts a fruity, alcoholic tinge through the air and they slide it surreptitiously out of view as I pass. I nod briefly to the faces I recognise, though I don't stop. Ethan walks between them and me as we skirt the walkways linking the great triangular buildings. South looms like a prison ahead. I don't allow myself hesitation as Ethan swings the doors open before me and we retrace our steps to the lift and up.

'Back so soon?' Daniel's voice crowds in as I make my way down the corridor. I sigh and turn around. He's wearing a hideous polo top with the sleeves rolled up and baggy, cargo trousers. I look him up and down distastefully.

'Did I miss the Casual Friday memo?'

'I'm sorry if we can't all prance about in white Chanel without the occupational hazard of faecal matter being thrown at us...'

'It's Dior, actually.'

'Couldn't give a shit. What do you want, D'accourt?'

'Temper, temper. Anyone would think you were bitter for not being invited to this morning's heads of department meeting.' The comeback is petty and beneath me, but it's been a long day and it's taking far more effort than I'd care to admit to just to stand here, looking serene with him so snide and the other thing waiting for me beyond the door ahead. Daniel frowns but covers it quickly.

'So you're off to try and tame the beast, are you?'

'Surely that's what you want me to do? I thought I was the whole reason why the *beast* was here...?'

'Don't flatter yourself,' he snorts, looking me up and down in return. 'You were a means to an end. Actually, before you go in, I wanted to ask you something. I was going to do so yesterday after our little tour, but you ran off so quickly...'

I raise an eyebrow.

'It's about your Youth Guard. What's the status there? I mean, how close is the programme to being launch-ready?'

'Very. But you'd have to ask Dr Lychen about the programme's launch date.'

'Of course.' His stare lingers just long enough to begin to prickle over my exposed skin. I turn again towards the door of the aviary.

'I just wondered what their level was like. The quality.'

'They're good. Almost at marketable level, in my opinion.'

'Excellent. Well then, I'm in need of a Primary Assistant and you won't mind my requesting one of them. The little blonde we saw at the track the other day. She'll do nicely.'

I don't react. I don't even blink.

'You will have to ask Dr Lychen. But we haven't discussed their being used as Assistants internally. They've been designed – trained – to bridge the gap between the traditional Guard and humans. For use in fields such as government, education, psychological care, that sort of thing...'

He smiles at me widely. When he blinks, it's too slow and I have to suppress a shudder.

'Well. I shall discuss it with Dr Lychen, of course.'

'Of course.'

When he says nothing more, I turn back to Nova's door, rolling the entire interaction out of my head, smoothing the spikes of irritation and making myself as bland and still as a robot. It's a move that has never failed me in the past and I'm using it with my life today.

I don't see Nova straight away as I enter the large high-ceilinged laboratory. The light is dim, though that's more because the sun is shining on the other side of the building to the window, which faces the gravelled walled driveway. I stare around, noticing more than I did yesterday. The room is lined with shelves containing food boxes, blankets, water bottles and large plastic tubs which remind me of dog beds. There are also tools of varying sizes, as well as computers and pieces of laboratory equipment that I can only guess were here before Nova moved in and haven't yet been rehomed. Two male workers conversing in the corner of the room throw me looks that are both sympathetic and relieved. Sorry, hashtag not sorry, Ariana would say.

'She's up there,' one of them, the taller and darker of the two, says, pointing to the corner of the floor-to-ceiling cage. I follow his gesture and spot a dark huddle upon the makeshift perch. 'Since she worked out she could fly, she hardly ever comes down anymore.'

'Except when Dr Skaid comes in, she loves trying to tear through the bars for his benefit,' the shorter, gingery scientist smirks, his grin widening when I return his smile briefly.

'Can I try talking to her?' I ask, adding just enough command so they can't really refuse, but not so much that they realise it.

'Of course! We have to stay, though. She's got to be continuously monitored by one of us. I mean, not us personally all the time, there's a shift change at six, but one of us Research Developers—'

'That's fine.' I smile, watching as they both relax visibly. 'Has she said anything else to anyone since yesterday?'

'No, she's been up there since your visit. It's fairly standard behaviour. Often they'll go weeks without so much as a second of eye-contact.'

'Mmm.' I move closer to the cage, rounding a corner until I'm almost directly below the huddle which used to be my bright-eyed sweet little protégé. I search for a face amidst the gloomy feathers but cannot see through the thicket of her wings.

'Nova? Are you awake? It's me, Bella...' I call. The huddle gives a tiny shuffle, but no face emerges and she makes no move to fly.

'I'm sorry I ran off so quickly yesterday. I was very surprised to see you. And a little sad, to be honest. I had no idea what had become of you, you see. Oh, thank you,' I smile gratefully as one of the workers brings me a chair. I sit down, smoothing my white dress as I do so and glance up at him, dismissing him with my eyes. He quickly hurries to the far side of the room with the other man. Ethan stands at ease behind me, eyes on Nova, body poised for danger.

'I'm sorry for a lot of things, truth be told, Nova,' my voice is quieter but I have given it enough power to carry up to her ears. She shifts again and I can tell she's listening.

'I never wanted to leave you behind. I wanted to take you with me. I know you probably think I abandoned you. I shouldn't have done that. I know what it's like to trust a person, to want to make them proud of you, to love them like a parent... and then be abandoned by them. I didn't want to do that to anyone but I know it probably feels as if I did that to you. I'm sorry, little darling.'

The movement comes so swift and nimbly it should take me by surprise, but I'm ready for it. She swoops from the perch in a flurry of huge wing-span – far greater than the height of Ethan or Ralph – and though the movement is fluid, it's nothing like the graceful balletic flight she could perform as a child. She lands on two feet; unlike her talons, they retain far more of their human shape and they do not bear feathers, though I notice her toenails resemble claws. Her legs, too, are bare, though short and thin as if they haven't grown at all since the age I last knew her. Her eyes are as dark and quick as they were yesterday and she keeps them trained on my face as she folds her great wings and tucks them around herself. If I squint, she almost looks like a smallish person cocooned and hooded in a great, shimmering cloak.

'There, I knew you were in there somewhere,' I murmur as she draws closer. Ethan takes a half step towards me and Nova's eyes narrow at the movement.

'It's OK. He is just here to protect me. But I don't need him to, do I? You aren't going to hurt me, are you? You *could,* I'm sure. Your wings are incredible. I'd love to see what you can do out in the open one day. Would you like that?'

She cocks her head and makes a small chirping noise with the tiny mouth nestled under her beakish nose. I sense a flurry of excitement among the two scientists on the other side of the room but don't take my eyes from Nova. She comes closer to the edge of the cage. I stand and approach as well. We are less than a metre apart now. I inhale slowly – a strange, wild scent of woodsmoke and trees filtered with human sweat.

'They say you don't speak,' I say, quietly. I can tell the men can't hear me now because they creep a little closer around the edges of my peripheral vision. I resist the urge to snap at them to stay away, knowing that any sharp word will send the creature in front of me skittering back up to her perch.

'They say you have never spoken and that you never flew until you arrived here... But I've seen you fly. And I heard you speak. You said my name yesterday, didn't you? You said Bella. Your mouth... it's still there. It's smaller than mine. Smaller than it used to be, perhaps. But it can still work, can't it? And your voice... It sounded like a chirp just now, but yesterday it was a shriek. I know you can speak, if you want to. But you don't have to. I won't make you. I *could.* You know that, don't you? You've seen me make people do things. I can do it by looking at them, concentrating on them, compelling them with my eyes and my voice. Sometimes just my hand. I do it because people made me able to. Just as they made you able to fly as a child without wings. But I don't have to. And neither do you. That's *our* choice, Nova.

'I'm not going to make you speak to me today. It's my turn, after all. It's been almost fourteen years since that summer, the one with the presentation. That was the last time I saw you. I wasn't allowed, afterwards... After Rudy died. They wouldn't let anyone in and, to tell the truth, I was relieved. I knew I was leaving by then, you see... And I knew that it would be all that much harder to leave you behind if I saw you first. It was selfish. I was completely selfish, Nova. I always have been. You deserved a chance at a life away from the ARC and I could have given it to you, but I knew that if I took you, they'd never let me keep you. It would have been hard to hide an eleven-year-old flying child and impossible to hide you from *them.* And I wasn't just protecting me... I had another child to think about at that point. My baby. You met her, didn't you? Ariana.'

Fury clouds her face once again and she gives a harsh shriek as if I've struck her. I reach out automatically and she thrusts herself backwards.

'*Ra-na!*' The word is twisted and bitter, but it is unmistakably human.

'Ariana,' I smile like a parent praising their child's first word. 'That's right. She's thirteen now.' More shrieks greet this trivia, some of them unmistakably sweary. Nova has twisted herself away, unfurling her wings, but seems unwilling to fly. I wonder what it is keeping her down here. My mention of Ariana seems to have infuriated and grounded her in equal measure.

'You didn't like her, did you? Is that because you thought she was me and were disappointed when you looked closer and she wasn't?'

'Noooo.'

'Ah. Was it because you realised who she must be and hated her for being the one who made me leave?'

'Leave... Leave! Leeeeeeeeeave. Leave, leave, leave. Leeeeeave!'

She throws the word at me, distorting it until it is void of all meaning, then she throws me a look of pure loathing before turning her back, spreading her wings and thrusting her strange, shrunken body into the air and up to her perch. It wasn't so much flying, I could see now, as beating the air into propulsion. I turn to the two scientists who are hovering at my elbow, eyes shining.

'That was incredible!'

'Remarkable, she's never so much as uttered a squawk—'

'...not in any meaningful sense, anyway...'

'But that was two, three words? Wow, just wow...'

'More if you count some of the swearing,' I say, placidly, watching the tight huddle up on the perch. 'I'd like to talk to Dr Skaid, please. Could you point me in the direction of his office, if he has one?'

'Of course, I'll take you there,' the darker man enthuses, almost colliding with Ethan in his eagerness to usher me along.

'Goodbye, Nova. I will come back soon, I promise. And I will find out about taking you outside.'

The huddle of feathers does not move, but there is a small sound which reaches my ears, a mournful bird-call, its sound undecipherably wild.

Daniel's office is small, smaller than my own, and has a transient sort of feel to it. The computer is Beaumont standard issue and all of the books on the shelf behind him are about theoretical physics. There's a potted yucca plant on the windowsill and a framed photograph of a gap-toothed boy. The only indication that this office belongs to Daniel is a small, patched blazer hanging on the back of a chair and the slight scent of petulant frustration.

'What is it now, D'accourt? I'm a little busy. One of the rat-boys has decided to go native and burrow a hole half-way through the lino. If you don't make it quick, the kids in the labs on floor two are going to get a nasty surprise on top of their heads...'

'Surely you have people who can handle such things,' I say, levelly, sitting on the chair facing the desk. Daniel sighs irritably and reaches over to the chair with his coat on it.

'Of course I do, I just want to make sure they're handling him properly… It's a delicate business, raising hybrids. The rodents in particular can be brittle. Their limbs don't take as well to elongation… Anyway, what do you want?'

'I saw Nova.'

'Ye-es, I saw you going in, remember?'

'She spoke a bit more.'

'Oh?'

'She said *no*, *leave*, an attempt at Ariana's name and I'm sure I heard a few swear words in a shriek.'

'Right,' he tries and fails to look uninterested. I see his right hand twitch as if itching to write the findings down.

'Your two research guys were in there too, they'll have recorded it all,' I say, enjoying his frown as I read his intentions so easily.

'And… I suppose you want to keep coming back?'

'Wouldn't you want me to? I seem to have made more progress in the last twenty-four hours than you have in a decade…'

'Yes,' he says, rolling his eyes. 'You're fantastic, Bella. Incredible. You're everything I could have asked for in a face-monkey to come and talk to my pet monster. Please keep doing so. There. Are we done here?'

'Be careful, Daniel… You don't want to get on my bad side.'

'What are you going to do, command me to go boil my head?'

'Don't tempt me.'

We glare at one another. He places his hands on the desk between us and gets to his feet.

'I want to take her outside,' I say, quickly.

'Out of the question. She's far too unpredictable.'

'We can use a leash if we must. At first. She needs to exercise her wings, she's getting nowhere in that cage in there... Surely your end goal is to have her actually be able to fly...'

'Yes...'

'Well how on earth do you expect to get her there if you won't let her practise?'

'Taming first. That's always been the goal. We tame her, bring her under control and then she can work on the flying thing. When we can be sure she'll actually, you know, fly back.'

'I believe that by giving her a little of the freedom of flight, you will exponentially speed up the *taming* process. And I believe I'm the one to do it...'

'Aren't you a little *busy?* What with your Youth Guard and your ambassadorship?'

I shrug. 'The Home Assistance launch has been scheduled for September. We decided that at the conference this morning. There's no hurry, now that the Care programme is underway. Gives us a chance to iron out any kinks which might arise... And, as we already discussed, my Youth Guard are almost launch-ready. They need less of me by the day...'

He narrows his eyes. 'GHAP was supposed to be a summer launch. You pushed it back on purpose. So you would have time for Nova... Didn't you?'

I shrug again. 'It's up to you. Let me know what you decide. Discuss it with Dr Lychen if you must. But I can only think it would be in your favour to have her progress as quickly as possible, if you intend to use her the way we all know you do.'

'And how is that?'

'As a spy, of course.'

He laughs contemptuously, but doesn't contradict me. I give him one of my sweetest smiles, even as everything else yearns to reach forward, palm the back of his stupid head and smash it smartly into the solid desk between us. Instead, I get to my feet gracefully, turn, and walk away.

27

May, 2019

Ralph wakes before the sun rises on Tuesday. He knows, from the moment his eyes open, that he will be having no more sleep. He pulls on a pair of clean jeans and dithers for a moment over his shirt, his memory snagging irresistibly on himself in a checked shirt, sleeves rolled up in the heat of an August evening, armpits clammy... the feel of Bella in his arms, her heart pounding all the way through her flimsy blouse to strike against his... Then he tells himself he's being ridiculous and grabs a plain clean white T-shirt. It's a little wrinkled because no one irons at The Manor, but at least it shouldn't get too sweaty if the warmth of the day overrules the weedy strength of the van's air conditioning.

For now, the corridors are dark and cool as Ralph steps quietly out of the bedroom he has occupied on and off since he was a baby. The walls are still the pale blue his mother painted them before he was born, though they are faded now and bear marks, dents, and discoloured squares from various posters and pictures. He took the more embarrassing ones down when he returned after the few years he spent living offsite and now there are just a few prints of lakes in Italy and a sketch of an atom one of the C children drew for him from memory.

Ralph paces gently down the corridor, stopping short when he sees the door to his father's room ajar. Shrugging, he continues downstairs. On the first floor landing he averts his eyes from the rooms where his not-really-daughter sleeps and his not-really-sister used to. The flagstones on the ground floor are freezing against his bare feet and he wishes he'd thought to put socks on. A soft glow comes from the door to his right where he and his family used to eat. The round table is still there and occasionally The Manor's inhabitants will all gather together when someone decides to cook a big pot of something simple for everyone, but it happens less and less now.

Ralph remembers the day Ramona left, the way she had reached for him – by then over a foot taller than her – and clasped him in an awkwardly bent-over hug. She had always loved him with a fierceness that was entirely disproportionate to the way he felt about her (as a constant warm, squashy presence who made really good food). 'Stay my love,' she had said, somewhat cryptically, before she had left, muttering something more in Spanish, the only parts of which he'd caught were something about a *diabla.* He'd never been quite sure what that was about, but he'd been able to make an educated guess over the years.

'Morning, Dad,' he says now, wearily, as he pushes the door to the dining room open. His father is sitting in the same large wooden chair in which he has always sat. A pot of coffee steams gently in front of him and there are two cups, Ralph notices with a little surprise. Doddery and predictable as he's become, his father still occasionally catches Ralph off guard with his little insights.

'I had a feeling you'd be up early today,' Dr Blake smiles soberly over the top of his glasses. His hair is all white now but only slightly thinner than it was a decade ago when he'd dismissed the last of The Manor's household staff and opened the doors to its many lodgers.

'So you know what today is?' Ralph draws out one of the chairs and sits heavily. He's about an eighth round the table from his father. Not so close to be awkward but not so far that they have no choice but to stare at one another.

'Yes,' Dr Blake replies, simply, pouring Ralph a cup of coffee and passing it across the table. When Ramona lived here it was all milk jugs and matching sugar bowls with small, silver spoons, but now the mugs don't match and the supermarket bottle of milk has been placed in the centre of the table, sweating slightly as the central heating slowly churns into the room from the newly lit boiler.

'So Felix told you… or…?' Ralph pours milk into his coffee until it swirls from the shade of Bella's hair to something closer to Ariana's. *Tawny, like her father's.*

'Yes. She is taking a few vials of Serum X. She's going to use it on Ethan.'

'Oh. She's changed her mind, then?' Ralph's thoughts trundle guiltily over the work he's been neglecting.

'She asked me to go over the research with her the other day and seems to think it's worth a try. Personally, I would have liked another few months working on it before applying to a Guard person, let alone Ethan, but, well… It should be safe enough for him. And it should at the very least give him a heightened awareness of memory and consciousness, though I'm not sure it will have the full effects she desires…' He shakes his head sadly at his coffee, as if it had deeply disappointed him.

'I'm sorry, Dad. I should have been around more to help these last few days… I've been… Well, distracted.'

'It's quite alright,' Dr Blake says quietly. Ralph avoids his gaze, feeling like a teenager caught with a packet of cigarettes they have no idea how to smoke.

'It's not really, though. I could have been helping you, doing something useful instead of moping about like an idiot, feeling sorry for myself... God, I feel so bloody useless all the time... Everyone else seems to be doing something meaningful. Felix hacking the computer systems, Dom's getting all that old ARC equipment online, he said he thinks he's even fixed your old scanner. Tess is helping him out... They've all taken on extra contracting work to help pay for this place. Even Ariana is getting on with it, taking buses to town on her own, helping Fee with the blooming codes. Meanwhile I haven't finished a piece of freelance work in weeks, the guys at the lab in Manchester are getting on my back...'

'Ralph... I don't want to sound patronising, but I do understand a bit of what you're going through... When your mother passed away... I knew it was going to happen, I thought I'd prepared myself for it. I'd even begun writing her eulogy in my head, months before... But it was afterwards that I hadn't factored in. The stretch of aching loneliness. The endless chasm where she was supposed to be. We are meant to love people, you and I. And when those people aren't there anymore, we don't work as well. We're like half-creatures, wandering the world only half-awake, half-functioning... I got to spend thirty good years with the woman I loved. You... You and Bella were ripped apart just at the moment when you had begun to discover one another. And again, last year... It's no wonder you can't think clearly...'

'It's not just that, though. Bella and I haven't been together for years... I managed perfectly well without her for over a decade...'

'Until you saw her again last autumn... Until you met

your daughter.'

'*Her* daughter.' He says it before he thinks and glances up guiltily to see if the slip has registered with Dr Blake. The old man twitches his eyebrows, but his eyes beneath them aren't shocked as Ralph's words sink into him. They're just... sad.

'Ah,' he says, quietly, as if Ralph has just completed a puzzle he's been agonising over for years but hadn't thought to ask for help with.

'You knew?' Ralph is surprised that he's not angry. Possibly the sadness of the old man is just too deep for him to muster anything but pity. Possibly he's just beyond feeling shocked anymore, about anything.

'I suspected. She... told me as much... in her way. When we saw one another last year, when I performed those tests. Bella was so... *angry* with me. Even after all that time. She said I didn't protect her or something like that. It got me thinking. Then when I met Ariana... She has a way of looking, sometimes. A cold, ruthless sort of logic that doesn't come from Bella.'

'That's what Fee said. But I don't know,' Ralph says, 'Bella's pretty ruthless when she wants to be.'

'But she's not cold. She thinks she is, that's the face she chooses to present to the world. Deep down though, the part of her which steers her heart is not cold at all. But with Ariana, what I've noticed more and more is this look she gets, when she focuses on something she wants... It's sort of black. Blank. There's a struggle there, too. She's a good girl, I know she is... except... sometimes I *don't* know. I fear for her. I really, really do. There's something growing in her that's going beyond us. Some sort of darkness, a confidence... the more it emerges, the more she seems to just... disappear. It's like she can compartmentalise her own emotions when they get inconvenient...'

'Bloody hell Dad. This is a bit much for six am, isn't it? I just thought... I just thought she was a bit of a moody teenager who doesn't like me much.'

'Well. Perhaps I'm simply a paranoid old fool and you're right.'

They lapse into silence, both drinking their coffee with dark thoughts swirling round their heads.

'What's your plan today, then? Show up, leave Ethan to Felix and confront Bella?'

'God. I don't know.'

'You're angry with her.'

'I'm angry with *him*. That *animal* who did this to her.'

'Yes. But you're angry with her too.'

'Stop it.'

'Ralph.'

'OK, fine. Whatever. I'm angry with her for not telling me. I've always been angry with her for that. I could have helped... I could have... Well, I don't know if I could have stopped him, but I could have helped her with Ariana. I would still have done it all, even knowing she wasn't mine. I'd have done it for her...'

'For Bella.'

'Well... yeah. Wouldn't you, if it was Mamma?'

'Yes.'

'Well, there you go then. It's ridiculous, really. It's been fourteen years – pretty much my entire twenties – and no one else has even come close.'

'I understand.'

'Well I wish you wouldn't. Quite frankly, the only thing sadder than loving the same absent woman for half your life is everyone else including your dad bloody knowing about it.'

Dr Blake sighs heavily, 'There is always some madness in love. But there is also always some reason in madness.'

Ralph rolls his eyes. 'Thanks for that.'

'Ralph...'

'Yeah, yeah, I know. Go easy. I'm not going to scare her off... I'm not going to go all wounded neanderthal.'

'I was going to say, don't lose sight of what you're there to do. Ethan is an unknown quantity; Felix needs you to be on alert...'

'Sure, I know...'

'Serum X is by no means a sure thing. She might not even get it into him without Bella's co-operation.'

'Bella suggested the meeting. She said she was trying to help Ethan.'

'Yes, but she has been away for a long time. With Lychen. Who knows what sort of toll that's taken on her mentally.'

'I thought you were the one saying she's not so bad underneath it all?'

'I said she's not cold. I don't mean she's good. I don't have the right to make any sort of claim for her decisions any more...' Dr Blake sighs again, sadly, and gets to his feet. He looks at Ralph for a while, long enough for Ralph to start to feel uncomfortable all over again.

'She still needs us, Ralph.'

'Who, Bella?'

'Her too. But I mean Ariana. She is under our care for a reason... I think it is vital that she doesn't learn the truth about her true father... At least not yet. I think Bella will agree.'

'Well. I guess I'll find out,' Ralph mutters, keeping his eyes down.

'Yes. And now, if you'll excuse me, I'm going to do

some final checks on the serum and ensure there are enough syringes in the pack for Felix. Ralph,' he turns, mid-shuffle towards the door.

'Yeah.'

'You'll do the right thing. I trust you.'

'Right. Thanks, Dad.'

Dr Blake makes his way round to the door. His movements are slow and cushioned in age, his stoop dwarfing his once tall frame. The time it takes him to reach the corridor is more than enough for a light-footed teenager to leap nimbly from the door, back up the stairs to the first-floor landing and into the furthest room on the right. Even though her heart is hammering so hard she cannot hear anything else.

28

May, 2019

The drive to London begins tensely, Ralph tight-jawed as he slots his seat belt into place in the passenger seat of the van. Felix, on the other hand, feels better than she has for months. Her hair – freshly dyed an ashy blonde, Ethan's favourite shade on her – has been washed and left to curl naturally close to her head. She wears some make-up, mostly on her eyes in a nod to her old gothic style, and is dressed in a dark purple, swirly-patterned top, leather jeans and combat boots. The jeans are old and rather too tight for the length of time she will be sitting in a vehicle, but they suit her nonetheless. Even Ralph blinks through his morose demeanour at her.

'You look... Wow.'

'What, Ral?' Felix snaps, betraying the steady buzz of nervousness hovering just beneath her good mood. 'I look what? Nice? Repulsive? Discombobulating?'

'You look young, I was going to say. I mean, not weirdly. But like you when you were younger... All you need is a bit of purple lipstick and spiky pink hair...'

'Yes, well. I'm trying to jog his memory in a *good* way. Some things are better left forgotten.'

'Yeah,' Ralph shoulders back into silence and Felix switches on the radio. She feels her spirits lift further as they crawl out of the driveway, and the looming mismatched architecture of The Manor is shrunken and boxed into the rear-view mirror.

'Did you see Ariana before we left?' she asks as they begin to pick up speed. Ralph shifts as if he is uncomfortable.

'No... I think she was still asleep.'

'Oh. I thought I heard her moving around in her room...'

Ralph shrugs and looks out of the window as they round a corner and make their way alongside a lake. The sun crests the peaks of tiny waves with sharp flecks of gold.

'Are you going to talk to her about... well, you know... the truth?'

Ralph sighs and stays silent for such a long time that they're miles past the lake and halfway down a narrow stone wall-lined road between two sheep-laden mountains before he answers.

'I don't know if I should, really. I mean, part of me thinks she deserves to hear the truth and that every day I don't tell her I'm lying to her... My dad thinks I shouldn't tell her, but he's the one that used to parrot some old saying at me when I was a kid. Something about how if you lie to me, I'll never be able to believe you again. I don't want her to think she can't trust me... I might not be her biological dad but she needs people she can rely on. Look at her real parents.'

'Well, quite.'

'And then, on the other hand I think, who the hell am I to tell her the truth? It's nothing to do with me, really. It's not my place to tell her, is it?'

'I prefer the first answer, less of a cop out.'

'Yes well, it's easy to have lofty ideas of right and wrong when you're speeding miles away from the problem. That reminds me, you checked the boot this time?'

Felix throws a wide-eyed look of alarm into the back of the van before relaxing her face.

'Course I bloody did. Nothing back there but Eth's old painting gear and about ten vials of Serum X.'

They lapse back into a comfortable silence, the radio buzzing in and out of signal. Ralph dozes off as they bump and nudge their way out of the Lake District's winding roads and onto the faster, wider A-roads leading eastwards. He wakes with a hollow sense of sickly anticipation as they join the M25. Felix chucks him a service station baguette as his stomach growls.

'There you go, figured you'd be hungry when you finally woke up.'

'Cheers. Did I sleep through a stop?'

'Yep. You must have needed it.'

'Yeah… I haven't really been sleeping too well recently… Since we talked to Bella, really.'

'I know. I've heard you pacing.'

He chews in silence for a while as they buzz through North London traffic.

'I just keep thinking about what she said… about the way she has to live now, the things that are expected of her, even if she doesn't want to do them,' he swallows bulkily.

'Mmm?'

'You don't think… Her and Lychen…'

'God, Ral. Can we not? I'm having enough trouble keeping my lunch down as it is.'

'Yeah… sorry. I'm nervous too.'

He reaches for the radio and tunes into a local station, trying to force the hollow, cheerful voices to permeate the ache in his chest. It's another hour before Felix is able to find an on-street parking space just a few roads away from the exhibition centre. It's not yet quarter to five, but Ralph's muscles twitch with anticipation as he stretches them out while Felix climbs into the back of the van. She passes him two vials and capped syringes for his pockets and places the rest into a small backpack.

Ralph cups his hands around the vials as they walk quickly towards the meeting place. Felix's stride is half his but she matches his pace easily and he's reminded of a time not so long ago when they strode together along a wind-swept cliff in search of Bella… The setting couldn't be more different he thinks, as he glances at the crowds of people hurrying to and fro along the busy road, the traffic a constant noise on his left, shops and cafes thronging with music, voices, and hundreds of fragments of lives completely alien to his own. How did we get here again, he wonders, as they hurry along, tight-lipped, looking for pieces of a puzzle containing the very same people it had almost a year ago?

'There's the centre, you can see the roof sticking up…' Felix points out, a little breathlessly.

'What was the name of the street she said, Marlow?'

'Marley. There it is, just behind that Pret.'

They wait for a crowd of foreign tourists to pass by before ducking, Felix first, around the edge of the dark, narrow little street. It's a cut-through to the main road containing the exhibition centre, too narrow for vehicles, too dark for shops. The ground is damp and cobbled and though there are several doors set along both brick walls lining the alley, there is an air of neglect and forgotten-ness about the place, along with a palpable scent of bins. At first glance it appears deserted, but as Ralph blinks in the sudden gloom, a large shape emerges from a doorway halfway down. A thick-armed, short-haired shape which is unmistakable, even to him...

'Ethan!' Felix takes three quick paces towards him before catching herself and slowing as a second, smaller but equally distinctive silhouette comes into view. Ralph keeps his pace deliberately measured as they approach. Ethan wears the same blank expression as the other Guard Ralph has come across, and he stands the same way – too tense to be normal, feet planted solidly, hands waiting by his sides. He doesn't look at Ralph or Felix as they come closer.

'Ralph, Felix,' Bella says in greeting. Her voice is the same as ever but as Ralph draws closer, he sees the changes in her instantly. She is dressed immaculately in a neat blue blazer and tailored skirt beneath, her heels high and unblemished by the grime of her surroundings. But her body beneath the neat trim seems smaller, more fragile than he remembers. Her face, too, appears more angular, her cheekbones more pronounced, more elfin. There is a new darkness, a weariness to her green eyes, though they pierce into him as sharply as ever. The overall effect only makes her more beautiful, he thinks, though it is a different kind of beauty, one that speaks of delicate fragility. Like the burst of brightness to a flame before it is pinched away. Or the death-flare of a supernova.

'Bella,' Felix mutters. 'Shall we skip the niceties? You know you look great, we look a shambles, yadda yadda. Hello, Ethan,' her voice curves from brittle disdain into something gentler, but more guarded as she stares at her husband. Bella gives a strange little twitch of her head and Ethan relaxes a small bit, glancing down at Felix. His expression doesn't really change, there is no sudden dawning of recognition, but his eyebrows move a millimetre closer together in the shadow of a frown.

'Hey you,' Felix breathes.

'I told you it was different with him,' Bella says, a little smugly. 'He's beginning to come back. Just a little. I noticed it the other week when I was talking about missing Ariana. Something about the conversation triggered a response – only tiny, nothing anyone unconnected would notice – but it was a way in. We have to be careful, though. Any indication that he's different and he'll be taken away. I don't know what they'll do to him.'

'Let me talk to him, on our own,' Felix says, softly, eyes still on her stoic husband.

'Alright, but just to talk… Ethan, go with Felix please. Let her talk with you.'

Ralph watches the consternation of the order cross Felix's face, but she doesn't say anything. Instead, she reaches an uncertain hand for Ethan's. He lets her lead him a few paces along the alleyway.

'She's got a serum she wants to use on him,' Ralph says quickly, his eyes dancing uncertainly over the shape of Felix, dwarfed by her husband, his father's reminder to protect her echoing in his head. 'Dad and I… mostly Dad, really… we developed it. It's not fully ready yet but we know enough to think it might help… bring him out a bit. We developed it in part from medications used on dementia patients…'

'Ethan will take steps to prevent himself being injured in any way,' Bella says, simply.

'Right,' Ralph turns almost reluctantly back to her. Her eyes. He sighs, realising his arms are wrapped around himself protectively. He loosens them and slides his hands into his jeans pockets.

'How is she?'

'Ariana? She's fine. Making friends, going to sleepovers, taking buses on her own...'

'From The Manor? Surely you don't mean the stop near Pickerton—'

'It's only twenty minutes away...'

'A lot can happen in twenty minutes, Ralph!'

'On a middle-of-nowhere country road in Cumbria?'

'She was abducted from a middle-of-nowhere country road in Cornwall just last year!'

'Yeah, by Lychen, to get to you... He doesn't need her now, does he? He wouldn't need to abduct her, anyway. If he knew who she really was, he'd just come and take her. None of us could stop him. Not even you.'

He hates the creep of bitterness in his voice. Scowling, he kicks a loose stone along the dirty cobbles beneath their feet. When he looks up, Bella is wearing a strange expression, he can tell she is trying to keep her usual impassive mask on, but it's like the strength of the turmoil beneath it is too great this time to be hidden.

'So Felix told you,' she says, quietly, no hint of accusation. No hint of anything.

'She had to, she knew I wouldn't be able to hang on till today to find out, not when you guys gave three-quarters of it away when I was sitting right there.'

'Right... It... I didn't— It wasn't my choice. What happened. I didn't betray you—'

'No, you just let me believe I had a daughter when I didn't. Don't.'

'Because I wanted her to be yours, Ralph. Don't you understand that?'

'I understand that you didn't want her to be his. And that I was the only other logical option.'

'That's what you think?' She turns away, her arms crossing in front of her narrow body. Her hair falls in front of her face as she looks down. He's only seen her like this once before; the night she ran to him, the first time they discovered one another. His hands remove themselves from his pockets, aching for her, aching to bring her into him, wrap himself around her as he had done then.

'Anyway, it doesn't matter,' she says, recovering, looking up once again and straight into him with a hardness which freezes his arms back to his sides. 'It's in the past. All that matters is that Lychen does not find out the truth. And neither does Ariana.'

'You think he'll want her?'

'I'm not willing to find out.'

They fall silent. Ralph glances behind him at Felix and Ethan. He's still standing rigidly and though Ralph isn't close enough to hear him clearly, his ears register the mechanical enunciation in answer to Felix's range of questions, her voice undulating like a river in comparison.

'What'll happen, if she breaks through to him? If she brings him back?'

'If she truly does, then that won't be up to me anymore. But I don't think she will. Not entirely. Our particular Guard bond is very deep… He knows things even I didn't realise… It will be extremely hard to break it entirely… It was designed that way so Lychen can keep tabs on my physical health, make sure the curse of Project A isn't creeping into me…'

'Ah. Yes, I did wonder why you hadn't dropped in on us or summoned Dad up to the Beaumont to do more tests.'

'I didn't realise myself until quite recently. It doesn't surprise me, though. Lychen's always had a thing about control. Over everything...'

'That's what the rollout of the entire Guard Assistance Programme is, isn't it? A Guard in every household, answerable ultimately to him.'

Bella doesn't reply, just blinks slowly in a measured way. Behind them, Felix's voice pitches higher in frustration. He glances behind them once again. Felix has a syringe in her hand, the other resting on Ethan's arm. She seems to be pleading with him. He answers in a monotonous, calm tone.

'I have a plan,' Bella says, so quietly that Ralph isn't sure she said it all. He tears his eyes back to her. She is standing slightly closer, hands on her elbows, watching the couple behind him.

'What do you mean? What plan?'

'Against Lychen. And Daniel. All of them... I'm working on something. My own project. I don't know how I'm going to use it yet... but it's something. *They're* something. Not a lot, and probably not able to do too much damage overall... But it might just be a way out for me. And if that serum works, it could mean everything... Let her,' she says the last two words loudly, so Ethan can hear. Ralph turns back in time to see the large man hold his arm out without pause. Felix throws Bella a look of frustrated contempt before plunging the syringe into her husband's deltoid.

'It will take a few minutes,' Ralph says, turning back to see Bella glancing at her mobile phone. She swipes several notifications away before he can glimpse any names.

'We need to leave as soon as possible. Questions will be raised if I'm not back at the facility by six-thirty. I have instructed my Guard driver to come and find me if I'm not in view at quarter to.'

'Beast, you don't have to—'

'I do. I need to go back. If we want to bring him down, if we want to bring an end to all of this and give Ariana a proper chance at a life without the fear of him looming over her... I need to be at the Beaumont. I have a plan.' She stares at him and this time he can't stop himself. He reaches for her and she's there in his arms, just as she was fourteen years ago, body vibrant against his, a puzzle piece neatly nocked in its partner's clasp.

'I thought—'

'I know what you thought.'

'Beast. I'm sorry.'

'I know. So am I. But it doesn't matter now...'

'It *does* matter. Don't you see? If I let you go now, I'm *giving* you to him all over again! Do you think I can live with that, knowing what he did, what he's probably still doing...'

'It's not your choice to make,' she pulls back from him and steps away, anger wiring dangerously into her eyes. 'What are you going to do, throw me over your shoulder and carry me back to the Lake District? I'm not some useless *doll*...'

'Why're you so angry?'

'Because I don't *want* you to save me. I don't need you to, I am more than capable of handling Lychen. I just want you to do what—'

'Do what you say? What, like everyone else? Is that all I am, some minion to command? Is that why you're really with him, because he isn't?' The words spit angrily and he knows even as they come that they're born of bitterness, of rejection and hurt and he's shamed, but fury is easier. Bella's eyes spit equal rage back at him and she raises her hands as if she's about to shove him, but then her attention is caught by something behind them. Her face transforms into wonder. He turns.

Felix and Ethan are standing in the strangest embrace he's ever seen. She has her arms around him and though his arms remain flatly by his sides, his rigid stance has gone and he's arched around her, his head resting neatly on top of hers. Ralph turns back to Bella in time to see satisfaction tussling with worry, fear and something echoingly empty that reminds him of himself, before she notices him looking and paints herself blank once again.

'It's twenty to six,' she says, quietly.

'Give them a few more minutes, for pity's sake...'

'Pity is a dangerous thing to time. Ethan!'

He straightens immediately, detaches Felix from around him and turns, his face clearing as he walks to Bella.

'Hey!' Felix chases him, attempting to grab him by the arm. He shakes her off.

'I'm going back to the Beaumont now,' Bella says quietly to the three faces in front of her. 'I won't be able to meet you again for a while. I have delayed the roll out of the latest Guard Assistance project and paused my ambassador role for the time being... I need to work more closely at the Beaumont.'

'Because of Nova?'

'Yes, partially. I cannot leave there without raising suspicion. I will always answer the phone if you need me...'

'Are your calls secure?'

'Yes. As far as they can be. Lychen knows I stay in touch for Ariana's sake. He trusts that Ethan will report anything untoward.'

'Ethan, come back with us,' Felix reaches for Ethan's hands. He looks at her and his face resembles its old self more than at any moment Ralph's seen it so far. 'Please. It's not safe for you there anymore. If Lychen finds out—'

'Bella will protect me,' he says, his voice still mostly

flat, though with tiny familiar flecks around the edges. Catching them is like trying to taste miniscule grains of salt in a pint of water.

'Bella, *please*,' Felix turns to Bella, tears streaming down her face. Ralph can't look, he stares at Ethan instead. His face is twitching between dismay and nothingness. Bella stares back at Felix. Her face is empty. Ralph knows she's already left the conversation, that her focus has moved on.

'It's up to you, Ethan,' Bella turns to the large man by her side. 'If you want to go with Felix, you can. I will say that I got tired of you, that you reminded me too much of my old life, so I sent you back to Futura. Daniel's not there to tell tales and Lychen will not bother following it up, he will be relieved to know that I'm severing emotional ties.'

Ethan looks from her to Felix, who has given up trying to swipe the tears off of her face and is simply staring, awash and blotchy. Ralph can't remember the last time he saw her cry.

'Please.'

'Bella needs me,' he says, quietly, measuredly.

'Ethan, *I* need you!'

'She needs me more. She has no one else.'

The two of them turn and walk away with short, calculated strides, and Ralph moves to catch Felix just as she collapses, her wail the sound of pure, sonorous agony.

29

Autumn, 2013

'Mama! Mummeeeee!'

I groaned as I rolled over in bed. The digital alarm clock threw the time – 04.12 – in glaring red letters. I blinked at the grinning face of my daughter beaming from the photograph next to the numbers, my own face a smooth picture of encapsulated happiness. I wondered, for a second, whether I'd imagined the cry. Then:

'Mummeeeee!'

I slid out of bed and padded quickly across my bedroom floor. I liked having my own room again after so long sharing. To an outsider it might have appeared that I'd not done much to put my stamp on the clear fresh white walls and cheap veneered furniture, but the tell-tale signs were there all the same, in the soft white rug beneath my bare feet, the tiny grooves on the en-suite bathroom door which only I would ever know for marks of the changing height of a small girl. The scent of sandalwood and cedar which came from the small white candles on the windowsill. The wooden shutters with which I'd replaced the plastic our first week here.

'What's up, little darling?' I gentled my voice over the spasm of frustration as I pushed Ariana's door open. Awash in vivid purple, her room was as different to mine as a room could be. Her simple wooden single bed was dwarfed by every fluffy stuffed toy she'd ever owned, the walls were covered in posters of Disney princesses – Rapunzel was the latest favourite – and the wardrobe door hung open, mountains of clothes spilling out where she'd been searching so desperately for her favourite pink pyjamas the previous evening. Ariana herself sat up in bed, blinking dazedly through a wash of tears, hair tumbling at all angles, small body shivering with sobs.

'I had a… had a… night*maaaaare*!' She wailed as I moved two stuffed penguins and a sheep to sit on her bed. She threw herself at me, all bony ribcage and elbows.

'Shh, it's OK… Mama's here…' I pulled as much of her as I could extricate from the tight wad of duvet and synthetic fur onto my lap, marvelling as I so often did at the sheer volume of her limby body, once so tiny I had cupped it in one arm against my shoulder.

'It was the man… the one you told me about… he was chasing me!'

'Shh! It's OK, no one's going to get you here…' I smoothed her warm, tangled mass of hair away from her forehead. Her eyes were already beginning to droop with tiredness. I held her for a few more minutes.

'But Mama, you said that he's looking for us…'

'Yes…'

'So what if he comes and looks here?'

'He won't… All I meant is that we have to be careful, Ri-ri. We don't let other people take photos of us, we only take our own… We don't go to strange places where people might ask questions… And we act normally.'

'And you have yellow hair and your name is Elodie?'

'And I have yellow hair and my name is Elodie.'

'Why don't I get a new name too?'

'Because you're my super lucky little Ariana-ri and the

The Child Left in the Dark

bad man doesn't know your name. OK?'

'OK,' her body was fully relaxed against mine by then and I slowly lowered her back onto her pillows, reaching under the duvet until my hand closed around a worn, familiar mat of fur. Her eyes glittered under the heavy sweep of lashes as I pulled Doggy out and tucked him in next to her.

'Try and go back to sleep now, little darling.'

'OK...' She turned and curled around Doggy, sending a small shower of teddies into a pile of books, which slumped across the floor. I sighed, resolving to clear out some of the lesser used toys.

'Mama?'

'Yes,' it was harder this time to keep the clench out of my teeth. My bed was paces away. I had a long day in the lab stretching ahead of me, a six am start.

'Do I still have to go to school tomorrow?'

'Yes, sweetheart. Now, *please*, go to sleep!' I turned back to her and met her eyes briefly. Her lids fluttered downwards instantly and she was lost to unconsciousness before the question had left her small round-cheeked face.

The afternoon was muggily warm and my head ached under my hairband. It felt like a restrictive band tightening around my forehead but I didn't dare remove it. My hair was due its monthly treatment and the fingers of brown roots were too long to be acceptable for anyone else to see. I leant my head back against the fuzz of the bus seat and shut my eyes for a few minutes, going through the internal check-list. *Dye hair. Sort out old toys. Purchase new hairband.* The bus slowed and let on a small stream of secondary school pupils. I watched them out of the corner of my eye as they laughed and stumbled their way awkwardly to the back seats, aware only of themselves, themselves, and themselves. *Buy a car.* I'd been trying to resist dipping into the trust fund Marc still paid into regularly, but my eyes couldn't help but snag on the other parents in their sleek SUVs, kids buckled firmly behind tinted windows. It wasn't as if buying a nice BMW was going to do anything to blow my cover, after all.

I had been happily employed at Flintworth University for just over three years now, starting as a laboratory assistant and rising to the ranks of academic researcher as I'd finished my PhD. I had veered as far as possible from the nature of my old work at the ARC without leaving the field of genetics and was now part of a small team researching common mutations. My colleagues melded well enough with young, shy Elodie Guerre who spoke with a throaty French accent and had a thing for old-school hairbands and hats. I'd invented a vague backstory about a dependent, elderly relative who needed my help in the evenings and they, for the most part, did not try too hard to make me come out with them on Friday nights. In return, I sifted through the eye-rovers and the hand-wanderers to those who could grant me the biggest advantages – the professors who could arrange the schedule so I could leave by three pm and work the extra hours from home – and I did what I needed to do to get by, stay hidden, fly under the radar.

The bus pulled up outside the familiar red-bricked little school. The Ofsted rating wasn't the best in the area, but at seven Ariana could read, write and boss around a small group of girls she'd known since reception, it was located just half a mile from the flat, and on one of the bus routes from the university. Ariana attended both the morning and after school clubs, which just about covered my journey to and from. Getting to my feet, I adjusted my hairband slightly and stepped lightly along the aisle and off the bus, smiling Elodie's shy little thank you to the driver as I went.

'Hello, Ri, how was your day?' I asked lightly, as Ariana barrelled out of the Year Three classroom. She threw her coat towards me and I caught it by the tips of my fingers before it landed in a puddle.

'It was just... *crap!*'

I caught the eye of one of the dads standing nearby and rolled my eyes, struggling against a sudden, alarming urge to swipe a hand neatly across the top of my daughter's head. Ariana's eyes were dark and shadowed with her early morning waking as she glared up at me. I offered my hand and, slowly, mutinously, she took it. I waited until we had reached the path leading around the edge of the recreation ground next to the school, then I spoke, allowing enough of my seething anger to creep into my voice to warn her.

'I don't want you saying that word. Especially not at school.'

'Why? You use it all the time. Like when you couldn't open that jar yesterday or when you're working on your computer.'

'Well, I'm a grown up. I'm allowed.'

Ariana muttered something under her breath. I sniffed slowly, allowing the sweet scent of pine needles and warm, dying summer air to calm my nerves a little. My head continued to pound under its band. I looked down and met her eyes, large and burning with a level of rage which surprised me.

'What's the matter? What happened?'

'Nothing.'

'Come on, Ri. If you tell me... I might be able to help.'

'You won't.'

'Oh, OK then.'

We continued walking, her hand a limp little stone in mine.

'You know, I was thinking about that ice cream we bought the other day. The cookies and cream one. I thought maybe we could have some later... watch your *Tangled* DVD... But if you've got the grumps, maybe it wouldn't be such a good plan...'

I kept my eyes straight ahead, focusing on the green-fingered pine trees lining the large open space. Dogs bounded off the lead, and the sound of kids running and kicking balls to one another filtered around the edges of my concentration. Out of the corner of my eye, Ariana peered up at me. I glanced down at her and very determinedly didn't smile as her anger battled with wistful hope.

'Really? Can we have popcorn with it too? And can I stay up late?'

'Only if you tell me what's bothering you...'

She sighed at the path in front of us. 'It's Lucy. She's having a unicorn disco party for her birthday but she said I'm not allowed to come because it's a sleepover.'

'Oh.'

'Why can't I go, Mum? It's just Lucy's house. It's not far away and she doesn't know any bad mens... No one is going to take photos of me...'

'Are you sure about that? I know Lucy's mum. She posts a *lot* of photos on her Facebook page...'

'Well, just tell her not to. Can I go, please? Please?'

'I'll think about it.'

She sighed and looked down, knowing that my answer was as good as she was going to get for the moment. Then she gave my hand a little tug and a swing and looked up, her face shining once again.

'Can we have pizza, too?'

It was only later, once we were home and Ariana was poring over her maths workbook at the dining room table while I slid the pizza onto a baking tray, keeping one eye on the open work laptop on the kitchen counter, that I realised I still had my hairband on. That my headache had completely vanished. I glanced at Ariana, swinging her feet under the table as her small tongue poked out of her mouth, eyes focused on some unknown thing as she counted in her head. Shrugging, I turned back to the oven and set the timer.

30

May, 2019

Darkness... Blankness... Animal...

The thoughts swirl angrily around Ariana's head as she paces up and down the small room, a half-packed bag by the foot of her bed. Every few minutes she stops and chucks another pair of socks or a jumper into the bag. Then the darkness overcomes her again and she can't concentrate on anything but movement, her fists clenching, her teeth grinding into one another. She feels as if her entire being is swathed in a large, amorphous fog of fire colours, undulating around her as she moves spikily from the window to the door and back again. Slowly, though, it begins to lift and she brings herself back. Packing. That's what she's doing, though the idea of leaving this place has only come to her half-formed. She sits on the bed, the swirls settling around her. Ralph is not her dad. Her mother lied to her again. Who is her dad? *There's a coldness that doesn't come from Bella... I want to kill that animal for doing this to her.*

Of course. Lychen. The name doesn't resonate with any shock, which tells Ariana that her subconscious must have got there first. Possibly while she was still crouched on the freezing flagstones downstairs. *Doing this to her.* She is the *this*. She is the reason Ralph wants to kill Lychen. She is the thing that ruined Bella. Ariana clenches her fists and thinks about the man who she has only met once. His dark, unknowable eyes. The way he seemed to pull her like a fish on a line across the busy cafeteria at Graysons. The utter unyielding command of him... so like her mother's, but so much colder. Dr Blake had been right about that. Her mother's power is not cold. But maybe her own can be.

Ariana shuts her eyes and tries to think clearly. She takes a long, shuddery breath. What does she know? She is powerful. She is special. She is bad. Well, at least she doesn't have to worry about stuff, if that's the case. Her mother has given up on her. Her fake father doesn't want to know – his behaviour towards her over the last few days tells her that, at least. She'd thought he was just nervous about seeing Bella again... Clearly not. This was why he hadn't cared about her taking the bus the other day, when she'd been so sure he was going to say no... Clearly he doesn't give a damn anymore... Well, that's good because neither does she.

Ariana gets to her feet and then stops. It's Tuesday. She could just throw on her jeans, pick up this bag and turn right instead of left at the end of the driveway, miss the school bus and catch the other one instead... But then what? Then calls would come, Dr Blake would worry, he'd call Ralph, he might even call Bella... Felix would use some sort of tracing thing to track her down by her phone... And she'd be collected, sat down and talked at by all of them, then they'd put her back here, ban her from getting the bus on her own, probably take away a few privileges as punishment, and her life would carry on in its dull little circle in this dusty old forgotten place and her mother and father would carry on their dazzling, pioneering lives in London. No. That wouldn't do.

Her mother and father. It's a strange idea, Ariana

muses as she reaches for her school shirt and shrugs it on. When she was little, she had daydreamed about her real father coming to find them in their sad little flat in Flintworth, sweeping her up into his arms and twirling her onto his shoulders. She had fantasized about him kissing her mother like they did in cheesy films, saying that he was so sorry he had been away for so long but he had been terribly busy buying the whole of Disneyland for them to live in... And when they'd got there it hadn't just been Minnie Mouse and Cinderella waiting to greet them, there had been a whole crowd of happy, twinkly-eyed grandparents, funky-dressing aunts and cool uncles and torrents of cousins who all wanted to play just with her...

When she'd got a bit older her fantasy father had morphed again into a James Bond-esque secret agent who'd found a way of tracing her through her phone, sending her secret messages only she could decipher... He'd pick her up from school in his Aston Martin and whisk her away to Paris or Rome... Then Conan68 had cropped up. No wonder she'd been so gullible. She still feels a gulp of shame when she thinks of all those silly Twitter messages. Pictures Tess reading them out loud to the rest of the people at Beaumont, laughter loud and cruel from her wide red-lipsticked mouth.

Ariana steps lightly across the hallway and down the stairs, her school bag on her back. She's running a little late, but no one has noticed. Felix is the only one around here with a vague idea of her schedule, though her dad (*fake* dad) used to make a bit of an effort in the early days, when she was still new at school and he'd drive her there. Before they'd arranged for one of the minibuses to make a stop at the end of The Manor driveway. It hadn't taken long for the novelty of having a daughter to wear off, she muses now, opening the door she had lingered behind earlier. It was probably a relief for Ralph, really. Finding out he didn't have to force himself to like her. Ariana crosses to a cupboard and grabs a couple of cereal bars and a carton of juice. Her stomach feels too weird to eat yet, but she knows she'll be hungry later. She still hasn't decided what she's going to do. Her insides feel torn. Part of her wants to scream and cry and do all sorts of crazy, embarrassing things that would make her mum roll her eyes. Part of her is all trembly and sharp, almost excited but in a sicky uncertain way... She can go. She *could* go anywhere... She has power. And then there's another part of her, the strange, quiet new part which just feels... nothing.

'Oh!' The voice behind her hitches with nervous surprise. She knows it's Tess before she turns and feels a savage satisfaction for making her jump.

'I thought... I thought you'd have left for school by now,' Tess mumbles, looking down and biting her lip.

'I'm just going now.' She moves towards her and Tess steps quickly out of the way.

'What happened to that lipstick you used to wear?' Ariana says as she draws level. They are pretty much the same height now, especially with Ariana wearing the two-inch heeled Mary-Janes she'd found last week in a hallway cupboard (which had turned out to be a second wardrobe of her mother's). Tess shrugs, trying to hold Ariana's eye and failing.

'I dunno... doesn't seem much point.'

'No. I guess not. Dom's not really the type to be fussed about that is he? And he's the only one who really matters... to you, I mean. Here. Isn't he?'

'Huh?'

'Well... I mean, he's the only reason you're still here,

isn't he?'

'I'm still here because it's not safe—'

'Oh, right, yeah… it's not safe because you told the big bad Blakes all the big bad secrets you knew about the big bad Beaumont place to make up for the whole kidnapping me thing… Do you really think anyone gives a toss? You're probably not even on their radar anymore. I doubt Lychen remembers your name. My mum wouldn't. It's sad, really. At least when you were one of them you had a purpose… Now you're just some sad old cow who wanders around here in her lame boyfriend's shirts and pretends to fiddle about with machines and stuff while everyone feels sorry for her because she used to—'

'Ow!' Tess frowns and holds her chest. Ariana thinks for a moment that she's being sarcastic, pretending that her bitter words have wounded her. But her face doesn't relax into a grin. It turns a sickly custard shade beneath her blonde hair. Ariana feels it then. A tiny pulse of energy flowing straight from her own chest, from the well of quiet blankness, filtering through the rage and anger of before to the woman standing across the room from her. She blinks and tells it to stop. Tess recovers at once, though she continues to breathe heavily as she stares at Ariana.

'What's with you?' Ariana snorts, tossing her hair out of her eyes.

'Nothing,' Tess mumbles, 'Just a weird pain…' She frowns again, but it's not in Ariana's direction. Ariana sneers again to hide her relief and leaves the room without a word, grabbing her coat on the way and urging her feet into a run as she throws the front door open.

What was that? Did I do that? She knows the answer before she's finished asking it. Because she's done it before, she remembers now. The memory is thick and indistinct, but the sensation trickles back all the same… That flow of energy from her to another, the tentative link of emotion… Vague anger, her mother's hand in hers… *Well. That could be useful.* She slows to a jog and then comes to a halt just as the familiar fumy minibus wheezes around the corner and pulls to a stop. She can't help but smile at the driver as she steps on board, even as a million new questions bundle and multiply beneath the surface.

31

June, 2019

Nova sweeps gracefully upwards, her wings beating in a stable rhythmic pattern, her body tight and lithe as a butterfly's. She twists in flight and swoops downwards, wings tucking neatly, pointed and poised, ready to lift at the touch of a feather... I glance sideways and give the rope the tiniest of tugs and Nova responds immediately, changing direction mid-dive, zig-zagging past a cherry tree to land on her feet three metres away. She staggers a little and looks up. I nod and she remains still as two Guard men approach from either side. One takes the leash and cuts it short around a metre from the harness around her feathered body, the other picks up the loose end and begins the slow process of retracing its flight path through the trees and shrubs of The Yard.

'Impressive,' Lychen murmurs to my right. I keep my eyes on Nova, making sure she has heard him. Her head remains lowered, but her feathers ruffle a little along her head and down her back in acknowledgement.

'The rope impedes her,' Daniel says on my other side. I do not spare him a glance. The three of us stand alone in the space between East and South East, the clearest section of The Yard. Even so, it will take the Guard man more than an hour to fully detangle the rope. Behind us, Ethan stands next to Delta and Bette, who officially entered Daniel's personal service two weeks ago. The Yard has been reserved for our private use for the hour, all other employees confined to the covered walkways to travel between buildings. They're not supposed to loiter, but there are more than a couple of clusters of people staring and whispering around the edges of my vision. Nova and I have been practising in The Yard for over a fortnight now, but the spectacle still draws a crowd.

'Build up of trust is crucial, I presume?' Lychen addresses Daniel. I keep my eyes on Nova. She is far more stable than she used to be, but I cannot fully trust her around Daniel.

'Yes, and although I do see the point of all this... *exercise*... I question what point it all serves if the subject is still, essentially, a wild beast?'

'Bella?' I feel his gaze without looking.

'As I have explained many *many* times to Dr Skaid,' I say, smoothly, 'the point is to encourage the bond of trust. This is a reward. A greater reward would be more freedom on the leash. You're right that it impedes her, but it is necessary at present. My experience with Nova has shown that once she has been allowed time to fly, to properly use her wings in the outside air, she is far more responsive to conversation...'

'Your *experience*... of what, the last three weeks?' Daniel sneers. I take my eye from Nova for a moment to throw him a withering look.

'My experience with *Nova* goes back more than twenty years, actually...'

'Give or take a missing decade in the middle...'

'During which time you did God knows what to her—'

'That's enough!' Lychen's voice slices through us both and we turn to him. His eyes are dangerously slim as he glares at Daniel and me like a disappointed headmaster.

'Workplace rivalry is all very well and good if it leads to greater achievements, but this petty squabbling is just puerile and, quite frankly, beneath you both. If you cannot find a way to communicate without it, I will take this project out of both of your hands.'

I glance from him to Daniel, who quickly twists his face out of its sulky glare. Lychen keeps his face stern but there is a small tic in his forehead which wasn't there before. Things have been different between us since our argument and his small revelation about his past. He still regards me with the same hunger, still watches me carefully and, if anything, his appetite for my body is more voracious than ever. But there is an anger which wasn't there before, a fury in his embrace which leaves marks on my skin and a tightness in my throat... Sometimes I watch him and can see the way he is grasping his self-control with two hands, clenched and vibrating with the effort even as the creature beneath them writhes and rolls for freedom. And it escapes, bit by bit, into his actions and his face... He explains more. He shows his frustration. He has small, unexpected bursts of anger, surprise, even joy. Yesterday I made him laugh. So, though my throat is sore when I swallow, and there is a bruise on my forearm in the shape of his fingers, I view it as progress – this slow, tentative unravelling.

'Shall we proceed? Bella, show me what the Subject can say.'

'Certainly,' I smile widely and turn to Nova.

'Nova, would you mind coming a little closer so I can talk with you?'

We wait. Nova remains silent and still, her head still downturned, her wings folded neatly behind her. Daniel shifts from one foot to another and I can *feel* his smug snideness emanating from him, though he doesn't dare say anything. *Come on,* I urge Nova, silently. Hers is not like a Guard connection; there is no sinuous pathway between her mind and mine, there is no answering touch at the corner of my brain. It's all outside of us, all trust and hope and messy uncertainty... Ralph's face swims into my head unexpectedly, his big, soft eyes pinched with the questions he cannot bear to ask of me, his hands gentle yet firm as they'd pulled me into him. *No. Not now.* I shake the thought away. There is no room for anything else right now. Slowly, Nova walks on small, bare feet across the grass. I watch her toes splay over the perfectly green blades, wondering if it's still a novelty.

'Thank you,' I say, softly. 'That was excellent flying. I especially loved the sweep downwards and back up. It reminded me of when you used to fly through the hoops. Do you remember?'

She stops walking and, slowly lifts her face. I take a step towards her, so she will keep her focus only on me and not the men by my sides. She is closer to me than anyone else now. The Guard holding her rope would not be able to stop her from sweeping a sharp, deadly claw across my chest if she wanted to. My hands hang by my side, palms up so she can see I'm not holding anything.

'Fff...' she says, her small mouth stumbling. I nod, slowly. She frowns and tries again. 'Ff... Fire.'

'Yes, that's right. There were hoops with fire around them. They didn't trouble you though.'

'Dancing... You... Tu...Turns...' She frowns again and shudders the feathers along her back. Those in her hair frizz upwards with what I'm coming to recognise as frustration.

'Yes. That's right, you used to do ballet with Madame Glioue, so we decided to incorporate some of the movement into your routine on stage. It was tricky work – there were a lot of advanced turns and it took you months to get them just right. I worked you hard.'

Behind me, Daniel sighs quietly with boredom. I don't let my anger show on my face, but I can tell that Nova has heard it. All the feathers ruffle upwards along her neck and the edges of her wings, which she begins to unfurl. She makes a snarling, clicking noise and the Guard man holding her leash steps forward, tightening his fist. I step away, sensing Ethan moving forwards towards us. Nova snarls openly as I move back, her talons raised at all of us now.

'Maybe that's enough for today,' I say, quietly.

'Really? That's it?' Daniel sneers, though I can hear the relief behind it as the other Guard man wheels a small, portable cage towards Nova. Seeing it, she squawks angrily and raises her wings, but the Guard holding her leash is ready, raising a small taser so she can see it.

'Nova,' I say, sharply. She turns to me, still poised for a fight.

'Go on now,' I say, keeping my voice calm, my eyes never leaving her face. She lurches angrily at Daniel, raising her hand-claw in what would unmistakably be a rude gesture if she had the fingers with which to execute it, before settling her feathers neatly back against her body and stepping into the crate. The Guard person bolts it behind her as she folds herself into her wings like a small, feathery child.

'Extraordinary.' Lychen turns to me as the Guard wheels her out of view. His eyes are shining and alive in a way I can't remember ever seeing them. He reaches for me as if he's about to take me in his arms, but stops himself.

'What you've done with her in such a short space of time... I'm very impressed.'

'Thank you,' I say, sweetly, smiling over his shoulder at the seething mess of resentment behind him.

'I wasn't sure if the delay of the GHAP launch would be worth it, I have to say... but you've worked miracles with the creature. If we're able to use the same application with some of the other specimens...'

'Well... It's a bit of a special case with Nova. I helped raise her, after all.'

'Exactly! It proves that the familial element is key in breaking through the communication barrier,' he turns to Daniel. 'I'm surprised it's not something you had thought of trying sooner, Skaid.'

'Well... it's not as if we had the creatures' former friends and family hanging around waiting to say, *Hello, how can we help?*' Daniel says through clenched teeth. 'In fact, the criteria for most of the test subjects was that they *didn't* have close relations who would look for them...'

'Well. Be that as it may, it's certainly an avenue worth pursuing now, isn't it?'

'Yes,' Daniel sighs.

'Good. Now... Bella, when do you estimate that the Subject—'

'Nova. Her name is Nova. That is what she answers to.' I watch him carefully. A frisson of annoyance at my interruption blooms over his smooth countenance. Just for a second, but I see it.

'Nova,' he concedes, smooth once again. 'When do you think she will be fully compliant with orders?'

'It depends... My orders? Probably within a month. She's almost there – you saw her get into the crate on her own volition, even with Daniel present. She didn't really make a meaningful attempt to attack him today. That's huge progress. If I can continue to bring her out here, let her have a little more length on the leash on my own judgment… Yes, I'm fairly certain she will be obedient within a month.'

'Just to you, though?' Daniel questions, unable to fully keep the sneer from his voice.

'It will take longer for her to obey someone else as well. It's a trust thing… She already trusts me. She is still angry with me, too… For leaving her behind all those years ago… but we're working on it.'

'Sounds like therapy,' Daniel snorts. Lychen frowns at him and he looks down.

'In a way, it is. We want her to talk, so I'm leading by example. I get more and more from her every day. She's managed a three-word sentence once or twice. Of course, it would help if I knew what I was working towards…'

'What do you mean? You're working towards her being compliant and able to communicate,' Daniel says.

'Yes.' I address Lychen rather than him. 'But I don't know why. I can only guess. If I knew your plans for her, perhaps I could concentrate on different skill levels. You want her to spy – I can focus on silence in flight, light-footed landing, being able to listen well… You want her to be an ambassador, an alternative face for your research? I can focus more on performance, eloquence, speech recital…'

Lychen nods, looking from me to Daniel and back again.

'I haven't decided yet,' he says, levelly. 'There are several avenues of possibility for a fully tamed human-bird hybrid. Just as there will be for the others.'

'Some options more lucrative than others,' Daniel

says. I look at him and I can see he has his own ideas for Nova. Ideas I can tell from the nasty little glint in his eyes that I probably will not like very much at all.

'We are getting ahead of ourselves,' Lychen says, glancing at his watch and gesturing at Delta. 'Continue what you are doing for now, Bella. Focus on extending conversation and, once the... once *Nova* is as compliant as possible, concentrate on transferring the trust to others as well. She will need to be answerable to all of us, eventually. They all will. Whatever the eventual outcome. Daniel, you will continue to observe but otherwise stay out of Bella's way, concentrate on how you'll apply this method to the other hybrids. Understand?'

'Yes, of course.'

I smile quickly at the ground as Daniel fights to keep the irritation out of his voice.

'That will be all,' Lychen says, already beginning to move back towards the walkway leading to North.

'No kiss on the cheek? You two do have an odd relationship,' Daniel says, too close to my right ear, as I watch Lychen walk away, tailed by Delta. Ignoring him, I turn and begin to walk in the opposite direction, towards North East.

'Still, I suppose PDAs aren't really your thing, are they. Unless it's in a dingy North London alleyway with Ralph Blake. Hmm?'

I freeze, my fists clenching as I turn around slowly. Daniel has tailed me like a dog and is grinning right into my face. His eyes slide downwards over my body and back up.

'I don't know what you mean,' I say, slowly.

'I think you do,' he replies, reaching out and stroking a finger along my shoulder and down my arm. I'm grateful, momentarily, for the bruising which has meant I've been wearing long sleeves for the last week, warm as it is. I feel Ethan burning to grab him, his body almost trembling with the need to throw the slimy weasel into the pond. *No,* I tell him, silently. *Only if he threatens me physically. Guards should not perceive general creepiness.*

'I'm guessing you haven't told dear Josiah about your little unscheduled meeting?'

'What do you want, Daniel?'

'I haven't decided yet,' he smiles, his hand still on my forearm, the clammy heat of it seeping through my cotton blouse. 'I'm quite enjoying *this*...'

'I would have thought, given my delicate work with Nova, it would be in your best interests not to aggravate me right now. It wouldn't be hard for her to accidentally end up off the leash while you happen to be nearby... Lychen knows how unpredictable she can be...'

A spasm of uncertainty flashes through his eyes, but then he narrows them and licks his lips.

'Lychen would have her destroyed. I'm worth hundreds of her. He knows that. He's the only one who ever did...'

'Oh, Daniel. Is this *still* about your childhood?' I place a hand over his and give him my most patronising smile. 'I'm sorry I didn't pay you more attention, OK? It's just, you were *such* a creepy little shit.'

'Careful, Bella. I can find you when your Guard pet isn't there. I know where you sleep. I know where your child sleeps, too.'

I take my hand away, unable to bear touching him any longer. I take a step away from him.

'My meeting with Ralph and Felix was so she could see for herself that Ethan is not coming back. So they would stop breaking into our facilities. A loose end, tied up. That is all.'

'So why hide it from Lychen?'

'He doesn't have to know everything I do. I am, occasionally, allowed to take the initiative.'

'Well then, maybe we should find out if that's how he sees it.'

'Go on then,' I shrug. 'But you know what he said, he's had enough of our pettiness... He won't exactly be happy with you for stirring up trouble for no good reason.'

'Ah, but I think it's a very good reason,' he leans forward again, though I can tell my reaction has made him less sure.

'Do what you must,' I say in a bored way, gesturing to Ethan. We turn and walk away. I can sense Daniel's gaze drilling into me from behind.

That was good. He is not so sure now. But he will use this against you if he can.

It is all he has. He won't give it up so quickly. How did he find out?

He was suspicious of you. He wondered why you would still be giving the talk on the GHAP if its launch was delayed. He had you followed. They were lurking at the entrance to the passageway, but they did not overhear the conversation.

The connection fades as we get further apart and my concentration begins to hitch and slip.

Try and warn me next time. This is the sort of thing you need to look out for with him.

Yes. I understand.

Thank you, Bette.

32

May, 2019

At first Ariana is quite careful around all the adults that have any chance at all of noticing her acting any differently. But they're all so wrapped up in their own drama that she might as well be invisible. Ariana doesn't hear Felix and Ralph come back from London on the Tuesday and doesn't see either of them the following morning. When she comes home from school on Wednesday, The Manor is quiet, but in a full, hushed sort of way rather than just empty. She peers into Felix's study to find most of the computers have been moved.

'Felix is in her room,' Dr Blake's voice tells her. She turns and regards her fake granddad sitting at his desk in his office-cum-living-room. He has his glasses halfway down his nose and is peering at her over the cover of a large hardback.

'What happened yesterday? With Ethan and Mum and everything?' Ariana crosses through the open double doors between the rooms and curls a leg onto the cracked leather armchair. Despite the warm weather outside, the room remains chilly. As if the stones themselves are partly made of winter. Ariana shivers a little as she kneels into a corner of the sofa, bare arms flat on the arm as she focuses on Dr Blake.

'I'm not *entirely* sure… But from what I gather, the

mission was only partially successful. Felix was able to administer Serum X to Ethan and he did, partly, appear to remember a little of himself…'

'Well that's good, isn't it?'

'On the surface… yes… but according to Bella, he had already begun to come back to himself at her encouragement… So it's unclear how successful the serum actually was.'

'But surely it's still good that he's coming back, no matter how it actually happened…'

'Yes, it certainly is.'

'So where is he?'

'Ah. Now therein lies the other bad news. He recognised Felix, but he still chose to remain with Bella, under her employ.'

'Oh. Oh… dear.'

'Quite,' Dr Blake raises his eyebrow in a way that tells her he knows exactly what she almost said. She can't help but grin, though the blank dark part of her sneers.

Hurt him. Make that big, wrinkly brain feel like it's about to explode out of his skull. He's a liar. He's lying to us every day he pretends he's our granddad.

But we need him. He holds answers in that big, wrinkly brain.

'So Felix…'

'…is rather upset.'

'And Mum? Was she… OK?'

'By all accounts, she seemed fine. A little strained, perhaps, Ralph said. But otherwise well. She asked after you, of course.'

'Good of her,' Ariana snorts. There's something more, she can tell. She narrows her eyes slightly, concentrating on what he hasn't said. He meets her gaze with a sort of determined blankness and she encounters a wall.

'So what happens now, then?' She asks, making her voice neutral.

'Well… we still have Serum X. It needs more testing; it was never really ready for Felix to use so soon. I want to spend a bit longer developing it. Ideally I'd like to get hold of a few Guard people to try it out on…'

'How the hell—'

'Well, one step at a time. In a few months, the reality may be that there will be a lot more Guard in the general community than now. Especially once they launch the Home Assistance package…'

'What about the hybrid creatures? Mum told me that one of them was her former student or something… Did she say anything to Ralph about freeing her and the others?'

'That I don't know. Ralph said she mentioned having a plan, but he couldn't gather much more than that.'

'OK. Well that could mean anything, couldn't it? She might want to free all the Guard people and hybrids and throw Lychen and Daniel into a pit of snakes, or she might just mean she wants to take over the whole operation herself…'

'Yes.'

'Yes?'

'Yes. I agree that it could mean anything. From what Ralph gathered, she doesn't appear to count herself to be on Lychen's side…'

'That's something, I suppose.'

'But she also didn't say she was on ours. As ever she did, Bella will walk her own path. But, like you said, we can only guess where she is intending that path to lead.'

Ariana sighs in frustration and sits back on her heels. She glances away from Blake, over to the books bowing the shelves, arching over the fireplace, piling up on the floor in front of the TV. *Ask him. Ask him now.*

'Hey... I have to do a family tree for history at school... Can you help me with it?'

'Of course,' he brightens visibly, getting up from his chair and reaching towards one of the groaning bookshelves. She almost feels guilty at the spring in his step as he bounces on his toes to reach a large leather-bound volume. She gets up and approaches the desk, slowly. He flips it open and she is surprised to see it's one of those old-fashioned photo albums people had before digital cameras and good phones.

'Here...' he flips through stiff pages of black-and-white people with moustaches and strange clothes until he comes to an image in the middle. It's an intricate family tree all done in black ink and curly calligraphy. *Blake*, it reads in the middle.

'Thanks,' she mutters, squinting to read the names. Her eyes snag briefly on her own – Ariana – until she realises it's not her at all, but Ralph's mother, the date of death listed as some five years before she was born. The blank voice hisses about lies and betrayal but she swallows it away. She can feel Dr Blake's attention on her, the last thing she needs is more suspicion. She sniffs and takes a picture of the family tree on her phone.

'We don't have to go back very far... but I was hoping you might be able to help me with my mother's side, too...'

'Ah...' Blake rakes a finger and thumb over the silver stubble of his chin. 'Of course... well, let's see.' He draws a blank piece of paper towards him from the stack next to the printer.

'There's Bella,' he scribbles her name at the bottom of the page, then adds two lines on the left. 'Her sister Maya, and brother Silas.'

'They're both from Project A too, right?'

'They were, yes... But both are dead now, sadly. The Project A curse, you know. What we tested your mother for when she was last here...'

'Oh... yeah...' My aunt and my uncle. Both dead. Did I know that? I must have. Surely I'd feel something if I hadn't known that? Surely I'd feel sad.

'Then there are your grandparents, Marc and Julia D'accourt. I'm afraid I don't know dates of birth off the top of my head...'

'That's OK,' Ariana stares at the names and then looks up at him. 'Are they still alive, my grandparents? Mum never spoke about them and always got cross when I asked.'

'Yes, I can imagine. She never spoke about them here, either. Even as a child. I spoke to them briefly last year, when Maya... your aunt... when she was in her final days. We were actively searching for Bella then, of course. We had reason to believe she had communicated with Maya over the last few years...'

'Yeah... when we ran away from Flintworth she said we might go and stay with Maya in Devon or something. I guess she didn't know she'd died.'

'No. Maya didn't disclose her illness to your mother, and she never told us where to find her.'

'So where do they live, this Marc and Julia?'

'They used to live in Weston-on-the-Hill. A small town in Surrey... I'm not sure if they are still there, though I reached them on their number there last year, so I expect so. I'm afraid I don't know their parents' names... I know

Marc's side is French, I'm not sure about Julia though. Would you like me to look them up? See if I can find some more relatives?'

'No, no thank you. It only has to go back as far as grandparents.' Ariana picks up the piece of paper with the names and drops her phone back in her pocket. She crosses the room and grabs her school bag.

'Ariana...?'

'Yeah?' She turns almost reluctantly. He's looking at her with that same benign blankness, deliberately guarded and yet kind, in an irritating way.

'It might be worth checking in with your mother before you get in touch with Marc and Julia. There's a lot of... complicated history... involved.'

The anger that he's seen through the lie rears like a dragon inside her and she grabs the reins, pulling it back down.

'I'm not going to get in... Anyway, why should I check with her? They're my grandparents, it's got nothing to do with her if I call them and tell them I exist, has it? It's *my* family too...' A tiny flame shoots from the dragon's mouth before she can stop it and she feels it hit him as a tiny flicker of pain clouds his eyes for a moment. He blinks at her without wincing.

'Just... tread carefully. OK? Trust your instincts.'

'Fine, whatever. It's just a project for history, OK? I'm not even going to call anyone anyway.'

'Start with Marc.'

She stares at him for a moment longer, the beast longing to send another poison mind-dart, just to watch him crumple, just to see the stupid knowingness slide off his face. Then she stamps on the impulse. She's not a monster. He's just a harmless, annoying old man. She turns on her toe, shoulders her school bag and walks slowly out into the corridor and up the stairs to her bedroom.

33

31.12.14

From: Dr.M.Daccourt@gmail.co.uk

To: el.guerre@hotmail.com

Subject: Happy New Year

Dear Bella,

I'm not really sure how to start this. I keep deleting things. Emails just highlight social awkwardness, don't they? Like: Hello, nicety, nicety, here's my point: yadda yadda, now another empty nicety and sign off. Who actually talks like that? Anyway, I'm just going to state the facts. I am a little drunk. Apologies. Dad gave me your email address. He is often a little drunk nowadays, which is probably why he and Mum have been arguing so much. You probably don't remember their arguments, I try not to bear witness if I can help it, but this one happened at a family BBQ from which there was, unfortunately, no easy escape. Mum roared, Dad sulked and now neither are speaking to each other. Apparently he's been having an affair, or was having an affair but isn't anymore – she told him to sod off back to his London whore or something like that.

Mortifying, I know. I got the rest from Si. He's around slightly more than me – he said that Dad was seeing someone in London for a few years and they all pretended they didn't know and everyone was happier for it in some bizarre, dysfunctional way. I went to talk to Dad and he said a bunch of stuff which didn't really make sense, but apparently the London whore wasn't a London whore at all and it was actually you and there was a whole lot of blither about the biggest mistake of his life and a poor little girl (also you, I guess?) and that he messed it all up and now you won't return any calls or emails, so perhaps I should try. So here I am, trying.

I should probably mention that all this took place over a year ago. I started drafting this email in 2012. July 15th, actually. Your birthday. Your 26th birthday. I'm not even sure if that was the same day that Mum and Dad had the argument which led to him giving me your email address (it probably was though, there's nothing like a 'Bella date' to set them off). Sorry. Was that insensitive? I'm just a bit shit at all this, really. I like my life all ordered and neat. I have a nice, neat little cottage in North Devon where I live with my partner Jade and three dogs. They're all small and none of them shed fur. Jade is a teacher, I work at Bristol University part of the week and from home the rest. I'm a neuroscientist but I'm plagued by headaches (ah, the irony!) which are made worse by stress, pressure, expectations, etc... I used to work in New York but had a bit of a mental breakdown a few years ago which led to me taking a huge swerve in the direction of The Quiet Life. Mum is still bitter about it, to be honest, but that's more to disguise her *raging* homophobia... but at least she still has her golden boy Silas, piling up the world records even if he's not allowed to compete...

Anyway, enough of me. I want to know about you. If you ever reply, which I'm sure you won't... how are you doing? What happened after you went to Cumbria to live with the Blakes? We still hear from them occasionally. Well, him, obviously. Now and again, to keep tabs on us and our gifts. Sorry, was that horribly callous? I suppose they raised you. I'm sorry about Ana. That must have been hard, you were so young, after all. What is your life like now? Do you have a family? Are you a prima ballerina in the West End? Is your (fake) name in lights like our mother always dreamt it would be? Are you glad to hear from me?

Do you even remember who I am?

I don't know how to end this. If starting was tough, at least getting stuck in made it easier to forget… But now – kind regards feels too stiff, love seems like a farce when I'm not even sure I'd recognise you on the street. That's a lie. Of course I would. I didn't need Dad to mumble about how incredibly beautiful you still are, it is burned in my retinas for always. The curse of the plain, older sister. Oh dear! Perhaps I had better simply say goodbye, and that I hope you *are* glad, even if it's just a little bit, to hear from me. And that you find it within yourself to reply.

Maya

30.4.15

From: el.guerre@hotmail.com

To: Dr.M.Daccourt@gmail.co.uk

RE: Happy New Year

Maya,

Of course I remember who you are.

I wasn't going to reply. I read your email three times and then I filed it away and did not look at it again because I knew that if I did I would reply and then I might start something that I said I never would again. You can thank our dad for that, though I'm sure he won't tell you why.

So why am I replying now, four months later? Well, I'm sure you can guess. Silas. I saw his picture in the sports section of the papers in the lunch room at work. I'm so sorry. I can't pretend that the news hit me hard – I hadn't seen him in so long. But it did make me remember. I remember him as a boy, all legs and impossible speed. I remember never being able to have a conversation with him when we were outside because he'd always be off – racing ahead far too quickly whether it was on his bike or his skates or just his own two feet. I remember him challenging us to a race along the rec ground in Weston, me and you running and him hopping with his legs tied together and his hands bound behind his back... and he still won. But he was nice to me too, sometimes. He stood up to our mother, when he could be bothered... And when it was raining and the river burst its banks that year, he carried me on his back the whole way home from school. Anyway. I guess you have more memories than I do. Were you close, towards the end? The article said that his death was from 'natural causes', whatever that means. Was he ill? Did you know? You don't have to tell me, of course. If it's too much.

I can't answer all of your questions. I am fine, though. I have a nice life, though it's quiet and, perhaps like yours, hasn't quite reached the glittering heights that were once dreamt for me. No name in lights, I haven't danced on stage in years and my name is a big, glaring mask that I hide behind. And here I must ask you something in return – please, please do not tell Dr Blake or Ralph – if he's in touch – who I am or that you are in contact with me. I am not hiding from them, but if they find me the people I am hiding from will, and that will be my end. Please, Maya.

And yes, I was glad to hear from you. Scared, too. Mostly because I worry who else Marc might have told about me. I don't think he would tell Blake, but no one has disappointed me more than Marc has, so I could not put it past him. But otherwise, I was glad and I am happy to hear that your life is neat and content. There is a lot to be said for living life under the radar. That is something I have had to teach myself over the last ten years.

Here I will stop. I hope the funeral goes as well as it can. I am sorry that I won't be able to attend.

Best,

Bella

6.5.15

From: Dr.M.Daccourt@gmail.co.uk

To: el.guerre@hotmail.com

Hi Bella,

Thank you for replying. I can't believe you're really there after all these years. It's almost like talking to a ghost. There are no pictures of you at Mum and Dad's, you see… Mum took them all down. Dad tried putting a few back up but they always came down and eventually he stopped trying. I know he kept some – still does, I expect – in his office and his computer and various other places. Don't worry, though, he won't tell anyone else about you. I made him promise that after I got your email. He was shocked I had heard from you, but pleased, I think, underneath it all, to hear that you're OK. And Dr Blake has no idea about you. He tried asking at the funeral but Mum walked off as if he hadn't spoken and Dad just said that we never heard anything.

The funeral. God it was awful. I still can't believe he's gone. We weren't overly close, to answer your question. I suppose I spoke to him on the phone if he happened to be at Mum and Dad's when I called, and we always saw each other at Christmases and during the summer and stuff... He came to stay with us sometimes, he liked to surf up here. Another thing he was excellent at, of course... But no, I wouldn't say we were especially close. Even when he came to stay, he and Jade would sit up playing board games and talking long after I'd gone to bed... She was closer to him than I was in a way. But the funeral was awful. Ralph Blake was there too; I had forgotten they had a son. I suppose he was like a brother to you. Good looking guy, kind eyes. A bit twitchy, though, always looking around at every cough or murmur of noise... I think he was looking for you.

Anyway. I got drunk afterwards. I don't usually drink much, contrary to what you might think, given I was a bit pissed the last time I wrote. I find it's not worth the extra headache in the morning... but I got drunk then. Probably not the best plan as I ended up shouting at Mum... I just couldn't bear to hear her wailing about losing a child, her precious child, etc... I *really* shouted at her. I don't even remember what I said but according to Jade I used the word hypocrite to excess. She was quite proud of me.

Jade, that is. She's never liked Mum. And Mum, of course, has never forgiven her for not possessing a penis. But that – and the oh-so-sweet irony of our narrow-minded mother disowning her perfect princess only for her remaining daughter to come out a few years later – is another story. (Though I think you should know that she tried very hard to make me wear dresses and take up ballet for a while after you left.)

What else did you ask? Oh, Silas. No, he wasn't ill. Not as far as I knew, anyway. I don't think he would have told me if he was, but he probably would have gone home to Mum and let her wait on him for a while if he had been. He was a bit of a man-child, really. Never had much in the way of serious relationships, though there were plenty of female 'friends' in attendance at his funeral, all in varying degrees of devastation... He didn't want to be tied down, though. He told Jade once, during one of their late-night games of Monopoly or whatever it was they played, that he tended to break up with women once they got too serious or if there was any mention of having children. He absolutely never ever wanted to be a dad. I actually think he was booked in for a vasectomy. He never told me why – that would have required a level of intimacy which, well, I've already mentioned that we never had – but it's not too hard to work it out, really, is it? The brain suffers all sorts of repercussions as a result of emotional trauma as a child... I don't want them either, really, if I'm honest. Jade gets all smooshy-faced when she sees infants. Our friends have just had their second daughter... and yes, I understand the urge. I held the baby and thought *wouldn't it be lovely...* But then I remember what it was like for us as kids. The feeling of being different, being unnatural... It's never left me (though adult prodigies are, mercifully, far less exciting to all but themselves). All those eyes, watching us for the things we could do. I still feel them. The awe, the wonder, the attraction, the repulsion... I know they told us our 'enhancements' would not pass to offspring, but how could I ever take that risk? Dr Blake spoke to me about it, briefly, at the funeral when he asked whether Silas or I had ever had a child. He mentioned that some of the other Subjects from Project A have had children who seem perfectly normal on the face of it all. I wanted to ask more, but Mum was off pretending he didn't exist and Dad was hovering awkwardly in the middle of it all and suddenly I felt very much like the middle sibling thrust unceremoniously into the unexpected glare of only-childhood.

It's lonely here. I don't like it.

So we can't talk about the important stuff, like where you live and who you live with, what your job is like and who the hell you're hiding from... Tell me other things, then. What was your life like up there with the Blakes? Did you meet any other Project children? There are rumours... there always have been, in the academic circles. Rumours of heinous experimentation involving animals and babies and all sorts of crazy things... Tell me about that. Distract me from my small little life with my crazy dogs and my broody partner...

Your sister,

Maya x

34

June, 2019

It is surprisingly easy to conceal my entire class – twenty still for this session, part of the agreement for Daniel's use of Bette is that she still be allowed to attend one hour of class a day – behind some of the interlacing shrubs by the pond in The Yard. They all stand, crouch or hover, none of them touching one another, all of them perfectly silent as we watch the small group of twenty-something scientists talking by the water's edge. I let my eyes slide from the observers to the oblivious and back again, noting that the only one who is a liability here is Lychen, standing ill-at-ease at the edge of the group. He catches my eye and holds it, his face carefully blank, but I glimpse the barely-concealed edge of impatience underneath. The clock tower atop East chimes two pm and the group next to the pond immediately begin to make swift movement in the direction of the lab buildings. One or two catch sight of Lychen as they join the path and hasten their steps. He says nothing, keeping his gaze on me and my Youth Guard as I turn to them.

'Hugh. What did we learn here?'

My blue-eyed Hugh, shorter than most of his peers and prone to quick, nervous movements when caught unawares, turns to me, his gaze twitching slightly. He once wore spectacles, according to his file, and although the need has been corrected, he retains a slight squint, a wrinkling around the bridge of his nose when he's thinking. Like now.

'Five female individuals, all mid-twenties in age and all around the same level of employee status – pay, living quarters, etc. The one with the blonde hair has worked here the longest, the others look to her for approval.'

'What is her name?'

'They called her Cece. So I would deduce Celia, Celine, Serena, Selena... Considering her approximate year of birth, I would surmise the most likely choice—'

'Too much detail. Cece is adequate. Tom, what group dynamics did you observe beyond the conversation?'

'The conversation was about a minor dispute in the West quarters, apartment six-c—'

'That's not what I asked,' I fix him with a steady glare. *This matters, Tom. He is watching.*

'Context, Dr D'accourt. The beauty is in the details.' He returns my stare, clear-gazed. I chance a quick look at Lychen to see if he's recognised the Blake-ism, but he remains stoic, staring at the dark-haired youth.

'Continue.'

'I concur that Cece is the leader, however at least two of the others expressed a subtle ennui with her perspective. They have heard her say these things before and are tiring of her manner...'

'Which is... Bette?'

'That she complains about things but doesn't take steps to change them.'

'Good,' I smile, and Bette echoes it, carefully. 'Eve, what about the redhead?'

'Her name is Allie. She is a rival leader. Olivia, the large brunette, and Leila, the one with purple glasses, have both met with her in secret and have had conversations about Cece.'

'How could you tell?'

'Subtle looks between them at certain points of the conversation implying complicity.'

'And in colloquial terms?'

'In-jokes. They've been mocking her behind her back...'

'Good. Liz, what would you do if Cece were your human?'

'I would tell her,' tall, redheaded Liz says, without a hitch of hesitation, though her eyes dart to Lychen and back again.

'Why?'

'Because her surface profile, gained through observation, implies that she would want to know. Her friends have hidden agendas, they lie... She would want to know.'

'Would Allie, if the roles were reversed?'

She frowns. I turn to Eve and raise my eyebrows.

'No,' Lychen interrupts. 'Ask one of the others. Ask... this one,' he points at Karl, a plain, stocky individual towards the back of the group.

'Karl?'

Karl opens his mouth slowly. His voice still bears the thick burr of his Scottish origins when he speaks.

'I would need to observe Allie more closely to be sure. But based on surface observation... I would not tell her. Her desires are more complex than Cece's. She prefers the world she sees, not the things she misses. This is partly why the others follow her. She is decisive but also happy to be blind to subtleties.'

'Good,' I smile at him, and he returns it readily. 'Unless

Dr Lychen has any further questions, class dismissed.'

They wait but Lychen waves a hand and, as one, the group disperses. Lychen steps closer to me as he watches them go, hands behind his back. The sun is beating down on us and sweat gleams almost imperceptibly on the back of his neck where his stiff collar meets his pale skin.

'Where are they going now?' He asks, softly, non-urgently.

'Some of them are shadowing other Guard and their masters... They will go and continue their shadow until the human dismisses them. Others will return to their living quarters to study. Bette, of course, holds her own engagement already.'

'Ah yes, Daniel says she is proving useful. Rather more so than he expected, as it happens.'

'Yes,' I say, simply, blandly.

'You have done well, Bella,' he turns to me. 'They are better than they were last time I observed...'

'Their progress has improved tenfold since we began observing human interaction around the Beaumont rather than just on video. There are subtleties to human behaviours that just can't always be caught on screen...'

'Indeed,' he raises an eyebrow.

'They're ready, Josiah,' I say, quietly, keeping my eyes on his. 'As ready as they'll ever be...'

'And where would you have me put them, these young, fresh-faced minions?'

'Wherever you require the closest control,' I murmur. He reaches for me and I let him. Our embrace is all angles and corners, there is no safe space for my body against his, no fitting of neat parts.

'But where would *you* have me put them?'

'Are you asking me for advice?' I peer up at him. The

sun is behind me and he winces as it hits his eyes. A duck squawks nearby and we both turn to look.

'Yes.'

'Well. I would put them at the top. But I would wait first. Let the dust settle on the Care Programme. Then launch Home and allow it to establish itself. That will be our biggest seller... Let its success speak for itself, then they will come to you...'

'Who will?'

'The government. The ministers. The royal bloody family if you so wish. Anyone willing to pay the top price for an elite generation of Guard who can understand the subtleties of human emotion with all the physical and mental integrity of former editions... We know how to do it now; we can make more. We can make an entire facility just for their manufacture, a purpose-built one where they can observe humans and learn accordingly...'

'It sounds expensive.'

'It will be. It will also be worth every penny.'

He watches me measuredly for a moment and then, with a sigh, he lets go of where he has been gripping me by my forearms. I move back slightly, resisting the urge to rub the sore spots.

'Daniel says the programme is flawed. He thinks there is an inherent risk in allowing Guard people access to knowledge of human frailties. Says they could use it against us...'

'Daniel... Daniel is used to working with humans at the very basest level,' I keep my voice level, but I can tell a little fire has crept into it. It flashes in Lychen's eyes in a response of both frustration and arousal. 'Moreover, he is suspicious of me. He is jealous of my progress with Nova, he is scared of what my success with her will mean for him.

You know this.'

'Yes. He claims he has reasons for his distrust that go beyond the personal. He claims that you have exploited my... feelings for you... Muddied my logic. Inspired lapses in judgment... hesitations, uncertainties... that I so abhor in others... And I see it too, Bella. You fulfil me, but you also infuriate me. You make me weak.'

'You wanted this. You wanted me. This is how I am.'

'I know...'

'Maybe there cannot be one thing without the other. Maybe I inspire you to be greater.'

'Weakness is never greater.'

'Is it weakness?' I reach for his face, my hand blazing against his cool skin. I pull him downwards and he catches my hand, crushing it within his. He leans the rest of the way and kisses me hard until we are both breathless.

'I don't forget my place. I don't forget who put me there,' I say, quietly.

'Good,' he replies, the wolf growling within, leaping to be freed.

I open my mouth to say that I need to be going now, that I'm due to take Nova out by two-thirty and Daniel is a stickler for time-keeping, but as the words begin to form my phone rings. Frowning, I take it from my pocket. Most calls go through the Beaumont switchboard desk and reach me during my office hours. There are only a handful of people who have the number of this phone and one of them is standing in front of me, still looking as if he can't decide whether to kiss me or throttle me.

'Oh,' I say in surprise as I read the name on the screen. 'Sorry, I'll have to take this.' I turn away from Lychen before I can look at his face. I take two steps away, feeling as if I have lit a fuse on a bomb before casually turning my back on it.

'Ralph? This isn't really a—'

'Ariana's gone, she's hurt Dad and she's gone.' He sounds like he's running and there's a wild whistling wind in the background that clouds my head for a few seconds before his actual words sink in.

'What do you mean, gone?'

'She's not here, Beast. Her bag's gone, she's not at her friends' houses... She's not answering her phone... Felix has gone out looking but I just heard from her and there's nothing. No trace.'

'Right. Right... OK. What happened, exactly? Something about your dad?'

'We couldn't find either of them this morning. We searched for them all over the house and all the cars were still here so we thought they must have gone to the ARC – Dad still has a key card... We found him unconscious in his old office. We called an ambulance, they've just left.'

'How do you know Ri had anything to do with it?' I speak quickly, staring unseeingly across the sunlit water in front of me. I can feel Lychen watching me rigidly, a malevolent gargoyle under the apple trees.

'We found her muddy footprints all over the floor and Tess said something... something about how a few weeks ago she'd been with Ariana in the dining room and Ari did something to her... gave her a weird pain or something, but without ever moving, just by looking at her... She thinks she did the same to Dad, only worse... And... well, she's been odd lately. Dad noticed it too. He said she was growing darker or something... I just thought it was Dad being Dad, you know, trying to see extraordinary things where there weren't any... But now... I think they're right, Beast. I think she did it. I found a piece of paper in the office too. It had your parents' names on it.'

'OK...' I realise I have a hand on my forehead as memories of Ariana's eyes staring in rage swirl into focus. Ariana furious at seven years old, eyes huge and accusatory as we made our way home from school; spitting hatred at twelve, hands pushing me across the unfamiliar tiles of the Cornish cottage with far greater strength than should naturally occur in the skinny arms behind them; Ariana in the entrance hall at Futura the last time I saw her, hurt tumbling from her like heat from a volcano – and the pain, each and every time. The instant relief when she'd calmed or turned away... The swirl of dark, blank anger edging around her words during our last, sporadic conversation...

'OK. So you think she's gone to Weston-on-the-Hill?'

'Maybe there, maybe Flintworth... She's packed a bag, Beast. This was thought-out, at least partially. I don't know if she meant to attack Dad, but I think she wanted answers from him... In any case—'

'We have to find her...'

'Yes, and you're a damn sight closer to Surrey than we are.'

'What time did you find Blake?'

'About twelve... we've been looking ever since. Felix is already on her way... I'm heading to the hospital.'

'Right,' I try not to think of the large, white house with the neat front garden. My pink little-girl bedroom, my parents sitting calmly in their comfortable chairs, cups of tea next to them, photos of my brother and sister on the mantelpiece... The images muscle their way into my head anyway.

'I know you don't talk to them, Beast, but please... if you could just check—'

'Yes, I'll go right away.'

'No.' The voice comes close to my ear, deathly quiet but clipped and clear. Ralph and I both pause.

'Beast?'

'I'll call you back,' I say quickly, turning to meet Lychen's cold, empty glare.

'Beast! Bella—'

I press the red button and replace my phone in my pocket without taking my eyes from his. My mind gallops furiously even as the cool, clenching fingers of fear begin to creep around my heart.

'Ariana is missing,' I say, levelly. 'I need to help look for her.'

'No,' he repeats. I feel Ethan step slowly into the sunlight from behind the apple tree where he has been waiting. Delta matches him.

'Ralph thinks she's heading for Weston where my parents live. Felix is still miles away but I could get there within the hour if I leave now—' I move and know, instantly, that it's a mistake. His hand whips around my right forearm, the fingers wrapping my bare skin – the last of the bruises have only just faded enough for short sleeves – and pinching it between them. I look at the hand and he does too, as if bemused by what it has done. But by the time his gaze meets mine, his expression is deathly resolute.

'You relinquished custody. You gave up responsibility. If Blake can't keep tabs on his own child, that's his problem, not yours.'

'But I want to—'

'And *I* do not want you to. I have been patient with your phone calls and text messages. Your distraction and the Blakes' interference with my facilities. Don't think I don't know they still treat the ARC like their own. Well, no more. I'm not asking you to choose anymore, you chose already, last year. I'm holding you to that choice.'

I bite back the urge to command he release me at the same time as I reluctantly hold Ethan from leaping to my defence. *There's another way. There's always another way,* I feel him murmur in my head.

But she's missing. Goodness knows where she is. I shouldn't have dismissed her when she called on me. I should have told her the truth.

She's OK. She'll be OK. You can feel that much of her. She's strong. Stronger than you are right now.

I know. I know I should back down, smile for Lychen, let him think I'm his. Dance away to see my pet hybrid as if everything is fine, buy myself some time to try and come up with a way out on my own... But instead, the clench of cold fear turns itself around in my chest and blooms upwards, melting and pooling and sizzling into rage. And before I can stop myself, the words are already there: 'Let me go.'

He drops my arm at once, a second passes and then the fury swarms across his face like oil sliding over water. The crack of his backhand shatters through my skull and I'm on my hands and knees in the dirt before I feel the blaze of pain across my face. Ethan is there at once, his large hands gentle as he takes one of my hands in his, helping me back to my feet.

'Escort Bella to her rooms. She is unwell,' Lychen says to Ethan, and then repeats it to Delta as well for good measure. He reaches into my pocket and takes my phone. I think of all the messages, the call log from last month, my mind scurrying beneath the pulsing tremble of my anger.

'Don't do this, Josiah,' I hiss, as Ethan gently begins to

walk me away. I twist until I can still see him, his face still shrouded in anger.

'I didn't do anything, Bella. *You* did this.'

My rage escapes in a sharp, animalistic cry. Which, of course, only pisses him off more.

35

June, 2019

'Hello? Hello? Listen, whoever this is, we're registered with the telephone spam people and you are *breaking the law!*'

Ariana opens her mouth to speak but before she can, the shudder overtakes her body and wriggles its way down to her hand. She jabs the red button until the voice – the only-slightly-quivery-old echo of her mother – disappears. Then she throws her phone onto her bed and groans in frustration. *Start with Marc*, he'd said. That would all be very well and good if he would answer the damn phone once in a while. Instead, she'd hung up on the increasingly irritated voice that could only belong to her grandmother – Julia – three, no four times now. Sighing, Ariana throws herself back onto her bed next to her phone. She stares sideways out of the window, at the cloud-scattered sky and the slow trail of a distant plane across it.

What's going on, Ri?

It doesn't come to her often these days, her mother's voice, but the furious tone of its older, frailer version seems to have re-ignited it.

I need to know. I need to know what I am. What this power is...

And you think they'll be able to tell you? They couldn't even handle me. And I am nothing like you.

You're nothing like anything, you're just a stupid voice in my head.

Ariana's gaze shifts to her desk, her maths book open on the surface where she'd left it on Thursday evening. Yesterday, Friday, she had stared at her maths teacher until he had become so distracted by pain he'd had to leave the classroom. The substitute, who'd arrived all flustered five minutes later, had not said a word about the homework due that day and Ariana had felt the small well of power within her glow in triumph as she'd grinned at her friends. *I did that,* she'd wanted to tell them. She'd wanted it so hard right then that it had taken some effort to keep her lips closed. *Why shouldn't they know?* the power had whispered. *What harm could it do?* But the moment had passed before the idea could take hold and she hadn't thought much more about it then. But now… Now it was back, swirling with irresistible arrogance.

I could show them. I could show them all that I'm not some useless, boring thing that can be shelved away in the middle of nowhere. Some problem child to be ignored, avoided, forgotten about…
Then what?

Her mother's voice is back, a guarded salve of reason against the wild passion of the power.

What do you mean, then what?
What about when they all realise you have this power? Do you think they'll let you keep it? Do you think they'll just nod and say, ah, turns out were all wrong about that Ariana? Oh well, silly us. You know what happened to the children who got too powerful at the ARC, don't you? The ones who ended up in those dungeon rooms?

The fingernails. The dark, smeared marks. The echoing heaviness of misery seeped and curdled within the very air itself.

That's different. They went mad.
And how did that start? By losing grip on their own sense of reality, perhaps? Having conversations with people who aren't really there?
Stop it. Go away.

It's only when the voice starts up again that she realises it's not her mother's anymore.

We need answers. We won't get them here. You heard Ralph... he doesn't really care about you, does he? If he did, he wouldn't have let you take the bus into town on your own. You didn't even tell him you were going last weekend. And what happened when you got home? Nothing. No one noticed, Ariana. No one cares. Not him, not Felix, not Dr Blake, not your mother. No one.
OK, I get it. Where do I go then?
If you really want answers about your mother and your father and where you came from, what you are, there's only one place.

And there it is. The answer. She sits up and, in one fluid movement, grabs her phone, shoving it into her jeans pocket. The bag at the foot of her bed is the same one she half-packed when she first overheard Ralph and Dr Blake's conversation in the dining room downstairs. No one has noticed that, either, even though it's been sitting there for over three weeks now. She bites her lip and places a few more things in it. Then she fastens Bella's old boots onto her feet, zips up the bag and slings it over her shoulder. She slips from the room and down the stairs, hearing the murmur of voices coming from the various offices on the ground floor of The Manor but not bothering to pause to listen. Nothing they say is important to her anymore.

The ARC gleams in its usual, oily-looking way. The mostly-intact windows are only slightly tarnished-looking. From the outside, as she stares up at it, Ariana thinks it looks like it could still hold all the vibrant, bustling activity it ever did. *This is where it happened*, she thinks, without quite knowing what she means, as she stares at the chained double doors of the front entrance. Through the glass she can see a chandelier still hanging in the large, arched lobby. She turns her head away from the mental image of the atrium full of scientists and trudges through overgrown tussocks of grass to the broken window of the ground floor bathroom.

There's no Dr Blake waiting for her today. The water puddling the ground is dirty with muck which has blown through the gap, and though the sun is gleaming warmly outside, the air inside the building is stiff, cold, and frigid, like it's forgotten how to be breathed. Ariana feels the goosebumps tremble along her bare skin and has to dig in her bag for her black hoodie. She doesn't know how she knows which stairs to take and which corridors to choose, she just follows her feet. It's almost as if her boots are possessed by their former wearer, following a track they know by heart. The thought comforts Ariana a little until she remembers that her mother probably didn't enter her place of work through the ground floor bathroom window… And, more likely than not, would have changed into her heels long before she reached anywhere that she might bump into someone important.

Up several flights of stairs and down countless narrow identical-looking corridors, Ariana finally comes to a stop outside a door that looks much like the rest of them. The name plaque has been removed, like several, but Ariana can see where it used to be. She places her hand against the cool, smooth wood of the door and shuts her eyes for a moment. The sensation is odd, a misplaced *déjà-vu*. She knows she hasn't been here before, as surely as she knows that this was once her mother's office. And yet... somehow the space she knows is locked away in front of her feels familiar... *This is where it happened.*

Where what happened?
You.

The door is locked. She does not need to grasp the cool, smooth metal of the handle to know that. She does not need to open the door to see, either. She keeps her eyes shut and leans her head against the wood and slowly, somehow, the image swirls into being in front of her. Her mother, standing a few feet from where she is now, her back to the door, her hair longer than she's ever seen it before and lit from the soft jewels of the chandelier above her head as if each strand were imbibed with the crystals themselves. She wears a flimsy-looking summer blouse over a skirt and she is reading from a thin sheaf of papers, her eyes glittering quickly across the pages. The sound of the door opening does not draw her attention, though her body moves slightly in the fluid, graceful way Ariana knows so well, telling her that she knows who has entered and, in a few seconds, will be happy to see them. The moment never comes. Ariana feels the force of the blow crack heavily across her mother's head. She opens her eyes and slowly takes her head and her hand away from the door in front of her.

Ariana doesn't think about where she goes next. She very determinedly does not think about anything at all as her boots trudge along the corridor, down some stairs and past three more sets of doors. Her chest and stomach feel all tumbled together and there's a burning sensation in her throat, like the scratchy awakening of a virus. The door in front of her is already open a fraction. She's surprised to see the vibrating shudder of her own hand in front of her as she pushes it further.

'Ariana...' The voice comes from the windows straight ahead. He stands, bending towards them in almost the exact same position he stood in April, when the mountains were still dusted in snow and he was just her grandfather. The days when all she had to worry about was the thought of phoning her mother and asking her to help rescue some freakish creatures of no consequence for reasons she can no longer be bothered to remember.

'Are you alright?' He is scrutinising her and, as she looks back, she recognises the bloom of fear in his expression. Is he scared for her or of her?

'I don't know,' she replies, truthfully. 'I don't know what I am anymore.'

'What's happened?'

She moves to stand next to him, her hands tangling together in the pocket of her hoodie. She looks out at the landscape, the glitter of distant water, the arid mountains and the red deer grazing on the moor below as if the ARC were no more than a large boulder in their midst.

'Nothing. Absolutely nothing. Except... I can do stuff with my eyes. I can make people feel bad if I want to. I can hurt them without touching them. I can make them tell me things. I can see things about them, read their wants and their needs without asking. There's a power inside me and it's getting stronger every day. I don't know where it came from and I don't know what it wants me to do... But it's changed everything. It made me get up and go and listen to you and Dad... Ralph... the other week. And it made me come here this morning... It showed me what really happened. Where I really came from... Just from touching a door.'

'What did you see?'

She looks at him and she knows she doesn't have to say it because the horror is right there in the depths of his ice-blue eyes.

'Ariana...'

'It doesn't matter.'

'But you must think... You must let me explain, I had no idea—'

'You don't need to explain anything to me anymore. You're not my granddad, are you?'

He sighs and looks down.

'But you do know what it is... this power... don't you?' She fixes him with a hard stare, knowing that she looks like Bella, only hardened. Bella less beautiful. Bella infinitely more powerful.

'I don't know if I'm—'

'Tell me what you do know.'

'I mean, it's more of a theory than anything... But I do know that during his time here, Lychen... He was always searching for the answer to what he saw as humanity's great failing,' he frowns out at the mountains, as if this same answer was scattered out there. 'You know about your mother, of course. Project A. The great, pioneering catastrophe... There was a strict vetting process for our candidates, and by candidates I mean the parents. It wasn't all about money, though that was essential... It was also about a certain level of stability. Some of the people we turned down... they gave us nightmares.

'The man you know as Josiah Lychen... his father was

one of them. I don't know what he did to the boy... but he haunted us, Ana and I. So much so that we kept tabs on the child ever since, saw that he grew up without further physical harm, ensured he went to a good university far away from his father. That's why he was offered his position here. He was always so polite, so controlled... Ana never took to him, but she was already ill by then. Her judgment often couldn't be trusted. I never saw anything to be feared, anything to be unduly alarmed about. I just saw a young man, damaged by his father's cruelty but otherwise brilliantly logical and with a keen sense of self-control. I didn't see the obsessive side until I caught him with a needle in his arm one day.'

'He was a drug addict?'

'No. Drug addicts can be treated. What Lychen is... I don't even know if there's a name for it. Psychopathy, sociopathy... neither seem to quite fit. But, in any case, he is obsessed with control, and not just over himself. And when he arrived here, we went and put him in charge of Project C, which had some of the most uncontrollable, unpredictable, emotional individuals imaginable involved... It was the perfect trigger.'

'So what was with the needle?'

'A proposed treatment plan for the children, he told me. In fact, I think he had already begun work on what would eventually become the Guard project. And in the absence of any existing Guard to experiment upon, he used himself...'

'What did it do?'

'Nothing, as far as I could see. Perhaps gave him a greater ability to command others, but I would say he possessed a large degree of that naturally. He was already cold and yet charming when he wanted to be. He never displayed any symptoms other than a general power-hungry ambitiousness, and that was already a fairly common trait among ARC scientists. I told him that self-experimentation was not advised and we never discussed the matter again. Indeed, I never gave it much thought until...'

He looks at her, frowning.

'Until Ralph told you I wasn't really his.'

'Ralph didn't tell me,' he remarks, quietly. His eyes have turned sad once again and she knows he is still seeing her mother.

'My mum told you?'

'Not in so many words... but yes, she let me work it out for myself. A fitting punishment, for not protecting her.'

Ariana turns back to the window.

'I don't care about that. I just want to know what this power is. Why I've got it.'

'Well... as I said before, it's all just a theory... I cannot be sure...'

'But you'd guess it was something to do with what Lychen was injecting?'

'Yes. That, mixed with your mother's genetic predominance...'

'I thought Project A traits weren't meant to pass on.'

'They weren't. The genetic alteration of each Project A Subject was not supposed to affect subsequent generations. But your mother wasn't an ordinary Project A candidate... She was a special case. She was Ana's case... I never knew at the time. I only found out last year, in fact, when I tested her blood for abnormalities... We always thought she was given beauty and grace, a hand-in-hand cocktail. And she was. But she was also given resilience and the strength of it was tenfold that of the other enhancements. It has manifested itself in her ability to control others and it has protected her from the usual Project A ailments, thus far...'

'Thus far?'

'We never did find the specific cause of Project A's failure, though in those cases we were able to examine in depth we were able to discern that their bodies weren't just rejecting the alterations, they were trying to reset the balance. That's why the causes of death were linked to their traits. The more extreme the enhancement, the harsher the punishment. Bella's resilience remains a Project A alteration. The most extreme one administered. If... when... it fails her... I don't know what will happen.'

Ariana shivers.

'Does she know?'

'I don't think so.'

'Shouldn't you warn her?'

'Would you want to know?'

'Yes. Probably. I don't know...'

'Well then. In any case, Bella does not listen to what I have to say anymore. I burned those bridges when I failed her as a father...'

'You should still try.'

'Why? You could tell her for me. That's where you're going, isn't it?'

'No,' Ariana frowns, not sure if she is telling the truth or not. 'I don't know. I haven't... decided yet.'

'I should try and persuade you not to, of course. You have school, it's not safe for you to travel across the country on your own, you're still a child... Your father, your real father, remains an extremely dangerous individual, possibly the most dangerous in the country. Except...'

'Except you can't tell me what to do. Except school

doesn't matter anymore. Except, actually, *I* might be the most dangerous thing in the country right now...' She glares at him, the churn of darkness swilling into an unknowable hatred. She doesn't know why. Ariana is no longer driving it, it drives itself. It yearns in anger for more than the vague images and half-answers he has given her. He turns to her with his palms out, and his eyes know, irritatingly, what is coming. He has known all along, she realises.

'What did he inject?'

'I don't know.'

'Where is the Beaumont facility?'

'Marc will give you a home. He knew you as a small child. He helped your mother when she left here, he paid for her to live and study in London... Julia never knew about it, but he told me when I spoke to him after your aunt's funeral last year—'

'I don't care about that,' she narrows her eyes and he staggers backwards, pain flashing across his face.

'Why are you doing this, Ariana? What purpose will it serve?'

'If you tell them where I've gone, they might stop me before I get there.'

'And what will you do, once you're there?'

'I'll know when I get there.'

'Try Weston first. Please. Just give him a chance...'

'Where is Beaumont?'

He slumps to his knees and a small, quiet part of her quails at the sight of him. The blackness swirls over it and she grabs for it, welcoming the ease of emptiness. His small, round glasses fall from his face and his too-big eyes blink into hers, his mouth moves and slackens and he crumples to her feet before he can say another word.

She shrugs, pulls the piece of paper with the stupid family tree drawing on it out of her bag and drops it next to him. The crunch of his glasses under her shoe does not pause her quick, even steps.

13.04.16

From: el.guerre@hotmail.com

To: Dr.M.Daccourt@gmail.co.uk

Dear Maya,

I'm sorry I haven't written for so long. I don't really know why I'm writing now, to be honest. It's been so long since your last email that me eventually replying has become more of a thing than not. Does that make sense?

I know it's taken me months to reply. Almost a year, in fact. But the truth is that even though I haven't put fingers to keys, I think about your words a lot. And mine. How I would reply. Because – without talking about the things I can't – I do think about it. Children. About how it was for us. How it would be for them. You asked about my childhood with the Blakes. The truth is that I was cherished and nurtured, disciplined and taught to the best of their abilities and never once did I ever feel like a normal child. I was never allowed to, you see. I was not supposed to. That is not the child they chose to raise, and they did choose me. I can't really explain how or why but they did. And I have no real frame of reference (I certainly never felt normal when I lived with you all in Weston either) so I can't say for sure whether I'm glad of the way I was raised. But I wouldn't choose it for a child of my own.

I did meet other Project children, yes. Not like us. We were the last of Project A. But there were other children. Project C, they were part of. Extraordinary individuals with very carefully constructed genetic interference to make them extremely suggestible... along with physical attributes which complemented certain gifts. But the really extraordinary thing was that these gifts were all suggested... They were inundated with suggestion that they could do certain things – fly, for example – and for every twenty who never did, there would be one who could. I was part of it all, Maya. I knew them. I helped raise them. In a way, I was one of them. I wonder, sometimes, if that was the greatest achievement of my life. Yes, I know I'm not even 30, but I sit here in this small flat in this uninteresting town and I wonder whether it has all peaked already. Sometimes the frustration of it all seems like it will overwhelm me, bubble and boil over within me until I can do nothing but scream... I was great once. I was the greatest. Respected, revered... feared, even. I was Bella D'accourt. And now... I wear an insipid mask and I hide and every day I feel like the person I was, the greatness I wielded, slips further and further out of reach... Until I can barely remember the taste of it, the feel of it... any of it. Until all I am left with are the insipid words which go with this mask: *There is a lot to be said for living life under the radar*. Huh. I suppose there is a lot to be said for living life with the radar ablaze at your feet, too.

I'm sorry, I appear to have taken a tangent. But perhaps you, with your 'quiet life' in the country with your partner and your dogs and your past glittering and remarkable behind you, can understand too?

How are things with Jade? Is she still broody? Did you talk to her about children? Does she know about Project A?

You are right, they did tell us that the Project A alterations would not pass through to a subsequent generation. I placed so much trust in that place, in the Blakes. Even when I worked at the ARC and saw for myself some of the corners which were cut, the arrogance and carelessness with which these 'pioneers' played God. (And yes, I played my part, I allowed myself to be caught up in the intoxicating hubris of being the aforementioned great and feared, etc.) But knowing what I know now, I wonder whether the designer baby dream was just another front for a bigger, overriding eugenic experiment. An experiment which only started with A and for all I know is continuing even now: which cords can almost be torn? How far can you stretch a human before they cease to be one? Which traits can endure? And what is the best measure of endurance?

How clever, then, the carelessness becomes. How convenient, to be able to hold one's hands up and say, Well you did sign this contract. We're sorry it hasn't gone quite according to plan, but while we're here, let's see what transpires.

I don't know. It's late. I'm tired. It has been a long day. It has been a long life.

Bella

14.04.16

From: Dr.M.Daccourt@gmail.co.uk

To: el.guerre@hotmail.com

What is your child's name, Bella?

⸻

15.10.16

From: Dr.M.Daccourt@gmail.co.uk

To: el.guerre@hotmail.com

I'm sorry, Bella. I didn't mean to scare you with that last message. You don't have to tell me anything if you don't want to. I might be barking up the wrong tree completely, of course. I just… It just sounded a bit like… Like you were trying to ask me something without coming out and asking it. With the whole children thing, the accountability issues of Project A… The thing about the best 'measure of endurance'. B, if someone did something… If the Blakes included something untoward as part of your genetic make-up and it's passed on…

But I'm getting ahead of myself. I'm babbling conjecture and rumours and whatever. But if I'm not – you can trust me. I hope you know that. And yes, for what it's worth, I do understand the sense of having peaked too soon… The frustrating, empty ache of one's greatest life achievements having passed. But Bella, if I'm right – about you having a child – surely this invalidates those fears? Surely this child, whoever she or he might be, is your greatest achievement? Your life's work? Is that not why you continue to wear the mask you so rage against?

M x

30.4.17

From: Dr.M.Daccourt@gmail.co.uk

To: el.guerre@hotmail.com

Well, Bella... It's been a year and nothing. I hope you are OK. There seems little point reiterating how sorry I am if I've said something. Of course I've said something. We both know I said something. So let's forget it, yeah? Please? Let's start over again with the niceties and the awkwardness. Hi. Now you.

M x

01.10.17

From: Dr.M.Daccourt@gmail.co.uk

To: el.guerre@hotmail.com

Hi Bella,

I don't really know why I'm writing. Things aren't so great for me at the moment. Jade moved out. Because of the baby thing. Our baby. I caved in about two years ago on the condition that she carry the child, that it contains none of my genes. None of this mess I have – this genetic/mental fuckery our parents put upon us. Anyway. She was fine with that... We found a donor, had IVF... Got pregnant on the second try... And we lost it six weeks later. The next one lasted a little longer. Nine weeks. There wasn't a reason. But after that... Jade wanted me to try. I'm younger than her, I'm fit and healthy. She couldn't understand why I wouldn't want to just try. I couldn't really explain it. She knew about Project A. She couldn't see the danger. She couldn't understand that it wasn't just Project A, it was the legacy of Project A, the darkness I felt – feel – in my head growing bigger every day. I don't know what it is – depression, maybe? Anxiety? She told me to see the doctor, I told her I *was* the bloody doctor. That there's no doctor alive who could look at me and understand what on earth could possibly be happening. Except perhaps Dr Blake and even without all you told me, I'd have to be genuinely fearful for my life before I let him back into my head.

I didn't back down. It broke her. It broke us.

I'm sorry to put this on you, Bells. I just… I don't know. I'm sitting here looking at my dogs and not really watching some programme on TV… There's a large glass of wine next to me and it's not the first of the day. And I'm just so fucking lonely. I can't talk to Mum and Dad because I blame them. Silas is gone. I have friends but they don't really get it. I tell them about me and Jade and I can *see* them siding with her. They say the right things and nod their heads just so… but they're also thinking *What the hell is her problem?*

Please reply. I just need someone. Please.

Maya xx

37

June, 2019

I pace up and down my bedroom, cross into the dance studio and walk its length three times until I feel as if the walls are beginning to squeeze in on me. I stride out again, through my bedroom and out onto the terrace. All the while Ethan follows from one doorway to the next, eyes upon me. I cross over to the balcony and stand there, gripping the rail. The sun has disappeared behind a thick thatch of cloud and a sharp wind chills around my body. I watch the small bumps rise atop the new bruise on my arm and slowly begin to breathe more easily. My mind slows its vicious swirl of feelings and I'm aware of a gentle nudge from the corner Ethan lives in. I look up. He's holding out the cashmere blanket wrap I haven't touched since early spring but which, for the weather and my outfit, is perfect. I let him wrap it around my shoulders, watching his eyes, wondering when my using him as a servant will become awkward. Wondering why it hasn't, yet.

'Thank you, Ethan,' I say, quietly.

'You were cold,' he replies, softly. I look around us automatically because at that moment he is so unlike a Guard he might as well have a *broken* sign slung around his neck, but of course we are alone. I know he knows he's showing his softness. I know it because I feel him knowing it. This time, I do look away. Not because I'm embarrassed or he is, but because the level of intimacy between us makes me horribly aware of Felix, out there, making her way back to us once again. And never able to reach the same closeness I have.

'How long will he keep me here, Ethan?'

Ethan focuses his eyes back into the cold stare of the Guard, his body becoming upright and rigid. I know he is accessing the part of him still wired to Lychen, touching and testing it for motive and reason. Then he sighs and comes back to himself.

'I don't know. My connection... it's almost gone. My regression has damaged it.'

'It's not a regression... You're returning to yourself, Ethan. Can Lychen tell?'

'No, he has no reason to know. I obeyed him without hesitation earlier. He won't know I've... changed... until I do something in direct contradiction to his wishes.'

'We'll have to be careful that you don't,' I murmur, looking back out across the sky, the clouds tumbling with brightness as they shield the sun.

'You are worried.'

'Yes. For Ariana.'

'But not for her physical wellbeing.' He frowns. I sigh.

'No. I haven't worried about that for a long time. Even last year, when she was taken in Cornwall, I could *feel* she was OK... And now she's so much stronger... and she's realised what she can do... It's not her body I worry about, it's her mind...'

'You are worried she will find out what Ana and your father did?'

'How can you see that?'

'I see you. Our connection... I believe that it runs far deeper than Lychen intended. His objective was that I could report on your health, but I also have insight into how you feel and process things... Something he did not deem worthy to consider when he stipulated the bond's parameters. I can see Ariana, too, in your memories. I can see that the gifts she has begun like this connection between us – that she was able to perceive others' wants and needs. As a child, she channelled it with simple emotions. She could make you hurt when she was cross with you, she could sense your pain without you voicing it, she could lighten your mood with her own, but only sporadically and without purpose, intention or control. But as her self-awareness has grown with adolescence...'

'...so has everything else. And now she has attacked Dr Blake. What will that do to her, when she returns to herself? When the rage ends?'

'I can only answer what you already know,' he says, simply.

'I know,' I sigh. 'It's better than talking to my dead mother, though.'

He pauses.

'What will happen to her when she reaches your parents' house?'

'My father will take care of her. He will try, anyway.'

'Your mother?'

'I don't know, Ethan. She may have mellowed in recent years. She may feel differently towards a grandchild. Goodness knows she won't get any more...'

'There is something else. You don't believe your own words.'

'No. I don't believe Ariana will go there. I don't think she left that piece of paper on the floor by accident. She's cleverer than that. She's careful. Besides, there isn't anything at Weston that she wants.'

'A home?'

'She doesn't want that, she wants understanding. She wants recognition. She wants to look me and Lychen in the eye and show us that we were wrong to dismiss her. She wants what any thirteen-year-old wants – respect for who they are. It's just that not many thirteen-year-olds pose the same threat if they don't get it.'

'So she's coming here?'

'I suspect so.'

'What will you do?'

'I will do what I've always done. I will protect her.'

'Against Lychen?'

'Against him. Against all of them. And herself, if I can. If she'll let me.'

'How?'

'I don't know yet. All I can do is hope she gives me a chance.'

He opens his mouth to say more, but then he stiffens upright, his eyes sweeping, blank, and takes a step back from the balcony. A second later, the doors to the terrace open. I turn. Delta strides quickly towards us, looking at me in assessment.

'You are to stay here for the remainder of the weekend. Ethan will bring you sustenance, but otherwise he will remain outside the doors.'

He turns to leave and Ethan immediately falls into step beside him.

It is a progress report. Lychen will be pleased to see you have calmed so quickly.

Yes, but the rest of the weekend!

It is a test. The intention is not that long.

It won't be that long. Ariana will arrive before morning. Perhaps before nightfall.

He walks out of the double doors. I will have to move closer if I want to communicate, but there is nothing left to say now. There is nothing left to do, either, but wait. I could have demanded Delta bring Lychen to me, but he would not have come. Nothing I can do will bring him here now, he will only come if it is entirely up to him. I can only hope that he does, before she arrives. I can only hope that I have truly pushed him far enough. And that I can push him a little further. *I can't see any other way of destroying him.* The words bounce back to me as if whispered by the furious clouds themselves and I cannot recall whose suggestion it was in the first place. There are so many voices now, so many touches of contact in my mind, sometimes it is hard to know where each thought comes from. And then, just as I focus on that one and think I can filter my own intention from it, another swarms in, a memory far more distant and enshrouded with a deep, life-wrenching agony unlike any I've ever known: *Do it for hate. Have his child and use it to destroy him.* I shiver. Now that *was* Mamma… Except it wasn't. None of it ever really was, after all. It was only ever me.

This is it, I think. *This is where it will happen. Whatever it is. This is where it ends.*

My hands wrap the edge of the balcony rail and suddenly the wind whips around me so viciously there is not a blanket thick enough to stop my shudders.

38

June, 2019

Ariana is half-dozing, her eyes focusing lazily on a shivering bead of condensation on the smeary train window, when her phone buzzes. She looks down at it, expecting Ralph's name, or Felix's. She's surprised to see the name *Grandpa Marc* flashing on the screen. She never stored the landline number she's been ringing and she certainly never would have been so lame as to store it under *that*.

'Hullo?' She keeps her voice low, trying not to betray her age.

'Hello…' The voice is low, rumbling and familiar in the vague sense of forgotten toys and half-remembered dreams. 'I seem to have a few missed calls from this number on my old landline. My ex-wife Julia wondered if you were trying to get hold of me. I'm Marc D'accourt.'

'Um…' Suddenly she's fully awake and aware of everything from the prickling felt of the train seat surrounding her to the uninterested glance of the old woman sitting across the aisle. She opens her mouth, not quite knowing what she will say, wondering why on earth she answered the call in the first place, but the man gets there first.

'This isn't… Is this… Ariana?'

'Um… yeah.'

'Oh my God, is it really? I had a feeling… Julia said

there was a nuisance caller, always staying silent... She thought it must be someone trying to get hold of me who didn't know I'd moved out. Oh *wow*. How are you, sweetheart? Do you remember me?'

'Er... not really...' But as she says it, an image swarms into her brain. Big hands, a shuddering laugh that seemed to warm her to her very toes. A packet of sweeties all twisted together in a finger-soft paper bag, the calls of children and wind in her hair.

'Did you used to buy me sweets in a paper bag? At the park?'

'Yes!' The voice is full of laughter and the images tumble more clearly than ever. 'We used to visit the sweet shop on the way to the playground after I picked you up from nursery. I never told your mum that... Fancy you remembering!'

'Yeah...' Ariana glances out of the window as the train races through a station. She glances at her watch. Only an hour left till they reach London.

'So... what's going on, love? Are you OK?'

'Yeah... sort of. Well. I don't know why I called really... I guess I had some questions about... stuff. But it doesn't really matter anymore—'

The train announces in a nasal voice that a buffet service is currently available in carriage B.

'What was that? Are you on a train?'

'Um...'

'Ariana, are you with anyone?' The voice has changed now. Ariana feels the blankness within her begin to stir as the rest of her dithers uncertainly. Why had she rung him in the first place? What had been the point? She'd told herself at the time that it was part of her quest for answers, but she knows now that it hadn't been about that, not really. It had been weakness. That quiet part of her grabbing for something lost, something distant and innocent. She should have known she couldn't have that. She wasn't that anymore. The voices had been right, there wasn't anything he could give her. Nothing she needed, anyway.

'I've got to go,' she says, quickly.

'Wait... Listen, love, are you in trouble? Do you need help—'

'Nope, all good, thanks.'

'Where's the train going, Euston? I can be there in an hour—'

Ariana cuts the call with a quick jab of her finger. Urgh. She'd known it was a mistake. She should never have answered in the first place. *But you might need him,* whispers a voice which has crept underneath the swirling anger. It's so faint she isn't sure if it is the one she imagines in her mother's voice or not. *I don't need him. I won't need any of them, once I've found the truth.*

She finds his number in her contacts and presses block. The voice, which has shrunk to a hiss and is now barely decipherable – muttering about being a child and needing money and questions being asked – flickers and dies. Her phone begins to flash again and this time it *is* Ralph. She switches it off.

Felix drives on autopilot. She feels as if she has spent years behind the wheel of this van, the same yawn of pain gnawing at her lower back as she squirms in an attempt to be more comfortable, the same thump-and-drone playlist on repeat, the same pattern of brake lights dotting across the grubby pitted windscreen. She welcomes the bland, sweeping boredom of it all; it distracts from the weeping sore of Ethan's face, turning from her in the alleyway. The hateful flash of pity in Bella's austere gaze. Her phone rings as traffic slows the van to 20mph on the M40. She plugs her hands-free set into her ear.

'Yes?'

'Fee? How's it going?'

'Fine until I got within spitting distance of Oxford. Now there're two pile-ups ahead. Southerners don't know how to drive. How's the old man?'

'Still unconscious. They did surgery because he had bleeding on the brain, but they managed to drain it and now he's in recovery. They're not sure how the bleeding occurred, they think it could have been an aneurysm, maybe a stroke... Certainly there's no *outward signs of trauma,* as they put it.'

'No, well there wouldn't be, would there. Sorry, Ralph, that sucks. Do they know what his prognosis is?'

'It's too early to tell at this stage. They don't know when he'll wake up... could be hours, might be weeks...' His voice trembles and she feels his swallow, lumpen and rough-edged.

'He'll be OK, Ral. He's strong. You all are.'

'Yeah. It's just frustrating... how do I know I've given them the right information? I don't know what happened – what if he hit his head? All I said was that that's how we found him and it's possible he had an argument with someone beforehand, but I could hardly say it was with a thirteen-year-old with crazy psychic powers who's now missing, could I?'

'Couldn't you? I mean, not about the powers thing, but would it be such a bad thing if we got the police involved with finding Ari? It's hardly as if we've done anything wrong here...'

'We can't... Lychen has contacts high up in the police, Dad said he offered to use them to try and track Bella down back in the day...'

'That was fourteen years ago...'

'Fee, I'm not going to chance it... If they're in his pocket and get to her first... Anyway, that's not why I rang.'

'It isn't?'

'No, I just got off the phone with Dom. He had a call at The Manor from Marc D'accourt – Bella's dad. He spoke to Ariana. She was on a train and hung up as soon as he mentioned Euston. She's heading to London, Fee. Not Weston.'

'Wait, he has Ariana's number?'

'I think she had his, I'm not sure, but in any case, Marc said he's heading there straight away. I figured it's a good idea, the more people we've got trying to intercept her the better...'

'Why is she going to London, Ral?'

'I mean... I'm hoping it's to find Bella. But there's every chance it's not. Her argument with Dad... She put him in a coma. She must have been really angry...'

'You think she knows about Lychen?'

'Yeah. I think she might.'

'Ah. *Crap.*'

'How soon do you think you can get to the Beaumont?'

'In normal traffic... maybe an hour and a half... As it is... God, I don't know. Two, maybe more?'

'Just try, OK? I'm sorry... I know it's a lot to ask. With Ethan and everything... are you going to be OK if you see him?'

'Don't worry about me, Ralph. I can deal with it.'

'And Bella?'

'Her too. This is about Ariana. I'll get her out if I can.'

'Thanks, Fee.'

She cuts the call as a police car screeches into her rear-view mirror. She looks straight ahead as she pulls to one side and lets it pass. Her ear is still warm with Ralph's voice and the images he's brought to her... Dr Blake lying still, face sagging lopsidedly in a hospital bed. Ariana alone, her hood pulled tightly over her distinctive hair as she disembarks a train in the bustling, predatory crowds of London... Another child, black-haired bright-eyed, Ariana's age but shorter, stockier, with Felix's smile and Ethan's caramel skin... *Oscar*. Felix passes a cool hand over her forehead as if trying to press the image away. When she looks up, the traffic ahead of her is finally beginning to move at a decent pace. She passes the accident – a lorry and an SUV, flashing lights, shell-shocked people in metal blankets – and begins to pick up speed.

39

June, 2019

Ariana keeps her hood up and her head down as she walks quickly through the crowds at Euston station. She looked up the Beaumont on her phone before she switched it off and knows it's roughly three tube rides away. In any case, her feet are doing that thing that they did earlier at the ARC and taking her onwards without much input from her. She buys a child ticket from the machine on the wall, using the card Ralph gave her for shopping with her friends... She knows they will be able to trace her through it, but that will take time and by then she'll have the answers she needs.

Lychen's face swarms across her brain as she feeds the ticket into the stile and passes through it, the set tightness of his jaw as he strode across the plush office at the ARC, his hand a blur in the air as he hit her mother... Ariana shakes her head. He was kind to her, once. Sort of. He had called her an asset and even though she had messed up their tracking system, he had told her mother he would be happy for her to stay with them. He'd offered to be a family, really. Even without knowing she was actually his... It had been Bella who had denied her that. Bella who had sent her away with strangers. *To protect you.* No. Not to protect her, to get her out of the way. So she could be the only one who shone. The only asset. Yes, that was it. Ariana grits her teeth as she shuffles down the steps, not noticing the old balding man climbing the stairs in the opposite direction, his eyes scanning the thick crowd, his whole body straining in anxiety. He might have seen her if not for the group of tourists rushing between them at the exact same time his head turns.

Ariana lets the power take over. It is easier than being afraid of the crowds and the noise, so much of it, so many bodies pressing in at all angles, so much clammy, regurgitated oxygen. She lets the dark blankness within her rise up and angle her body stiffly against the pole so she doesn't stumble as the train moves. She lets it whisper instinctively to wait until the doors open before moving to get off. She doesn't realise that the ease with which she rides the lurches and jolts of the London underground comes from an inherent muscle memory from early childhood. When her eyes skate over Peckham Rye on the overground map, they don't linger or spark a shadow of recognition. She has no idea, on the surface, that she lived in London for more than a quarter of her life. But her body does.

It's not quite dark by the time she reaches the station nearest the Beaumont facility, but the shadows are beginning to grow. People wander lazily towards pubs lining the streets, their outdoor tables already beginning to fill despite the edgy breeze in the air and the odd spot of rain. Ariana, who had to relinquish her hoodie or risk suffocating from the oppressive heat of the underground, pulls the black garment around her once again. She enjoys the icy plops of rain on her face for a moment or two, before studying a road map on the side of a bus stop. She gathers her blankness around and within her like an invisible, impenetrable cloak and sets off.

The Beaumont gives nothing away from the outside.

Tucked in an industrial area behind a carpet factory and several plain office buildings, the outside perimeter is just high concrete walls with a narrow single lane driveway of gravel. A large iron gateway blocks this off. There's a buzzer on the wall, which Ariana presses, staring straight into the lens of a security camera. Let them see her. She doesn't care.

'Yes?' says a blank-sounding, nasal voice. Ariana recognises it instantly as a Guard voice. A small part of her shivers in fear, but she's glad that it's only a very small part underneath the swirling hatred of blank grit.

'My name is Ariana D'accourt. I'm the daughter of Bella D'accourt. I would like to see Dr Lychen, please.'

There is a long pause. Ariana frowns at the gates, willing them to open with her mind. They remain stubbornly closed.

'Proceed to the front entrance. You will be met and escorted. Do not attempt to enter without an escort,' the voice commands, impassively. The gates swing open easily and Ariana walks through them.

✳

I'm sitting on one of the terrace chairs attempting to read a magazine by the time the double doors open and Lychen strides through them. I've changed into a pair of tight-fitting jeans and a bardot-sleeved white blouse. It's too cold, now that the sun has been swallowed by clouds, to be outside, really. But I'll be damned if I'm going to sit in my bedroom like a chastened child to wait for my punishment. Besides, in this position I can communicate with Ethan on the other side of the door. Not that he can tell me much from there, but I do get a few seconds' warning before Lychen joins me. I shake my hair loose of its clasp and slip my feet into a pair of leather sandals as he opens the door. He is still dressed in his suit and tie, his face tight and miserable. He eyes me warily.

'Wine?' I gesture to the bottle of Rioja and two glasses I'd had Ethan bring half an hour earlier. Lychen crosses over to it and opens it before I can, as if worried I might slip something into his glass. He pours two generous measures and hands me one, watching me sip it without breaking eye contact.

'I'm glad you've calmed down,' he says, as he takes a measured swallow from his own glass and places it down on the table.

'I've had time to reflect,' I say, slowly. 'I was wrong to try and command you earlier. I had agreed not to.'

'Yes.'

'I hope you can understand that it came from a place of desperation. Of worry.'

'Well. There is no need. Blake has the matter in hand, I'm sure.'

'Have you checked my phone? For any updates, I mean?'

'No. I have had rather more important matters to attend to,' he says, wearily. He sits down and takes another large gulp. I raise my eyebrows, surprised.

'Oh?'

'Three of the care homes have reported complaints with their Guard. Apparently their lack of empathic intuition has created a few problems.'

'Well... That's something we're addressing with the Youth, at least. It shouldn't be too hard to adapt the Care Assistants accordingly. And presumably none of the other facilities have had any issues, so that's still a resounding success by all accounts.'

'Quite.'

A strange sound filters through the air to us. A furious squalling mixed with high-pitched, anguished shrieks.

'What's that?' I frown, disarmed.

'That's another of the pressing matters. Daniel has been experimenting with taking some of his other hybrids out of doors following your success with the bird— with Nova. He's managed to unearth a cousin of the porcine hybrid, but the creature is not showing any sign of recognition let alone any inclination to communicate. He thought if he took him outside and let him… explore… with the relation, he might have more success.'

'And…?'

'And the blessed animal broke his leash and charged straight into the pond. It took six Guard men to retrieve him, the cousin went into hysterics and had to be taken to one of the sensory labs to calm down and—'

The shriek comes again, this time more high-pitched and furious than before. It doesn't sound like the noises I've heard coming from the pig hybrid. In fact, if anything, it sounds like—

'Is that Nova?'

'Yes,' Lychen sighs, and passes a hand over his eyes. He doesn't exactly slump in his chair as bend, slightly, so that he is less poker straight than usual.

'She's out too?'

'She was scheduled for exercise this afternoon with you. I don't know why Daniel decided that it would be a good idea to take the pig out at the same time…'

'Probably just trying to mess with me.'

'Perhaps,' he sighs, too weary to even frown at my pettiness. 'In any case, she was all leashed and ready but of course you weren't there, the lab handlers were distracted by the return of the pig hybrid and there was a messy struggle... she managed to fight her way out, the pig only just got back in... Daniel was arguing with one of her handlers that she might as well take exercise as well now she was leashed and ready, the handler was protesting that bad behaviour shouldn't be rewarded. I left when they began to use foul language.'

'They shouldn't be here, none of them... Nova needs a purpose-built facility now. She needs to be able to fly in the open air without six million people crammed into the city beneath her...'

'Yes. I can see that. But our funds can only stretch so far. It isn't cheap running this place and the Futura. The Guard project returns have yet to make a dent in the debt we generated developing them.'

I watch him. His glass is half empty. There are definite shadows within the waxy skin under his eyes and, for the first time, I can see the sprout of wrinkles around the edges. I take another sip of wine, letting the rich liquid slide over my tongue and down my throat, settling over the frazzled edges of worry that I'm hiding so well.

'You do realise that there is a solution which won't cost you a penny tucked away up in Cumbria, don't you?' I say. I watch the words settle into his face and deepen its frown as I'd known they would. He opens his mouth to reply, but at that moment Delta appears at his side to murmur urgently into his ear and Ethan, still outside the doors, tugs at my attention. *She's here.* Lychen says something back to Delta, who strides away. I place my glass down on the table, fighting to keep my body – wired for fight – still and sinuous in its chair. Lychen finishes the last of his wine in two gulps, places the glass next to mine and tops them both up before speaking.

'It seems your concerns for Ariana can be laid to rest, at least,' he says, smoothly.

'Oh?' I paint my face surprised.

'It would appear she has made her way here, alone. She is being escorted across the premises as we speak,' another shriek from the direction of The Yard reaches us. I wonder whether Nova has caught a glimpse of Ariana or whether she is just furious that I haven't come to oversee her flight for today, that I haven't fulfilled my promise that she will be allowed off the leash very, very soon. I should feel sorry for the hapless people attempting to control her, really, but I can't spare the feeling underneath the surge of adrenaline thundering on the shoreline of my awareness.

'She's here?'

'Delta has gone to meet her now,' he says, watching me carefully. I stand up, allowing my hands to flutter around my elbows. I shake my hair out of my face and angle myself towards the double doors, waiting. Here we go.

40

Autumn, 2018

I waited in the car until I was absolutely sure Ralph hadn't been lying. And then I waited a little longer. I had requested an ordinary vehicle, nothing that would draw attention. I had wanted to come alone but, of course, I hadn't really expected Lychen to agree. Not so soon. Not when the balance between us, so new again, so familiar, had only just been reset. Still, the Guard people took the front seats and, as neither had spoken a word since the car had rumbled down the long, gravel driveway of the Beaumont and through the iron gates, I could almost fool myself that they were just normal bodyguard/chauffeurs.

I checked my reflection in my pocket mirror. My hair was loose. It felt strange to wear it like this out in public, where anyone could spot me. I still had glasses, three wigs, and two spare pairs of contact lenses in my large handbag. I reached past them and took out my dark sunglasses, telling myself that they were for the brightness of the day outside, not to make me feel safer. It was not rational to need sunglasses to make me feel safe, not anymore.

I glanced out of the window as the hearse drew up outside the church. The pallbearers lifted the nondescript coffin onto a small trolley and, as they began to wheel it down the path, I glanced automatically at the passenger seat next to me, my hand reaching for hers. Nothing there, of course. She was gone. I took another breath as the coffin disappeared from view. My throat was sore as I swallowed; I did not know if it was a lingering symptom from the dust and dirt Ethan's pipe-bombs had shattered into my windpipe less than a week before or from the new spray of bruising gathered there.

'What are your orders?' I asked, quietly.

'No straying out of line of sight. Commence return journey before sixteen hundred hours.'

'So I can't go inside the church?'

'Not without accompaniment.'

'Fine,' I breathed, sizing them up with my eyes. 'You, on the left. You follow me at a distance. Do *not* let anyone notice you. Keep me in your line of sight by all means, but do not indicate that we know one another. Wear sunglasses, keep your head down. Act like a normal person.'

'Affirmative.'

I waited a few more moments and then slid neatly out of the car. The Guard I had selected, the smaller and slightly less conspicuous of the two, climbed rigidly out of the passenger seat and waited for me to begin walking towards the church before he followed.

The day was bright and sunny but with the unmistakable twinge of approaching winter in the tips of the breeze. The church was small, nestled in a green landscape dotted with trees, shrubs, and graves. The concrete path undulated with roots. I wondered if I had been here before, as a child. If I had, I didn't remember. I glanced behind me at the Guard as he plodded methodically behind me. Strange, I thought, to feel a completely different kind of fear of discovery now. One that was far more complicated than I was used to. I tugged my new black woollen coat lower over my wrists and, as I reached the small, stone archway of the church's entrance, I gathered the fur collar closer around my neck. The bruised skin tingled a little where it was covered. I had not been able to stop my initial resistance, it was so a part of me, so enmeshed with the memories and darkness. I had been punished for trying. And now there was an agreement in place. The bruises would heal, and they would not be replaced. But this was not about that.

I waited until I heard singing and then I placed a gloved hand against the door, pushed it open as lightly as I could, and slipped through. Luckily the congregation was sparse and no one turned as I headed for the last pew and slipped around its outer edges. Glancing behind me, I saw the Guard man entering as quietly as I had, scanning the crowd and, once he spotted me, standing at ease at the back of the church. For a moment I was glad of his total impassivity teamed with the formality of his suit. He could easily pass as an undertaker.

It took me less than ten minutes to decide that I shouldn't be there. That the *brilliant mind* the minister spoke of, the tragic genius who travelled far and wide, loved her family and volunteered at the local old people's home... None of this matched the sad, warm flow of words I had read a thousand times over the last five years. I didn't even recognise the picture on the front of the programme. Bobbed hair, round-faced, eyes nervous behind their thick lenses – she was nothing of the tall, smooth-limbed girl I remembered racing me to the climbing frame, quick eyes always glancing back to make sure I was there, I was keeping up, I wasn't doing anything odd. Who was this stranger who had spent the last year of her life building animal sanctuaries in Africa and helping vaccinate deprived communities whilst I laughed throatily at my aging lech of a line manager, let him casually brush his crotch against my body in the lift and told myself I was doing it for my daughter? My increasingly resentful, hollow-eyed *life's achievement*. Where was the sad, lonely, alcoholic depressive?

What did you expect? You haven't spoken to Maya for over two years. You haven't seen her for more than twenty.

I know... but still... Something, I suppose. Some spark of something familiar. Something that might... I don't know.

Might make you feel something?

Well... yes. Something sad. Something mournful, like all these other people. She was my sister, after all.

Yes, she was. And you ignored her when she asked for help.

Because she knew about Ariana.

Did she? Or was that just an excuse?

Well, it doesn't matter now. It's not like she killed herself. She died of a brain tumour. The minister even confirmed it. It wasn't a lie. It's true. Project A will probably kill me too, one day.

You never thought it was a lie. Not really. That's not what you came here for.

I came to say goodbye to my sister.

No.

I came to tell her sorry, to ask her forgiveness.

Not that either. Maya has nothing to do with why you are here.

I waited until another hymn – *All Things Bright and Beautiful* – brought the congregation to its feet. I waited until the petite woman in the large, black fascinator and this season's Dior dress suit began to wail loudly into the shoulder of the large, balding man in the front row. I waited until I admitted to myself I had been staring at her more than anyone else in the church, then I slipped quickly out of my row, along the back of the aisles and out through the front door, the Guard man on my tail. I led him slowly back to the car, but I did not tell the driver to leave. I checked my watch. Lychen had given me three hours. I still had one left.

I *didn't* know why I had come, despite Mamma's claims. I had received the message late the night before –

> Maya's funeral is tomorrow at 2pm, Weston Baptist Church. Dad wanted me to let you know. We have been told our presence would not be welcome, so there's no worry you will bump into us. Ariana is doing fine.

I had swiped the message away without thinking about it, but later that night, when I lay in still-unfamiliar darkness, swallowing painfully against the new weight in my throat, panic still flowing and flighty from his touch, I'd thought *why not.* There was no one I had to hide from anymore, after all. Why shouldn't I pay my respects to my only sister?

It was only now, as I stared out of the car window as the church doors opened and the congregation began to stumble forth into the unexpected brightness of the afternoon, that I realised why I had really come. What I needed to do. Mamma had been right – I had been right – it wasn't about Maya. It wasn't even about me, at least not entirely. I was here to do what I had said I would do all along. I was still breathing, after all, wasn't I?

The balding man, his hand gripped tightly around the shoulders of the woman even as he averted his gaze from the delicate dabbing of her eyes, steered her along the path out of the church. Mourners muttered things to the couple, but no one stopped them, no one reached a hand to grip theirs. No one broke into their tight, contemptuous embrace.

The legacy of Project A...

A tall elegant woman with smooth red hair and a similarly flame-haired baby on her hip broke away from the crowd and approached the couple. I could tell, even without hearing them, that she wasn't passing on her respectful condolences. Marc let go of his wife, holding his hands up as if apologising. Julia swarmed forward, all spindly legs and melodramatic gestures as she thrust her delicate lace handkerchief at the woman. The redhead – Jade, I presumed – simply stared her down disdainfully, said a few words and then turned smartly to leave. Even her child watched with pity as Marc took up his wife's arm once again and lead her away in the opposite direction.

I waited until they began to walk towards the car. Then I opened the door once again and, before I could think myself out of it, stepped out and into their path.

41

June, 2019

The first things I notice about my daughter when I see her for the first time in eight months are the lost things. The baby-roundedness of her jawline. The full apple-red cheeks. The wild hair. The uncertainty of her stride and the warmth in her green eyes. All gone.

The creature who strides scornfully through the double doors, imperiously ignoring the Guard people on either side of her, her eyes pinioned on mine, is almost a stranger. Her hair is shorter than I've seen it in years, its springs tucked back behind her ears. Her face is harder; set and almost chiselled. And she's grown. As she strides towards me, I realise that she's as tall if not taller than me now. Her baggy hoodie doesn't quite hide the new curve of her chest and, though still leggily slim, her shape is veering more towards hourglass than beanpole.

'Hello, mother,' she says, her voice deeper than I remember but still hers. I smile at the dramatic teenager-ness of her, the defiantly crossed arms, jutting chin, solidly planted feet in—

'Are those my old walking boots?' I say in surprise.

'Is that all you have to say to me?' She snaps, her gaze flicking from me to Lychen, who has stood up and is watching her inscrutably. I think about the last time I saw her, the magnetic pull between us as she'd run into my arms, the tickle of her hair under my nose, the sweet, safe softness of her.

'You look wonderful. It's so good to see you,' I say, keeping my voice low. The two Guard still stand either side of her but drop back to wait against the double doors as Lychen makes a gesture off to my left. Ariana looks back at me and I see a flicker of the little girl behind her careful shield, a flicker of longing to step back into safeness, let me hold her. She twitches and I unfold my arms a fraction. The movement draws the shutters down over her gaze and she glowers. Something cold pushes against my body like a slap of ice.

'Forgive me if I don't exactly believe you,' she says, coldly. 'You've been lying to me my whole life, after all. Why would you start telling the truth now?'

'Ariana, let's—'

'Has she told you, yet?' She turns to Lychen. He frowns.

'Ariana—'

'*No!*' This time the icy push knocks me backwards off my feet and onto the hard, rain-spotted ground. She stares at me with a cold fury which I have never seen before. It's utterly devoid of anything I knew of her and, for the first time, I'm terrified.

'I'm done, OK? I'm done with your sweet-voiced little lies and manipulations. It won't work anymore. Not on me. I don't need you anymore.' She spits at me before turning to Lychen, who has taken two steps towards me but stops when Ethan reaches me first. I take Ethan's hand and let him help me back to my feet.

'What's this all about?' Lychen turns to Ariana in mystification. 'I cannot allow—'

'You're my father,' Ariana says, keeping her voice level

but not quite able to banish the small wobble beneath the words. It hurts me more than her strike, that wobble. It tells me that there is a little of my daughter there, still, underneath this strange, emotionless presence. It tells me that she's still there and she still struck me down and showed no remorse.

'What?'

'You're my real father. You and her, you made me... That night back in August fourteen years ago. I know what you did. I saw it.'

'You *what?*' I say, gripping Ethan's hand tighter, my horror swirling like a growing tornado.

'I went to the ARC this morning... I wanted to find out what I am... Where I came from. Really. I overheard Ralph and Dr Blake a few weeks ago, they were having a little pep-talk on the morning of the day you met up with him... I heard Ralph saying that I wasn't really his. Dr Blake knew, Felix too. Seems like no one knows how to tell the truth anymore, so I found out for myself. I knew where to go... I went to your old office at the ARC, I put my hand on the door and I *saw.* Him, coming in, hitting you... I worked out the rest...'

'But...' My brain races to overtake the blooming siren of panic. I don't dare glance at Lychen. I can feel the shock radiating from him like cold heat but already it is beginning to change, to burn into anger. 'But surely... if you know what he did... you understand a little bit of *why* I lied to you...'

'I understand that you used him to control me. You fed me lies and nightmares for years so I wouldn't give you away...'

'It wasn't like that—'

'Oh what, you were trying to keep me safe? I don't

need protection, in case you hadn't noticed, *mother*.' She gives a jolt of her chin and I have just enough time to throw my hands up in defence before I find myself on the ground again, this time thrown further away from Ethan. It takes a second or two to feel the pain searing in a blaze across my hands and cheek. My vision blurs but I can see Ethan's large shoes hurrying towards me, until—

'No,' Lychen's voice is cold and hard. 'Leave her.'

Ethan hesitates. I urge him to do what he says.

'Why've you come here?' Lychen turns to Ariana. I watch through a veil of blurred edges and red spots. I don't remember hitting my head, but when I move to try and get up, the terrace lurches and swims.

She's keeping you down.

I'm not even sure who says it – is it Ethan? Or Mamma? In any case I can't move. I watch from the ground, my hands clenching on the tiles. The panic, to my surprise, begins to subside a little as if in relief at the relinquishment of control. I try to think through the blurry dizziness, Ariana's words coming to me as if through a dense hedge.

'...don't want to play happy families or anything like that. You're still a scumbag rapist as far as I'm concerned. I just want to know what it was you did to yourself back at the ARC, when you first started working there. Blake said you used to experiment on yourself. Trying to give yourself superpowers or something. I want to know what it was.'

'You believe that is what is causing your telekinesis?'

'Telek— what?'

'Moving things with your mind. That's what you did, is it not?'

She laughs; a cold, bitter mockery of sound which rips at my heart.

'I can do much more than just move things... I'm more powerful than you could ever imagine. I see patterns and codes. I hurt people without touching them. I can think pain at someone and they feel it.'

'Just because it's moving things which you can't see, doesn't mean it's not telekinesis,' Lychen's voice has lost a little of its shock and is full of the scorn he usually reserves for employees who have especially disappointed him, usually by doing or saying something emotional.

'I see no great power here, just a young girl with a source of potential within her that she is wasting on wild displays of messy emotion.'

I blink and my vision clears a little. Ariana is staring at him with a mixture of sourness and intrigue. He has his back to me, so I can't guess what he's thinking or feeling. Just beyond him, I sense Ethan watching me and urge him to stay robotic. As I do so, I realise the clarity of my thoughts and the stability of my hands on the ground. My face still burns and I can feel blood running down my chin, but I don't feel close to passing out anymore.

'Was that what you were injecting, then? Telekinesis?'

'You think we had the resources to simply bottle genetic ability like it's a magic potion?' He gives his hollow, humourless laugh. 'This isn't *Harry Potter,* you silly little girl. I used to develop chemicals designed to enhance latent genetic properties within people, similar to how the Project-C children were prepped for their individual talents. I wanted to see if it could be done with adults. It wasn't my main focus of research and so I didn't have the resources for extensive experimentation. So I used myself. Nothing substantial transpired – I improved my power of influence over people, perhaps, but much of that was down to manner and confidence – and I put it aside once I began focusing on something new.'

'So what was it? Why did it skip a generation? Will it last or am I like the Project C children whose abilities all left them...'

'I don't know,' he says slowly, carefully.

I reach into my pocket for a clean tissue and bring it to my bleeding cheek.

'But I could help you find out.'

'What do you mean?'

'Stay here for a bit. Let me look into this extraordinary talent you've got within you. Let us see what you can do with it. I've not seen much of it... but from what I gather, I believe you've only tapped the very edges of its potential... I have the resources to find out all the answers, Ariana. If you want them.'

Ariana shrugs. I bring the tissue away. I feel the blood beginning to clot as the sting subsides. Slowly, I get to my feet. Ariana's focus switches back to me and, for just a moment, I see the same little girl flicker. Remorse.

'He'll use you and spit you out when he's done,' I hiss, my voice strange and torn. I keep my eyes on hers, preying on that uncertainty which has crept back into her gaze. 'He'll turn you into one of *them*,' I gesture at Delta, blank-faced between her and Lychen.

'I'll let her be whomever and whatever she wants to be,' Lychen snarls, turning to me, his face a whirl of raging contempt. 'Who am I to hold her back?'

'He'll never love you, Ri. He's incapable of love, he'll just want to control you, that's what he does... That's what he's been doing to me and I stayed and I let him and I lied everyday with my entire *life* so you wouldn't have to...'

I feel Lychen's gasp and know, without looking at him, that his careful blankness has all but gone now. I can feel him burning with white-hot rage, painfully human and swarming with underlying pain as my words knife his deepest parts. In another time and place I might have enjoyed the feeling of it tumbling from him in all its chaotic glory, but right now all I can focus upon is her. I reach for her with everything I am.

Please, Ariana. You have this power for a reason. Don't give it to him—

The words have barely registered on her face as I send them to her when she reacts, the confusion peeling away like a curtain.

'Stop telling me what to do!' For the third time, I'm flung backwards. This time I feel the shock of the balcony railing against my back before I register the pain in my body. I gasp and everything slows down. Ethan stares from me to Ariana and I can feel him wrenched between trying to help me or stop her from hurting me more. He turns towards her. At the same time, Lychen takes the few furious strides he needs to reach me. Ariana's push subsides and I sag loosely against the railing for a moment before his hand reaches, icy as it was the night he flung me onto my desk fourteen years ago, and finds my throat. He lifts. My body screams.

'I loved you,' he hisses, his voice bound by painful fury. 'I *loved* you.'

I gasp, my airway battling the urge to tell him – make him – let me go. He wraps another hand around my upper arm. My feet kick outwards. Ahead, Ethan turns from Ariana and we all realise he won't get here in time.

'You're not who I thought you were,' Lychen says, quietly. His face turns deathly still. Then, with one swift movement, he thrusts me up and over the balcony. I give away the chance to struggle, and reach, instead, for the chance to search for her one last time, her eyes round with shock, her mouth open around my name, her hand outstretched but too late... too late.

There are screams as I fall, but they are not mine.

42

June, 2019

Ethan feels it the moment it happens. He'd gone for the girl, his straightforward Guard mind telling him with its utterly unemotional logic that she was the biggest threat, that she was the one who needed to be neutralised. He had let the clear logic of it overpower the small flicker of turmoil and stomped towards her, intending to wrap himself around her and take her away from Bella. But he'd been wrong. It wasn't his fault. Nor was it the fault of the small, blooming reminder of humanity that had begun, more and more, to swim to the surface of whatever it was he was now. Guard people were programmed to make decisions based on the most likely outcomes. He had easily pinpointed Ariana as the major threat, she had attacked his charge three times now. But he'd been wrong.

He had seen it on Ariana's face first, had found himself acknowledging the irony even as the horror had begun to sprout as he turned and watched Lychen lift Bella by the throat. He could feel Bella struggling to breathe, could feel her airway tighten even as he realised, with surprise, that she wasn't panicking. Not like she had been earlier. Instead, she was utterly calm. As if this had been part of her plan all along. He had frowned as he began to run, knowing it was always going to be too late, because Lychen knew where he was and Delta was moving as well, moving to block him like a man-shaped bollard. And for a moment everything was still; Bella was suspended in the air above the balcony, unable to breathe, her eyes searching for her daughter's. Lychen held her still and close like a strange, death-grip embrace. Ethan ran and ran and didn't get anywhere.

There is a lurch, a flurry of fluttering hair and a small leather sandal which flies over all their heads and Bella is gone and for the first time in eight months, Ethan finds himself untethered, free of her tight leash on his mind and body and he opens his mouth and howls.

Someone shrieks. At first he thinks it's the girl, but when he spares her a glance he sees her frozen, her face a prism of shock, her hand outstretched still. Lychen is a pillar of stone against the balcony rails. Ethan moves forward as if wading through sand as the shriek comes again, animalistic, terrified and as he reaches the railings something niggles in his newly-whole mind. *No thump. No thump.* Even tiny Bella would make some sort of noise as she landed. Ethan knows the layout of the Beaumont. Beneath the balcony of the North headquarters is nothing but pavement and road, skull-shattering hardness. Even with this niggle of reason, he looks down and forgets how to breathe.

There is no crumpled body far below. No small broken doll. There are wings – impossibly huge, golden-coloured wings – arms grasping a tangle of limbs and feathers and it all lands on the ground as he watches. He takes one second to blink, breathe and realise that they are alive. She is alive and so is Nova, for that is who has her, of course. Then he turns, not caring that he is blazing anguish and relief and more all over his face right in front of Lychen, who appears to be in some sort of trance anyway, and he runs.

Felix is stuck in traffic once again. She can see the walls surrounding the Beaumont and knows that if she takes the next left she will come across its front gates, but she also knows that there is no chance she will get any further that way. They tried once, several years ago now, when Lychen first started making the Guard people. Ethan had been with her, of course. They'd driven in Ralph's old Fiesta up to the front gates and told the person who'd answered the intercom – a real person back in those days – that they had an appointment. This had confused the other party long enough for Felix to hack into their security system and bugger up some of their surveillance. She'd caused a fair bit of trouble that day without them ever getting past the front gate.

The traffic inches forward. Felix glances from the clock on the dashboard to the left turn at the lights. She has an emergency back-up plan in the form of a blue flashing light she can fix to the roof of the van, but it really is only for extreme emergencies... And she isn't completely sure that this is what that is. After all, if they're right about Ariana she's more than capable of holding her own. Still, her train would have arrived hours ago. She's willing to bet money that Ariana has found her own way inside the fortress of walls to her left. Felix sighs, thinking furiously. She doesn't have a plan. Now she's here, the jittery uncertainty mixes with adrenaline and she wonders what on earth she could possibly do to help anyone, let alone Ariana. Just make sure she's OK, she thinks. Just make sure she's OK and maybe check on Ethan too... And if you get a chance to punch Bella in the face... Someone screams loudly nearby and the car in front brakes sharply. Felix glances out of the smeared windscreen to see a strange, dark and fuzzily indistinct shape tumbling through the air. She has just moments to glimpse impossibly large wings which are beating in an odd, jerky way as if broken, before the car in front pulls forward and the one behind honks loudly. Felix grits her teeth, gulps bulkily and reaches for the blue light in her glove compartment.

Five minutes later she pulls up on the pavement in a backstreet off the main road. A massive, golden bird is standing nearby, its wings still outstretched as it leans over something. Luckily, the road – more of a one-way alley than a proper street – is deserted, though one or two passers-by are already beginning to gather at the far end, squinting at the flash of Felix's blue lights. She switches them off quickly and darts out of the van. It takes her a few more seconds to understand what she's seeing and connect the strange, womanly bird creature to the child she'd known back at the ARC, but she forces herself to recover when she notices the body on the ground.

'Oh Jesus,' she groans, kneeling down. Bella's face is covered with matted blood and hair, her arms and midriff are all ripped and bloody. 'What the hell happened to her?'

She doesn't really expect an answer from Nova, whose head jerks back and forth, but she makes a strange, growling noise at the back of her throat, stops and then tries again.

'Fell...' she grunts, eventually.

'Well, yeah,' Felix checks for a pulse. It takes a while to find but it's there, fast and faint, like a tiny animal's. She looks up, past Nova to the distant balcony rising from the sharp points of the North building.

'Go... Now... *Go*,' Nova hisses, jerking forward and trying to grab Bella with her hands, which Felix now notices are more like talons and instantly rip new shreds in Bella's clothes. Felix looks from them to the cuts blooming along Bella's arms and partially-exposed torso and instinctively reaches to stop her. Then she hesitates. She can sense Nova's agitation, her glances to the van and past it, to the entrance of the alleyway where more people are gathering. Felix's brain ticks furiously. No Ariana. No Ethan. None of this is what she came here for. Ralph would have hauled Bella into the van and been halfway to the M25 by now... but this is *Bella*... Felix bites her lip and glances behind her. Then she shrugs off the clean white shirt she is wearing over a vest and wraps it around Bella's upper body. The blood immediately blossoms across the white.

'*Go... Now!*' Nova reaches for Bella again, her entire face screwed up with tense concentration.

'Yes, I know, I know. I'm just... I just need to think...' *Come on, come on...* And there, at last, comes the figure she's been waiting for. Thick-set and steady on his feet, Ethan breaks from the small crowd at the head of the passageway and sprints towards them. He stops short as he reaches them and for a glorious moment, his eyes meet Felix's and they're his, truly, properly *his,* full of confusion and love and concern... She grins and he looks from her to the bloody mess of Bella on the ground. Without blinking, he scoops her up, turns towards the van and runs for it. Nova half flies, half sprints behind him, as if uncertain how to do either entirely correctly. Felix waits one more second, the grin frozen on her face as several impossible horrors scream to be heard, before following them.

Delta reaches the far side of the alleyway just in time to see the rear-lights of the van disappear into the adjoining road. He blinks, taking in the number plate, the cracked rear bumper and the glimmer of blue lights. Then he turns on his heel and jogs, evenly, back to the Beaumont.

43

June, 2019

A little after three in the morning Ralph finds himself turning into The Manor's empty driveway. The entranceway is lit, but it is the only source of light other than his yellowing headlights, which throw the higgledy-piggledy architecture into looming shadow and odd bulges of stone. Ralph aches for sleep with every fibre of his frame, feeling his back curve into its looming stoop as he climbs out of his car, but at the same time his brain whirs with all that's happened in the last few hours. His father, lying motionless in the hospital bed. Ariana, gone. Ariana, knowing the truth and running straight to Lychen. And Bella... The call had been perplexing to say the very least, mostly because it had come from Ethan, whose voice Ralph had thought he would never truly hear again. *Bella's hurt. We're bringing her home.* He'd asked for more details, but there had been a strange chattering in the background and Felix had said something indistinct and the line had gone dead.

The night is cool and clear, the stars patterning the inky sky. Ralph lifts his face upwards and breathes deeply, enjoying the sensation of stillness, the trickle of chilly air with the hint of velvety blossoms within it. He begins to stride towards the house just as the rattling, groaning sound of the van greets him. The adrenaline leaps to the fore once again and he's jogging towards the rumbling vehicle before his mind can catch up.

Felix barely has time to cut the engine before Ralph reaches the dirt-strewn rear doors and thrusts them open. The first impression he gets is a lot of feathers, then the large, ruffled form of Nova scrambles clumsily past him and immediately unfurls her large wings. Ralph stares as she beats them once, twice, her face held up to the sky as his was only moments earlier, before she begins running in a bobbing, uneven way, her wings thrusting her up and off the ground untidily.

'What the—'

'Let her go,' comes Bella's weak voice from inside the van. Ralph turns so fast that his exhausted body nearly topples over. Bella is a mess. Her face is half-covered by an already-bloodied bandage and it looks like the remains of the van's first-aid supplies have been exhausted on her arms, upper body and left leg, which is duct-taped to a make-shift splint in the form of a paint-stirring stick. Ethan clambers out of the back of the van and instantly turns back to lift Bella, who winces.

'Ethan, you're… here,' Ralph says, somewhat redundantly, passing a hand over his head and feeling very strange. He turns to Felix, who has joined them with an odd, brooding expression on her face.

'What the hell happened, Fee?'

Ethan strides towards The Manor without looking at either of them, Bella held neatly in his arms. From the shadow of the oak trees, Nova makes a strange, soft coo of sound. Ralph feels as if he's slipped into some sort of bizarre dream-like dimension with all the pain and tiredness of reality but none of the sense.

'That,' Felix mutters, 'is a *very* good question.' She

slams the doors of the van shut.

'Well... didn't anyone say anything on the way here?' Ralph glances from the dark, woman-shaped bird in the nearest tree to the front door, where Ethan and Bella have already disappeared.

'Well... Bella was out cold when I found her and Nova... After watching them both fall out of the sky while I was still trying to navigate the North Circular. She doesn't seem to have suffered any major head injuries. Ethan thinks her leg is broken and she's pretty torn up, but I think that's more due to Nova trying to save her.'

'Nova was saving her?'

'As far as I can gather, yes...' They begin to walk towards The Manor, keeping their voices low but neither knowing why, exactly.

'Didn't Ethan tell you...?'

'Ethan spent most of the journey tending to her royal highness and trying to keep Nova from ripping us all to shreds.'

They find the front entrance and the downstairs rooms shrouded in darkness. Felix heads straight for the curving staircase and, after a moment's hesitation, Ralph shuts the front door behind them, but does not lock it. He follows Felix up the first flight of stairs, his brain staggering to keep up with all the madness. It's only when he sees the second door on the left open, an unusual sight in itself, that he realises where Ethan has taken Bella.

Felix waits for him and they enter together. The room is softly lit by disused lamps. Bella lies back on the soft, purple eiderdown, her hair tangled and matted like Ralph has never seen it before, her face a ghostly white beneath the livid bandage. He finds himself unable to look directly at her, it feels like a violation. Instead he glances around

The Child Left in the Dark

the room, taking in its dustiness, the smear of bloody footprints across the old rug, the wardrobe still slightly ajar from whenever the last time Ariana was in here... Ethan is peeling some of the bandages from the wounds on Bella's arms and surveying the damage beneath.

'Is he still... bonded?' Ralph frowns and, turning to Felix, sees the same expression mirrored on her face.

'I'm not sure. I didn't think so at first – his face and his voice are so different to how they were before. I think either the serum had some delayed effect or she did something to bring him back... but then... look at him. He seems to know what she needs before she even moves... I don't think I've heard them say a word to each other the whole time... not that I'd have heard much above the noise Nova was making. You should see the state of the van...'

'Is Nova...'

'Safe, as far as I know. Not exactly one for conversation. Or vehicular travel, for that matter... but once Bella woke up she calmed right down, even said a few words I could recognise. I don't think she's a threat to us...'

'And she's alright out in that tree?'

'She's fine,' Bella's voice comes weaker than before, but with the old steeliness that Ralph knows so well.

'She saved my life.' She shuts her eyes and lies back on the pillow. Ethan replaces the bandages and comes over to Felix and Ralph.

'She's lost a lot of blood and her leg is broken. I think she needs to go to hospital but she is insisting she'll be OK here. I can immobilise her leg properly, luckily it's a clean break—'

'Do you have X-ray vision or something?' Felix's voice cuts through them all like a blade. Ralph glances from Bella to the ceiling, wondering if Dominic and Tess are awake and listening, anxious not to intrude, desperate to hear what's going on.

'I have medical training from being a Guard. And I just... I know what's going on with her.'

'Are you still bonded?'

'I don't know,' Ethan looks down, clearly uncomfortable. 'Something happened when she went over the edge of the balcony... I feel different but... I can still feel her...'

'Look, never mind that now,' Ralph cuts in as Felix opens her mouth furiously. 'What happened, Ethan? Where's Ariana? Is she OK? Marc D'accourt said he was trying to get to her, did he manage to? I haven't been able to get hold of him since...'

'Ariana arrived at the Beaumont this evening,' Ethan says, his voice sounding far more Guard-like now that he was dealing in facts again. 'She was escorted up to Bella and Lychen's quarters in the North building just after six. She came alone and appeared to be in good health...'

'What happened then? Did she do... this?'

'She did attack Bella... I don't know how she did it,' his large face creases into a frown and he becomes instantly recognisable once again. He turns to Bella. Ralph follows his gaze. Bella is watching them out of the one heavily-lidded eye not covered by the bandage. A tear blooms from its edge and rolls down her cheek. Ralph crosses to her in long, quick strides and crouches on the floor next to the bed, taking one of her hands.

'Did she do this?' He murmurs again, quietly. He still feels the strange dream-like sense of ethereal reality. It permits him to ask the impossible questions, hold Bella's hand without feeling awkward. Let all the worry spill into his face.

'She... I think she pushed me backwards. Using her mind.' Bella's voice is so low, so quiet that Felix and Ethan come closer as well so that they can hear.

'My face...' she raises the hand that isn't in Ralph's up to the bandage and winces as she finds it.

'She did that the second time she struck you,' Ethan says, his voice different again. Gentle, like he's talking to a precious child. 'It was like a slash through the air. It whistled. And then you couldn't get up. She was holding you down.'

'Why? What did she want?' Ralph stares between them.

'She was angry... She knew about Lychen. About *how.* Everything. I tried to tell her... But she'd had enough. She wasn't *there.* Not my Ri. Not really.' Bella's voice fades and she shuts her eye. For a moment Ralph wonders if she's fallen asleep, but then her breath comes in one long, shuddering gasp and there's a glimmer of green as her lashes flicker open.

'She wanted to know about something Lychen did to himself when he was working here,' Ethan says, his voice sounding louder than it is because it is so much stronger than hers. 'She said Blake had told her that he experimented upon himself and that this was the key to working out who she was and how she could do what she could... Lychen said that he could show her all the answers, that he could teach her how to harness her new power... She seemed to be intrigued by the idea. Bella tried to warn her against trusting him... That's when she pushed her against the edge of the balcony.'

'And...?'

'I tried to stop it. I went for Ariana. She was the clear threat. But it was like he knew exactly what I was going to do... It was like he was waiting for me to go for her...'

'Lychen?'

'Yeah. He went for Bella. Took her by the throat. Threw her over the top before I could so much as take a step.'

'*Lychen* tried to kill her?' Ralph stares from Ethan to Bella. She doesn't speak but gives a small affirmative twitch.

'They've... There's been a lot of tension between them recently. He accused Bella of making him weak, she had found a way of pushing him, needling him, using his obsession against him. Then today he refused to let her help try and find Ariana...'

'Ah. So that's what I heard. And that's why you never answered your phone again. Oh, Beast... If I'd known, I'd have come.'

'You had... your dad...' She says, barely whispering.

'Hell. If *he'd* known I had gone to him instead of you, he'd have had a stroke all over again.'

She shuts her eye again, not so much wincing as radiating a deep heart-sick pain. Ralph feels himself leaning towards her, his hand gripping her soft delicate fingers. Behind him, he can sense Ethan leaning as well.

'She... in warning Ariana not to trust Lychen, she all but admitted that she's been lying to him about their relationship over the last few months. Added to the fact Ariana had mentioned your meeting up a few weeks ago, it seemed to be the final straw for him... Even so, I saw his face when she went over. He meant it, but he was terrified, too. And when he saw that she wasn't dead... When Nova came out of nowhere and tried to catch her, he was relieved.'

'Sounds too human for Lychen,' Ralph snorts. Bella

opens her eyes and looks beyond him, at Ethan. Something wordless passes between them. She shuts her eyes again.

'We should let her rest...' Ethan says, firmly. 'Her wounds are not deep, they need washing and perhaps a few stitches but she should be fine. I can do it—'

'You've done enough for her,' Felix says, firmly. '*I'll* do it. Lord knows I've stitched *you* up more than enough times over the last few years when your little explosive experiments have gone awry. You two go and try and get some sleep. You both look like hell.'

Ralph sighs and slowly unfolds himself. He pulls his hand from Bella's but to his surprise she tightens her fingers slightly on his.

'Ralph...' he leans close so he can hear the strange, hollowed-out version of her voice. 'Has it gone?'

'What's that?'

'If it's gone... maybe he'll let me... maybe I can go.'

Ralph looks from her to Ethan and back again in perplexity. If Ethan knows what she means, he doesn't say.

'Shh... Just try and get some sleep, OK. You're going to be fine. You're safe. You're home. And don't worry about Ariana. He won't hurt her. She won't let him.'

He doesn't say that they'd all thought the same about her but he knows they're all thinking it. He follows Ethan out into the hallway as Felix tails them and then strides towards the bathroom where they hear her opening cupboards and taking things out. Ethan turns towards the room he's shared with Felix for years, his face looking lost as if he can't quite remember what sleep is and how one goes about getting it.

'Good to have you back, Eth,' Ralph mutters, trying to sound as if he truly means it. Ethan looks at him as if he knows exactly how he really feels.

'I'm sorry,' he says.

'Why?'

'About your dad. I'm sorry. And about Bella. I should have saved her...'

'You did enough.' Ralph turns from him because he can feel his face already betraying him. He trudges away, up the stairs towards his bed and grateful, long-awaited oblivion.

44

June, 2019

Ariana doesn't want to be in her mother's bedroom. She paces back and forth, body fizzing with energy, images swirling around her head. She catches sight of herself in one of the ornate mirrors and sees her mother, her eyes wide as Lychen hoisted her up… over… Ariana cries out and the mirror gives a jagged crack as it splits apart and half falls to the floor. Still her mother's eyes haunt her. She hadn't looked angry or scared. She hadn't even seemed all that surprised. *Why hadn't she stopped him? Why didn't I?* She whirls around and stares at the large, four-poster bed, the bottle of water and crystal glass next to it, the hairbrush and make-up on the vanity nearby… The scents of sandalwood, cedar, and jasmine find her nose as she sees all the familiar perfume and lotion bottles.

'I need to get out of here,' she tells the room. Her voice is oddly static and low. 'I need to go…' She crosses to the double doors and hauls on the handle, but it's locked of course. After Bella had fallen and Ethan had sprinted out of the double doors, Lychen hadn't seemed to know what to do. He'd stood at the balcony edge for a few seconds before turning to mumble something at the biggest Guard person, the one Ariana had taken for his own personal assistant, who'd followed Ethan. The other two Guard people, the ones who'd found Ariana at the front gates and escorted her all the way up here without ever uttering a word, had gone with him. Ariana had run across to the balcony just in time to see a flash of wings when Lychen had put an icy hand on her shoulder and drawn her backwards.

'She's not dead,' he'd said, quietly. 'Delta will retrieve her if he can.' He'd steered her towards the doors behind which she now stood. 'Wait in here until I'm ready to deal with you.'

Ariana had let him guide her through the doors and slide them shut behind her because she had been in shock. And she had thought that the simple matter of the Guard people going down to the street and bringing back her mother and whatever bird creature – the bird-girl? – had presumably flown into her wouldn't take too long. Half an hour, tops. It had been almost three hours now and though she was exhausted, she knew that she would not be able to sleep in this bed. Her mother was everywhere in here. And she'd thrown her across the bloody roof. Was she sorry? Sometimes. Sometimes when the scent of sandalwood crept into her nose and she spotted the little laminated bookmark she'd made for her mum when she was five poking out of a paperback on the bedside table, she felt wretched. Other times, though, the anger returned. *She lied. She lied my whole life. She deserved to be punished.* Punished, not thrown off a balcony, reasoned another part of her. *But we didn't do that,* argued the blankness. And the pacing resumed.

Two am finds Ariana sitting cross-legged in front of the cracked mirror. She is trying to remember how she broke it. She stares at it and thinks *move*. Nothing happens. She tries clearing her mind and willing it to move. Nothing. She imagines tendrils of energy spurting from her eyes and lifting the shards. They don't so much as shudder. She balls her fists. It doesn't help that every glimpse she gets of her own eyes makes her think of Bella. It doesn't help that she is beyond exhausted. That every time she shuts her eyes her body lurches sideways until she spasms awake.

Maybe it just doesn't work like that. The power is about seeing patterns, isn't that what Felix said? But what the hell does she know anyway, there weren't patterns to see in that door we looked through at the ARC...

Less than 24 hours ago and yet it feels like several years have passed.

Lychen said it was telekinesis.

She shuts her eyes, falls asleep and jolts awake. She won't ever call him Dad.

But he didn't lie to us. And we can use his help.

Her mother had said Lychen would turn her into a Guard.

Mum lies. She has never, ever told us the truth. We can't trust her.
But Lychen tried to kill her, he shot Ethan last year. She can't trust him, either.
We can if we take the feelings away. We can't live on our own. We are thirteen. We need a grown up. He's our father. He can help us and no one will question it. He can give us answers.
How can she ever feel safe here? How can she ever feel safe anywhere, ever again? Sleep. Awake. Sleep. Sleep. Awake.
We make ourselves safe. No one will ever hurt us again. Let them try. Let them try.

The glass shards shudder and throw the soft lighting of the room into gleaming echoes of fractured green eyes.

Ariana gets to her feet and turns her glare to the sliding door. The lock gives a loud wrenching noise and the door drags backwards. She steps over the threshold and stops short. Lychen is sitting in one of the metal patio chairs, a glass of amber liquid in his hand. He is wearing a fresh clean shirt and greets her with a little salute of his glass.

'Good,' he remarks, curtly. He gets to his feet, drains the glass, puts it down and strides towards the double doors.

'If you'd care to follow me, I have a gift for you.'

Ariana thinks about wondering what on earth all this is about, but finds that she is too tired and too drained to really care. She follows him through the double doors and down the richly carpeted staircase. There are no Guard people about. Ariana glances at her father out of the corner of her eyes.

'Why did you leave me in there?'

'To see if you would come out.'

'You were testing me?'

'Yes.'

He leads the way down a corridor past several rooms and down another set of stairs. The building is lit, but deathly quiet. It feels as if they are the only two people awake inside it.

'What happened to my mother? Did your Guard man person manage to bring her back?'

'No. By the time Delta reached the pavement, Bella had gone. Along with one of our top research assets. The avian girl, Nova. I believe you've met.' He turns to her blandly, as if making a commonplace introduction.

'Yeah. Mum said she used to be her student or something.'

'By all accounts it appears as if she attempted to rescue her. I do not know if she was successful. In any case, Daniel is furious.'

'Good. I don't like him.'

'No.' Lychen sighs as if very, very tired, though his face is as smooth and unblemished as if he's just had twelve hours' sleep. 'I don't like him much either, but he is useful.'

'Why?'

'He gets things done. He doesn't let emotion get in the way. He pushes boundaries. And he is a former C-Subject so there is a massive untapped source of potential within him.'

Ariana snorts. He turns to her, eyebrow raised. They're on the ground floor now, the plush corridors set with up-lit pillars and ornate paintings. He's standing in front of a dark window through which she can glimpse twisting plants and blooms of flowers.

'What?'

'I've lived with a former C-Subject for the last eight months. I didn't see much *untapped potential*. He was supposed to be some sort of computer-reading freak but he didn't even see some simple coding sequence before I did.'

Lychen smiles. It's not the same as the proud-dad smile Ralph would give her, but it's swift, powerful and impressed. 'Well. Not all C-Subjects were born or raised equally. And none of them are equal to you. Come. He's down here.'

He leads her through a darker corridor and down a few stone steps to a subterranean level. It's cold down here and the corridors are less obsequiously luxurious, but there is still something impressive in the thick stone walls. They pass a window through which she catches a glimpse of a large pool glimmering with underwater lighting. A door on the other side of the corridor is labelled *Gym.* Next comes a *Sauna* and a *Treatment Room* and, at last, Lychen stops outside a door labelled *Court Two.*

'There's never a tennis court down here?' Ariana asks, incredulously. Her curiosity has, for the moment, overtaken her determined blankness.

'There is. The underground level of this particular building far exceeds its above-ground width. But *this* is a squash court.' Lychen opens the door and holds it for her. Ariana passes through. The room is wincingly bright and high-ceilinged and there is a man tied to a chair in its very centre. He raises his head as she steps towards him, frowning. She opens her mouth to ask who he is, to tell Lychen that there must have been some mistake because this is some stranger. Then she stops. Because there *is* something familiar about him. His grey hair is straggly around a large bald patch on his head. Though sitting, she can see he's powerfully built and tall... His eyes are soft as they meet hers and when he opens his mouth, she finds that she knows exactly what his voice will sound like before he even speaks.

'Ariana?'

She turns to Lychen.

'That's my granddad?'

'Ah. You recognise him. Good. Neither of us were sure you would. He was following you. At least from Euston... He's the one that alerted the others to your whereabouts. He's the reason Bella and Nova were taken away. He turned up here shortly afterwards... I thought I should leave it up to you what you want to do with him. If you like, I'll have him untied and taken out of here, given a meal and a bed for the night. I could simply turn him out onto the streets of London. Or…'

'Or?'

'You can make use of him. Hone your skills. Sharpen your ruthlessness and resolve the way your mother always failed to.'

She looks at him. He wants her to do it, she can tell. She doesn't need to see the hunger in his face, the hardness with which he is watching her. She can just feel it as truly as she can feel the waves of quiet despair coming from the bound old man in front of her.

'Ariana… Please. I was there when you were *born*. I used to push you on the swing—'

'Shut up! I don't want you to talk to me.'

He stops talking, his eyes bulging slightly and his mouth gaping like a fish. Lychen snorts. Ariana turns to him.

'What do you want to do?' he asks quietly.

She thinks. Her brain swarms and shudders with tiredness. She sways a little as a yawn wracks through her. She tries to think.

'I want to decide tomorrow. I'm tired. I want to sleep. But not in *her* room.'

'Alright, I shall summon the Guard.' Lychen pulls a phone out of his pocket and taps something into it. She can't tell if she's disappointed him. Probably. But she's too tired to care much. 'Her room *is* the most luxurious,' he adds, without looking up. 'Apart from mine.'

'I don't care about that. I just need a bed. And let him go to sleep too. Somewhere basic. But give him a bed. He's an old man.'

Lychen nods, briefly. Two Guard people appear in the open doorway behind them.

'Ariana, please… your mum would—'

Ariana turns to the man on the chair, her entire body thunderous with anger.

'Don't you talk about her! I'm *sick* of everyone always talking about *her*. She's not here anymore! She doesn't matter anymore! And if you want to... If you want me to treat you well, you better just shut up about her right now, OK?'

She waits long enough to see the pain shoot across his face, then she turns on her heel and marches up to the nearest Guard man.

'Take her to the guest suite on the second floor,' Lychen says, from behind her. And she can tell, without looking at him, that he isn't disappointed in the slightest.

45

Autumn, 2018

Julia saw me first. Of course. She was the one who had been searching the longest. I stood on the grassy verge next to the parked car and waited until they were five paces away. Then I removed my sunglasses and let her find me. I could see it on her face, the moment I happened to her. The shock, of course, came first – a great, walloping sag of it across her entire visage. It was followed swiftly by a glance to Marc, to see if he had seen, to see if she might get away with pretending she hadn't…

'Bella?'

Marc had grown leaner in the last few years, the paunch of his stomach and roundness of jaw replaced by wrinkles and sadness. I wondered if it was the loss of his children that had done it to him or simply living with her.

'Hello, Marc. Julia.'

Marc's face seemed to ignite, the beam groaning out of his wretched, greying skin almost painfully. Julia had recovered a little by then, though she kept a grip on Marc's arm, her white, crepey hands clutching as he moved towards me. I didn't know if it was this or the quick narrowing of my eyes which pulled him up short.

'Bella, I can't believe it's you. I didn't think I'd ever see you again! I – I can't believe it!'

'Marc,' Julia turned to him as if he had stopped at

nothing more than to observe an interesting insect in his path. 'Marc, the guests. The wake.'

Her voice sent me back to being nine. To being something small and defective, dirty and powerless. I let the icy memories in, whirl in a tightening band around my heart and back out. On the outside, I didn't twitch. I didn't so much as blink.

'Julia, this is our daughter! Our Bella! You haven't seen her for twenty… Twenty-three years! Have you *nothing—*'

'I have no daughter! I buried my daughter, today!' Julia's voice twisted in a pitchy, hysterical whine. I noticed a few of the straggling congregation glance our way and knew that she was aware of every one of them as well. When she glanced back at me it was only for a moment but I let her see the withering pity on my face. I let her see what a pathetic, shadow of a thing she had become to me. I watched her quail and I let her see my enjoyment. Then I turned back to Marc and I did not look at her again.

'I haven't got long—'

'Come,' he said, desperately, shaking off the insipid Dior dress next to him. 'You missed the funeral but come to the wake, at the old house—'

'I didn't come for Maya,' I said, quickly. 'I came for Ariana.'

'What? What's happened to her? Did *he* find—'

'No. She's safe. She's with the Blakes. But I need you do to something.'

'Anything, name it – anything!'

'I put your number in her phone. I didn't tell her who you are, but your name is there. If she calls… go and get her. Please.'

'Bella, you don't have to ask—'

'There is a facility called the Beaumont. It's run by

Beaumont Futura Industries. You will hear a lot about them in the next few months. They're about to roll out something called the Guard Assistance Programme; it's going to be huge. You will see me working for them, too. On the internet, TV, radio... I'm to be an ambassador. None of that matters. The facility is in South London, the nearest tube station is Borough. If she calls you and you can't get hold of the Blakes... That is where she will be going. That is where *he* will be, do you understand?'

'Yes, of course. Beaumont. Borough. But, Bella—'

'She might not call,' I looked away from him, from the dawning realisation of his dread, everything I had ever told him all clamouring with the new information to make sense. 'But I think she will. If she works it out. If she finds out the truth... She will want to know where she came from. Eventually the questions will lead to you, to the decisions you made with Ana... But it might not even be her who calls – if *anyone* does, saying she's missing... That's where she'll be going. You're closer than the Blakes, you can get there faster.'

'Of course, of course. But Bella, what about you?'

'Yes, hopefully I'll be there, hopefully I'll be able to stop her before he gets to her—'

'Bella... You said he'll be there. Lychen. Does that mean... Did he find *you*?'

I didn't answer. Instead, I checked my watch and replaced my sunglasses over my eyes. I began to turn to the car. I felt his desperation, his presence lunging towards me like a clumsy toddler lurching for its mother. I let him find me, his arms large and warm and completely enveloping. I did not wince, even as he crushed my bruises, I did not put my arms around him either, but I let him wrap around me until I disappeared and for a moment, I shut my eyes and was gone.

'Bella—'

'He doesn't know the truth. He doesn't have her. Not yet.'

'But you—'

'I have to go. They're waiting for me. They'll hurt you if you try to keep me here.'

I pulled away and, slowly, he let me go. I was surprised to see Julia still there behind him, an indistinct blur of agitation hovering awkwardly. I turned and opened the car door.

'Bella?' Her voice around my name, the cold inflection of question. I hesitated for less than a second before I wrenched the car door open and slipped inside.

'Go,' I told the driver, simply.

46

June, 2019

The pain comes in undulating peaks and troughs. I slip in and out of sleep and wakefulness, always seeing the same things. Ariana's blank eyes. Lychen's face twisted in anger and pain. Ethan, wrenched with anguish. I watch Felix bustling around the room through hazy vision and wonder if I'm dreaming. My old velvet eiderdown feels achingly familiar beneath my fingers. The bedside lamp is different, though, and the old purple curtains have been replaced with a plain, cream blind. My wardrobe is the same and the sound of the old pipes wheedling through the walls transports me decades into the past. I shut my eyes. Ariana gazes blankly. My sandal flies shockingly upwards. Empty space punches through my internal organs. I open my eyes and Felix is near, her face rigid as she slowly but determinedly peels away the bandages covering my right arm. I wince and she looks up.

'No easy way of doing this… but it's got to be done. Believe me, it's not exactly my idea of a fun Saturday night either.'

I fail to summon the energy to reply. As she dabs my ripped skin I look away and grit my teeth to hold in the scream of pain. She dabs, dries and wraps and I doze in an excruciating river that dances from my arm to her fingertips and back again.

'This one shouldn't need stitches, just a good clean I should think... I don't know what he'll do now. Will he come here, do you think? Will he keep chasing you? I don't know. On one hand... he tried to do a job and it failed. Perhaps he will want to finish it. Finish you. On the other... it sounds very much as if he was acting out of anger and passion. Could well be that once he cools off, he thinks *meh* and simply turns to the issue in hand. Ariana. Which is worse? If he really decides he wants you dead, you and I know there isn't anything that can stop him. Except perhaps her. And that doesn't seem all that likely, given recent events... This one doesn't need stitches either.'

She finishes with my second arm and lifts away the fabric covering my torso. The sharp bite of air on my open wounds draws my eyes downwards. My midriff is crisscrossed in bloody cuts where Nova tried to grasp me. I look away.

'But then, of course, this is you. And I can't imagine anything worse for someone like you than to be dismissed. Unimportant. What a novel concept, eh? Almost like a person disappearing in mysterious circumstances and then remaining unfound for twelve long, boring years... That didn't sit well either, did it? Hmm. Yeah, I'm going to throw a few stitches in here, I think. Looks deeper than the others. It might not be pretty but, hey ho. Maybe you'll leave a little for the rest of us now, eh?'

I wince as she presses unnecessarily hard on a laceration above a bruised rib. After a moment or two I feel the stinging bite of a needle and I can't stop the sharp cry this time. She pauses, but when no one comes, she pushes the needle through the other edge of the wound. I moan. It feels as if she's ripping me apart all over again.

'Yeah... it's going to smart a bit. Here we go, I'll just do one more to be safe.'

I cry out again, the sound pitifully weak as the agony tears deeper. I blink her into focus, her face a white strain caught between anxious glances at the door and a savage enjoyment which I've never seen before.

'There you go, I'll leave the suturing there. Can't have my dear husband running in and accusing me of mauling you. Now I'm going to need you to sit up so I can wrap your chest. On three, OK. One, two, three. There we go, I'll be as quick as I can.'

It's incredible how normal her voice is. It makes me wonder if I'm imagining all the rest of what she's saying and doing. The look of pleasure. The low, mumbling stream of words that seem to come from somewhere very close to the centre of all the hatred, jealousy, confusion and conflict she's ever felt towards me.

'See, I've been doing a bit of research all these long months. They put me to work on hacking into the Beaumont even though we all knew it was pointless. Ralph and Dr Blake always trusted you… As far as they were concerned, there wasn't much we could discover about that place that you wouldn't willingly share anyway… After all, isn't that why you agreed to go and live with Lychen in the first place? To keep us all safe?'

She snorts as she fastens the edge of the bandage to the rest of my securely wrapped middle with a piece of tape. Then she lowers me back down, her hands solid and warm if not exactly gentle. I shudder as I slide back into the pillows and by the time I open my eyes again she's hovering right above me, a new flannel in her hand as she removes the white cloth from around my face. I wait, knowing she won't lie.

'Hmm,' she surveys the damage for a moment or two.

'This isn't from Nova, is it?'

I blink slowly. My left eye, which had been covered, swims in sudden exposure but after a moment or two she hazes into clarity. There's a bitter disappointment in her gaze, which lifts my spirits slightly.

'Missed your eye,' she mutters, dabbing away. 'Not too deep. Might scar. Probably needs stitches. Delicate area though, the face. Needs a professional really. Not sure what would be worse, someone making a real hash of it or just leaving it to scar. Decisions, decisions. What was I saying, anyway? Oh yes, my research. See, something never sat right with me about last year... I was there through it all, remember? The plain little techy B-character. I saw your drab little life with my own two eyes. Your boring little job at the boring little university. Your dull little flat... Compared to all this... and the Bella I knew, who set the stage alight with the tip of her toe and the whisper of one syllable... It didn't really add up. And there was something else... A conversation I had with Ralph just after I found you and you left for Cornwall... D'you know, I just don't think I'd feel *right* attempting to stitch this up. I'm going to leave it. We'll see what happens, eh? Might get a nice old infection brewing if we're *really* unlucky...'

She finishes washing my face and turns to find a clean pad of gauze. My cheek burns with whatever ointment she's used and I swallow painfully, trying to summon the energy to speak. She turns back and, with the press of the gauze on my skin, wrenches another low moan from my throat.

'So, as I was saying... Ralph and I were discussing how easy it was to trace you using Ariana's phone. Ralph was all for the possibility that either you didn't know she had the phone or that you didn't know what she had been doing with it. And *I* said, what if it's neither? What if we were simply playing into some big, grand plan of yours? Well, I still say that. I'm not sure if you're reckless enough to let Ariana talk to just anyone on the internet... but I still remember the look you had when you spotted me in that lecture theatre. You looked right at me and you didn't even *blink.* That's not the reaction of someone who has put their heart and soul into hiding for ever and ever...'

She finishes taping the dressing to my face and smooths some of my hair away almost tenderly before sitting back and surveying her work.

'Well, that's the worst of it cleared up. I should think that will do you for the night. I'm not sure what we should do about your leg. Ethan says it should heal alright as long as we keep it still. Perhaps we can get hold of one of those boot things off the internet...' She holds her hand above the leg and I can feel her sore temptation to bring it down, to smash my world apart with bone-shattering agony... But we both know I'll scream, and that the men will come running, and questions will be demanded, and far harder to answer than my earlier cries of pain from the stitches. Besides, she's not done with me yet.

'The really interesting thing only cropped up quite recently. You had me feeling sorry for you, after you let Ariana go, you see. I was almost on your side. I stopped digging for a bit. I looked after her when she had all those nightmares. Held her. Taught her some computer tricks. I even talked you up to her. I told her that I understood your decisions. Even after I knew about Ethan, I didn't completely hate you – perhaps you hadn't had a choice in the matter, I thought. Perhaps you really were keeping him safe.'

She snorts derisively. 'Then. Well. The other week

happened. He chose you. You *let* him choose you. And, well… Let's just say it gave me a nudge. These last few weeks have proven pretty fruitful, once I managed to get through your old email passwords. I remembered, you see, that little conversation we had in your car last year. When you told me about Maya, your sister, and how the two of you had been corresponding until she started to get too close to the truth, or something… I always thought it seemed a bit strange, that you'd cut her off so abruptly just because she *began to suspect* you had a kid. In any case, those emails made for some *very* interesting reading… What was it you said? Something about feeling your old life slipping away, missing being the centre of greatness and there being a lot to be said for bobbing back over the radar, leaving it burning at your feet…

'Quite poetic, really. I wonder if the others will see it the same way… Oh, I know you never admitted to anything. It was all just postering and pondering and whatnot. But I do wonder whether you knew all along that you had gone, perhaps, a little too far. That maybe *that* was the reason poor Maya never heard from you again. I'm sure you told yourself it was because of Ariana… Except… Maya said she would forget all about it. That she'd never mention it again. Then she *begged* you for help, Bella. Who doesn't respond to something like that from their own sister? Unless they're terrified of the consequences of what she knows…

'I'll get the truth, you know. I will. I may not be so charming or efficient at getting what I want as you, but I'm a plodder and when I get the facts, they will be on paper and indisputable. And then they will all see what I see. Because you weren't born for that life of keeping your pretty little head down and being a sad, bitter mother of an increasingly ungrateful kid… I'm not sure *how* you did it yet, but I will find out. And I'll tell all of them.'

My mind is beginning to cloud over with sleep, but I heave the heaviness away with the biggest shove I can muster. My voice dregs out of the depths, cold and hoarse.

'Why?'

'Because you took him, you sadistic little bitch. You were adored by all of them – Ralph, Blake, Lychen... and still you stole *my* husband and made him your slave and still... even now he's back to himself again, he loves *you*.'

'I didn't—'

'No,' she says, holding her hand up and then pulling it through her cropped hair. She shakes her head and sniffs away the sudden rush of emotion in her face. 'I'm going now. I've had enough. And you need your rest. If you can get any. Oh, you know,' she puts a finger to her chin in mock contemplation. 'Now I come to think of it, there's a whole case full of painkillers upstairs in Blake's bathroom cabinet. Morphine, analgesics, numbing cream... the lot. How very absent-minded of me. Oops.'

She gives me a cold sneer that doesn't reach her hard, deadened eyes, turns ungracefully on her heel and walks away. I shut my eyes and sink, heavily, back into the slow, roiling waves of torment, wondering why I'm still breathing.

47

June, 2019

Someone must find and administer the painkillers at some point because I spend the next few days and nights drifting on a strange, heady cloud of muffled sensation. Occasionally the pain spikes through and I feel my heart respond to it before anything else, thrumming in my ears. I don't speak much. I don't open my eyes unless completely necessary. Instead I lie still, I feel the lacerations covering my body begin to knit themselves back together and I listen.

I hear the arguments between Felix and Ethan blooming even through the thick walls. I hear the soft footsteps of Dominic and Tess as they peer into my room like curious, trespassing children. I hear Ralph's voice on the phone to the hospital, sighing over the lack of change in his father's condition. I hear Felix's voice mumbling to herself and to me as she ostentatiously checks my wounds, haphazardly removes my stitches and changes dressings. And slowly, slowly, I listen to the different points of contact in my head and begin to understand them. Ethan lurks in his old spot. Our Guard-human connection was torn by the strength of his turmoil when he watched me fall from the balcony, but he remains here. By his own choosing, which is the point of everything, I am beginning to see. And Felix is right. He sits by my side when everyone else has gone to sleep. He holds my hand as tenderly as Ralph. His presence and his love beats like a constant warmth at the edge of my mind. I will have to deal with him at some point soon, before Felix's jealousy tips her into action stronger than threats, rough hands and morphine withholding.

Gradually I feel my brain beginning to whir back to itself as the pain recedes and the painkillers are reduced. When I'm ready, I touch from Ethan's spot to the corner occupied by the Youth Guard. Immediately I feel them all – all twenty strands linking my mind to theirs – light up with a clamour of questions.

Where are you? What happened to you? Are you safe? What should we do? Shall we come?
I am safe. I am fine. I am healing. Do nothing. Wait for further instructions.

I wait until I'm sure I can feel them simmer back into normality. I can almost see through some of their eyes if I really concentrate – Bette is standing just behind Daniel and I can see the loose strands of hair covering his head from the back as she pauses to listen to me – and I can feel their reactions. Not so much relief – they don't feel, after all, not like that – but more like clicks of satisfaction at a question finally answered. I feel them all and they feel me too. And I slide from the interaction as smoothly as I entered it, swiping away the window, tapping onto the next.

Ariana. It was a horrible shock for her, when I spoke to her in her head on the rooftop. She had thought I was just an echo of her own thoughts, as Mamma is to me. Our bond has always been stronger than she realised. I made it that way a long time ago and so did she. She is part of my resilience, after all, and I am part of hers, whether she likes it or not – the clear voice of reason telling her to pull herself together when she finds herself cold and alone in a strange place, the constant reminder that she has always lived in a world which requires her to protect herself at all costs. She thought she was the only one whose powers had grown over the last few months. I feel for the link to her mind tentatively, one strand of sensation at a time. She sleeps, her dreams a tumble of longing and energy. I haven't tried to feel her during daylight hours yet. She needs time to heal away from me and it is enough for me, right now, just to sense that she is safe and whole. It is enough, for now.

I keep my eyes closed as the voices of real life stammer and start around me. Someone mentions depression. Someone else barks that I just need more time. I ignore them and burrow back into the inner worlds. Their subconsciouses batter and bray tediously – love, jealousy, rage, confusion, longing, frustration. I bat them all away and return to the deepest, darkest corner of my mind. The place where he lived. Where I could feel, albeit briefly, the flashes of him which told me the truth, however horrifying. His is the slipperiest link of all, the thread a fine gossamer which I can only glimpse if I don't really try, let alone grasp. It has to come to me, while I concentrate and he doesn't, drifting across the gap of blankness like a tiny spider floating through the air on a miniscule, diaphanous strand of silk. And even when it works, when it connects, the results are often a confusion – desires unacknowledged and jumbled in their unnamed forms. Fury battles grief. I sift and wait and listen and eventually it comes clearer. I did not die. I should have. He warned me. I pushed him, and yet... And yet. The thought of me alive but beyond his grasp wracks his mind with torture. I should have died; only the possessor can destroy their possessions.

It takes several days of exertion before I can muster the energy to address the connection directly. I do it in the middle of the night when the veil is thinnest and his defences are dormant. His shock, even so, is almost enough to shake me off entirely. I hang on, though the strand dances and twists between the tips of my concentration. I put everything I have into the five words I speak, loud and ringing and haunting his wide, staring eyes:

I will come for you.

END OF BOOK TWO

J M (Jenny) Briscoe is a sci-fi author, journalist, blogger, and stay-at-home-mum based in Berkshire, UK. She writes a strong female lead, bakes a mean birthday cake and has been known to do both simultaneously. Her publishing debut, *The Girl with the Green Eyes*, was longlisted for The Bridport Prize: Peggy Chapman-Andrews First Novel Award in 2020, reaching the top 20 of over 1,600 entrants.

Jenny lives with her husband, three children, and two fairly indifferent cats. She is currently working on the final novel in the *Take Her Back* trilogy.

Follow J M Briscoe on Twitter @jm_briscoe, subscribe to her author website www.jmbriscoe.co.uk and blog www.jmbriscoe.com for updates.

THE GIRL WITH THE GREEN EYES

J M BRISCOE

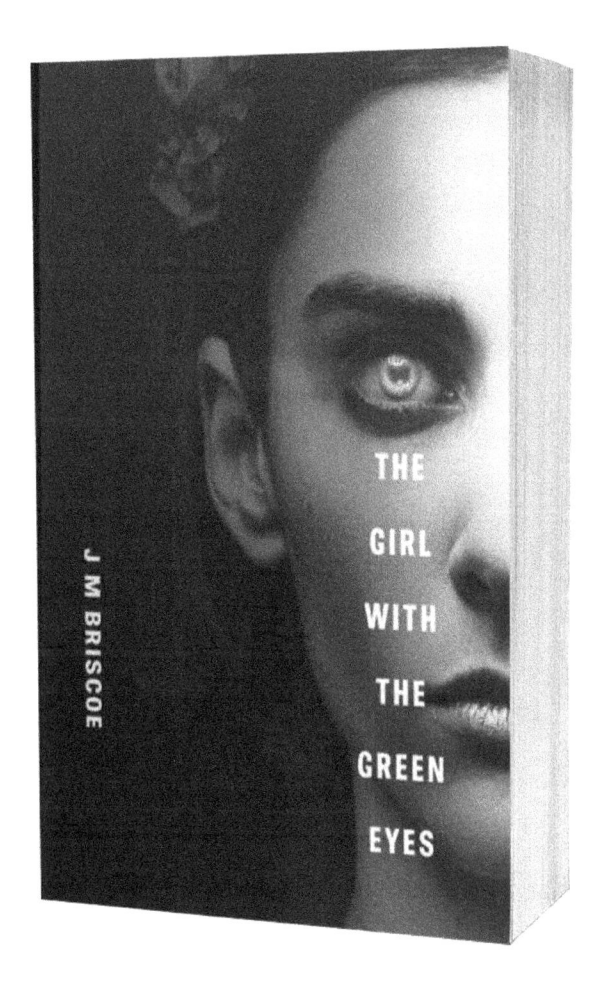

Bella is defective, you need to take her back.

The first book in the Take Her Back trilogy.

BAD PRESS iNK,
publishers of niche, alternative and cult fiction

Visit

www.BADPRESS.iNK

for details of all our books, and sign up to
be notified of future releases and offers

Also from BAD PRESS iNK

WHILE NOBODY IS WATCHING

MICHELLE DUNNE

They called it peacekeeping.
For Corporal Lindsey Ryan it was anything but.

The first book in the Corporal Lindsey Ryan series.

A migrant crisis. A corrupt harbour town. Who will stand up for those who have become invisible to the rest of the world?

The second book in the Corporal Lindsey Ryan series.

The Blue Hour

M J GREENWOOD

Caring for the elderly was never meant to be like this.

Lightning Source UK Ltd.
Milton Keynes UK
UKHW021532161022
410571UK00016B/159